BLOOD PRICE

By Nicole Evans

A Prices Asked and Paid Novel

First edition, 2024
Copyright © 2024 Nicole Evans

Cover Illustration by Zoe Badini
Typography by Norman Olasiman of Stardust Book Services
Formatting by Rae Davennor of Stardust Book Services
Editing by Jeni Chappelle and Danai Christopoulou

ISBNs:
eBook: 979-8-9905707-0-2

Print: 979-8-9905707-1-9

*To every person who has ever bled and was made
to feel lesser for it, required to speak about our blood in
hushed whispers, embarrassed tones and met
with disgust or doubt.*

*There is nothing wrong, unclean or gross with or about you.
I see you. I hear you. I believe you.*

You deserve better.

Please note that some content in the novel may be triggering. A list of warnings, to the best of my knowledge, are listed below, as well as posted on my website.

On the page: Verbal abuse, anxiety, blood, graphic injury, death, murder, depression, guilt, death of a parent, death of a sibling, death of a child, pregnancy, animal death, foreplay
Mentioned: animal sacrifice, child abuse (past, referenced), war
Minor: hunger (starvation)

In the back of the book, you can find a list of pronunciations, credits for who helped bring this book to life, a list of fellow authors to support, acknowledgements and an author bio.

Thank you for taking the time to read BLOOD PRICE. Please leave a review and share the word, so it can reach more readers and I can keep writing more stories.

CHAPTER ONE

"I, Ashilde of the Slátra, I who is she and she who is me, pronounced *sangrild*, one who bleeds..."

The words left Ashilde's lips in a whisper, coming almost unbidden—the start of a promised oath, yet to be spoken publicly, but with the ceremony nearing, she found herself practicing the words whenever she could. As if misremembering the words to something so sacred, a promise so binding, was the greatest fear Ashilde had about being named her clan's Faethegnar.

She shivered, clutching the edges of her cloak closer to her person. Ash blinked to recenter her vision, lost in distracted thought instead of scanning for threats—the entire reason she was here. She glanced around, hoping neither of her companions noticed, as the trio stood underneath the forest's canopy on the outskirts of their village. They weren't so far out that they couldn't still see the large, white wooden walls enclosing the Slátra's village, but they were far enough away that they were fully immersed in the forest that bordered their land:

large, white-trucked trees with leaves a deep red, slowly falling to the ground as the season began to shift from fall to winter, in a month's time.

Her eyes fell on Davyn first, a man who was both her beloved and their clan's healer. Dressed in a fur cloak and in boots caked with mud, his massive frame was bent on the ground, fingers gentle as he inspected another plant Ashilde couldn't name, only knowing its value if it made its way into the satchel he carried.

Up ahead of him was Hildrid, one of their hunters. She was dressed in hunting leathers, her bow resting in her hand. She scanned the area around Davyn, ensuring no predators lurked in the shadows, strands of blonde hair slipping free from the tight, braided knot sitting atop of her head. She brushed a strand away, her fingers brushing against the paint covering her eyes and traveling down her cheeks. Two pairs of thin lines, painted white to stand out against her black skin, traveled down through each eye, denoting her status as a hunter, all four lines coming together to meet at a singular point on her chin. Ashilde's, painted red, only had one pair of lines, traveling through her vibrant green eyes, down her pale white cheeks and meeting together at the base of her chin, before becoming a singular line that trailed until it met the base of her throat. A warrior's mark, one blessed by the gods to kill other humans, in the same way Hildrid could kill animals as a hunter.

Between herself and Hildrid, both could protect Davyn from any threat, be it animal or human. Though the replenishing of ingredients was hardly at huge risk of attack during times of peace, peace was still a new concept, even two generations in. Not just for the Slátra, but for all the clans of Armadin. It was tradition that no *sangrendi* traveled outside their walls without a pair of *sangrild* to protect them. That tradition remained. In her thirty-three summers—over half of them spent as a *sangrild* warrior, bleeding monthly as her proof and price—Ashilde had lost count how many times she'd left to traverse their border as an escort.

Yet this was the first time she struggled to focus on her task, her mind too distracted otherwise.

Not *exactly a resounding example of what a true Faethegnar should be*, her mind whispered, a mixture of her own fears and the voices of those who opposed her nomination—not least of which being her sister.

Thankfully, Hildrid pulled her out, before her mind could ensnare her in thoughts too dark against the soft morning's light, flickering like candlelight between leaves blowing against the wind. "It will be fine," she said, her voice deep, not looking at Ashilde. Her eyes never stopped their scan, her bow always ready at her side.

Ashilde laughed, running her hand through her red waves she'd left down that morning. "Is it that obvious?"

Hildrid gave her a look, brown eyes shining. "You're quiet, but not usually *this* quiet, especially on rotation with your favorite hunter and the person who warms your bed at night." Her smirk faded to a concerned frown. "It's pining down what nerves you that I struggle with, since I know you won't tell me."

"As if she could only pick one thing," Davyn said, joining them as he threw the satchel over his shoulder. His skin was even whiter than Ashilde's, who at least got sunkissed in the spring and summer months, during her work and training outside. Davyn, instead, was quite content to remain in his hunt with his plants, books and garden.

For a moment, her heart skipped a beat as his eyes met hers, ice-white to her grass-green. He had a thick, black beard and hair—shaved short along the sides and back of his head, its length only kept up top. His face paint matched the markings that all Slátra bore:

a solid strip of color across the eyes—his painted red, though the colors of white or black were often also used, dependent upon skintone—with a row of small circles forming a line across the top of the paint on his forehead. Where his markings deviated was by the singular, thin, red line painted underneath his eyes and across his nose and cheeks—a healer's mark.

It didn't matter how many times he looked at her. He never ceased to take her breath away.

Unless he said something to annoy her, which was the quickest way to ruin a moment where she was lusting after him. Which is what Davyn chose to do in that moment, the crinkles forming around his eyes as he smiled, giving away he was aware of it, too.

"The ceremony nears. The vote is not unanimous, though those who dissent are not opinions worth worrying over. A new month's price to bear, this time in front of us all. The pressure of leadership." His grin widened, his teasing obvious. "Did I miss anything, my heart?"

"Well, when you put it so succinctly, it seems I have nothing and everything to worry over," Ashilde said, shooting him a glare that held no bite. It was no surprise he could guess the path her thoughts had tread. She'd spent most of their evenings the past fortnight curled up in her bed, voicing her concerns and her worries about becoming the next Faethegnar, only quieting after his arms gripped her tighter.

"But yes, you did miss something," she added, if only to distract them from diving too fully into her concerns. This wasn't a conversation she particularly wanted to have with Hildrid—despite the fact she probably was already aware, considering Ashilde had been conversing with her wife, Freydis, about it just as often as she did with her own lover. "The last ceremony naming a Faethegnar didn't run so close to risking the absence of our hunters."

The hunter grunted in acknowledgement. Once they returned to the village, Hildrid would lead the rest of their hunters—a small band of five—out to scout for more resources. Namely, animals, both as meat to stock their stores and as sacrifices for their gods, before winter's bite kept them borrowed deep within their longhouses. It was the last hunt of the season, always the most important. But with her monthly blood cycle nearing—the cramps waking her in the mornings signaled its coming—it'd only be a matter of days, if that, before she'd announce to their Seidsian that she was bleeding once more. If Dagfinn, their current Faethegnar, confirmed his cycle was missed, then his prediction would be true and the naming of a new Faethegnar would take place.

The gods would have deemed his blood price paid, after four long centuries.

It would start as a solemn affair, before becoming a celebration to rival any living Slátra could remember. It'd been so long since one of their members lived long enough for their blood price to be fulfilled naturally through time, instead of paid through the sacrifice of death, protecting their clan from the other eight within Armadin. A result of peace; one they were still learning to accept, to trust.

Hildrid gripped her shoulder. "We'll be there," she promised. "A good hunt awaits us. The gods will see it done, allowing us to be present with you. And support you, even against those foolish enough to not."

Ash smiled her thanks, but it didn't reach her eyes. She wished she shared the hunter's faith. Or optimism.

"But we delay their start by dallying here," Davyn said gently. "I've replenished what I needed. Let's return, if only so Hildrid and her hunters can come back just as swiftly, removing at least one thing from your worries."

He offered his hand to her and Ashilde took it, squeezing it and soaking up the warmth he offered so effortlessly. With a nod, she agreed to return home, wishing that all of her concerns were so easily solved.

***

"Sod, Torhild, go and get Little Goose. Or else they'll miss Hildrid's leaving."

Ashilde watched Freydis command two of her hovering children, shooing them away with one free arm while she continued to check over her wife's armor. Ashilde sat on a stool, moving her leg as the children ran past her in giggles, a smirk on her face. Hildrid caught the look and rolled her eyes, finally turning and catching Freydis's hands in hers.

"I'll only be gone a few days, at most," Hildrid said gently. "You don't need to fret over me every time I leave for a hunt."

Freydis *tsked*. "My fretting is what you love about me."

Hildrid grinned, tracing a finger down her wife's cheek. "As if I could choose only one thing."

Ash looked away as Freydis blushed, giving her closest childhood friend as much privacy as she could, while sitting in Freydis's home. After returning to the Slátra's village, Ashilde and Hildrid had parted from Davyn, as he had plenty of work to do. A lingering kiss was his promise that he'd give her more comfort later that evening, a silent plea for her to stop worrying.

Ashilde had promised Freydis she'd stop by and help her ready her trio of children for a smaller ceremony, happening later that evening. Her youngest, nicknamed Little Goose for their love of the animals at the dens Freydis worked, had announced a few days ago they were ready for their Kallen Day, their naming ceremony. Every child, upon birth, was given a nickname that suited them, but only the child themself could know who they truly were. So, the nickname and the address of "they" was used, until the child was ready to give both their name and their address in front of the clan.

As the children returned, Sod and Torhild leading Little Goose by the hands, Ashilde frowned, as the youngest wrapped their arms around Hildrid's legs. It was clear they had been crying.

Hildrid immediately dropped to her knees, gripping Little Goose by the shoulders. "Pup, what's wrong? Today is a wonderful day!"

Little Goose's breaths came in shuddering gasps, as they tried to calm down. They wiped snot on the back of their hand. "I ... should've ... w-waited..."

"Oh, pup." Hildrid pulled them into a hug, kissing their cheek. "You know I hate to miss your Kallen Day. But you're ready, and our gods are so excited to learn your name. I am, too, you know? It'll be the first thing I ask when I return." She pulled back and rubbed their hair. "Now. Why don't you and your siblings come with me to see me and the other hunters off? I'm sure your mother can spare you for a bit, can she not?"

Freydis tapped her lip with a finger, as if considering, though the spark in her eyes gave away that she couldn't deny them. The immediate, begging cries from her children proved they didn't catch onto her ploy. "Well, if your birth mother *insists*," she said, earning thanks and gratitude as her children screamed in delight.

Ashilde leaned back against the table, her frown deepening, allowing herself to become lost in thought while the family finished their goodbyes. Hildrid and her hunters were eager to leave for the hunt, it was true. More leaves fell every day, and layers were beginning to be needed as they stepped outside. Winter would come, whether they wanted it or not. Yet, they had time enough to delay a day, for Hildrid to stay and witness her youngest's Kallen Day. But, if they delayed, then they would most certainly miss the ceremony naming Ash Faethegnar—something she'd been complaining about just this morning, not even realizing the price Hildrid was paying to make it.

Selfish, selfish woman, she thought, making up her mind. She stood to tell Hildrid to delay, only to find the hunter had already walked over to her, offering her arm. Ashilde grasped it at the elbow.

"Don't even think about it," Hildrid said, her voice low as Freydis ushered their children outside, complaining that they needed to put on their cloaks if they were to accompany their birth mother to the gates. "Their Kallen Day is special to me, but the naming of a new Faethegnar is special to the entire clan. It's important we are there to witness it."

Ash shook her head. "Hildrid—"

"Our gods chose us to be strong enough to carry these burdens, make these sacrifices," Hildrid said, hand absentmindedly touching her stomach. "We've all done it. Let me do it again."

But you shouldn't have to. The gods are unfair in what they ask.

The words remained unspoken on her tongue, swallowed by years of practice. Their gods—Róta the Ravenmother and Waldemar the Wolffather—and their tenets were everything to the Slátra. Following them was how they protected themselves from a wrath history had shown they weren't afraid to use, if displeased. To go against the gods was to put the entire clan at risk—something Ashilde could never bear to do, for she loved her clan more than anything.

So, no matter how much it irked her to do so, she continued to keep her misgivings and her questions against those they worshiped to herself.

She caught Freydis looking at them just behind Hildrid's shoulder, wearing a look Ashilde knew all too well.

Well, mostly to herself.

Ash tightened her grip on Hildrid's arm. "Good hunting," she said.

Hildrid squeezed back. "See you soon."

Ashilde hung back as Freydis and Hildrid said their goodbyes, waiting for her friend as she watched her wife leave once more. While the hunters left to hunt often—despite most of the clan only complementing their meals with meat, instead of using it as the main course—only the final hunt before winter carried the weight of pressure this one did. She caught Freydis whispering a quick prayer, lingering in the doorway, with her head bowed and her eyes closed.

Ashilde wished she believed the gods would listen.

Freydis came back inside, shutting the door to capture the warmth from the hearth. She gestured at the table and stools, where Ashilde resettled herself, her axes and her spear resting against the side. "Sorry you had to be here for ... all that," she said, waving her hand toward the door.

"It's no trouble. I felt I was intruding, more than anything," Ash admitted. "But you asked me to come. How could I say no?"

Freydis smiled as she knelt over the cauldron, ladling soup into large, stone bowls before pouring tea. She brought the meal and drink over for both of them, before finally settling down to sit across from Ashilde. She heaved a sigh of relief, and Ashilde knew it was gratitude to rest her feet and enjoy the silence, so rare within their household. Raising her children, even with the help of the entire clan, was no small feat.

It was a silence that, being childless, Ashilde knew all too well.

Ignoring a mixture of guilt, shame and sheer

confidence that always tasted too sour on her tongue, Ashilde dove into the leek soup instead, letting the warmth slide down her throat. They ate in companionable silence for a moment, Ashilde not wanting to break her friend's rare peace. She managed to steal a look at her.

Her friend was the most gorgeous woman that Ashilde had ever met. Her skin was darker than a night sky, with long hair as white as snow. Her blue eyes rivaled Davyn's for beauty, an ocean dark against his ice light. Currently, her hair was wrapped in a trailing braid that rested against her shoulder. A dress of deep green wrapped around her curvy frame, and the scent of animals—of horse, sheep, cow and bird—always lingered around her. Her laugh lines were still present around her eyes and mouth, and she ate her soup with a clear hunger.

She didn't seem to carry the weight of someone left behind, as her wife left on a hunt. A weight that she'd learned to hide, not out of fear for Hildrid's safety or abilities. Out of their band of five, Freydis's wife was the strongest of them all, her accuracy with a bow practically uncanny. No, it was the weight of being born with a body like the Ravenmother's, growing up with the expectation of becoming *sangrendi*, yet never being able to bleed. Freydis was two years older than Ashilde at thirty-five summers.

Yet she'd never once bled between her legs.

It was not unheard of. It was—in word and teaching— not frowned upon. There were plenty of roles needed within the clan aside from the *sangrendi* warriors and hunters to protect them. A fulfilling life could still be led. But teaching did not always result in reality. Not bonded in their youth, their friendship came as both of them were slowly othered in the eyes of some of their clan. *Bloodless Freydis, a betrayer of her duty,* it was sometimes whispered. *Childless Ashilde, unwilling to give what the clan needs most.*

Both had endured the whispers, the judgment. Both, outwardly, had claimed they'd healed from it, moved past it, embracing who they knew themselves to be.

Both of them were liars.

Considering, as they ate in silence, Freydis didn't have the glow of a mother excited to learn her child's name during their Kallen Day, Ashilde wondered if an old wound was getting the better of her. And without Hildrid to comfort her, perhaps she'd asked Ashilde to be here, instead, as the only one who could possibly come close to understanding what it was like.

"I'll never deny your summons," Ashilde reconfirmed, finally breaking the silence. "But, you already have everything ready for Little Goose's Kallen Day ceremony tonight, and I didn't help a lick." She set her spoon down, the motion causing Freydis to look up at her. "Is everything all right?"

Freydis laughed, a true sound, making Ashilde sit up straighter. Her musings and reading of her friend had been wrong. So why had she been summoned to her home?

"I knew you'd give your help more readily than accept mine, so I used it as a ruse."

Ashilde's body twitched, not used to such trickery from Freydis. "Frey," she said, tone wary. "What—"

Freydis reached over and took her hand. "I worry after you. Davyn does, too."

She frowned, completely caught off guard. "Davyn set you up to this?"

Freydis's own frown rivaled hers. "As if the man could set me up to do anything I didn't already want to do myself. Yet you being here during our goodbyes confirmed it. You're doing it again."

Ashilde stilled, wanting to pull her hand away. She'd

much rather help comfort Frey through her troubles than confront her own. Freydis's grip tightened on hers, however, anticipating it.

"Doing what?" Ash forced herself to ask, not truly wanting to hear the answer. But, after being part of her family's private moment and sharing a meal, Ashilde knew she couldn't deny her friend this conversation. Not when she also knew Freydis wouldn't give up until they had it.

"Taking it all on again," Freydis said. "Taking too much. I can see it in you, the way your eyes unfocus and your lips curl downward as your mind overtakes you. You do not need to bear the weight of everything upon your shoulders."

"I don't know what you're talking about."

A *lie*.

"Hildrid told me of your discussion in the forest this morning. Just as Davyn and I have conversed these past few weeks. There is so much you cannot control, Ash. The timing of the hunt, Little Goose's Kallen Day or your upcoming naming as Faethegnar, for starters. The reaction of the clan, the coming of your price or the choices we have to make."

Ash snorted. "It's good to see that any conversation I have is not private."

"Not from those who care about you. Who know you." Freydis squeezed her hand, forcing Ashilde to meet her eyes. "Your doubt is undeserving. Dagfinn does not make his choice of successor lightly. Nor without consult from the gods. You can do this. You will be a great Faethegnar for our people."

Excuses lingered on Ashilde's tongue, echoes of words her sister had thrown at her upon Dagfinn's announcement almost a month ago, naming her the next Faethegnar. She hadn't yet killed—the first Faethegnar in Slátra's history. She'd failed to protect those she'd loved before. How could she be in charge of protecting everyone now, when she hadn't saved the one she'd loved more than anything? She'd chosen to not give birth. The only one capable of doing so who hadn't. Aside from Dagfinn who, despite being born in a body that was capable, he announced it was wrong, asking to be addressed as he rather than the she that was traditionally paired, when having a body akin to the Ravenmother's. The clan had understood, knowing that his choice to continue to bleed when the gods willed it was a greater sacrifice than any of the other *sangrild* could know, all being born in bodies they were comfortable in. How could they do anything but understand?

Not for Ashilde, though. Her childless choice was seen as selfish, unheard of, wrong.

None of it was enough to change her mind.

Yet it was used to question her ability to lead her people.

Freydis—and Davyn's—concern was kind. But there were so many reasons she was unfit for such a role, undeserving. Worse of all, none of them were strong enough for her to deny her desire for it; to convince her to turn it down, earning yet another first in Slátra's history if she did. For there was nothing Ashilde wanted more. It was what she had spent the last two decades working for, striving toward. To become Faethegnar, to pledge herself completely to the protection of her people, was the only chance she could truly atone for the failures of her past.

Blinking, Ashilde came out of her thoughts to find Freydis staring at her. Not unkindly, though a small curve of her lips clued her into her friend's words before she spoke them. "See what I mean?"

Ash sighed, unable to deny it. "I ... appreciate your concern, Frey. Truly. But it's my price to bear."

"On top of what the gods already ask of you? Isn't that a little harsh?"

Not harsh enough by half. "What else would you ask of me? What else could I do?"

"Go to Dagfinn. I know you've been avoiding him since his announcement. Express your concerns, and let him give you the comfort you seek."

Ash blushed. Was she truly so obvious? For Freydis wasn't wrong. Ever since Dagfinn announced his price was almost paid—and the Seidsian confirmed it, being the only person able to speak with the gods— and named her his planned successor, Ashilde had avoided her longtime mentor and friend. Publicly, she'd accepted the nomination, but privately, she questioned it; questioned if she deserved it, if she could bear the guilt of accepting it when she knew the truth that she didn't. Yet, sitting with Freydis now, the moment days away, only waiting for her bleeding to start to allow the ceremony to begin, she knew her choice was as resolute as ever.

The gods asked her to bear incredible things. Unfair things, her entire life. She bore the secret of her doubt in them, her questioning their wisdom and the guilt of her failures. What was more guilt than she already knew?

Finally, she pulled her hand away from her friend, who let her. "I love you, Freydis," she said. "But please, trust me in this. I know what I'm doing."

"If you insist," Freydis said, not bothering to hide the doubt in her tone. Ashilde ignored it, unable to help Freydis understand, as she recollected her weapons and her cloak. "Just … remember you don't have to do it alone, alright? Please."

"I'm not alone," Ashilde said. "I have you and Davyn, my warriors and the clan behind me. Well, most of them." She gave a grin she didn't fully feel, attempting to hide the hurt she felt at her sister's obvious rejection of her nomination.

"And Dagfinn," Freydis added, as Ashilde reached the door. "Talk to him, Ash. Please."

Ashilde wasn't sure if she was strong enough for that conversation. "We'll see," she said, the promise a lie slipping through her teeth as she slid through the door, leaving the kindness of her friend behind, knowing what she'd do instead. She'd continue on as she had been, avoiding her mentor and the conversation they needed to have before the ceremony.

Everything will be fine, if you can just make it to the ceremony, she promised herself.

Yet that promise tasted just as bad as her lies, a taste that lingered with her the rest of the day.

CHAPTER TWO

Whether it was fate, or the gods or just bad luck conspiring against her, Ashilde would never know. And it didn't much matter, anyway, for it didn't change the outcome, as Dagfinn cornered her later that evening.

She was too shocked to be upset, angry or nervous when he did, surprised he had found her at all. Ashilde hadn't planned to arrive at the burial mound cradling her mother's body at the end of the day. In fact, the rest of the afternoon had been rather pleasant. She'd found a few of her warriors not already on patrol—or bedridden, as a few had already started their *dolorsandri*, their blood price—and trained with them, falling into a routine that was so familiar, it kept the thoughts of a changing future at bay. She'd immersed herself so fully, she'd barely had time to clean up before the clan had gathered in the Mess Hall to celebrate Little Goose's Kallen Day.

Or Arnvid, as he now wanted to be called.

The ceremony had raised everyone's spirits, and

Ashilde had held Freydis as she cried both tears of joy for her son and tears of frustration that her wife was missing that moment, for the good of the clan. The rest of the evening had been spent in celebration, in dancing and song and good ale. Yet, as the mood continued to rise, Ashilde had found herself with the strange sensation of wanting to be alone.

So, she had snuck away, seeking advice and wisdom from a mother who had been too dead to offer either for the past two decades.

There, Dagfinn found her, kneeling on the hard, cold ground, among wilting flowers and a biting breeze.

"May I?" he asked, though if the carrying of two mugs were any indication, he'd assumed her answer when he made the climb to the mounds.

"Please," Ashilde said, gesturing beside her. She accepted the cup he offered her as he knelt with a smile, pausing to glance at the mentor she'd avoided so thoroughly. He was broad shouldered and of a large frame, a head taller than Ashilde herself, not short by half. He kept his brown hair cropped short, a slight shade darker than his brown skin. He used white paint in the strip across his eyes, while the dots above and warrior's mark through his eyes were painted a bright red.

Wearing only a leather jerkin, his chest was flat, bound by a special binding their weavers made, for those whom the gods gave a body not fit for them—the only mistake the gods could make that the clan acknowledged and attempted to fix. By a miracle Ashilde didn't always understand, the gods allowed it, not punishing the clans for going against a binary created by them.

She shivered as the breeze picked up, fully taking in Dagfinn's cloakless shoulders, showing the dark, tattooed markings he'd acquired over the years, in his time of Faethegnar. Including the rune centered on his chest, reserved for the Faethegnar alone, intricate in its design, depicting the raven and wolf of their gods dancing in a circle around the runic symbol of protection.

"How are you not freezing, Dagfinn?"

His honey-gold eyes glanced over at her with kindness, his mouth upward in a smile. "Our elders warned me that, upon my price being fulfilled, my body's natural heat would rise. I thought them fools, when they suggested it." He glanced down at his arms, where his sleeves were rolled up to his elbows, exposing hard muscle. "I guess they were right."

"And you're about to join them," Ashilde said, unable to hide the pride in her words as she matched his grin. Despite her choice to avoid him, she couldn't deny her love for her mentor. He'd been the only leader she'd ever known, the one who trained her on every weapon in their arsenal, picking up the training her mother had started, after her chance to continue was cut short. He'd also been the one to approve and encourage her desire to master the spear, in honor of her mother, who'd also chosen the weapon, even if the axe and the sword were much more popular and common among their people.

She laid one hand on the ground, paying respect to the one she missed so much.

"That I am," Dagfinn answered her, lowering his hand to the ground beside hers. "A chance I do not take lightly, as it was denied to so many of us. A chance I am hopeful you'll get to see, too, as you start your own legacy."

She swallowed. "It's what I've always wanted," Ash whispered.

The air was quiet around them, aside from the echoes of celebration in their village below. "But?" Dagfinn prompted, giving her the option to ignore the space to process her growing guilt. An option that, just yesterday, she would have seized without hesitation.

But her conversation with Freydis, one that echoed so many nightly discussions with Davyn of late, was still fresh upon her mind. Their worry for her. Her doubt in herself. All of it, against her unyielding desire.

"But what if I don't deserve it? What if I'm not enough?"

She glanced away from the ground to look at him, as Dagfinn leaned back to sit on his heels. He took a sip of his ale, before answering. "Do you doubt my judgment? Or the gods?"

"I don't doubt yours," Ashilde said quickly, meaning it. "I never have."

His eyebrow quirked up at what she left unspoken. Ashilde cursed for making it so obvious.

"But the Seidsian only confirmed the gods agreed your price is over," Ashilde said, hoping to cover her opinions on the gods with something else that truly *did* bother her. "During your announcement, she did not confirm the gods' approval. Nor offer her own."

"Ah. Talking with Brynhild, I see."

The mention of her sister's name made her tense up, preparing for an attack that wasn't there. This time. "Avoiding her too, more like," she admitted.

She hadn't spoken to Brynhild since her sister had cornered her after Dagfinn's announcement, spitting out her disagreement with his choice. One she had not been quiet about, among the clan, in the weeks since. It hadn't been easy, avoiding her, considering they were both *sangrild* and both warriors, so many of their duties were one and the same. Not for the first time, she'd wished the gods had made Brynhild's *dolorsandri* light, marking her a hunter rather than a warrior.

At least that would have made her avoidance less obvious.

But, her sister had apparently been content with spewing her hatred to others, rather than Ashilde herself, for once. Ash hadn't realized how nice a reprieve it was.

"So, her words and the Seidsian's silence have you questioning whether or not to accept?"

Among other things, yes.

Her eyes darted to the burial mound while her hand rested against her stomach. If only it could be as simple as other's opinions of her, this wouldn't be so hard. Adding those on top of her opinion of herself...

"Almost," she said instead, not ready to bear all even to Dagfinn. It was hard enough speaking with Davyn and Freydis. "I plan to accept, if you are serious about your choice in me. I war with myself ... wondering if that choice is wise, without the unanimous faith of my clan behind me."

Dagfinn chuckled. "You think mine was unanimous?"

Ashilde gasped. "There's no way it couldn't be."

"Let me give you your first lesson, as a leader," he said instead, not giving her more details. But Ash wouldn't soon forget and planned to bother him in the future about something she didn't know of his past, during a time before she was alive. "Do not hesitate for the council of others. To take it all upon yourself could ruin you."

Just talk to Dagfinn, Freydis had begged. Apparently, she had been right.

Refusing to let herself go into another guilt spiral, Ashilde met Dagfinn's eyes. "What council do you have for me, my Faethegnar?"

A smile quirked on his lips. "A question, first. It will inform my council, though I suspect I already know the answer."

"Then ask."

"You claim the clan doesn't support you fully, yet you still plan to accept the mantle of Faethegnar. If that discontent continues into your leadership, how does it influence your choices?"

Ash opened her mouth to respond immediately, but

forced herself to close it and confirm her answer. Yet, even taking a few moments to think, it didn't change from her initial instinct. When she answered, she spoke honestly. "Their opinion of me doesn't change what I owe them. I swore to protect my people and serve the Slátra, no matter the cost. It's what I've trained my entire life for. To become Faethegnar is to promise that upon my soul, for my entire clan to witness and our gods to uphold. Their opinion of me doesn't absolve me of that duty."

Dagfinn let a moment pass before reaching out and clutching her shoulder. "That is why there is no other possible choice for Faethegnar than you, Ashilde, daughter of Gunnvor. I feel no trepidation, no regret, in my choice."

Ashilde didn't hide the tears that brimmed her eyes. "Thank you, Dagfinn. I will do everything I can to be worthy of this honor."

"I know," he said, looking away from her and toward the burial mounds beyond. "It's because you will not forget this title is a price dressed up as an honor that I know I chose well. Take comfort in that, Ashilde. As much as you can."

Looking ahead with him, she breathed deeply, feeling her body relax in a way it hadn't since the announcement. "I will."

***

Back in the village, Ashilde wasn't surprised to find the two people most important to her in their usual spot. Even despite the ongoing celebrations—the Slátra never needing much excuse for a cause to sing and dance late into the evening hours, after so much of their past knew nothing but bloodshed—Ash was quite content to slide into her usual spot, as if it were any usual day. She ducked into the corner of the animal dens on the far north of the village's perimeter. Davyn and Freydis were already there, sipping their ales surrounded by a warm fire and many sleeping animals. One of the dogs lay snoring in Freydis's lap, while a horse whinnied a greeting.

"She says you're late," Davyn said, smiling. Ashilde shivered, nothing to do with the cold at all, instead relishing that she could still love him so deeply, all these years later.

"Stop translating for her, Dav," Freydis said. "How will we ever convince her to use Waldemar's gift more if you're always there to speak on our animals' behalf?"

Ash stuck her tongue out at Freydis, who giggled, despite the truth in her words. While the Ravenmother was much crueler, in the eyes of history and Ashilde's own, her mate, Waldemar the Wolffather, was always treated much kinder. Perhaps not in small part due to his granting each clan a gift, after a tragedy their histories labeled the Banishing. Some called it an apology. Others, something owed, for what their ancestors lost.

Ashilde didn't know what to make of it. Only that the Slátra, given the ability to speak telepathically with beasts, were robbed, compared to the gifts of other clans. Gifts that were much more practical in battle. Freydis argued that, being as they were at peace—and had been, their entire life spans—was it truly so bad, to embrace what was given to them, a connection that no one clan could have? Ashilde always refused with the same answer.

Peace could only be maintained if she was always prepared for war.

And war had been her intention tonight, taking up the battle to scold her friend and lover for conspiring against her. Yet, as she curled up against Davyn's side, and he draped his cloak around her shoulders as his strong arm wrapped around the curves of her waist, she felt the desire to pick a fight with either of them wane away.

She was stubborn in her belief that the gods were not kind to them. The examples were endless. From the death of her mother far too young, to never giving Freydis the ability to bleed and become *sangrild* herself, to the weight they put on those they did make *sangrild*—like the hunters, missing out on celebration so the rest of the clan could survive the winter in peace, with bellies full and the gods' appeased; her prayers were often raging with questions rather than filled with asking for guidance, or giving thanks.

But tonight?

Tonight, she *did* thank them. For giving her so much in her life that she loved so strongly, protectively.

"Where did you go, anyway?" Freydis asked, breaking her out of her reverie.

"I was ... speaking with Dagfinn."

"Oh?" she asked, raising an eyebrow that said, 'I *told you so*' without any gifts necessary to read its intent. "And did he give you the peace of mind we hoped for?"

"Yes, no thanks to either of you," Ashilde said. "For now."

Davyn kissed her on the forehead. "We'll take for now, as long as you remember, when your peace is broken once more, that you have more people to lean on than you think."

"As if either of you will let me forget."

"And, as long as you take this," Freydis said, leaning over and pulling out something very large, hidden from underneath the wooden bench.

Forcing herself to sit up and out of Davyn's warmth, Ashilde reached her hands out tentatively. "And what is this?"

Davyn laughed. "It won't hurt you, my heart."

"No, we think you'll be doing the hurting with it, instead," Freydis added, grinning, before she hushed the pup in her lap, whining at all the sudden movement.

Moving gingerly, Ashilde unwrapped the loosely tied knots of rope wrapped around the cloth, laying the item on her lap, its length twice as long as her legs. Even though she guessed what it was the moment she saw its shape, unveiling it still took her breath away.

The spear in her lap was freshly made, but expertly so. Their weaponsmith had outdone themself. The wood of the shaft was white, matching the sturdy wood from the white ash trees that grew in the forest around them, enclosing their village. Her fingers brushed its length, following it up to the blade: a dark, sharp iron, almost as black as Freydis's skin. An inscription decorated its edges, hammered up the length of both sides of the blade.

To our Faethegnar, who has protected us without shedding another's blood, the left side read, before continuing down the right. *May this weapon protect you, should you ever have need to draw it.*

The final word was smudged, which surprised her. A weapon of this caliber was not one that would have mistakes. It wasn't until she realized it wasn't smudged at all, but instead, tears clouded her vision, making the runes hazy to read. Ashilde choked out a laugh, Davyn's arms wrapping tightly around her shoulders as Freydis moved to kneel in front of her, wrapping her arms around them both.

"Thank you," she whispered. "Both of you. I will do everything I can to be worthy of such a gift."

"Oh, Ashilde," Freydis said, laughing through her own tears.

"You already are," Davyn finished.

Clutching them both tighter to her, Ashilde hid a grimace as a cramp—a long, deep cramp, hitting her very core as her stomach tightened and her back spasmed—reminded her of the price she'd always paid and the weight it was about to take on.

If you've ever thought to listen to me, heed me now, she prayed to Róta and Waldemar, surprising herself in the process. *Let me succeed in this. Let me be strong enough to protect them; protect them all.*

She would not fail another again.

CHAPTER THREE

Pain racked her body.

Ashilde inhaled, purposefully sucking in air through her nostrils, her bottom lip pinned between her teeth, keeping her breath steady, held. Another wave of cramps hit, targeting her lower abdomen and back, like a blade was trapped within her, slowly scraping from the inside, desperate to carve its way free. She didn't exhale until the attack subsided, the sharp sting of the blade transforming into a drum, becoming a dull, thudding rhythm within her stomach—a beating reminder that her relief, as quaint as it was, was only temporary.

She sank deeper into the water, lines of dark red trails slipping into the dirty liquid, no longer clear as the paint on her face began to wash off. Her arms rested against the stone, fingers clenched against the basin's edge releasing their hold, if only slightly. She wished, for just a moment, that she could spend the day submerged in the water, lost to her own private pity and pain.

But today, Ashilde simply didn't have the time.

Her *dolorsandri*—and the ceremony naming her Faethegnar—had arrived.

Her heart hammered in a mixture of nerves and excitement. *You need to get ready. And soon.*

"In a moment," she whispered, before taking a deep breath and releasing it, willing her cramps to cease. She'd wasted too much time already, waiting for her price to lessen. The first day bleeding was always her most painful, but this? This took that pain to new levels. Another wave hit, the pain attacking with acute precision—like that of a tool, freshly sharpened on a whetstone—accentuating her pain to the heightened state of near unbearability.

Moaning underwater, Ashilde curled her body inward, arms slipping down from the basin's edge to wrap gingerly around her legs, pulling them forward into her sore stomach. Nails sunk into the side of her calves, leaving marks behind on her muscles, one nail even drawing a pinprick of blood. She didn't feel it. Ashilde's focus remained fully on the pain erupting from inside of her, expanding to attack her lower back and thighs.

So distracted, she didn't hear anyone enter her home.

"Warmongers, the both of you," Ashilde muttered through clenched teeth as she raised her head back out of the water.

A cool hand, soft compared to her callused fingers, brushed strands of stuck red hair away from her forehead, before caressing her cheek. Ashilde opened her eyes, greeting Davyn with a smile that didn't mask the pain she felt.

"I hope you're not talking about me," Davyn said as he knelt down on the ground, leveling his face with hers, his tone teasing, even if concern laced through his eyes.

"You shouldn't be here, my love," she said softly.

It'd been three days since the hunters had left

and they'd celebrated Arnvid's naming day. The night before last, she'd begun to bleed, only lightly, signaling her price's true start was nearing. She'd announced it to her Seidsian, who promptly made preparations for the ceremony. It was customary, for that final day prior, that the new Faethegnar stayed in solitude for the entire day and night, offering prayers for wisdom and guidance from the gods.

Ashilde had been in too much pain to even attempt it.

Davyn had already prepared for the ceremony, dressed in his best clothes, his cloak lined with fur along the shoulders accentuating his naturally large frame. They'd slept apart, as was tradition—the first time in years. She hated it.

He kissed her softly. "The gods will forgive me for this one transgression."

The same gods who she'd been cursing as he walked in. He didn't need to know that, though. She was in no mood to fight with him today.

Besides, there were other concerns.

"Any word?" she asked Davyn, before hissing through her teeth as another cramp took hold.

"I can go get some willow bark?" he offered for the pain, ignoring the question as to whether their hunters had made it back in time. Yet it answered it just the same. She shook her head, answering his question.

"They didn't make it," she whispered, her stomach twisting in a way completely unrelated to her *dolorsandri*.

"It'll make the celebration even grander, upon their return," Davyn said, always seeing the light where Ashilde had trained to focus upon the dark. "Come, my love. Our people wait for their Faethegnar."

Her heart pounding at the title being attached to *her* got her moving, despite her pain. Standing, she shivered as she escaped the cold water of the basin. Davyn glanced at her, his eyes slowly drinking in her body, a combination of thick curves and thicker muscle. Heat warmed her cheeks as she shoved him away with a giggle, distracted from her fears and her pain for just a moment. His grin gave away his intentions to do just that, though it didn't completely distract her from the heat in his eyes and the promise he held there—of celebrations of a different kind, once her naming was over and they were alone.

Ashilde stepped out of the basin and walked across the room, toward a basket on the floor that held linens specifically used during her *dolorsandri*. She wouldn't need to wear one for long today—the ceremony required her to bare all—but her blood flow was strong enough to justify wearing one while she got ready, at least.

Using a jar of sap they harvested from the trees, she applied it to the base of the linen, before lining it against the crotch of a pair of tight black pants. She slipped them on before pulling on a loose shirt, her stomach pulsing all the while, a familiar, monthly rhythm.

Turning back around, she collided into Davyn, who immediately wrapped his arms around her. Startled for only a moment, she returned his embrace, her head resting against his broad chest, his black fur mantle tickling her cheek. Pulling away slightly, he leaned down to kiss her, before cupping her face into his hands, forcing her to stare into the ice of his pupils.

"I am so proud of you, Ash," he whispered. "Even in peace, a clan needs a Faethegnar. And you will be a great one."

She smiled, warmed by his praise and his faith in her.

Together, they moved over to the rug and sat, after she gathered her paint. Davyn sat behind her and began braiding back her hair without a word, while Ashilde reapplied her face paint: her eyes and the lines traveling down them to the base of her throat were a deep red, while the small round dots spaced eventually across her forehead were black.

Davyn styled the sides of her head with trailing twin braids, pinned together at the back of her skull to join the rest of her hair he'd pulled up and tied into a tail, allowing most of her hair to hang as a mess of wavy red curls against her back. He kissed her neck to signal he'd completed his work. Standing, Ashilde put her jar of red paint back on her shelf, shuddering a sigh, as she stole a glance at the spear Davyn and Freydis had given her, just a few days prior.

"It's time, isn't it?"

Davyn nodded.

She exhaled, slowly. Hoping her nerves didn't show, Ashilde gathered the long, thin white cloak crafted specifically for this purpose, made from spider silk. She stripped her barely worn clothes, her linen already stained, red smears glaring back at her. Leaving her clothes on the wooden floor, she slipped the cloak on, the garment more ceremonial than purposeful, with its sheer design and thin layers. It felt as if she wore nothing at all. She raised the hood to hang over her face.

Davyn kissed her one more time. "Meet you there?"

They couldn't approach the shrine together or the others would know he'd broken the rules to visit her. As if they didn't know already. She nodded, not trusting her words.

It was time.

"Give thanks to the gods. I'll see you soon," he said, turning and leaving her home.

She glanced over at her private shrine: a small wooden table, surrounded by candles meant to be lit during prayer, and a bowl of water to wash the hands clean. Figurines—wooden, stone and cloth—of wolves and ravens overburdened the three tiers of shelves built above the table, signifying gratitude to the Ravenmother and the Wolffather, for all that they had given them.

It wasn't a coincidence that she hadn't made any herself.

Ash turned ever so slightly, preparing to kneel at the shrine, but stubbornness stopped her. An old hatred, born from her own trauma and guilt, lingered like coals within her, always hot and ready to ignite with the slightest provocation. Though publicly, she went through the motions of worship with the rest of her people, privately, she held too many questions, too many doubts, to truly give those actions any weight. The gods had never done anything for her. Instead, they asked and commanded, threatened and took what they pleased.

"I don't do this for them," she whispered to the empty room.

Ignoring the shrine, she walked out the door.

***

The air outside was still as Ashilde walked across the village, normally alive with noise. Instead, the village felt eerily empty. The sight of children running between the thatched longhouses and huts; the distinct rhythm of hammering wood or clashing steel; the smell of freshly baked stew; all of it had vanished, swept away as if by the wind, not a soul in sight.

They wait for you.

Ashilde continued her march through the empty village, her bare feet sinking slightly into the ground, still wet from last night's rain. By the time she passed through the cluster of homes and began climbing the single, soft sloping hill leading south, she could already feel the blood between her legs begin to stain her upper thighs, rubbing together without the fabric of her pants to pad them. Keeping her back straight and her head high, she pushed forward, ignoring her discomfort and the feeling of vulnerability trying to snake its way underneath her skin, refusing to ponder at what her people might think of her in such a state. Nakedness wasn't uncommon—many shared the bathhouse together, after all—but this? This was different. This was baring her soul to be judged and hoping no one found her wanting.

Ashilde set her mouth in a line, as if fighting against her own nervous thoughts.

Dare them to question you, she fought, faking confidence with every step. *You haven't given everything, only to fear what those you serve think of you. Give them someone to be proud of. Become worthy of them.*

Cresting the hill, Ashilde found her people.

They had gathered before her at the main shrine for the gods, one simple in design, but grand in purpose. It consisted of a large stone slab centered on the top of the hill, placed purposefully so both the sun and the twin moons could shine directly upon it, during their zeniths. On the back stood a raven made of stone, wings outstretched, spanning far enough across to cover the entire slab. Below it, a wolf curled up and slept, discolored in spots where blood from the sacrifices dripped onto its head and body, despite how hard they'd tried to scrub it clean.

Ashilde didn't think Waldemar liked his chosen animal to be covered in blood.

Even if it came from the blood of animals Róta demanded in their honor.

Inhaling deeply to settle herself, Ash walked between the benches, meeting the faces of her clan who watched her. She caught glimpses of her fellow warriors to her left, all dressed in their finest leather armor to celebrate this rare occasion, not bothering to hide wide grins and brimming eyes. Aside from Brynhild, whose scowl was as sharp as any weapon.

Today, Ashilde refused to feel its bite.

Freydis grinned, tears flowing down her face, surrounded by her children, who waved at her and whispered excited praise. Ash waved back, earning some laughs from the others behind her. She held onto that joy, that pride, pretending that she didn't notice the empty seats where their hunters should have sat; pretending that Hildrid's promise wasn't broken, by not being here; pretending that it didn't hurt, even when she knew that their mission to collect food and sacrifice for their people was greater than any ceremony the Slátra could hold.

Instead, she turned her eyes forward once more, focusing on the trio of people standing beside the shrine. Davyn stood off to the side. As the clan's only healer, they needed him close, in case she passed out. She gave him a quick smile, which he returned tenfold, not bothering to hide his pride as he, too, used the back of his hand to wipe his tears away. She turned to face the other pair before his love undid her: the Seidsian, leader of their clan, and Dagfinn.

The Seidsian stood as tall as her frame would allow, her body thin and hunched, holding a spear as a walking stick. She wore an elegant dress dyed red with a black fur cloak wrapped around her, her necklace of raptor talons passed down from each Seidsian before her hanging heavy on her neck. Her face, an ashen white, was a mask, her opinions unreadable. Ashilde was forced to take comfort in the knowledge that, if her Seidsian—or the gods, for that matter—truly disagreed with Dagfinn's choice, this ceremony wouldn't be happening now.

Beside the Seidsian, Dagfinn wore a simple outfit consisting of breeches and a low-cut, sleeveless shirt, allowing most of his tattoos to be on full display. Stationed beside Dagfinn on the shrine was a jar of black liquid and a small needle, glowing red at the tip from being heated.

Meeting Dagfinn's eyes, she waited for him or their Seidsian to speak.

Just breathe.

After a moment, the Seidsian spoke up, her voice like perfected iron, surprising in its strength, coming out of a brittle sheath. "Today is a day like no other. Today, we thank the service of Dagfinn, who has given us many years as both a leader and protector of the Slátra clan." She turned and nodded toward Dagfinn, who bowed his head in response. "The gods have blessed you, my friend. Today, we will celebrate you and all you have accomplished, and celebrate the next path in your life, one that so few of our ancestors ever reached."

Turning again, she faced her people. "But first, it is time to welcome our newest Faethegnar, a woman who has earned the honor through years of hard work, dedication and sacrifice."

The Seidsian paused and a jolt of fear laced within Ashilde, waiting for Brynhild or perhaps someone else she'd recruited to her cause, to speak out against the proceedings and Ashilde's nomination. Yet, the people sitting behind her remained silent, except for the shuffling of feet and the occasional labored breath.

The Seidsian, apparently pleased, looked down at Ashilde. "Are you ready, Ashilde?"

Ashilde swallowed. "I am."

The Seidsian nodded and took a step back, letting Dagfinn take over. He motioned Ashilde forward, and she walked to stand in front of him, bending her head as she pulled the hood off of her face. He twisted to pick up the ink and the needle, his own tattoos stark and bright to her eyes, knowing her own body was about to be similarly marked.

He looked past her, over her shoulder. "I am

Dagfinn," he said, addressing their people. "I am he and he is me. For over forty summers and forty winters, I have served as your Faethegnar, leader of our small, but fierce band of warriors." Hoots from behind encouraged his words. "As well as the hunters who are gone from us today, once again proving the lengths we go to, to protect our people."

That brought the quiet stillness back, the cheers of the warriors dying out to a solemn acknowledgement, none of them a stranger to the sacrifices asked of them, nor the ones each had made.

"I am *sangrild*, one who bleeds, as the gods have gifted me since I was eleven, on that fateful Wyrdan Day. Every month, I paid my *dolorsandri*, bleeding heavily, so that, if the gods asked it of me, I could kill any person who dared to come and attack the Slátra." He paused and offered a large grin. "Today, I am *sangrild* no more. The gods have witnessed my sacrifice and deem my oath fulfilled. Today, I become *sangrendi!*"

Cheers erupted behind Ashilde, accentuated by clapping and whistling, growing to a roar that sounded much mightier than the fewer than two hundred souls gathered there. She was warmed by it, her nerves settling somewhat, the goosebumps covering her body betraying her pride.

After a moment, Dagfinn motioned for the cheering to cease. When silence prevailed once more, he returned to look at her. "Ashilde, you have been chosen, by the people behind you, the warriors you have trained among and the gods we worship, to take the mantle and lead in my stead. Do you accept this charge, which is as much a gift as it will be a burden to you?"

Ashilde met his eyes. "I do."

"Then, in the names of our Ravenmother, Róta, and Waldemar, our Wolffather, and witnessed by all of the people gathered here, promise it."

Swallowing, Ashilde spoke slow, but steady, thankful for the moments she'd practiced her oath.

"I, Ashilde of the Slátra, I who is she and she who is me, pronounced *sangrild*, one who bleeds, by the gods since I was thirteen on my Wyrdan Day; bare my *dolorsandri* for you all openly today, as proof of the price I pay." She paused to breathe a single, deep breath, before she continued. "I take upon me the oath to protect not only alongside my fellow *sangrild*, my warriors and my hunters; but also to protect the *sangrendi*, those whom the gods have not given the ability to bleed. As *sangrild* and as Faethegnar, I swear to kill on behalf of those who cannot, in the name of protection, self defense or the art of war."

Slipping off her cloak and letting it fall to the ground, she knelt, her knees sinking slightly into the wet grass. "Today, I pledge to put the needs of the clan before myself. Today, I pledge to bear any price that is asked of me, to protect my people. Today, I pledge my body and my soul to the Slátra, in the form of becoming your Faethegnar." As an afterthought, she added, breaking away from the scripted oath, "I will do everything I can to be worthy of it."

After a moment, Dagfinn nodded, before glancing past her once more. "People of Slátra, what say you?"

Cheers of encouragement and approval answered. Not as loud as the cries of joy and pride for Dagfinn becoming *sangrendi*, but Ashidle was unable to turn around to see who was less than thrilled by her promotion. But it didn't matter. She'd meant what she said to Dagfinn, at the burial mounds. She would serve her people, no matter what they thought of her. She would continue to sacrifice everything for her clan.

"Then, through the gods-blessed magic of our Seidsian distilled into this liquid, I will mark this day on your skin, Ashilde, labeling you protector, so that all will remember not only what you are, but also what you have pledged. Today begins your journey as Faethegnar."

This time, the pronouncement was answered with a nervous silence, as Dagfinn turned and dipped the hot needle into the small jar of black liquid. Any warrior or hunter who had proven themself would have those deeds remembered by staining the skin permanently. Ashilde didn't understand the process particularly, only knowing that the liquid and instrument used had to be crafted by the Seidsian herself, as the only member of any clan to have any sort of magic gifted upon her.

Rumor claimed it was extremely painful.

As Dagfinn leaned over and pressed the hot needle into the soft skin in the center of her chest, rumor transformed into truth. Ashilde squeezed her eyes shut as tears threatened to slip out, biting her lip to keep from crying out. She knew Davyn waited nearby, to rush her back to his hut, if necessary. And though it wasn't unheard of, for a newly-chosen Faethegnar to pass out during their first marking, it was often read as a sign of disapproval from the gods; a warning that the people had chosen poorly and their new Faethegnar wasn't strong enough to bear what would be asked of them.

Ashilde refused to let that happen.

Instead, she squeezed her hands into fists and breathed in a rhythmic pattern, in and out, through her nose, staying stone still, shivering slightly each time Dagfinn paused from marking her skin to dip into the thick liquid once more. The first design was the simplest of what would hopefully be many in the future: the rune of protection, encircled by simple drawings of the wolf and the raven.

Dipping the needle in once more, Dagfinn bent low and whispered, "You doing okay?"

Eyes still shut and lip pinned between her teeth, Ashilde nodded.

"You're doing great," he said encouragingly, as the needle bit back into her skin, as he continued to draw long, smooth lines against her chest. "You know, when I—"

He was interrupted by the strident sound of a horn, sounding off in the distance.

A flash of sharp pain erupted against her chest as Dagfinn quickly turned at the sound, forgetting to pull out the needle and accidentally dragging it against her skin, tainting her mark. Ashilde's eyes flashed open. She struggled to inhale as she met Dagfinn's stare, widened in horror, as whispers began to gather strength behind them, her chest burning.

"Was that...?"

But Ashilde couldn't finish her question, as a second call sounded, this time further away, as if near the front gates. It was a horn that she'd only heard in demonstration, when Dagfinn had taught her why each of their fighters were required to carry warhorns, whenever they left the village. It had been a quick lesson, for they only had one purpose: to sound an alarm.

"Our hunters..." Dagfinn breathed as the whispering of the clan grew louder, rising to a panic.

Ashilde stood quickly, turning around. Her warriors stared at her, stunned for a moment with inaction. Despite training for their entire lives for a moment like this, that's all it'd ever been; a training session, a possibility, a worst reality. They had never been attacked before.

But it didn't matter.

They were being attacked now.

Their band of hunters were out there, alone. If whatever was mounting an attack was human, their hunters couldn't kill them; not without paying the ultimate price.

Leaning forward, Ashilde grabbed a bow sitting

against the bench where her warriors sat, not bothering to ask who it belonged to. "Get them to safety, then follow me," she commanded quickly, before raising her voice to address her people. "Follow your warriors! Go to the Seidsian's home, all of you, and stay together, until one of us tells you otherwise!"

Without waiting to see if anyone followed her orders, Ashilde took off, bow in hand, down the hill and towards the front gates. She ran with wide strides, her balance slightly uneasy against the wet, muddied ground and her own chafing thighs. Cramps assaulted her from within, and she gritted her teeth as she dodged around a garden, passing the central fire pit where they were to gather in celebration, later that evening.

The warhorn sounded again, shrill and stark, before being cut off too soon, casting an immediate silence outside the gates.

She feared they would be gathering tonight instead for a sadder purpose.

Picking up her pace and praying her warriors had gotten everyone to safety and followed right behind her, Ashilde stumbled slightly as another intense cramp rocked her. Glancing down, a thin trail of blood trickled, leaving a trail behind her.

Ignoring the growing discomfort of not being wrapped in protective layers of cloth, especially as a cool breeze whipped against her naked body as she rushed, Ashilde finally reached the outskirts of the village. She strapped the bow across her back, climbing the ladder with steady hands as she shoved all her emotions away, centering herself to focus, preparing for anything. She pulled herself up onto the walkway, not noticing the splinter that had lodged itself into her wrist as she'd climbed, nor the blood continuing to drip down her leg, making her foot slick.

Immediately kneeling, Ashilde glanced left and

right, confirming her solitude. *At least they haven't managed to breach the gates.*

Swallowing, she stood and pressed herself against the edge of the wall and glanced beyond it, mentally counting the arrows collected in the quiver sitting atop the gates. In the clearing along their walls, she saw nothing. In the forest beyond, to her left, she saw nothing. She heard the splashing of waves from the distant cliffside, but she saw—

A scream interrupted her scouting, filled with anguish and pain.

Ash shot up, pulling her bow off her back and readying it as she twisted to look directly below her, her stomach pressed uncomfortably close against the wall. Her eyes widened as her breath caught, almost choking her, taking in the scene below.

She'd found her missing hunters.

Four were now corpses. Only Hildrid remained, held at knifepoint by three attackers who had ambushed them; the real source of her horror.

It was ... impossible, but the status of the three men was instantly clear. While their clothing of thick, wool coats overlaying leather armor could have aligned them with any clan, the lack of markings on their faces was the only clue she needed in identifying them. Every clan used facial markings to help denote status and allegiance, varying in colors and design, but all following a similar pattern. The lack of any markings at all was just as universal, reserved for only one thing.

Rhuanics.

Those who were banished from their clans after being renounced by the gods, cursed to live their lives in exile and spend eternity in the Pit upon their death.

The brute holding a bloodied knife—unpainted, once again showing their status as an outcast—looked up at Ashilde and whistled. "Do you always greet enemies in such a fashion, Slátra? If I'd known, I would have asked Waldemar to let us attack your borders sooner."

Ashilde couldn't care less about her naked state. Clothing and armor would have wasted time and cost lives, she'd reasoned without needing to think about it, taking off as soon as the warning sounded. Apparently, it hadn't mattered.

She'd been too late, regardless.

Ashilde's body remained rigid, as she forced every feeling deep.

She couldn't allow her guilt to surface. Not now.

"You will face unspeakable consequences for what you have done," Ashilde whispered, staring into Hildrids' eyes. Her hunter, her *friend*, met her gaze, no fear reflected there, only a hardened resolution. One that broke her heart.

I can save you, Ashilde promised, opening her mouth to bargain with the Rhuanic, to spare the only life they hadn't taken.

It didn't matter.

Her arrow flew the same instant the man's armed moved, slicing his knife deep across Hildrid's throat, grinning as he did so.

His grin remained as Ash's arrow pierced through his eye, dropping Hildrid's body as he screamed. She hit the ground with a hard *thump*, not attempting to stop her fall.

Ash lost all sense of time, any awareness of her surroundings. She only came back to herself moments later, after her fingers grasped at the air, no more arrows left to pull from the quiver. She took in the scene below, seeing the Rhuanics laying on the ground, dead, arrows through their chests, their shoulders, their eyes, their hearts, their skulls.

The bodies of her hunters surrounded them.

Hildrid.

Ashilde screamed, shouting from the top of the wall for help from her people, from her warriors, from *anyone*. Climbing back down to the ground, she rushed to reach the circular wheel, cranking it to pull open the gates. She only opened it wide enough for her to slip through, her body protesting as she dragged roughly against the wood, leaving her skin irritated and splintered, before Ashilde was moving again. She sprinted until her shaking body failed her, sliding onto the ground freshly stained with blood.

Four of them were certainly dead, either lying in pools of their own innards or staring blankly at the sky as it grew overcast, unable to see the changing weather. None of the animals they'd left to hunt were with them, nor their wagon or their horses. Their weapons were scattered upon the ground, while the warhorn lay splintered in two.

Finding Hildrid laying between the slain Rhuanics, Ashilde pushed outside the corpses of those she'd slain, quickly collapsing beside her friend. Lifting her body up, she cradled Hildrid in her lap, wrapping her arms around her thick shoulders and arms. Blood staining her neck rubbed onto Ashilde, making her grip slip. She clutched at Hildrid tightly, looking for any sign of breath, any movement of her chest, any gurgling in her throat or fluttering of her eyelids.

She can't be gone. Davyn can save her. Davyn can—

Ashilde moved strands of hair past her face, not wanting to meet a stare that couldn't answer back. She choked on a sob, her vision blurring with tears, unable to accept the reality before her, knowing that her lack of acceptance didn't change it. She kissed Hildrid's forehead, her clan's markings smudged from sweat.

Cradling her head, Ashilde whispered in Hildrid's ear, "His name is Arnvid."

Ashilde continued to cradle Hildrid as she sobbed, her

mind playing a constant refrain she wasn't fully aware of, just yet. But the understanding would come and it would hurt. Her fears had been right. She couldn't protect them. She couldn't protect anyone.

She was always too late.

Chapter Four

Ashilde didn't know how much time had passed and didn't hear them approach. She didn't notice the metallic scent training the air, carried along by a careless breeze also carrying the sounds of crashing waves and rustling leaves, both deafened to her ears. She stared at the ground, but she saw nothing.

All Ashilde noticed was the weight of Hildrid's body against her legs, shocked that her hunter's cheek felt so cold against her naked thigh, only for her mind to catch up and remember.

Hildrid was dead.

Fur blanketed her shoulders, startling Ashilde. She jumped up, her fists swinging, forgetting to grab her bow. She'd *kill* whoever dared interrupt her vigil. Her face was tear-stricken, dirt covered her knees, while a mixture of blood—Hildrid's across her arms and her own, between her legs—stained her skin. Instead of landing a killing blow, she collided with Davyn, who grasped her shoulders hard, stilling her.

"It's all right," he whispered, pulling her out of her shock with a lie louder than the deafening silence of the dead.

She shook her head, silently asking him not to say anything else, not allowing herself to fall into his embrace. Instead, she pulled away from his grasp and moved to look behind him, to find the warriors—her supposed charges, before she'd become a failed Faethegnar—gathered together, still dressed in thick, ceremonial leathers and armed to match, carrying an assortment of spears, axes and short swords.

The rune in her chest burned, as if trying to purge her of her shame, instead of making the sense of failure within her swell even more.

On her first day as Faethegnar, she was responsible for the death of the clan's hunters.

Every single one of them.

She was met with a mixture of expressions: from the taut lips of stunned shock to the wide-eyed stare of disbelief. Even from Dagfinn, who stood behind the others, axe in hand; ready to pay the ultimate price to protect his people, even after becoming *sangrendi*, if it had come down to it.

Only Brynhild openly bore the look of hatred, a fire in her eyes; only Brynhild showed her what she deserved to see. But Ashilde was unable to bear it, her mind too tattered, her heart too hurt and her reality too shaken.

She looked away, instead meeting the gaze of her Seidsian.

As the only living member of the Slátra to have ever experienced the war, she could read the battlefield before them clearly and without much wasted time.

"Ingrit, Torunn," Dagfinn said as the Seidsian surveyed, his voice firm. "Go inform the clan they are safe, but also of what happened here. Spread the word: we gather at the shrine tonight, after evening meal."

Both warriors shared a glance that spoke in a way that only those married to one another could understand,

and nodded, before turning around toward the village.

"Bodil, Unna, go with Davyn to get the wagon. You will assist him in preparing our hunters for their funeral song. Magnhild, please go gather their families and do what you can for them. We delay our council to give them time to grieve. Let them."

The trio turned away without hesitation, though Davyn stole a glance back at Ashilde, his brows furrowed in concern. She gave the smallest shake of her head. *Not now.*

Ashilde had frozen up at the appearance of her warriors and their Seidsian so soon after losing all of their hunters, despite calling for them moments before. Dagfinn had been forced to step in and lead, as he'd done so often before. And was once expected to, as Faethegnar. As *she* should have, regardless of her emotions.

She couldn't explain the guilt and shame she felt when Davyn looked back at her. She wasn't sure she wanted to. He seemed to understand and left with the others.

After, only she, the Seidsian, Dagfinn and Brynhild remained.

Her sister didn't hesitate. "How dare—"

"Brynhild," the Seidsian interrupted, not even raising her voice, taking over from Dagfinn. "Drag the Rhuanics away. Dump them into the ocean."

Brynhild turned to look at their leader, crossed her arms. "Seidsian—"

"Strip them of their belongings and take what remains to my hut," she continued, not even looking at Ashilde's sister.

For a moment, Ashilde thought Brynhild would argue, the way she opened her mouth to voice her displeasure. Instead, her words were taken away by the wind, chilling Ashilde for the first time, the adrenaline from the attack all but spent. Brynhild's jaw set firm as she turned away, anger reverberating off her smaller frame as she stalked off, not sparing Ashilde a second glance as she ignored their leader's instructions, instead returning back within the confines of their home.

Ashilde turned back to the Seidsian, who's eyes flashed from a pale green to the stark silver for an instant, the first hint that she experienced any emotion other than the calm she'd shown so far. She glanced at Dagfinn, who nodded. She knelt beside one of the slain hunters, closing her eyes to whisper prayers to Róta and Waldemar. She also didn't move her cloak, allowing it to trail in the blood as she moved between the dead.

Dagfinn approached her, not meeting her eyes. Insead, he stood beside her, staring out into the distant ocean.

"Your heart has always been pure, and your dedication to your people has made me proud," her mentor began. "But not today."

Ashilde flinched, the words stinging worse than the sharp stabbing of her cramps within and the pulsating flare from her broken mark on her chest combined. "Because I couldn't save them."

Dagfinn glanced over at her, one eyebrow raised. "Because you acted in haste, without thought."

This time, Ashilde's hurt transformed to anger, her voice lowering an octave as she met his stare, not unaware that her Seidsian could hear everything they said. "Without thought? I came to save our hunters from an attack! I rushed to prevent this fate!" She threw her arm at the bodies lying dead beside them. "Our hunters are dead. *All of them.* The implications are ... are..."

Dagfinn did not hold back, his eyes flicking to look at her briefly. "Are something we will discuss tonight, *as a people.* What would have happened had you been met by not three Rhuanics, but three trained warriors? Could you have killed them all yourself?" Before Ashilde could promise that she certainly could have, Dagfinn pushed on. "What about a dozen? Two? They would have sliced you down, and the numbers of those sworn to protect the clan would have dwindled even further, bolstering our problem."

Ashilde blanched. "They sounded the horn *three times*. I just ... if I couldn't save their lives, I wanted to save their souls. I—"

"But even in your haste, you were too late."

Ashilde flinched as if struck, the promise she had made herself just this morning that she would never fail another again stark in her memory.

"Worse, you commanded those who could have helped you to tarry, when there were enough to split up so you wouldn't have to venture alone." Dagfinn glanced back toward the cliff and the sea, as if his words weren't tearing her insides apart. "Met with only three, you've slain them all and avenged your fallen sisters. But at what cost? With the strength of the warriors at your back, you could have overwhelmed them and taken them alive. Tell me, newest Faethegnar of the Slátra: of all the answers you seek currently, how many could one of those Rhuanics answer, were they still alive?"

She didn't even want to think about it, but after being prompted, they all rushed to the surface of her mind, bidden like a beast to its master's call: *who were these Rhuanics? Why had they come? And from where? Which clan had they once been a part of? Was this attack purposeful or was it a one-off chance? What did they want?*

Ashilde swallowed bile that rose into her throat.

You fool.

Dagfinn nodded, as if he could read Ashilde clearly and see the guilt that she currently felt rising within her, understand the nausea threatening to take hold of her and unleash itself upon the already-spoiled ground. Only a few nights ago, he'd been comforting her that his faith in her was warranted, that he believed in his choice. She'd believed him.

Instead, they'd both been wrong.

The Seidsian stood, then, surprising Ashilde when she approached and raised a hand to caress Ashilde's cheek; a motherly gesture, rarer than the brief words the Seidsian chose to speak, often instead staying in silence to better commune with the gods. Dagfinn stepped back slightly, allowing the Seidsian to take over. Ashilde stiffened, bracing for the next blow.

"You will learn from this," the Seidsian said, removing her hand and speaking with firm authority. "All that Dagfinn has reminded you is true, including your failures today. A warrior's first lesson is to remember why she fights. You fight for your people. You fight to ensure the clan survives. Sometimes, that means making hard choices in the moment that could even cost lives, in order to protect the clan's future." She glanced down at the hunters, recognizing their sacrifice, before looking back at Ashilde. "Now, our future is in question and we are in mourning. But winter waits for no woman's grief. I've set the others to work. You will dress and do the same."

Ashilde nodded, not trusting herself to speak, as her own guilt—an emotion that came to her too often, yet still hurt, as if it was their first time meeting—weighed heavily on her chest, creating a physical pain in her heart. Her cramps hit once again, as well, making her wish she could return home and do nothing but give into it all; replay the mistakes that had cost her hunters their lives, and her clan vital information they needed to understand today's attack, from the comfort of her own bed.

Instead, her Seidsian spoke again. "You will do what your sister could not. Strip them and dispose of their bodies. Then, you will return straight to your home and you will submit yourself to prayer. You will wait until Dagfinn comes for you."

Ashilde nodded, knowing she had no other choice.

But then, the reality of the Seidsian's words hit home, as well as the greater pain she hadn't realized yet. *Freydis.*

"Seidsian, please. Freydis, I must—"

"Will be with Davyn and the others, mourning the loss of her love. You will pray, until I send Dagfinn to tell you to stop. Am I clear?"

Ashilde hesitated. The Seidsian moved her hand to press against the center of her chest, *hard.* A sharp pain shot through her core, the ruined rune burning against the pressure. Ashilde bit her lips to stop from crying out.

Stunned, Ashilde finally relented, agreeing to the Seidsian's price.

"Then go."

Ashilde turned to move, but Dagfinn grabbed her arm, stopping her. "I'll tell Freydis you cannot comfort her now," he whispered. Ash choked back a sob, undeserving of the kindness. She wasn't sure if she could take the pain of Freydis believing she'd abandoned her during her darkest day.

Instead, she pulled Davyn's cloak tighter against her, and watched as her leader and her mentor left the battlefield, leaving her behind with the dead.

For the briefest of moments, Ashilde wished she was among them.

***

Ashilde's knees were sore as she knelt in front of her prayer altar. Layered now in a loose shawl over breeches and an oversized shirt, she remained alone in her home, the walls around her—which normally brought her comfort and peace—feeling suffocating for the first time. She stared at the figurines representing her gods and couldn't come up with the words that her Seidsian commanded her to speak to them.

She only felt anger and sorrow as her mind filled with questions; oh, so many questions, yet never finding any of the answers.

Instead, her fingers traced the rune carved into her chest—incomplete, its purpose now unclear. It wasn't meant to be a symbol of status, like the markings on her face served. No, it was meant to be a promise, a pact that ran so deep within her, made between her and her clan, that she could never be rid of it. It should have reflected the promise to protect.

Yet, missing half of the runes to complete her promise, what did that make it now? What did that make *her*? The first Faethegnar to fail her people, despite all the ancestors who'd protected them during generations of war? The first Faethegnar to have the title not just stripped, but removed the very same day it was given? Her one shot at redemption for her mother's death, gone, the cost being more than she could ever pay?

A knock on her door surprised her to her feet.

Dagfinn entered before she could acknowledge it.

Ashilde lowered her eyes in shame, her heart suddenly thundering. The Seidsian had promised she'd send the former Faethegnar to collect her. By the way he walked in, with his shoulders slumped and his face an impassive mask, she feared he brought worse news than simply a summons to the council.

Instead, a warm, deep voice said, "Come here, child."

In a blink, Ashilde found herself in his arms, her tears long since dried away, but her body shaking in a broken surrender as she gasped. Dagfinn caressed her hair in a calming manner, letting her unload everything she'd forced down and away without a word or any ounce of judgment; a much different reception, compared to their last meeting just that morning. But not the first time she'd cried in his arms.

When she finally collected herself and the

shuddering stopped, Dagfinn pulled away and cupped her face in his hands, before leaning forward to press his forehead against hers.

"Do you mind if we sit, for a moment? We have a little bit of time before the council gathers and I ... well, I have some news."

The pit in her stomach grew, but Ashilde swallowed it as best she could, motioning for Dagfinn to follow her as they moved to the other side of the room, where she'd set up a small, circular wooden table, bordered by a matching pair of stools. She hadn't gathered water that morning from the well, too preoccupied preparing for the ceremony. After a moment of fidgeting with her hands, she clasped them together and forced them into her lap.

"I'm sorry I don't have anything to offer you to drink," Ashilde said quietly.

Dagfinn raised an eyebrow, giving her a look she knew well. She swallowed, hard. Even if the Seidsian had determined it was a sign from the gods that she could not become Faethegnar, her people would still need her, in whatever capacity she was able to give.

You have the rest of your life to grieve and berate yourself, she thought. *Focus.*

She met Dagfinn's eyes. "Has she come to a decision of what's to be done with me?"

He nodded, a sign of approval, rather than a confirmation of her words. "She has—and there is nothing to be *done* with you. The Slátra don't turn on their own, not even when it becomes dire."

"Not even when it costs the clan our hunters?"

Looking away, he sighed. "You are a good warrior, Ashilde. I meant what I said this morning, but ... I also meant what I said, back at the burrows. I do not regret my choice. You took charge and you made a decision that ended up being a mistake."

"You didn't stop me. Why?"

"You are Faethegnar. It was important for the people to see me respect your leadership. Not to mention that I can't exactly kill, anymore." He sighed. "Though I welcome it fully, being a *sangrendi* will take some getting used to."

Ashilde nodded, suddenly ashamed of the blame she'd tried to place upon her mentor. He reached over and took her hand.

"You'll learn, or you will continue to fail and those you love will continue to pay the price for it. It is harsh, but that is what it means to be Faethegnar—even if your first day has been harsher than most."

"I'm still proclaimed Faethegnar?" she asked, unable to keep the surprise from her voice.

"Yes. The Seidsian prayed to the gods, asking if they wanted a different answer, yet none was given. Since no one has come asking for your replacement, then it is agreed: you are Slátra's Faethegnar."

Ashilde flexed her hands, wishing that the tightness in her chest would ease with the news. It hadn't. "You hesitate. Why?"

This time, her old friend couldn't face her, looking over at her shrine. "I asked the Seidsian to allow me to come and finish your rune. She denied me. It is to remain unfinished."

The weight sunk into her stomach, making it hard to breathe. "A reminder?"

"A warning," he said, his voice grave. "Of what, she didn't elaborate. Only said to trust in the gods and their will."

Ashilde barely hid her mask of displeasure at his words. There were many people she trusted. The gods were not part of that list.

Instead, she kept her face impassive as she reached over and touched Dagfinn's wrist. "Thank you for bringing me this news. I'm sure it will be announced at the council, but ... I know it wasn't easy to deliver."

He turned his hand so he could grasp hers in his. "I can only imagine how you feel, Ashilde, but I know it is nothing pleasant; grief, anger and uncertainty are a dangerous mix. But, if our ancestors can conquer greater trials than this, then so can we. Together."

"Together," she said with a small smile that she didn't feel. "When does the council gather?"

"Soon, just as the sun sets. Many have gathered to eat, first. I will go there myself, after this. Join me?" he asked as he stood.

Ashilde stood alongside him, but shook her head. "I must finish the prayers the Seidsian asked of me." She grasped Dagfinn's arm, gripping it tightly in farewell. "I'll see you at the council. Thank you, Dagfinn."

"Of course, Ashilde," he said, turning away and heading back towards her door, before pausing as she pushed it open. "My Faethegnar," he added as he walked out.

Ashilde watched as the door shut and felt nothing.

CHAPTER FIVE

Despite her promise to Dagfinn, Ashilde left shortly after he did, moving in the opposite direction.

The sun had finally started to dip closer to the horizon, the soft blue of the day transitioning to the vibrant reds, pinks and grays of the coming evening. She didn't go to the Mess Hall to eat, as she felt no hunger and had no appetite, despite not eating all day. She didn't stop by the healer's hut, where she knew Davyn worked to clean and dress the hunters for their funeral rites, despite wanting nothing more than to feel his embrace. She didn't even go to the training ground, where a blunted blade and a practice target usually offered her respite when nothing else could.

She didn't go check on Freydis, unable to bear the sorrow her friend felt.

For the first time since her mother died, Ashilde didn't feel like she deserved to be with her people. Her penance could start by staying as alone as she felt.

A coward on top of a failure? You're learning more about yourself every day.

Ash stumbled, shuddering against her own mind's cruelty, not used to being its target with such venom, such accuracy. She emptied her mind of thought, focusing on putting one foot in front of the other. Ashilde climbed up the hill, leading away from the heart of the village, until she reached its highest point: the shrine to the gods. The place where she'd been named Faethegnar. The place she'd made her first mistake that'd cost them everything.

The irony that she had sought sanctum at the one place where she usually avoided was not lost on her.

Ashilde sat on a stone bench, shivering slightly against the air as it started to chill, her mind flashing to earlier that morning—could it have really not even been a full day yet? Images of the friendly faces, filled with excitement and pride as she walked between them, only to be ruined as everything twisted into horror and panic at the strident sound of a warhorn.

Ashilde pulled her legs up onto the stone and wrapped her arms around them, resting her chin on her knees, as her cramps continued to pound within her stomach. Bearing her price and forcing her thoughts and emotions away by concentrating on regulating her breathing, she waited for the rest of her people to arrive, eager for the answers they'd bring to all of the problems she'd created.

Instead of fixing it yourself?

Ashilde blinked away tears.

It seemed even her own mind was against her.

It didn't take long, however, before others began to show up, either talking quietly among themselves or staying as silent as she was. They began to fill in the benches around her and behind her, but none beside her. Ashilde sat straighter upon their arrival, lowering her feet back onto the ground, but she didn't do anything to acknowledge them, just staring at the shrine ahead of her, at the bloodstains that marred it. Images of her hunter's faces continued to flash in front of her eyes and no amount of blinking erased them fully.

"Ash!"

The choked sound of a surprised voice crying out her name forced her to turn around, as Little Goose—Arnvid—stood beside his mother, his siblings standing behind her, all of them clinging to Freydis's skirts as if letting go would cause them to lose the other mother they had left. Ashilde let out a choked sound she didn't recognize. Freydis stared at her, not in anger, but with a sorrow deeper than Ashilde had ever seen.

Ashilde stood to rush to them, to embrace Freydis and wrap her children in a hug she wasn't sure she'd ever be able to let go of. Freydis even took a step toward her, as if she'd welcome the comfort.

But then Brynhild stepped up from behind Freydis, the line of people coming to the gathering growing behind her. She placed a hand on Freydis' shoulder, stopping her, before motioning toward the bench.

"It's about to begin," Brynhild said, not unkindly, but in a way that Ashilde knew all too well meant there was no option for an argument. Her heart shattered as Freydis obeyed, quietly moving her children to file onto the bench, before Brynhild took a seat beside them, her partner and their children following. She met Ashilde's wide-eyed stare, then, daring Ashilde to try and reach her friend.

Ashilde, feeling the eyes of all those who had gathered, backed away, sitting back down alone at her seat with a numb brokenness.

Eventually, the quiet hum of those who gathered grew to a steady beat, as the mixture of reminiscing their hunters and voicing their fears and anger at the day's events continued. It created a cacophony that was only silenced as the Seidsian herself walked up to the shrine, Dagfinn, the rest of the warriors, the hunters' families and Davyn in tow behind her. They spread out to sit as the Seidsian remained the only one standing in front of the crowd.

Only Davyn moved to sit by Ashilde, immediately taking her hand and wrapping it in his.

Ash took a moment to look at him and saw his own exhaustion written on his features, from the lines protruding from his eyes to the way his soft smile wavered as he looked at her. But as he squeezed her hand, Ashilde felt life breathe back into her for the first time since before the ceremony.

The Seidsian turned to face them, illuminated by the dying sun behind her that had just sunk behind the wall, creating an ethereal-like glow around her frame.

"This morning, we experienced a tragedy unlike any our ancestors had, despite tragedy being the only constant they knew," the Seidsian said, her soft, fragile voice reverberating through the stark silence, her people hanging on her every word. "I hear your pain and I understand your sadness. I promise you, we will honor our fallen and celebrate their passing together."

Pausing, the Seidsian took a moment, letting her eyes pass over the gathering, lingering on each member in turn, allowing the silence to draw out. Ashilde felt the atmosphere shift, a sense of calm slip over the Slátra that, moments ago, had been slowly building chaos, fear and doubt shifting among a sea of hushed conversations. Even the children, down to the smallest, days-old babe, were silent.

And all the Seidsian had done was look at them.

That was her power.

But Ashilde couldn't help but notice how the Seidsian, too, shared in the collected exhaustion from that day, despite standing with her back rigid and her expression blank. Her eyes provided a glimpse within, showing the toll she'd paid, how heavy her burden had become. She'd lost five daughters—by clan, despite not by blood—and all of her hunters in one day. Yet, she had changed into her finest: furs made from the skin of the giant white bears, worn leather armor that helped her to survive numerous battles and war, alongside the same jewelry hanging off her neck that she'd worn that morning, made from raptor claws—representing predators that no longer stalked Armadin, wiped out by their ancestors. A reminder of what their ancestors had conquered and what they, too, could now overcome.

"But first, we must understand what has happened, so we can determine how to respond. And respond we must," she said, her voice becoming iron. She glanced over at Ashilde. "Despite the interruption, you were chosen as Faethegnar and Faethegnar you will remain, the unfinished mark on a chest an accurate depiction of what has happened today. Do you accept?"

Ashilde swallowed. "I do."

"Objections?"

Ashilde was surprised it remained silent, though the shuffling in seats behind her made it clear this wasn't accepted unanimously.

The Seidsian didn't linger, moving on. "Men have killed our hunters. Men who have renounced any ties to clan or land. Is this true?"

Ashilde sat up a little straighter. In her stripping of the bodies, she found nothing to disprove the claim. "Yes, Seidsian."

"To the Slátra, they are branded Rhuanics," the Seidsian proclaimed. "Róta and Waldemar would not permit such blatant disregard to their rules. They deserved their fate: dead and left trapped beneath the sea."

I would have asked Waldemar to let us attack your borders sooner.

Though Ashilde trusted the Seidsian more than anyone, doubt lingered within her, pulling her shawl closer, as she remembered the Rhuanic's easy words, spoken without hesitation. She was no stranger to questioning the gods. If they listened to her prayers, they would recognize that was all they were: a barrage of questions, begging for explanations of personal mistakes, juxtaposing laws and unfair rules. Yet, despite her questioning and her anger, she believed the gods wanted what was best for their people, deep down.

Which is why Waldemar somehow ... *approving* the Rhuanics' existence made no sense.

Especially since they were only branded Rhuanics for going against Waldemar's own teachings, from whichever clan had outcasted them.

She kept her face impassive as she shoved the memory aside, though her body remained rigid, a foul aftertaste suddenly souring her mouth. It was a private discussion, for her and the Seidsian alone; no sense in alarming her people. Still, she cursed herself silently for letting the earlier reprimands from both mentor and leader alike distract her from disclosing such a specific and potentially important detail before the evening's council.

"Dead," the Seidsian continued, "but not forgotten. There are many mysteries that surround these men: who they were, where they came from, which clan they've forsaken, why they attacked, what drove them to do so. I assure you, I'll lead the search for these answers myself, starting with my prayers tonight."

Murmurs of approval answered her, backed by the faith they all had in their leader.

"Now, in this moment, I must ask all of you to join me in a hard task; difficult, but necessary, forced upon us." Her stare swept over the gathering once more. "Our hunters have been slain. In the grossest of realities, we must acknowledge that our ability to gather meat has died with them. It is this problem that we must now solve."

The air shifted again and even the Seidsian's presence wasn't enough to quell the anxious storm beginning to brew.

It was the topic no one had wanted to talk about, no one wanted to acknowledge. It didn't matter whether they chose to or not. It wouldn't change their new circumstances.

Yesterday, the Slátra had five hunters: women blessed to kill animals.

Today, they had none.

Without those animals, they would have nothing to sacrifice.

Without a sacrifice, they risked not only Róta's direct attention, but also her wrath.

A wrath that, last time their god exerted it, resulted in the Banishing: a storm so intense, so devastating, it not only ruined all the lands of Armadin aside from the Segan—the god's blessing, where they now lived—making them inhabitable, but also wiped out the entire Skalda clan.

Ashilde swallowed and slipped her hand out of Davyn's, wiping the sudden sweat off her palms. She wished it was something as simple as a lack of food, a shortage of furs. They usually gathered more fruits, greens and nuts than they killed meat already, so the lack of meat to their diet would be an adjustment, but not an issue. For some, it wouldn't have even been a change. Blankets could be shared, layers could be added, more logs added to burning fires, to deal with the fast approaching winter.

But without an animal to sacrifice monthly, they would be breaking the only rule Róta had given them, as a result of the Banishing: a demanded animal sacrifice, as a reminder of what the Skalda had done—and a promise, of what the remaining clans would never do.

To ignite her wrath could be the end of the Slátra, forever.

She slipped her still-sweaty fingers back underneath Davyn's palm, resting on his knee, searching for comfort. He didn't look over at her, instead looking around the faces of their clanspeople around them, with their narrow lips, wide eyes and shaking hands betraying their worry. But he squeezed her hand tightly, intertwining his fingers again with hers. He knew as well as she did—as well as they *all* did—the bind they were suddenly in.

"I open the invitation now for conversation and ideas. We will return to our homes to privately grieve and mourn once we've come up with a solution," the Seidsian declared.

Silence answered her, but only for a moment.

"Could we ... try to begin each child's Wyrdan Day sooner?"

Ashilde glared at the speaker, her sister's husband.

There were few moments in a person's life that resulted in ceremony: Borinn Day, the day of their birth; Kallen Day, a child's naming day; Asttan Day, the day partners swore their love; and their Wyrdan Day, a day where a child who would become *sangrild* bled for the first time.

According to their teachings, any child between the ages of nine and sixteen has a chance to experience their Wyrdan Day, though none without a body matching the Ravenmother's ever had. If they reached the age of sixteen without bleeding, they were considered unchosen for the honor—and the burden—of becoming a warrior or hunter, and thus proclaimed *sangrendi*.

Ashilde resisted the urge to snort. It wasn't a process a person could stop and start on a whim. It wasn't like a child's naming day, where they approached the Seidsian and informed her when they were ready. No, the *dolorsandri* was triggered by the gods or withheld by the gods, often without rationale or reason as to why one experienced it when another did not.

If they tried to determine who would be blessed with the *dolorsandri* against who wouldn't, alongside trying to guess the level of blood flow before a child first experienced it, and guessed *wrong*, then that child's soul was forfeit. For to kill without paying the blood price was to damn your soul to the Pit, instead of spending eternity in Skírrdrauin.

They had many children. At least half their number were younger than the age of ten, many of the Slátra using the peace their ancestors hadn't known to replenish the number of their clan, hoping to raise the next generation of *sangrild*. Ashilde, for more than one reason, had chosen not to help the clan in that way. It was a choice she stood by, knowing in her heart to be the right one.

But now, as calculations began of what could be asked of their children, guilt flared.

"No," Ashilde said, the numbness she'd wrapped herself within throughout the day shedding like a cocoon, giving way to her strongest emotion: anger. "You will look me in the face and ask me to put my soul on the line, before you ask our children to risk theirs."

Many people looked away from her quickly, after her response. Her sister's husband had the decency to look ashamed, blushing after she called him out, but Ashilde couldn't fault him, not completely. It was a natural thought, if crass: just replace their hunters with new ones. But all of their children were just that, none of them old enough to have a chance to have their fate revealed by the gods, and no certainty that any would experience their Wyrdan Day before the next sacrifice was due, in a fortnight's time. Not to mention the training required to be prepared to go out into the wilds.

And all those who would have trained them in the art slain in only a few heartbeats.

In shutting that down, Ashilde had hinted at another

alternative, but silently disregarded it just as quickly. She was willing to kill animals, even as a warrior, and pay the price of her soul to do it. But to corrupt her soul would mean her death, in one month's time, for carrying souls not meant for hers to carry.

Her own *dolorsandri* would kill her.

That was a heavy price to ask any of their warriors, but a foolish one, too. Even if they were willing—and she believed most of them were—they would only survive as a group for a few months; a year, at the longest, before all of the warriors had died off, too, one month at a time. Then, the clan would be left without *both* hunters and warriors.

She shivered.

"We will not risk the eternal lives of our warriors nor our children," the Seidsian said, cementing that decision in stone. "We need another solution."

Another voice called out, too far away and hidden behind others that Ashilde couldn't pinpoint who spoke. "How about speaking with the beasts we already have; ask them to hunt for us?"

Bodil, the oldest of the warriors, spoke up quickly. "You want to ask animals to go hunt their own kind on our behalf? Open your ears and you'll hear them laughing." The crow that perched on her shoulder rubbed his head against Bodil's cheek, before releasing a harsh, singular caw, as if in agreement. "They are no more our pets than we are their masters. To ask them such a favor would cost us the friendships our gift has graciously given."

"Not to mention, what predators do you think we keep here?" the penmaster asked, an older man who leaned against his walking staff. "We have dogs, sure, but coddled, they are. They'd get themselves killed before they'd do any good for us."

Murmurs of agreement echoed.

No one expressed the idea that they could sacrifice *them*.

Thinking of her own mare Ashilde often rode, she shook her head at that solution, too. Even if she was upset that their gift paled in comparison to those of other clans, she'd still formed a distinct attachment to her horse—even if she didn't speak with her, like many of the Slátra did. Sacrificing them would buy them time, but not enough to be worth the pain.

Instead, an idea sparked. Ashilde spoke before she could bury it with fear. "We could ask for help," she said, barely raising her voice.

Silence answered her.

The Seidsian glanced at Ashilde, commanding with a stare to elaborate.

Ashilde felt an additional weight added to her shoulders than what she usually carried, as the eyes from every clan member narrowed in on her. But she also distinctly felt Davyn's thumb continue to trace circles on her kneecap, his hand still covering her own. It was enough to ground her against the weight and give strength to her voice.

"This problem is much greater than simply replacing our fallen hunters and figuring out how to appease the gods through our sacrifices," Ashilde began, ignoring the burning in her chest as her broken rune flared. "The very foundation, the very rules that govern us, have been broken."

People grumbled at that, but a quick, sharp turn of her head and a glare that could break steel cut them off. Her anger stirring, Ashilde stood and turned to look at her people, something she hadn't had the strength to do the entire day while she wore a veil of shame and regret.

No longer.

"Today, men killed, willingly damning themselves to the Pit, in order to take out our hunters. I worry of a greater storm approaching, one we need all of our wits and our resources to prepare for. All obvious options in acquiring meat ask for costs that are too high: for our children, for our animals, for our warriors. We cannot combat heresy with heresy. We must *think*, both long term and immediate."

"What are you suggesting?" the Seidsian asked, not unkindly, but her tone made clear she wanted a feasible solution and she wanted it now.

"We have too many questions about those who attacked us and not enough answers. And we cannot gather meat for ourselves." She purposefully paused and glanced around the gathering of faces, meeting eyes, if she could, noticing how they pleaded for answers. "I suggest we send out a scouting party to the other clans—as many as we can reach—and ask them if they have experienced similar devastation. If they have not, we ask for the assistance of their hunters to help us through the winter—long enough for us to work out a more long term solution, while also gathering answers."

As expected, after the idea sprouted in her mind, the council erupted into chaos, with shouts of dismal and gasps of disapproval echoing all around her.

The clans had been at war with one another ever since the Banishing, the event that shook the core beliefs of them all and separated the clans even further. All of them prided in being self-sufficient, believing their own interpretation of the gods' actions and their decrees to be the *only* correct interpretation. After generations of war and skirmishes left each clan weakened to the point that they barely had the numbers to survive on their own, let alone fight one another, a shaky truce had been called—out of necessity alone. Ashilde's was the first generation to grow up within the rebuilding years, instead of being born into war.

To ask for help from another clan was to admit and

show weakness; an invitation to bring war back into their home, encouraged by old grievances and the first generation untested by battle, if other clans found the Slátra easy enough to destroy, upon discovering their new reality. Not to mention it would be the first time any of them had traveled outside their home and into the borders of lands that didn't belong to them, visiting clans they'd only heard, at best, nightmares about.

Ashilde knew the risks, of course.

But she was in no mood.

She met the eyes of her Seidsian, hoping she saw the strength of Ashilde's determination reflected through a narrowed gaze and straightened spine. *I'll do what no one else is willing to do. I'll do what must be done. For our people.*

"We don't have time for petty pride," she said, her voice rising above the cacophony. "Nor, I think, do we need this discussion. You asked me to be your Faethegnar. I ask you to trust me in this. I will not let you risk the souls of our youth. And unless you can ask me, to my face, to risk mine, then I refuse to do that, too. I leave to travel across the Segan at dawn and meet with as many clans as I can, before the next sacrifice is demanded, in two weeks' time. Anyone interested in joining me, may."

The stunned silence followed her as she left the gathering and walked down the hill back through the empty village and toward her own home, as darkness descended upon the village. No one chased after her to argue—not the Seidsian, none of the warriors, not her sister, not even Davyn. For what argument could they give? They had already exhausted all other options. Ashilde knew, in her heart, that asking for help—even begging, if it came to it, was the only possible solution.

Even if it meant testing the limits of this truce truly for the first time.

Determined, renewed with a sense of purpose weighed by sorrow and guilt, Ashilde knew she would not sleep that night. Now, there was too much to prepare, too much to do, to ready herself to travel across lands she didn't know; prepare to say goodbyes to those she loved most. As she made it to her door and slipped inside, Ashidle knew the risk, just as much as she knew she couldn't do anything but accept it.

There was a great chance that, when she walked through the Slátra gates, she wouldn't return.

CHAPTER SIX

Ashilde walked alone underneath starlight, slowly meandering between their mixture of longhouses and cottages, allowing the sconces slowly burning away outside doorways to be her light. Her eyes lingered on the homes, making a mental list of spots that could use patching, gardens that could be replanted and various other duties she'd want to assist with, once she returned home.

If you return home.

This time, the chill jolting down her spine had nothing to do with the lazy breeze.

Crossing her arms across her chest, she walked along the curved dirt path, leaving the cluster of homes behind and instead facing a row of specialized longhouses, where no one lived, but many of them worked. Their ancestors had set up the village in this manner purposefully: from the smithy, weavers and healers' hut on the right, the Mess Hall, bathhouse and market on the left; to the pens, stables and training grounds that wrapped around the north side of the village; all of it made up a secondary border, protecting the homes in the center.

Ashilde had already made her rounds earlier that evening, collecting everything she'd need for her journey into a small pack currently sitting by the edge of her bed. She'd promised Davyn she'd meet him and Freydis at his hut. Her friend's comfort was long overdue and Ashilde, selfishly, hoped Davyn might give her some comfort of her own.

But first, she needed a respite only one thing could give her; the weight of a weapon in her fingers. Her fingers flexed.

Perhaps swinging her sword at an opponent who couldn't break her soul might do something to help repair it—or start to, at any rate.

As she approached the small enclosure, the sound of clashing wood alerted her that someone else had the same idea.

Ashilde slipped open the wooden gate and let it fall shut quietly behind her, her cramps thankfully quiet within her—a good thing, since her stomach quickly twisted as she discovered her sister, still dressed in her leathers, hacking at a wooden dummy with a blunted practice sword, the sheen of her sweat on the back of her neck glistening against torchlight.

Brynhild was shorter than Ashilde by a head, with a lean frame, compared to Ashilde's thick curves—though both carried the thick muscles years of training had provided them. With light blonde hair, pulled back to nest atop her head, and silver eyes, she looked exactly like their mother, while Ashilde was told her red hair and green eyes came from her father.

Barely remembering him, she had to trust the comparison.

Ashilde stopped before she got too close. "Brynhild," she called.

Her sister flinched, yet didn't turn around. Ashilde hadn't seen her since the council, hadn't spoken to her directly in … gods, she wasn't sure how many days she'd spent avoiding her. All she knew was that Brynhild had, instead of listening to their Seidsian's demands, gone to distract the children of the slain, so their parents could mourn their partners in peace, even for a few moments. Her heart had swelled when she heard it, unsurprised by the kindness in Brynhild that she only witnessed, never felt.

Something not to be changed tonight, as Brynhild finally turned around, silver eyes flashing. "You *actually* mean to go through with this?"

Blinking, Ashilde said, "It's the best option, Bryn."

"Don't call me that," Brynhild spat, before she tossed a wooden sword at Ashilde.

Ashilde quickly caught it, frowning. She hadn't even realized she'd slipped, calling her sister by her nickname; a name Ashilde had called her ever since Brynhild announced herself on her Kallen Day. Once, her sister loved it so much, she demanded everyone adopt the shortened version of her chosen name. Before she'd had time to grow up and realize what Ashilde had done, how she had failed.

Before her sister could hate her for it.

Brynhild shook her head, struggling to say what bothered her. Instead, she picked up another practice sword off the rack beside the dummy, moving in front of Ashilde in a challenging stance.

"If I beat you, you give up this foolish notion," she declared.

Before Ashilde had time to respond, she attacked.

Ashilde barely had time to raise her blunted weapon before her sister's weapon came at her face in a sweeping arc. Ashilde caught it, her arm twinging from the impact, before she shoved backward, pushing the blade and her sister away in the process, who took a step back as she adjusted. Ashilde glared.

"This is not a drill or a game, Brynhild."

"They wanted to come, you know," she said instead, before taking another swing.

Ashilde blocked this one easily, now that she knew to expect it. Relenting, she offered a blow of her own, though not one motivated with enough force to actually *hurt* her sister, unlike what her sister was trying to do to her.

"Who did?" she asked as the pair of them fell into a rhythm of par and swing, block and swipe, bash and slash.

"The hunters' partners," Brynhild replied, already slightly out of breath. Who knew how long she'd been out there alone, working out her own rage and frustration?

Ashilde winced as Brynhild caught her wrist with a quick tap, her heart breaking slowly as her sister grinned at the pain. Her sister's hatred, she should have become accustomed to, given it'd been years since their mother's death. Yet, seeing fresh evidence of it never ceased to bring Ashilde pain, especially when the good Brynhild did for the clan was never ending.

Ashilde had lost memory of when any of that good had been directed at *her*.

She lowered her stance and went on the defensive. If attacking her directly was what Brynhild needed to process the day's events, she could do that for her. Brynhild took the bait and began to hammer away at her defenses, gripping her weapon in a two-handed manner to give her more powerful, albeit slower, strikes. Ashilde took a moment to focus on surviving the blows. It didn't take long for them to become slick with sweat.

"They would be welcome to come with me," Ash finally responded. "Perhaps it could give them some comfort."

"You'd lead them into enemy territory, without the ability to defend themselves?" Brynhild glared. "You'd just leave more orphans behind."

Ashilde winced, but tried to let the jab slide off her, like water. Instead, it stuck like mud, picturing Freydis's children running to see Hildrid off just a few days before. They'd never get to see their birth mother again.

"It's not ideal," she admitted. "But we're at peace. They deserve any closure they can get. If I can give it to them, I—"

"And who will send our hunters off tomorrow, hm? Who will help them reach Skírrdrauin, if not their partners?"

Pit, she has a point.

After the death of a clan member, they celebrated the life of the fallen through ceremony and song: their funeral rites. It was the job of any living loved ones to offer the final prayer over the burial pyre, before burning the body of the dead and releasing their loved one's soul to Skírrdrauin, the realm of the gods.

Ashilde took a step back, lowering her weapon. "Why do you bring this up, sister?"

Brynhild paused, though her fingers twitched along the base of her sword, her grip tightening, itching for her next attack. "I thought you should know that some wanted to come with you," she said, her voice lowering slightly, a rare sign of guilt from Bryn.

Ash frowned. It hurt that no one took up her offer to join her, especially none of her fellow warriors who should. She hadn't given it much thought, not wanting to follow what she'd felt was a natural line of thought: their lack of aid reflected in their opinion of her, lessened by her failure.

Now, she wondered if something much different was at play.

"What did you do?"

"I did the first thing necessary in my own bid for Faethegnar: I told the truth. No one should leave the borders of the Slátra, especially on such an imprudent errand when we already know the answer."

It was Ashilde's turn to grow angry, unsurprised that Brynhild planned to challenge her to the role of Faethegnar. "Foolish child."

Her guilt often outweighed any other emotions she felt toward her sister. As such, Brynhild—only three years younger—was usually the only one to raise her voice, between the two of them. And she used that power. Often. But the day's toll had caught up with Ashilde and she was *tired*.

With a lunge, she struck out, startling Brynhild as she went on the offensive.

"Did you offer another solution, then?" Ashilde asked as she struck rapidly, causing Brynhild to quickly begin falling backward, barely fending off the quick and precise onslaught of one who'd trained night and day to earn the skill. "Or are you simply waiting for Róta to wipe us out in two weeks' time, making us the first clan since the Skalda to be killed by her hand?"

"I'll ... come up with another solution. A *better* one," Brynhild floundered, her lack of confidence obvious. "One that doesn't involve relying on other clans, insulting our ancestors' memory by seeking help from those who killed so many of us." Her eyes left their flurry of weapons to meet Ashilde's, filled with heat once more. "Or pretenses of bravery."

Ashilde misstepped, her sister's words breaking her anger and concentration. "Is that what you think this is? A chance to ... to *prove* myself?"

"Oh, don't act so innocent," Brynhild spat, parrying her last blow with ease. "Running out alone this morning, *naked*, while commanding the rest of us to wait, when we could have met the Rhuanics as a united force? All because you want to 'protect' us?" Her sister snorted.

"Everything I do is to protect the Slátra," Ashilde whispered, seething beyond the point of yelling.

"*Everything.* You know that."

"Oh, because you're so good at it?"

Her words hit harder than any blow she could have delivered with her weapon. Ashilde knew her sister didn't like her. She knew she didn't forgive her, most likely never would. But she wasn't used to her being so cruel.

"I'm going," Ashilde said, dropping her weapon to the ground. "And I will not fail."

Brynhild threw her hands up in the air, exasperated. She threw her weapon against the rack, not bothering to pick it up as it bounced off and landed in the dirt. "You're a greater fool than I took you for," she said, before striding back toward the gate. "I see right through you, Ashilde. Playing sole savior isn't enough to bring her back."

At her back, Ashilde whispered, "And hating me will?"

The only sign her sister heard was a slight hitch in her step, which she quickly corrected, before she slammed the gate shut behind her, disappearing into the night.

***

"I'm so sorry," Ashilde whispered, her face already tear-stricken, as she crashed into Freydis' arms. She'd left the training grounds soon after her fight with Brynhild, seeking comfort even when she didn't deserve it. Entering Davyn's hut and discovering all of his tables—usually over-ladened with books, scrolls, bottles and herbs—instead holding only five bodies, covered in burial quilts, shook her.

Finding Freydis standing near the only one uncovered, Hildrid's face clean but the jagged line across her neck glaring, Ashilde broke.

Freydis clutched at her arms as they buried their faces into each others' shoulders. Her friend's sobs were sharp, violent. Ashilde clutched her close, swallowing the onslaught of apologies she wanted to unload, to let Freydis cry without the added burden. Ashilde threaded her fingers in her hair, cradling her head as the shoulder of her tunic began to become wet with tears.

She didn't know how long they stood like that, clutching each other as if it was the only way to remain anchored. It wasn't until Freydis shuddered a breath and pulled away that Ashilde let her go, looking at her face to see tear stains amongst bloodshot eyes.

"Freydis—" she began, but her friend cut her off quickly.

"Apologize again and I'll thrash you, Ash. By the gods I will."

The venom in her voice was one Ashilde wasn't accustomed to. She barely kept herself steady.

"I don't want to hear your guilt. I don't want to know how she was murdered," Freydis continued, her body shaking. "All I want is your promise that you'll avenge her. You find out who sent them and why and you make them suffer."

"Freydis…" Davyn came forward, out of the shadows and Ashilde's heart broke anew. His eyes were tired, his shoulders slumped, his exhaustion as clear as Freydis's fury. But his voice carried a thread of warning. Apparently, they'd had this discussion before. "She can't—"

"She can and she will," Freydis said, whipping around to glare at him with a bite Ashilde had never seen before. "Brynhild forbids anyone to accompany you; claims it would be unfair to the children, to potentially lose both parents." She spat the words, her disagreement evident, before her shoulders shuddered and, finally, her anger dissipating as if she didn't have the strength to continue. "Please, Ashilde. I can't … but I *need*—"

Ashilde pulled her forward into another embrace, clutching her arms tightly. Even if Freydis had no children, she couldn't kill without sacrificing her soul. Ashilde had no idea the levels of grief she had to be feeling, at both losing her love and never being given a *dolorsandri* to avenge her with. But she didn't have to explain it for Ash to understand.

"I promise, Frey," she whispered, pulling apart to grasp her face as she spoke her vow aloud. "I will do everything I can to find out who is behind this. And they *will* suffer."

The brokenness in her friend's eyes hardened into resolve, as she nodded her approval. "Then I must go. My children..."

She didn't bother continuing. Instead, she pulled out of Ashilde's arms and walked toward the hut's door, glancing at Davyn as she moved. "I'll be back with the sunrise."

Then, she left, leaving the pair of them momentarily stunned, to see one of their trio so irrevocably broken.

Davyn was the first to move, walking over to where Hildrid lay, pulling the quilt back to cover her face. Ash walked up to him and took his free hand, gripping it tightly with her own. He looked over at her and sighed, though he squeezed back, however weakly.

"'How are you doing,' feels too foolish a question," Ashilde admitted.

That brought a small ghost of a smile to his lips. "With no answer quite sufficient. Are you prepared for tomorrow?"

"As much as I can. Come with me?"

Despite all the horrors of the day, spending the night wrapped in his arms was a blam Ashilde couldn't deny she needed, desperately.

Her heart shattered slightly as he shook his head. "I must keep vigil here," he said softly. "I have many prayers to complete before the funeral tomorrow."

Ashilde didn't know if it was exhaustion or anger that caused her to speak. But she regretted her words as soon as she uttered them. "As if the gods cared about any of us enough to listen. They—"

Davyn turned to her, his ice-blue eyes sharp enough

to cut. "Blasphemy in your own home, Ash, but dare not do it here, among our fallen dead. I will not allow it."

She recoiled, though the heat of his eyes cooled the same moment regret bubbled up in her stomach. She was usually so much more careful about her critiques of their gods around Davyn, who held such an unwavering faith in them. He was right. She was a fool to bring it up now and risk a fight amongst the bodies of the hunters she'd failed to save.

"Ashilde—"

"Goodnight, Davyn," she interrupted, pulling herself away before his hand to pull her in for the comfort she desired. Instead, it was all she could do to avoid running out the door, escaping back to the pseudo-safety of her own home. As if her own mind would be any kinder than what she'd just experienced, between Brynhild's hatred, Freydis's vengeance and Davyn's faith. As if she'd deserve it, if it somehow was.

CHAPTER SEVEN

The next morning, Ashilde woke not from nightmares—no matter the horrors she'd face, her sleep never experienced dreams, let alone nightmares. Instead, it was the cramps within her that caused her to stir, throbbing pointedly as soon as she opened her eyes. The events of yesterday hit her fully as she sat up, her gaze immediately landing on her pack, her fitful sleep punctuated by a sudden, deep exhaustion—the kind only carrying the expectations and future of an entire clan could weigh. Paired with waking up alone, the memories flooded back and Ashilde wished, for a moment, to crawl back into bed and let them consume her.

Instead, she forced herself up.

Ash silenced her mind, instead focusing on readying for the journey. She washed and cleaned herself, reapplying her face paint and lining up a fresh linen in her trousers. She dressed in a simple pair of black breeches with a matching, sleeveless undershirt, before slipping into one of Davyn's oversized green shirts—to keep the herbal scent of him close to her, if nothing else, despite their argument. She hoped, when she returned, they could mend properly.

For now, there wasn't enough time.

She checked each of her weapons—a pair of throwing axes, her bow, her new spear and three knives—strapping them onto her belts. Ash hoped she wouldn't need them, but she'd rather carry her entire arsenal on her person than be without.

She was about to turn and leave before she paused, staring at a small wooden box—plain, unmarked, making it easy to overlook and ignore—placed beside her linen basket. Inside was the only item she had left of her mother's, aside from her armor. It was a gift: a necklace, carrying a singular, stone pendant, painted red. Brynhild had the matching bracelet she wore daily.

Ashilde had always felt undeserving to wear the necklace, hadn't thought of it in years.

But what she was about to do would have long lasting consequences for her people, while putting herself at great risk; traveling across the Segan for only the second time in her life, meeting with clans she only knew through passed-down memories from a war not long enough past.

She could use her mother's strength today, of all days.

With shaking hands, she slipped on the necklace, before slamming the lid shut once more.

Turning, she picked up her pack, bundled tightly, and slipped on her cloak. Swallowing her nerves, she pretended she couldn't notice the unaccustomed weight suddenly wrapped around her neck. Inside her pack were more linens, as she wouldn't stop bleeding until the end of the week, as well as dried meat and a few fruits, her waterskin, flint, a map of Armadin given to her by her Seidsian, rope and a few other, smaller essentials she didn't want to be without.

Ashilde paused for a moment and sighed. She'd lingered long enough.

She slipped out of her hut, not bothering to pray to her gods, and stumbled to a stop before she was fully out the door.

The village had gathered before her, forming two groups on either side, leaving the middle path open for her to walk. All of them stared at her, but it didn't bear the same weight she felt during the council yesterday. Instead, a few wore open smiles, while most appeared solemn—whether from their shame at asking her to travel alone on their behalf or due to their fear of the uncertain future to come, was beyond her to distinguish between.

Her face flushed crimson. After her people had all but ignored her yesterday, she planned to slip away quietly with the morning sun, while others began the day's tasks. Ashilde had tried to become content with the idea that, even without their support or their approval, she had to go through with her plan, to save them even from themselves.

To find a gathering to see her off was as surprising as it was humbling.

Her stomach unknotted, just a little.

Ashilde pushed her feet forward. She squeezed hands and clasped arms, patted shoulders and offered smiles to their well wishes as she talked with each person who gathered to watch her leave, her heart growing warmer with every conversation. It didn't take long for Ashilde to realize nearly everyone was there—including the partners of the slain hunters, all gathered together, stone-faced and swollen-eyed, the younger children clutching desperately to their last surviving parent. She hugged each of them, foreheads touching as they whispered gratitude and hope into her ear.

She lingered with Freydis the most, kissing each of her childrens' forehead in turn, before reaching up and clasping Freydis by the head, pulling her close to whisper in her ear.

"I hold my promise close to my heart," she whispered.

"I know," Freydis said, the softness in her voice more akin to the Freydis Ash knew. "Come back to us."

Ash choked back a soft cry. Not trusting her voice—not willing to promise something she wasn't certain she could keep—she nodded instead.

Reaching the end of the procession, following it as it led to their main gate, Ashilde nodded to the Seidsian, before grinning up to her fellow warriors—including Dagfinn—all of them gathered above on the ramparts, one arm across their chests in a silent salute, fists clenched shut in solidarity. Even Brynhild stood with them, though her expression showed how she truly felt about this entire display.

Ashilde blinked back tears.

For once, Ash didn't let her sister's hatred bother her, instead overwhelmed by the support of the family she'd chosen. She had no doubts, now.

The clan trusted her, even despite the events of yesterday.

She would not fail them.

"We have gathered to see you off, Ashilde, Faethegnar of the Slátra," the Seidsian proclaimed, her voice booming across the village. "Go with the blessing of the Slátra and know that your journey is constant in our hearts and first in our prayers."

Ashilde bowed low. "Thank you, Seidsian."

"Ah," the Seidsian said as Ashilde rose. "Not alone, then."

The line on the right parted to make way for the pair of readied horses that needed to pass, though Ashilde's gaze focused on the man leading between them.

There you are, she thought, her heart speeding up at the sight of Davyn, dressed in traveling breeches and a long-sleeve shirt barely seen beneath his long black cloak, his own pack readied and draped over his shoulder. He stopped the horses before closing the remaining distance between them, smiling so honestly that Ashilde couldn't help but match it, despite immediately noticing the bags under his eyes, his messed up hair and unkempt beard—not to mention their harsh goodbye the previous night still fresh in her mind.

"We can hardly afford to send our healer," she said softly, so only he and the Seidsian could hear. "Especially on the day of mourning."

"I go where you go. You know that." He took her hand into his palm and kissed her fingertips. "Nice shirt."

She quickly brushed her thumb across his fingers. She knew they'd need to talk later, but later could wait. Instead, she let his warmth fill her, willing to be selfish in his moment. With him traveling at her side, the journey felt no less daunting. But at least she'd feel a little less alone.

He let go of her hand, before bowing to the Seidsian. She nodded her head to him and gestured for them to mount, the mares fidgeting with anticipation.

"Go, the both of you, if only so you may return all the more swiftly back to us," the Seidsian finished, stepping aside to let them pass. The rest of the clan was silent as they passed underneath the arched gateway.

As they came out the other side, Ashilde stole a glance behind her. On top of the wall, her warriors had turned to face her, still lined in a row, arm at attention across their chests. She could easily meet their eyes and she did, every pair, until finally ending on Brynhild's.

Her sister glanced away as the other warriors cried out, shouting varying messages of encouragement and hope.

Then, as one—this time, her sister included— all of the warriors collapsed down to their knees, arms lowered to touch the ground, heads bowed in unanimous respect.

Ashilde raised her spear that she still held in her hand, offering a quick battle cry in response, the well of confusion she'd felt the day before running dry, quickly refilling with a pride and love for her clan that made her heart soar.

Turning, she kept their pace at a walk, her eyes brimming with tears, as they left home, traveling out into the Segan. Her people's support renewed her sense of purpose, hardening her will to iron.

She would not fail them.

She could not.

***

They rode through the morning at a brisk pace, traveling under clear skies and open grassland, alongside a wide path separating the coastal edge from the forested heart of Segan. The path might have once been clear, but after almost two generations of disuse, it was overgrown by weeds, making it only barely distinguishable from the graying grass surrounding it. Ashilde was able to discern when the path split, one direction continuing straight along the coast, while the other hooked left toward the forest. She slowed her horse to a standstill, looking at Davyn for input. They hadn't spoken since leaving their village, both taking in the quiet morning among familiar lands.

That was about to change.

As he stopped next to her, Ashilde noticed sweat dripping down the shaved sides of his head, while the unruly black hair piled atop his head and down his neck was also slick with it. His pale white neck was already turning a soft red.

"You need to get outside more," Ashilde said, smirking when Davyn scowled back at her, before wiping sweat from his eyes. His cloak might have kept him a little *too* warm, even as Ashilde sat content in weather that was neither too cold nor too hot to bear.

It was an old joke between them. Davyn preferred to spend most of his time studying inside the healers hut he'd turned into his home, more interested in learning about plants and poultices than he was spending the day under the sun, like she did. Yet, as his scowl widened to a grin, it gave her a sliver of hope to hold onto, no matter how small.

His teasing faded as he let out a sigh. "Are you ready?"

Ashilde glanced around, taking a moment to think. The land they currently stood on was considered Slátra territory. Though they stood on the edge now, even here felt familiar. Despite never leaving their territory, they both had spent plenty of time outside of their walls; whether exploring underneath the red leaves of the tall, black-trunked trees that made up the forest ahead; or, toes buried in the sand of the beaches below, leading to blue-green waters. Every aspect of Slátra soil was known.

To take another step would be to leave that familiarity and safety behind.

Yet you must do this, Ashilde reminded herself. *You need help and information. The Rhuanics had to come from somewhere.*

She promised Freydis answers. She couldn't shy away from getting them when they'd only just begun. She wouldn't.

Ash turned her attention back to Davyn, patting the pack shoulders by her mare. "The Seidsian allowed me to take her map detailing the Segan. I've studied what I could, in the limited time I had. Going north would allow us to see three, maybe four clans." *And allow you to avoid the Fundi on the coast.*

Davyn bit his lip. "We can't know how we'll be received."

She shrugged, feigning more nonchalance than she

felt. "It's impossible to tell. But, which would you prefer, Dav? To test our peace amongst the clans for the first time or risk Róta's wrath by missing a sacrifice?"

"I know," he said, stroking his mare's neck as she began to prance in pace, most likely sensing his agitation. Or, speaking with her about it directly, through their gift.

Ashilde's mare sat still beneath her, accustomed to her silence.

Davyn took a moment to calm his mare before he replied, "I just ... I struggle to believe Róta would punish us for something out of our control like that. We didn't instigate anything. Surely, she would recognize the difference?"

Ashilde frowned. Davyn referenced the Banishing that started the war between the clans in the first place. The Skalda clan once showed favoritism between their gods, preferring the kinder, gentler example set by the Wolffather, to the point where they began to hunt ravens for sport; proof of their devotion to Waldemar.

The Ravenmother had not been pleased.

Ashilde could still remember hearing the tale for the first time. Even sitting close to a roaring fire, leaning against her mother's leg as she nursed her new infant sister, Ashilde only felt a deep chill as the Seidsian spoke of skies darkening by black clouds, the darkest their ancestors had never seen. Torrents of wind poured out of the sky, destroying everything in their path, while bolts of white fire struck the ground, setting ablaze anything it hit, accompanied by an onslaught of rocks made from ice. The ground shook and split open, screaming for help, yet their ancestors could do nothing but flee south into the massive forest.

The Skalda never made it.

The survivors found that they couldn't return to their once homeland. Part of the forest they'd escaped through, now called the Flatrí, had become darkened and cursed, a death sentence for any who tried to venture back through it. Upon that discovery, the Seidsians of the clans all heard the same message from the Ravenmother: despite being allowed to live, they were banished from their ancestral lands and had to start anew, in the small slice that was left for them. As punishment for the deeds of the Skalda, clans would also need to sacrifice a healthy animal once every month, to show their devotion to *both* gods.

Failure to do so would mean the skies would unleash again, and this time, she wouldn't hold back her fury.

Ashilde shuddered. "No," she said, coming back to the present. "I don't think she would."

Davyn frowned. "Ash," he whispered, as if the gods were listening to them right now and would strike her down for her doubt. "Please. The gods want what is best for us. Look at what they've given us!" He spread his arms wide. "You must have faith."

"Gods who punish us for questioning, who ask me to suffer monthly to protect my clan, who allow Rhuanics to exist with no punishment? Who punished the death of a raven, yet didn't intervene as all the clans went to war over territory—limited land that *they* forced us to share; almost destroying us all as we became addicted to battlelust?" Ashilde spit on the ground. "You'll have to have enough faith for the both of us, my love. For they will get none from me."

"Ash!" he whispered, aghast. Even though they'd spoken of this before, she'd never been so blatant about her feelings towards her gods.

Yet all her hunters were dead.

And they did nothing.

She no longer cared what they thought of *her*. All she did, she did for her clan. And she would find answers.

"Come," she said, turning away from her partner, not

wanting to continue this fight. Not allowing him time to say anything, Ashilde clicked her tongue. Together, the horses took off through the grass, sprinting hard until they quickly breached the forest, trees spread wide enough for them to run around the trunks, but still presenting a challenge to navigate; something that would require all of her focus, to ensure her horse wasn't tripped up by root or twig.

Ashilde leaned forward, her argument with Davyn leaving her stomach in a knot. She was happy to dedicate her entire mind to ignoring him, focusing on the ride instead.

It kept all other thoughts at bay, at least for a little while.

CHAPTER EIGHT

They arrived at the borders of Hvass territory shortly after dawn the next day.

Ashilde and Davyn had stopped and slept under a clear sky, the stars glistening bright enough to provide distraction when Ashilde couldn't sleep. After an early start alongside the sunrise, it only took a few more hours traveling through the forest at a slow pace to arrive in Hvass territory, following the notes laid out on the Seidsian's map.

Yet, even without the guide, Ashilde didn't think they would be able to miss it.

The slow but steady incline that announced the rising forest was the first sign that they neared borders of land not their own. Familiar trees, slightly taller than the outer walls of the Slátra village, were rooted through most of the climb, but the space between the trees slowly began to grow as soon as the bark shifted color, from the stark white of the trees back home to a dark black. As they climbed, the next tree would be slightly wider, a little taller, following this pattern with every passing footstep, until they finally arrived among where the Hvass called home.

There was no gate or walls to announce their territory. Instead, as Ashilde and Davyn finally crested the top of the large hill, they were greeted by the sight of trees taller than any others in all of Segan. It was a small group, only a few dozen in number, clustered together in the center of a circular clearing. They were massive, with black trunks the width of entire homes back in their village, towering high above the sky line created by the rest of the forest. The dark red leaves were gone, replaced with green vines that hung down from the top of the trees like ropes.

She glanced over at Davyn, who stared with his mouth wide open.

"I'd heard stories that the Hvass lived among the trees, but I didn't imagine ... *this*," he breathed.

Ashilde surprised herself with a laugh, as she slipped off her horse. "I may doubt the gods, but this? This is a good reminder that the magic of the Segan is very, very real."

Despite forcing all nine of the remaining clans to live within a more compact area of Armadin after the Banishing, signs pointed that the gods had indeed blessed it in a way their ancestors hadn't known. Many of the predators who once assaulted the clans—raptors, dragons and even the great Sea Beast—didn't follow them here and hadn't been seen in centuries, rumored to have been wiped out by the storms that destroyed so much else. No clan had ever struggled to hunt or gather enough food, either, despite each having a smaller area to call their own hunting grounds than their ancestors once did.

Their Seidsian taught it was a silent apology from the gods, for forcing them into such confined spaces to begin with, making the plants plentiful and the animals grow faster, with more offspring with every generation. Ashilde wasn't sure if she believed *that*, particularly—the idea that the gods, Róta in particular, would apologize for anything, seemed too far-fetched to her. Yet, she couldn't deny Segan *was* magical, in many ways.

The trees the Hvass lived in were proof of that.

As Ashilde began transferring gear off her horse, strapping her weapons and pack onto her person, choosing to use her spear as a walk stick, she caught Davyn squinting. "You really think they live up there? Among the sky?"

"If we're lucky, we'll find out here in a moment," she said, before stepping close to him to whisper in his ear. "But keep an eye out. We have no idea where the Rhuanics have come from."

He frowned. "What sort of signs would there be?"

"I don't know," she admitted. "But whatever they are, we can't miss them."

Ashilde swallowed, wiping sweat off her palms onto her pants. Since she'd woken up, her body was on edge, her muscles tense, ready to snap into action the moment she needed them to. Even her own blood flow had stopped, thanks to the stress of meeting with another clan for the first time.

She turned back to Davyn, knowing he felt the same anxiety, seeing the lines of worry become more prominent on his face. "We'll present what we know and see how they react, if they grant us audience or don't try to kill us—"

An arrow landed in the ground between her feet, cutting Ashilde off.

Her head whipped forward to find a warrior, their facepaint—a bright white compared to Ashilde's red, contrasted by their black skin and the dyed green of their leathers, the latter mirroring the green of the vines—similarly patterned to denote their status as a warrior. They stepped out from the trunk they'd been hiding behind, another arrow already nocked. They were fully armored, as if dressed ready for war every day.

"What business do you have in Hvass lands, Slátra? We want no business with those who worship the gods here," they called.

Ashilde sucked in a breath. They would openly declare themselves as Rhuanics?

Calm head, Ash. It's not just you at risk here.

She glanced at Davyn, who'd gone still, but trusted her to take the lead. She couldn't let her tongue—usually unguarded and sharp—put his life at risk.

"A matter to be discussed with your Seidsian, if she'll grant us audience," Ashilde said, not letting go of her spear, but not angling it as a threat, either. Instead, she raised her opposite arm, offering her hand. "I am Ashilde, Faethegnar of the Slátra. I am her and she is me. If you fear my intentions, come and test them for yourself."

The warrior, who had walked toward them warily as Ashilde spoke, cocked their head to one side. "You can call me Borghild. I am her and she is me. You're armed enough to fight half a horde. You'd do well to keep your distance." She glanced away. "That one will do."

Her partner looked over at Ashilde, but she nodded. If the warrior dared to even think about trying to hurt him, she'd be dead before the thought made its way from her head to her heart.

Ashilde stared, eyes locked in on the young warrior, as the warrior lowered her bow and walked up to Davyn. The Hvass' gift from the Wolffather was the ability to read emotions and memories through touch. If they had evil intentions, the woman could detect them with the barest brush of fingertips. It was the easiest way to discern why they were truly here and the quickest way to establish trust—even a guarded one.

Still, she didn't like another armed warrior approaching Davyn.

Ashilde clutched her spear a little tighter, her entire

body coiled like a snake, preparing to strike.

The warrior's fingers brushed against Davyn's hand, taking his entire hand into her outstretched palm as she laid her other hand over his, barely covering it. The warrior closed her eyes and began to concentrate. On the outside, Ashilde witnessed nothing. But less than a minute passed before her eyes snapped open and she pushed herself away, releasing Davyn in a hurry, as if she could no longer bear the connection.

"Come," she said, purple eyes wide and voice hoarse, as if she'd just exerted a great effort. "I will take you to the Seidsian immediately. Though, dare accuse that these Rhuanics came from our borders and I'll kill you both myself."

Turning, the warrior walked away before Ashilde could comment, her bow lowered and her strides long and purposeful. Ashilde moved to walk beside Davyn as they led their horses to follow. "You held nothing back."

He shrugged. "She needed to trust us, not waste time trying to figure out whether we were friend or foe. Letting her see the full memories of the past few days was the quickest way to do that."

She nodded, though such honesty worried her. That warrior, after taking them to the Hvass' Seidsian, would tell the rest of her clan about the slaughter that happened on Slátra soil. Though it was unlikely it would spread to other clans, Ashilde had hoped to keep the knowledge as confined as possible—especially if the Rhuanics had indeed only targeted them alone and hadn't come from, nor attacked, one of the clans they visited. The more people who knew about their weakness, the better chance someone would decide to use it against them.

But it was a necessary risk. If a clan did decide to attack, the Slátra would do what they must to survive.

Even kill them all.

"Tie your horses here and then follow me," Borghild called over her shoulder.

Hurriedly, they did as she bade and then continued to follow her, Ashilde not relinquishing any of her weapons, especially since that had not been asked of her. Reaching the tree, the warrior shouldered her bow and grabbed an actual rope that hung down among the vines, climbing with practiced ease. Ashilde secured the rope as it swayed under the warrior's weight and movement. Sneaking in a quick tug to make sure the rope was sturdy enough to hold them all, she lifted herself off the ground and climbed, Davyn following more slowly behind her.

They climbed until her limbs shook and her muscles felt alive—and not in a good way— but Ashilde was proud that she didn't allow those sensations to cause her to lose her hold. Instead, she pulled herself up and huffed once, before standing. The Hvass warrior nodded, appreciating strength outside of her own clan, before walking across a large tree branch like it was flat earth. Ashilde waited for Davyn to reach the top, keeping an eye on the warrior as she left them behind.

"Can you walk across this?"

Davyn snorted, breathing heavily from the climb, his arms shaking. "Not like we have much choice, do we?"

"Just ... be careful."

He smiled, despite his pain. "Of course."

They made their way across the tops of the trees, following the large branches that connected and twisted to form what she recognized as a natural path, even if it was one she wasn't used to taking. Their crossing didn't have any of the grace or poise of the warrior who lived among the leaves, but Ashilde didn't much care about appearances, as long as they made it across.

Even as she walked across the branches, she made a note to search her surroundings as carefully as she could.

Immediately, she noticed a distinct absence amongst the Hvass' home. She heard voices echo between bird calls, yet she didn't see anyone amid the cluster of wooden homes built surrounding where the trunks ended and the branches began. It wasn't the absence of people that stuck out to her, but instead, the lack of any sign of raven or wolf—symbols used as decorations and reminders of their devotion to the gods.

Not here, however. No paintings, no carvings, no trinkets, no figurines. No designated area to offer sacrifice. The usual symbols used to worship Róta and Waldemar were nowhere to be found.

And yet the gods haven't struck them down.

The thought didn't rest well with Ashilde, but as she slipped, forcing Davyn to quickly steady her, she realized now was not the time to ponder such impossibilities—not with nothing but some wood and a lot of air between her and the ground too far below her feet.

When they finally reached their destination, Ashilde was quick to busy her shaking arms, putting her spear back into her sling across her back; not wanting to reveal any evidence of her nerves, nor her gratitude to be walking across planks built around the trunk's top, creating a steady—and solid—platform. They walked around the circular planked path before Borghild stopped, just short of the open doorway to a hut made of black wood, covered only by hanging green vines from the trunks above. She took a step toward them.

"I'll wait here to escort you back down," she said, her voice quiet. "Speak with the Seidsian inside." Her voice dropped another octave. "For your sake, I hope she agrees to help you."

The sentiment surprised Ashilde, especially considering the warrior threatened to kill them mere minutes before. "There's a chance she won't?"

The warrior didn't answer.

Ashilde didn't try to read too much into the mixed messages. But she couldn't help wondering what sort of clan they'd come into. Borghild's words, and the lack of traditional markings among their home, suggested they were self-chosen Rhuanics, and thus should have been destroyed by the gods, especially if this wasn't a new development, but generations in the making. Yet, their leader kept her title as Seidsian, a name adopted after being chosen to lead a clan, giving up their chosen name in favor of their new rank. It was expected that any identity they had in the past would be sacrificed in dedication for their new role as the voice of the gods among their people.

She was surprised a Rhuanic would still go by such a sacred title.

Ashilde slipped in-between the vines, Davyn following on her heel. Inside, the Seidsian sat on a large, white bear pelt. The trunk of the tree interrupted the room in the center, where it grew up and out an opening that was cut through the ceiling. Otherwise, there wasn't much inside, suggesting this was used only as a meeting ground and perhaps not a home where someone lived. A small, circular table with cups and a bowl of water, alongside a plate filled with fruit, sat on their left. Otherwise, the room was empty, save for candles littering the ground, balanced on bronze cups flipped upside down, burning brightly.

Although she couldn't imagine lighting a fire inside a structure made entirely of wood that was perched atop a tree, she was thankful for the light. They hadn't built any windows and it was only the faint candlelight that allowed her to make out the Seidsian's face at all.

She did not look pleased.

Ashilde stopped halfway across the treehomed–hut, Davyn lingering slightly behind her. The Seidsian stood before Ashilde could get a good look at her or properly kneel, brown eyes dark and fretting, not pausing to look at any one spot for longer than a few seconds before darting away once more, already dressed in her winter furs over a long white dress.

"You would not make it past Borghild without her allowing it," the Seidsian said, her voice deep and strong. She was younger than the Slátra's. That was no surprise, as *everyone* was younger than Slátra's Seidsian. Yet no wrinkles creased this one's face, making Ashilde wonder how long she'd served in the role. "Either give me your hand and let me see why you've risked our truce by coming here or get out. I don't want to waste daylight with conversation."

Ashilde stuck out her hand even as her mind recoiled. What foul creature had the gods chosen to give guidance to the Hvass? For a woman who was meant to understand and know someone's emotions, she sure seemed empty of possessing any pleasant ones of her own.

The Seidsian took her hand before Ashilde could change her line of thought, picking up on her musings even without the ability to read exact thoughts inside her head. "Judge all you want, child. I care not," the Seidsian spat, even though she couldn't have been half a decade older than Ashilde herself was, if that.

Her head cocked to the side, considering, the silence lasting only for a moment. "Hm. Yours is a tale of sorrow and horror even those the likes of us have never known."

Ashilde felt her hand be thrust away as the Seidsian released her. "It seems the gods have finally deemed it time to begin dealing out their judgment. I cannot help you, and neither can the Hvass," she said.

At the same moment hope died in her chest, anger flared, taking over. "That's it? You understand everything my people are going through in mere seconds, without even allowing me a chance to speak?"

"Understand it? No," the Seidsian said, shaking her head. "What understanding can one have, these days, when the gods remain silent, even after men are willing to risk their eternal lives to kill?" Ashilde swore her eyes flicked toward Davyn in a distrustful manner, but they darted away too quickly for her to be sure. "But do I understand your plight? That, I do."

Ashilde took a step toward her as the Seidsian lowered herself back onto the bear skin. "What do you mean, the gods remain silent? Do you not speak to them, as all Seidsian do?" Her anger moved quickly, fueling her tongue before her mind could catch up. "Or do they deny your prayers, as they would any Rhuanics?"

"Ashilde!" Davyn hissed, but she didn't move at his interruption. Instead, she kept her expression a mask as she stared at the leader below her.

The Seidsian surprised her with a laugh, deep throated and raw. "You come to challenge us, child? Accuse us of attacking your clan? For what purpose?" She leaned back, exposing her torso. "I promise you this: if I had wanted the Slátra dead, you wouldn't be here. These Rhuanics who attacked you did not come from us."

Ashilde wasn't convinced. "And yet, the first clan we come across have forsaken the gods. Would you not question, in my position?"

"You'd be a fool *not* to question a coincidence like that," the Seidsian said. "Almost as great a fool as one who would threaten a fully armed clan in their own territory." She leaned forward again, with a nasty gleam in her eye that made Ashilde's throat constrict. "You still believe those claims, bring your people with you and test it with a blade. Smarter course, that."

Ashilde flushed crimson, but refused to give into her embarrassment. "So you won't help us?"

"First you threaten and accuse, then you beg for assistance?" The woman shook her head. "My people owe no allegiance to you, Slátra. Never have and never will, not that you'd ever understand it." The Seidsian closed her eyes, a decisive gesture. "I do not need to hear the voice of the gods to know what they are planning. Judgment comes swiftly, child. Best simply sit and bear it, instead of trying to fight it."

"But—"

"Ashilde," Davyn whispered, touching her gently on the shoulder. Ashilde didn't want to respond, wanted to fight harder, ask more questions, make more demands.

But it seemed their audience was at an end, as the vines parted and two warriors, this time, appeared to escort them out.

"Now go," the Seidsian commanded, still not opening her eyes. Though she smirked before she added, "You have others you can ask for help, yes?"

CHAPTER NINE

*F*ailure. *That's all I am, all this journey is.*

The Hvass' harsh and quick rejection set the tone for their journey. A week had passed since they'd left Slátra's borders, and they'd visited three clans in total, every one of them denying the aid they so desperately needed.

Not disastrously so, Ashilde reminded herself as she sat on her horse, pulling her cloak tighter around her body. The weather grew colder with each passing day, the sky today gray and overcast, doing nothing to help improve her mood. Davyn rode beside her, but both were lost in their own thoughts.

True, they hadn't secured the help of a hunter, nor got any closer to discovering where their attackers came from. But no clan expressed a desire to ruin the peace that existed between them simply to gain an upper hand on the Slátra, in their weakened state. It was luck divinely caused, all things considered—though Ashilde bit her lip, unsure if she could trust their words, especially as they traveled further away from their borders, unable to know for certain they wouldn't return to a home ransacked, raided and ruined.

Ashilde shook her head, as if she could shake such thoughts away. The images that accompanied them were almost too much to bear.

"Love," Davyn said, his voice soft and kind, banishing her frightening thoughts away like light invading the darkness; a positivity he relentlessly held onto, even as she felt heavier with guilt, with each passing day.

She looked at him and offered a small smile, but he saw through it.

"You haven't been sleeping well," Davyn continued, meeting her eyes as he trusted his horse to continue forward without his prompting. "You toss and you turn, and your knuckles are always clenched, your jaw set, shoulder rigid."

Ashilde let out a rough chuckle. "I'm, ah, not hiding it very well, am I?"

Davyn smiled at her, though it didn't erase the concern in his eyes. "You never have. You always take up so much, place too much weight upon your shoulders." He leaned forward. "Especially now. The result of this trip—whether success or failure—does not rest upon your conscience alone. I will not let this break you."

Ashilde frowned at that. She knew her love came from a place of kindness, but he was wrong, in this instance. For *he* wasn't the one who acted in haste and cost their clan information. *He* wasn't the one who not only failed to save their hunters, but also became at odds with the warriors she called family by acting out of turn and attacking alone—even if they'd forgiven her for it. No one but her could claim those actions, which meant no one but her could bear the burden of not only this trip, but the result, as well.

Not that she'd mention that to him. The way she carried guilt was a topic only Davyn or Freydis confronted her with, and it usually resulted in harsh words and tears on both sides, as her dearest friends failed to understand how she was responsible for her own actions and failures, while she, according to both of them, failed to be kinder to herself.

But the broken runes on her chest burned beneath her clothes—a soft, constant reminder—making her guilt impossible to ignore.

Ashilde glanced around them. The trees within the forest had returned back to their normal size days ago, though they had begun to shift again, away from the black bark and green leaves that'd spent most of the time traveling through. Instead, the leaves had shifted to hues of blue and purple, becoming larger and thicker, creating a canopy above them that would have blocked out the sun, had there been any sun to shine on them that day. The bark became a shining gold, glowing against the dew of the ground.

The Dreyma clan would be close.

She didn't want to argue with Davyn right before she met with their last hope, before time would force them to turn around and return home, bearing the consequence of her failure. She needed all of her wits about her and experiencing his rare anger—or worse, seeing his disappointment—would be enough to unnerve her.

"What do you make of the gods' silence?" Ashilde asked instead, finally speaking again.

"Ashilde—"

"Davyn, please," Ashilde said, meeting his eyes once more. "Not now. Please."

She didn't miss the tick at the corner of his mouth as he threatened to frown, but the way his shoulders relaxed slightly, she knew she'd won reprieve from his concern—for now.

Her stomach still twisted in discomfort, however.

It felt a hollow victory.

"By the Seidsian's claims?"

Ashilde stroked her mare's neck to help calm her beating heart. This conversation was dangerous, but her mind was moreso. She needed a way to process, some comfort that she wasn't making the wrong decision. "Surely you noticed the ... *differences* between each clan, in regards to how they viewed our gods?"

He nodded. "Of course I did. They didn't even hide it!" Her love actually shivered, reminding her that this bothered him as much as her, but for much different reasons.

Ashilde didn't understand it. The gods had demanded to not only be worshiped as equals, but to be worshiped, period. Yet so far, they'd seen everything but. The Rekja, who they'd met with only a few days ago, may have claimed equal worship, in word, yet it was obvious they favored Waldemar much more. Ashilde had never seen so many wolf-like statues in her entire life, thinking the god's chosen animal outnumbered even the people who lived in huts beneath trees, rather than atop of them like the Hvass. The Solskin, meanwhile, the second clan they'd visited who preferred the dwelling of caves, were the opposite, obviously worshiping their fiery goddess with a passion. And, of course, the Hvass had rejected both gods, vocally, becoming Rhuanics in their own right.

Yet all of them still stood, breathing and unharmed.

"The gods do nothing. Does their silence—no, their *inaction*—not bother you?"

"Nothing that we can see," Davyn replied.

Ashilde sighed in frustration. "What if they *will* do nothing, Davyn? What if ... what if missing a sacrifice won't mean our ruin, especially when other clans have become rhuanical and been left unscathed?"

Davyn paused for a moment, considering. "Do you really believe that?"

Ashilde cursed. "I don't know what to believe. I only know what I can't risk."

Despite the evidence against it, to go against the gods *did* risk Róta's wrath—a wrath capable of destroying so much more than just the Slátra. With none of the other clans reporting any Rhuanic attacks, it all gave her an uneasy feeling she couldn't shake. There were too many questions and not enough answers.

It made her want to scream.

"What about what the Seidsian said? The Hvass', I mean."

Davyn's brow furrowed even further. "I'm ... not sure what to make of that."

"Our Seidsian has never mentioned that to you?"

"What?" He whipped his head around to look at her. "Ashilde, you can't be serious. The gods speak with the Seidsians. The Hvass were just trying to unnerve us."

She bit her lip. "But what if she wasn't?"

"Hey," Davyn said, speaking gently, encouraging her to look at him again. She did. "I know it's hard to remain steadfast, to have any faith at all, in gods who appear to not listen and go against their words. But, if and once they *do*, the Slátra will be protected, thanks to the efforts of not only the clan, but also because of what *you* do." He offered her a smile that, surprisingly, made her smile back. "We can try to take solace in that, hm?"

"We can try," Ashilde said, which seemed to be enough for him, as he leaned back and began looking around.

"Not to move on too quickly," he said, "but does something feel ... off, to you? It's like the air is..."

"Warning us? Yes," Ashilde said, feeling the goosebumps cover her entire body and this time, not from the cold. "We've reached the outskirts of Dreyma territory. It's the Flatrí."

Though the forest around them had thinned, beginning to give way to the area the Dreyma had cleared for their home, if she looked over to her left, she could see it. In the distance, the forest became compacted, transforming from the relatively safe, well-traveled woods of the Segan to the edge of the Flatrí: an uninhabitable wilderness that was the first marking of the lands destroyed during the Banishing.

A blackened forest, a jungle of vines and trees and leaves so tightly knit and interwoven, it looked like a black wall that blocked out not only the horizon, but one side of the world, even though it was the peak of midday. Neither of them had ever seen the inhabitable lands—labeled a maze, the gods' warning—but, even still at a distance away, she could feel the taint in the air from their poison.

Many generations ago, her people once lived somewhere within there or perhaps even beyond it, amongst the Hafleden. But Róta's wrath had turned it into a labyrinth of horror, one so impossible to navigate and so devoid of life, no one living had made the journey through it, to even map what it looked like now, since the Banishing. Living day by day right beside the lifeless mass, uninhabited only because nothing could stand to live within it?

Ashilde had no idea how the Dreyma managed it.

She felt Davyn's hand slip into hers. She glanced away, looking over at her partner, who leaned from atop his horse to reach out to her. "You still with me, Ashilde?"

Raising his hand to her lips, she kissed the back of his palm. "Always," she whispered, offering him her rare smile. "It will take more than a cursed forest to stop me, even if it is..."

"Terrifying?" Davyn said, still smiling, but it didn't reach his eyes. She didn't fail to notice the sweat sticking on his palm, even as he pulled his hand away to sit properly on his mare. "I don't think there's a word to describe how content I am to get no closer than this to a place so cursed and barren."

"Agreed."

With that, they lapsed into an uneasy silence, until they finally arrived at the Dreyma's gate.

It stood tall, made from black-trunked trees from beyond their border. Each column of wood, tightened together to form the barrier wall, had been sharpened into tips. The gate was large and straight, and with the spikes of black wood, it created a menacing figure, something to inspire terror from an attacking force. On either side of the gate, however, two quilts hung, each woven with the Dreyma's blue and purple—to match the leaves of the forest that surrounded them. One depicted a wolf standing guard, while the other had a flock of ravens soaring across the sky. A sign of the first clan to, in at least appearances, follow the same tenets of equal worship the Slátra themselves did; the tenets the gods demanded of them all.

Ashilde slipped off her mare. Immediately, she became aware of the presence of arrows pointed at her from above. She glanced up, so they could see her face, not bothering to hide her warrior paint, refreshed each dawn. She had little doubt they would fail to recognize the coloration of her markings, recognizing her as a member of the Slátra. A clan that was a sworn enemy of the Fundi, the Dreyma's closest neighbors to the east. While none of the clans were on friendly terms, the Fundi were hated by most, but none more than the Slátra, or pit, even Ashilde herself.

The bows were lowered from her head to her heart. A sign of respect, at least, while still prepared to kill. She understood that, though she couldn't help her blood boiling as she was distinctly aware of one arrow aimed at Davyn. If they dared even *think* about harming him—

"You travel here with only days before the first snow is expected," one of the warriors called down. "Desperation drives you."

They spoke without question.

Ashilde nodded. "I wish to speak with your Seidsian, if I may, alongside a representative of your hunters."

An eyebrow clearly rose at that. "Weapons must be surrendered."

"You may try."

Carrying every weapon she owned on her person, it would take half the afternoon for her to unload at the Dreyma's request. She met the warrior's eyes after the warrior gave her the run down and apparently, they came to the same conclusion. They made a quick gesture with their arm, before disappearing from view. The gate opened a moment later, the heavy doors pulling open slowly by the chains that drew them from within.

On foot, Ashilde and Davyn led their horses inside, as the warriors climbed down from the wall, on the ground to escort them in seconds, weapons already aimed once more. One of them even dared to keep one aimed at Davyn, as if he would lash out and attack them, instead of Ashilde. She silenced her initial anger at the threat, surprised when hope replaced it. Had the Rhuanics attacked them, too? Is that why they were so on edge? Were the Dreyma the ones who would finally give them the answers they sought?

"Why have you come, Slátra?"

"An answer for your Seidsian alone."

The warrior, glancing at their silent companion, surprised her with a shrug. "Come, then," they said, as the second warrior took off, going to warn of their arrival. "I'll take you to the Seidsian and you can have your audience, odd as it is. But break any promise of peace, and your man will be taken down before you can attempt to give that glare any bite."

Her expression hardened.

Davyn appeared unconcerned, when she glanced at him after the warrior looked away. He offered her a small smile before checking out the onlookers who stared at them, openly gawking at the newcomers in their land, the first from a different clan that many of them most likely had ever seen. Ashilde paid them no mind and cared not for what they thought, nor what rumors would spread as it appeared the warriors had caught a pair of Slátra wandering outside their borders.

The truth was far more damaging.

A simple hut, though large in size, housed the Seidsian. It was built in a similar fashion as the Slátra's were, a single-level home with a thatched, triangular roof. A shield hung on the wall on the opposite side of the door, decorated with black and white paint, the edge cracked. The Slátra trained with shields, but didn't use them as much as the Dreyma apparently did. Ashilde, personally, preferred to go without.

The warrior pulled open the door, the door creaking. Ashilde didn't hesitate to enter, already feeling the warmth of the fire give strength to her weary body. Davyn stayed outside with the horses, this time. After the rough treatment their mares had gotten from the Rekja, he didn't entrust them to the care of anyone else. There was no point in getting comfortable, besides. All the other meetings had been quick and any offer to stay for the evening, protected within another clan's walls, never given. She expected much of the same from the Dreyma, even while daring to hope for a different answer.

Ashilde knelt on the ground across from the fire pit after the two warriors joined her, showing respect that all Seidsians deserved—especially one who worshiped the gods as demanded.

Their Seidsian sat on a wooden bench, eating their meal on a table beside where the fire pit was built. Windows were open behind them, casting shadows across the room, as the flashes from the sconces on the walls flickered with each whisper of the breeze.

As Ashilde knelt, the Seidsian didn't bother to stand, instead turning to look at their new arrival. They wore a dyed dress of purple and gold, with no jewelry to complement it. Their white hair was long and thick, reaching down to their back.

"Rise, warrior," the Seidsian said, their voice airy where her own Seidsian's was cold. "I am the Dreyma's Seidsian and she is me. I've never had a visitor in my lifetime, and you come armed. Tell me, why I shouldn't throw you out?"

Ashilde did not waste time, though she remained on her knees. "Have Rhuanics attacked your clan recently?"

The warrior to her left inhaled sharply.

"Define them," the Seidsian commanded, turning her body to face Ashilde head-on, now.

"Men who kill without fear," Ashilde said. "A trio, dead now—though their total numbers or their origin remain unknown."

"If you dare suggest that those heathens came from our stock—"

"Silence, child!" the Seidsian cut in, interrupting her own warrior. The one quick to threaten Davyn, Ashilde noted. "If you cannot listen before you cast your judgments, your presence is not necessary. Out with you."

Ashilde felt an intense, sudden heat—and it didn't come from the fire in front of her, remaining only until the harsh slamming of the door alerted to the warrior's departure. She kept her expression muted, despite feeling smug.

The Seidsian stared at her, hazel eyes shining. "My warrior told me you requested my hunters. I have not yet called for them, wanting to speak with you, first. What do you require of them? Do you seek aid against these Rhuanics who attacked you?"

So they hadn't attacked the Dreyma. But the Seidsian hadn't dismissed her claims outright, either. Promising, if only silently. "Not necessarily. We seek aid against ... against the damage they have already done."

"Speak plainly, warrior. Or you, too, may depart."

Ashilde glared without remorse. Respect she would show, but she could only combat her nature for so long, before it showed itself. "Our hunters were slain. All of them. We seek assistance in the coming winter, to keep up a supply of sacrificial meat only, to appease our *great* gods."

"Is that all?"

Her glare remained, if only to try and drown out the fear that suddenly hammered in her chest. The Dreyma were her last chance. If they denied them aid, her people could perish, if Róta was indeed watching.

The Seidsian opened her mouth to speak, but was interrupted as someone opened the door in a hurry, almost knocking into Ashilde's kneeling form in their rush. The Seidsian's eyes flared a reprimand, but the interrupter dared to speak before she could.

"It's Anóra," they said, almost breathlessly. "She—"

The Seidsian cut off a warrior with a look as her entire body tensed, but she managed to remain calm as she returned her attention to Ashilde. "I'm sorry. We cannot help you."

No. "Wait," Ashilde said, crawling on her knees, prepared to beg. "What's happening? Please—"

"See them out," the Seidsian said, standing and walking purposefully out the door, leaving the rest of her food untouched and Ashilde on her knees. She quickly stood and followed. Outside the tent, the gawkers who had watched them arrive had disappeared, the entire village suddenly empty, like no one else lived there. Ashilde's heart hammered as she met Davyn's wide-eyes and she made a flash decision.

Ashilde reached out and grabbed the Seidsian's arm, who looked back at her in a fury. "Please," Ashilde continued. "Davyn is a healer. Perhaps he can help whatever ails your people."

Davyn, bless him, kept his face impassive, despite being as confused as Ashilde most likely felt, especially as she offered his skills to strangers.

Indecision made the lines of the Seidsian's face go taut, casting a glance over at Davyn. Only a second passed before her face smoothed out, her mind made up. With a nod to Davyn, she commanded Ashilde, "Stay here and wait. I will return with your answer shortly."

Though desperate to know what was going on, Ashilde swallowed her indignation and her pride at being left behind. Instead, she offered a nod of her own and moved out of the way, as warriors and Seidsian alike left. Davyn waited for a moment, meeting her eyes. She mouthed a quick, "Go," before he, too, disappeared, leaving Ashilde alone with her thoughts. She found them darker than the Flatrí bordering Dreyma lands, and even curiosity was not enough to distract her.

With nothing else left to do, Ashilde went back inside and waited.

***

The Seidsian returned, alone, a few hours later. She did not hide her exhaustion well, with her worry lines around her eyes deeper than before she left the tent, creating new wrinkles on her face. Ashilde stood up from the bench she'd sat on as she entered, slipping her mother's necklace she'd been flidging with to hide underneath her shirt once more. She barely forced herself to stay mute as she waited for the older woman to return to her seat across from her, sinking rather than settling into the furs that adorned it.

"You stayed," she said, finally meeting Ashilde's eyes.

"You asked," Ashilde replied simply, not sitting

down, this time.

The Seidsian nodded, a new appreciation on her face. "And yet you do not overwhelm me with questions."

"Is Davyn okay?"

Another, smaller nod.

"Then there is only one other answer I seek," Ashilde said, denying her personal curiosities in favor of her clan's needs. "And it does not require me to pry into your clan's affairs."

"You request to borrow one of our hunters to hunt for you."

Holding her breath, Ashilde met the Seidsian's gaze.

"Your Davyn helped give my grandchild a peace she hasn't known in weeks. Something none of my healers have ever been able to do," the Seidsian admitted, causing Ashilde's heart to hammer in hope. "I—"

She paused, lips parted as her eyes glazed over, hazel suddenly going silver, before they rolled into the back of her head. Her entire body went rigid, and her hands fell limp onto the table with a *thud*. Ashilde froze, her body becoming pinpricks of concentrated pain against her own rigidness. She'd never witnessed this, but everyone had heard whispers of what it was like.

The Seidsian was speaking with the gods, who weren't so silent after all.

"The tests are just beginning, for both the Slátra and for you, Ashilde," the Seidsian said aloud. "Oh yes, we've been watching you. A clever idea, to ask the aid of others. But also a useless one. Go home and report your failure to your clan. It will not be your greatest one."

With a blink, the Seidsian's eyes rolled back and returned to their natural hazel state. She swallowed, once, though her entire body shook, giving way to the emotion the Seidsian struggled to keep contained. Her focus returned to Ashilde, causing her heart to lurch more than the strange words she spoke had. Her expression was one of sorrow.

"Any aid we could—and should, after what you did for us today—have offered has been denied," she said, quietly, suddenly weak. "Take the stag we caught and killed yesterday, then be on your way."

Ashilde couldn't believe it. "But … what just…"

"You've been singled out by the gods, though for what purpose, I do not know." The Seidsian looked away. "I will not have you within my borders when they decide what to do with you."

Chapter Ten

A week later, they arrived back within Slátra borders on the first day it snowed. Ashilde had forced them to ride at a hard pace—not only because she wanted to make sure they got the stag the Dreyma gave them back in time to sacrifice to the gods, but also because she needed guidance on what to do next. Davyn offered his support and sympathy, after she told him what the Dreyma's Seidsian had said, but it wasn't enough; wasn't what she needed.

It will not be your greatest one.

She needed to speak to her own Seidsian.

As they approached the gates, two warriors—Magnhild and Bodil—were on guard, standing atop the wall. Magnhild gave an excited shout as she disappeared below to go open the gates, while Bodil waved, 'her' bird still perched upon her shoulder. The older warrior, Ashilde could tell, wasn't blinded by excitement at their return. Instead, she eyed the stag tied behind Ashilde and the absence of a third person with a frown.

Ashilde swallowed.

She'd allowed herself to be so distracted by fear from the Dreyma's proclamation that she hadn't even considered what it would be like to tell her clan she'd failed. And not just in solving the problems of the clan.

Your promise to Freydis. You barely even thought about it, so focused on securing aid. You have no answers for her.

She wanted to puke.

Instead, she dismounted alongside Davyn, who took her hand, trying to offer whatever comfort he could. Her sudden dread was momentarily forgotten as Magnhild slipped past the open gates and threw herself at Ashilde, wrapping her in a tight hug.

Ashilde returned the embrace with a startled laugh. Magnhild was usually quieter, being the youngest—only seventeen summers—among their warriors, but this sign of affection was something she didn't want to turn away, especially today of all days.

"You made it back," Magnhild said, pulling away with a huge grin on her face, before she realized what she said and rushed to explain. "I mean, not that I *doubted* you would, of course! It's just ... two weeks is a long time to be without one of our own. I want to hear *everything*," she continued, barely pausing to catch her breath. "I want to know all the details, what it was like, more about who is helping us—"

Ashilde's smile faltered at her last words, but Bodil's interruption was enough of a distraction that Magnhild failed to notice.

"We all want to hear stories and tales, Magnhild," Bodil said, stepping between them and offering one arm, which Ashilde clutched gladly. "But, I think it's better that Ashilde report straight to the Seidsian, first."

Magnhild wilted like a flower against the frost, her excitement drained by the practicality of Bodil's words. "But—"

"Don't you?"

Magnhild nodded, though she didn't appear happy about it. "Yes, you're right. Of course."

Davyn stepped in. "Mind helping me with the horses, Magnhild? I can at least tell you all about climbing the trees of the Hvass and seeing the Flatrí for the first time, though I imagine their perspectives are far more interesting than mine."

Magnhild's eyes widened in excitement. "Oh, would you, Davyn? I would love that!"

She quickly moved over to Ashilde's mare, greeting her with enthusiasm and double checking that the stag was still secure, before clicking her tongue, asking the mare to follow her. She glanced over at Ashilde. "It truly is so good to see you. I've missed you—we've *all* missed you."

Ashilde smiled. "I've missed you all too, Magnhild. I promise I'll come find you as soon as I'm done with the Seidsian."

The younger warrior left, looking over at the mare—speaking with her, most likely, trying to get the mare's own version of events. Davyn paused to lean over to Ashilde and kiss her on the cheek.

"Everything is going to be fine," he whispered.

Ashilde's throat tightened, unsure of how to respond. She watched Davyn leave, too, leaving her with Bodil.

Bodil's expression softened as soon as they were alone. "I take it that it didn't go well?"

Ashamed, Ashilde could only shake her head.

Bodil let out a sigh, though she reached out and squeezed Ashilde's elbow, hard. "Come, I'll escort you to the Seidsian. That way, maybe everyone will be less likely to ambush you. I doubt all of them will be as naive as Magnhild."

Ashilde appreciated it and said as much, despite the sting. She didn't want her people to think she was avoiding them, or that she wasn't thankful to be home, for she *was*. She just needed a moment with her

Seidsian to process everything, first.

Then, after, you can confess your failure to Freydis, before being confronted by your warriors. And her sister, who would be the only one in the entire Slátra who'd be thankful for her failure.

As she began to follow Bodil, it felt like a normal winter day. She could already smell the scent of fresh stew carried on the air, hear the calls of children playing nearby, intermixed by the distant echo of laughter—a heartening sound, as the small flakes of snow drifted and fell all around them. Despite the cold, many were still outside their homes, as the work to keep their clan alive and well didn't end once the weather turned sour. A few who saw her walk past were surprised, doing double takes and offered waves and shouts of greeting. Ashilde nodded back, while Bodil discouraged any further approach with a firm shake of her head, immediately wiping off smiles for frowns of concern.

And just like that, the air had begun to shift, feeling the weight of change.

They walked between homes until they reached the last one on the edge of their living quarters, built so the door and the windows all faced the hill where the gods shrine sat above them; that view, alongside being the house furthest away from the main gates, made it the perfect home for a Seidsian.

Bodil stopped just outside it. "The warriors have been taking shifts in pairs to watch the wall," she said. "I'll gather everyone up there. Come find us when you're done?"

"Of course," Ashilde said.

Bodil surprised her with a quick hug of her own. "Magnhild wasn't lying: we're glad you're home. That won't change, no matter what the outcome of your journey turns out to be."

Ashilde blinked away tears as Bodil pulled away, the

bird squawking and fanning out its wings in protest of being so close to someone else. Bodil stroked its beak to calm it, commanding it to hush verbally, before she turned away, heading past the Seidsian's home toward the training grounds, leaving Ashilde alone.

She wiped the sweat off her palms, staring at the house. It had quilts displayed on either side of the door, one displaying the power of a raven's flight while the other depicted a wolf howling to the twin moons, both woven by the Seidsian's hands. A long, wooden walking stick leaned against the door frame, while a collection of seashells were held together by a thin strand of rope, tied up to the overhang, the shells clashing together to make a soft song against the breeze.

Ashilde had been here more times than she could count. It was a second home for her—for everyone, among her people. Yet, despite Bodil's assurances, she had no idea how her leader would respond to her failure, or if she had the answers that Ashilde so desperately sought.

And you won't know standing out here in the cold.

Taking a deep breath, she walked up the trio of steps leading up to the door and pushed it open. Entering the main room, she found the Seidsian sitting on the floor in a pile of rugs, with a few children who apparently hadn't been interested in playing outdoors surrounding her, listening to her every word. The Seidsian had paused, her thin, bony arms raised high in the air, animated as ever as a storyteller. A warm fire burned within the fireplace, and the room smelled of lavender.

The Seidsian's icy stare glanced up at her, hardening for a moment before she looked back down at the children gathered around her.

"I guess you'll all be left in suspense at what Harkul did next," she teased.

Cries of disappointment answered her, but quickly

abated as the Seidsian sat up straighter, cutting them off with a swift motion of her hand. "It is important that I speak to our Faethegnar immediately," she said, earning a few startled looks from the children, most of who hadn't even noticed Ashilde had arrived. "But finish your daily tasks and come straight back to me. Whoever finishes first will get to hear the ending before everyone else."

At that proclamation, Ashilde had to remain still before the children took her out in their hurried dash to escape, none bothering to say hello. The Seidsian stood and walked over.

"It is good you have returned whole," she said, gesturing for Ashilde to follow. Together, they sat down among the rugs, ignoring the perfectly good table and chairs off to their right. "Davyn is well, too, I take it?"

Ashilde nodded. "And things here?"

The Seidsian answered her with a raised eyebrow.

Knowing neither of them wanted to truly waste time with false pleasantries, Ashilde didn't hesitate, reporting her tale with precision and swiftness. Even so, it still took her a better part of an hour—even lacking any interruptions on the Seidsian's part—for her to give the full account, her voice catching every time she reported a denial in response to their plea. Ashilde finished with the Seidsian of the Dreyma clan's proclamation, slipping in a few concerns about what their clan could possibly do to keep the gods appeased—remembering, also, to finally mention the strange proclamation the Rhuanics who attacked them taunted, hinting at still being servants of Waldemar.

The entire time she spoke, the Seidsian had remained expressionless, her gaze empty, her hands folded in her lap. Finally finished, the Seidsian blinked, once.

"It's simple, then. We continue gathering the harvest," she said. "We will adjust."

"But—"

"Go now, Ashilde," the Seidsian interrupted, stunning Ashilde into silence at her brash dismissal. "I need time to think and speak to the gods myself, before giving you the guidance you seek."

Knowing better than to argue with her own Seidsian, Ashilde bowed and left the hut, making her way to her own home with a single-minded focus. Either no one saw her or they all immediately noticed her face, guessing either the results of her quest or her mood from what was written there—with her eyes narrowed in on the ground and her lips taut—and chose not to interrupt her. She was thankful for the respect, as she slipped into her hut and shut the door behind her.

Shaking, she quickly stripped off her pack, dislodging her weapons and her gear. In a blind rush, she pulled off Davyn's shirt, which now smelled more like hard travel than his earthy, herbal scent, dropping it on the floor alongside the rest, almost ripping off her mother's necklace in an effort to remove the reminders of her journey off her body. She caught herself just in time, instead taking it off gently before returning it to the box it belonged to quickly, as if it burned her.

Ashilde collapsed onto the floor, not making it to her bed, wrapping her arms around herself as the full weight of her failure sunk in, deepening thanks to the confusion instilled within her from the Dreyma's warning.

It will not be your greatest one.

Ashilde tried to puzzle out any meaning between the two different Seidsians: one who spoke cryptically of her own downfall, predicted by the *gods themselves*—gods that, prior to witnessing their speaking to a Seidsian, she believed to have abandoned them—while the other hardly said a thing when she should have spoken for hours. Her Seidsian hadn't even offered a reprimand! She wasn't known for her warmth, but Ashilde had never seen her so cold, so distant. Both responses seemed important. There was meaning there that she should have been able to unravel.

Yet she was too distraught to try and figure it out. Ashilde had failed her clan, failed her people, *again*. She'd put them at greater risk for invasion or war by spreading their new weakness across half of the Segan, when she'd promised to bring them a solution. Instead, she brought them nothing.

And now the gods predicted something *worse* would happen to her? To *them*?

What failure could be greater than this?

Ashilde gagged as her heart pounded, picking up speed at the thought of what that could be, images of her friends—her *people*—being cut down, sliced through and slaughtered by Rhuanics, flashing unseen, yet very real, in her eyes.

A knock on her door distracted her. She didn't respond. A few seconds later, she heard the door open and close, before footsteps echoed, carrying Davyn inside.

"Want company?" he asked.

Ashilde hated to admit it, but she did. She knew she'd promised Bodil that she'd go to the warriors after meeting with the Seidsian, but the Seidsian's lack of response unnerved her, and she wasn't sure she could bear seeing the disappointment, confusion and fear on her warrior's faces. Not yet. She prayed they understood. Freydis, too, who she owed a visit perhaps even more than her companions.

But Davyn already knew of her failures. She didn't have to fear his presence would be accompanied by the disappointment or anger she wasn't sure she could handle.

Looking at him, she nodded.

Davyn smiled, before he offered her a small frown. "And you're sitting on the floor because...?"

"It seemed as good a place as any, at the time."

He walked over and slipped between her and the

bed, his hands moving to massage her shoulders, attempting to work the tension out of them. She knew it was no use. He could do that all night and her back would still be tight with knots. But she didn't stop him, instead leaning further into him.

Her mind itched to continue thinking about everything gone wrong; to worry about how her people would manage to stay strong and survive the winter without their hunters; to realize how alone they were, their calls of aid left unanswered; to question her own predicament, one she couldn't even begin to understand, not fully; to fear the unknowns of the Rhuanics and what their purposes were; to wonder what the gods wanted from her and how they were going to test her people, as if they hadn't been tested enough in the past month already.

Instead, she sighed, as if the motion could release the thoughts away. "Do you remember," she asked, "when we were kids, and our parents first tried to set us up?"

He wrapped his arms around her stomach and rested his chin against her shoulder, still smelling like dirt and sweat. If he was upset that she hadn't opened up about her discussion with the Seidsian, he didn't show it. "I was ... eight, I think? You were eleven. And already, your strength with a spear and your promise to be a great warrior was whispered among the clan. You had a reputation." She felt his smile, heard it reflected in his words. "I was terrified of you."

Intertwining her fingers with his and staring down at their combined hands, she said, "I thought they were joking. Even as the matchmaking had begun, I didn't think it could happen to me. I cursed you and ran, like a child."

Davyn was silent for a moment. "But when you saved me from that leopard? You didn't run then."

Ashilde's cheeks warmed at the memory, but she found herself smiling as she recalled it. "You know it was the hunters who really saved you. I simply pulled you out of harm's way, so they could kill the beast."

The memory came to her clearly, as if she could simply close her eyes and step inside it, to relive it in real time.

The hunters had gone scouting, teaching the younger members of their group how to identify and follow the tracks of their prey. Davyn had wanted to accompany them to gather herbs. Ashilde had volunteered to accompany as a precautionary guard, claiming she had wanted to escape the confines of the village for an afternoon.

Truly, she had wanted to study Davyn a little bit more.

Their relationship, if it could even be called that, had been rocky to start, at best. The fault was mostly hers. She had poured everything she had into her training to become the best; the most equipped, the most talented, the most feared. She had the legacy of her mother to live up to and then ... well, *after*, she knew she had to focus on nothing but her training; only through that dedication could she atone for being too weak when she should have been strong. She didn't have time for a partner, even if Davyn had agreed with their parents' schemes, his interest in her clear. She thwarted him for years.

Then, when he had turned sixteen—and her nineteen—he cornered her.

She was so surprised at his sudden, uncharacteristic audacity that she had no idea what to say or do. But he spoke quickly, never touching her, simply blocking her in with his massive frame as he rambled. He told her that if she didn't want to be his partner, she didn't have to. He cared about her, even if she didn't care about him. So, he gave her a choice: if she wanted him as her partner, she could ask him and he would say yes. If she didn't, he wouldn't hold it against her, but he couldn't pursue another, either—and not just because many their age had already paired off, in groups of two to four. Instead, he'd dedicate himself to his studies as a healer, the same way she obsessed over her status as a *sangrild* warrior.

He'd left, before she could give him an answer.

Ashilde smiled softly at the memory, her cheeks coloring, remembering how stubborn she'd been.

She hardly talked to him for the next year, but every time she saw him, her heart sped up—a new sensation, one completely unknown to her. She became concerned for his well-being. Neither of them ever said anything to the clan about their discussion, so to everyone else, it looked like nothing had changed. She was still being stubborn, as her mother had once complained, and Davyn was still being patient, as her mother had always praised.

Then, of course, everything changed.

The day the leopard attacked, she chose him.

"That's not how I remember it," Davyn said, picking their conversation back up and pulling her out of her reverie, speaking softly against her ear. "I'd wandered off, searching for ... you know what, I don't even remember what plant it was I was looking for."

Ashilde glanced back at him. "Truly, you don't? It seemed so important for you to find. You were obsessed with it."

Davyn laughed, a soft, pure sound. "It was rare, I remember that. And I never found it, because a leopard was foolish enough to attack me, despite you being there." He shook his head, grinning. "It never had a chance."

Despite his joviality, Ashilde shuddered against him. That day had been one of the darker days in her life. She'd barely noticed the leopard until it was almost directly on top of Davyn. They hadn't seen such a creature in their entire lifetimes, predators of the past usually not found in Armadin. They—creature and woman—had launched themselves at the same time, the leopard silent in its sneaking while she screamed at the top of her lungs, desperate for the hunters to hear her. She had tackled Davyn out of the way and then stayed on top of him when the leopard attacked again, tearing her back into shreds with its claws before the hunters arrived and killed it.

Davyn himself had carried her back to the clan, his arms covered in her blood, and took care of her wounds the entire two months it took her to heal.

It was during that time of healing that she allowed herself to fall in love.

And he knew it, then.

Just like he knew it, now.

Her breath hitched as he pulled one hand away, sneaking it underneath the back of her shirt, his fingers tracing over the scars there. She closed her eyes as her body became covered in chills.

Davyn whispered into her ear, "You saved me from that leopard. And since then, you've saved me from so much more. You realize that, don't you?"

His hand continued to inch upward.

"*Davyn*," she breathed, twisting to look at him.

He instantly slipped his hand from underneath her shirt and cupped her face instead. "Ashilde," he said, smiling.

There was no sorrow in his eyes. No regret. Once, she both feared and expected those emotions as a response to her choice, but she'd since learned those fears were unfounded.

Ashilde trained to be the best warrior in her clan because it was her penance; because she couldn't live with herself if she'd become anything *but*. She dedicated everything she had to it. Even when she chose Davyn, her choice and sacrifice as a warrior still came first. It always had. That was proven when he asked her to marry him, officially.

And she said no.

That night was one of the most painful in her

memory. She saw his heart shatter, his confusion oozing off of him in waves. He had spent the night in her home, but neither of them slept. They cried together for hours, spoke for many more. The issue, she assured him, wasn't him or a lack of love for him. It was an issue against expectation.

Once vows were taken, they had to be consummated, sexually, within a fortnight. A sign of commitment, exclusivity—regardless how many partners one pledged themself to. It was also expected, in particular, for any who had the body of the Ravenmother, usually capable of producing children. The sooner a marriage was consummated, the sooner the next generation could be born, rebuilding their too-low numbers.

Ashilde, in all her life, had never wanted children.

It wasn't just the process of the birth, which seemed too painful and too risky. They'd lost more than one *sangrild* to the dangers of childbirth. It wasn't even the fact that she feared what choice she'd make, if she ever had to choose between her child and her clan. Despite seeing all of her fellow warriors and hunters train, work and sacrifice while pregnant, Ashilde could never picture it herself. Both reasons were enough. But they weren't her truest ones.

She simply didn't want the burden.

The burden of responsibility. Of time, of energy, of resources, of emotions. Though any child she bore would be raised among the clan, it didn't change the responsibility she would have toward them and the emotional attachment she knew she'd develop. She enjoyed the rigors and routine of her life too much—her training, her patrol shifts, her late nights with Davyn and Freydis—to sacrifice any of it for the attention of a babe.

Once explaining her position, Davyn supported her, despite his disappointment. They both knew he would have made a wonderful father. Yet, she'd never forget his words, spoken through tears in their long discussion.

"My love for you is greater than any desire I have for myself. I will sacrifice the world to be worthy of you."

So, they'd come up with a plan. He remained her partner and they never formally went through their marriage ceremony. They remained exclusive to one another, despite their freedom to pursue others in the eyes of their gods, if they chose. And they'd never, ever fucked.

In everything that had resulted from her choice; from the judgment of her clan, to the whispers she wasn't doing her part, to the accusations that she was "cursed" like Freydis and unable to bear any children; none of it compared to the pain she experienced, knowing the only true way to guarantee she never caught with child was to never know Davyn completely. She yearned for it, more than anything.

"Hey," Davyn said, leaning forward and forcing her to meet his eyes. "You keep slipping away from me. Do you want to talk about it?"

"No," she said, not wanting to travel down that tired conversation. "I just ... there is too much, Davyn. And I can't stop thinking about it all. Can't stop—"

Davyn interrupted her with a kiss. It was gentle and sweet, but when he pulled away, she also saw the heat in his eyes, and her heart melted as it also broke a little inside.

She hated the necessity of her choice. She yearned to know Davyn so fully, with every fiber of her core. She knew his desires matched hers in intensity and there were many nights when her fingers were just not enough to sate what she wanted. But his desires, every time, were outweighed by his respect, the same way her desires were outweighed by her resolution to herself; the only time she'd *ever* not sacrificed for her clan.

But sometimes, they found other loopholes against their own rules, too.

Davyn leaned in and kissed her neck, before nipping at her earlobe. "Then let me help you stop thinking, if only for a moment. May I?" he whispered, his voice dropping low enough to make her toes curl.

Ashilde knew she shouldn't. Every time they tested themselves, it became harder and harder to suppress her desire to have him, giving every inch of herself to him and know what it was like to fuck without abandon or worry. But her body was so tense, her mind so filled with worry, that she just wanted it to all *stop*; for it all to be silent, if only for a few moments.

His tongue was the perfect answer.

She leaned in and kissed him fiercely, only pulling away long enough to answer him. "Please," she breathed, before she turned and straddled him, her mouth finding his once more. His fingers slipped into her hair as he returned her kiss with fervor. She bit his lip and teased him with her tongue, making him moan slightly as he kissed her lips, before trailing bite marks down her neck, his hands caressing her back, tracing the scars she bore there.

Finally, he wrapped his arms around her and lifted, picking her up as he stood, before turning and throwing her onto her bed. She laughed, every stress and worry forgotten as Davyn climbed on top of her, kissing her once more. Only this time, he started at her lips, before he began to slowly trail down her body, kissing over her clothes between her breasts—pausing specifically to kiss her broken rune on her chest, making Ashilde almost break down and cry—before continuing down her stomach, distracting her once more, pausing just below her waist. Her breath hitched, her body tingling with anticipation.

She felt his fingers grasp her hips, before tugging at her pants. "Tell me you want it," he whispered, his breath hot against the small amount of her stomach that he'd exposed, teasing her.

"Fuck, Davyn, *now*," she panted and that was the last command he needed, before he swiftly pulled her pants down her to ankles, abandoning them there before pulling himself back up and dipping his head between her thighs, parting them gently with his hands. He kissed inside each thigh, licking trails following her stretch marks and making her shiver with his teasing.

Before she almost couldn't take it anymore, he finally wrapped his fingers around her hips as his tongue flicked in and tasted her. Ashilde's hips jerked up at the sensation she craved so deeply.

Holding her down more firmly, Davyn gave her the only kind of attention that could make her mind go utterly blank, licking her until she bucked violently, sucking her until she cried out, unable to handle that much pleasure all at once. He didn't stop until her entire body shuddered, then proceeded to tease her for a little while longer, until Ashilde giggled and begged him to stop.

Pulling her pants back up and making sure she was comfortable, he slipped the blankets out from underneath them, before settling in beside her, pulling her close as he wrapped himself completely around her. It didn't matter that it was only midday and everyone would be wanting to speak to them. It didn't matter that their world was distorting itself past the point of familiarity. Together, they had comfort and they had strength.

And they would figure out what to do, how to persevere.

They didn't know how to do anything else.

CHAPTER ELEVEN

That evening, Ashilde finally reunited with her warriors. All eight of them sat together on top of the walls overlooking their village. The light snow had abated, but as the sun began to dip below the horizon and the torches along the wall glowed brighter, winter's chill threatened to sink into their bones, even despite the large fur coats and blankets they wrapped around themselves. They wouldn't stop guarding the walls until the twin moons were high in the sky and tonight, they took the last shift together, if nothing else but to be together again; like they used to, before.

They ate, having collected food from the Mess Hall. The meal was still fruitful—scraps of preserved meat included, though their stores were closer to empty than full—allowing an air of denial to hang over their situation like fog. None of them tried to clear it, but instead, accepted it with desperation, a needed reprieve.

Ashilde sat with her back against the wall, her fingers sticky and wet from the berries she'd pulled apart to eat. She'd already shared with everyone her version of events—leaving out only the Dreyma Seidsian's proclamation. Since, they'd lapsed into an uncomfortable silence. She took the moment to glance at each of her sisters in turn, mentally checking up on them as they silently processed her failure.

Magnhild sat closest to her, on her left, a colorfully-dyed quilted blanket wrapped around her legs. Her muscles were starting to become truly defined from her training, as she'd only joined their ranks a year ago, experiencing her Wyrdan Day at sixteen. Short and a little bit cocky, Magnhild always lifted their spirits, despite also being the shiest of them all.

Ashilde's heart grew heavy at the obvious bags underneath Magnhild's eyes; the lines of stress that protruded, erasing the smile lines Ashilde was so fond of. There were other, less obvious signs of stress and worry: the soft, incessant tapping of her foot, the gentle rubbing of her knuckles, and the way she didn't meet Ashilde's gaze, even as Ashilde stared at her.

Worse, every warrior reflected the same toll, only in different ways.

Moria wouldn't stop fidgeting with her fingers, constantly brushing against her stomach, still not fully showing, but she'd announced to them a few weeks ago she was pregnant. Ashilde couldn't imagine how amplified her fears must have felt, with a new child on the way and their clan experiencing such uncertainty for the first time. Unna would take a bit of food, then stare at her quiver she'd laid against her thigh, her finger tapping against it while her lips barely moved, before looking back at her plate, picking up another piece of meat and repeating the ritual over again. Ingrit had laid down, her head in her wife's—Torunn—lap, slipping off to sleep between every bite. Torunn, in turn, had taut lips and fleeting eyes, constantly petting Ingrit's head, flinching at every sound, which woke her wife up instantly, always on alert. Bodil, meanwhile, stood rigidly, her back to the rest of the group, choosing to take watch while others ate, whispering to another from her flock of birds ever-perched upon her shoulder.

All of them bore the weight of the unknown, while Ashilde's head swam with the guilt of starting it all.

Finally, she braced herself and looked at Brynhild, the only one who showed no signs of any nerves. Instead, she sat closed off, away from the group. She refused to look at Ashilde—and hadn't yet. Not once, since her return.

"You should eat," Ashilde finally said.

Brynhild smirked, still staring at her hands, her plate of food discarded and ignored beside her. "Because I'll be wasting a precious resource if I don't? Because this might be some of the last meat we eat for months?"

"Brynhild!" Bodil scolded, twisting around so quickly, her bird took off, cawing loudly in protest as it flew into the night.

Ashilde raised her hand, steading Bodil. She hadn't experienced much backlash from anyone, yet, unless she counted the Seidsian's quick dismissal earlier that afternoon. She'd expected—and prepared for—plenty, so when she received nothing but empathetic support and understanding, she hadn't truly known how to respond. Instead of the intended comfort, her guilt solidified even further, like a stone settling inside her, weighing her down.

It didn't surprise her that her sister would be first to challenge her.

"You're angry," Ashilde said, her voice calm. Getting heated now would solve nothing.

But Brynhild did not see that.

Brynhild whipped around, meeting Ashilde's eyes for the first time, revealing hers, rims wide and brimmed with unshed tears. Her entire body shook with contained rage as she hissed her insults. "You left us for almost two weeks with one purpose and then you came back with nothing! Your plan failed when *you* said we had no others. Now, we're left with the question of whether we risk our children, unbled and fates unknown, for the sake of appeasing gods who don't listen to us anyway."

A few of the others hushed her instantly at that remark, but Ashilde didn't bother. She shared those fears, even if she felt Brynhild's blame was misplaced. She'd done all she could do and she *had* got them a sacrifice for that evening, buying them at least another month. Didn't she understand that? Couldn't her sister know she carried enough guilt on her own, without adding more?

"You'd really think I'd ask any of them to take such a risk before I risked it myself?"

"Perhaps you should," Brynhild muttered. "Do something right for once."

"*Brynhild*," Ingrit hissed, sitting up, fully awake now. In fact, all the warriors stared at the fight brewing between the two of them, some in complete shock and others with a more subdued expression; perhaps not surprised by Brynhild's outburst, as if she'd spoken to them before.

Or perhaps they agreed with her sentiments.

Ashilde bit her lip as Brynhild shook her head. "No, Ingrit, I will not keep quiet. Because I know what will happen. To save everyone, we'll have to risk it all; *us*, the warriors. The last of the *sangrild*. Yet have we not sacrificed enough? Is the price we pay every month to keep this clan safe not *enough*? What right do they have to ask that of all of us?" Her eyes darted back toward Ashilde, defiant. "Why do I have to pay the price for *your* failures?"

A hundred different retorts flashed through Ashilde's mind, each one less compassionate than the first, though inside, it felt like her heart was breaking. She could understand fear. If any situation the Slátra had undergone deserved such a response, it was losing their hunters and risking the wrath of Róta. She could even understand that fear transitioning into anger.

But with Brynhild, it was never that simple. Was she attacking Ashilde for her failure regarding their current situation, or older grievances? Ever since the death of their mother, Ashilde had become a target for Brynhild, who she lashed out at without hesitation. She could be doing the same thing here, covering her old hatred with new reasons.

Or, perhaps Brynhild was truly scared to be asked to die for her clan.

Instead of shrinking against Brynhild's onslaught and accepting more of the guilt she threw at her, Ashilde steeled herself and spit out a response that surprised everyone, including herself.

"Go then, Brynhild, if you cannot handle what the clan asks of you."

Brynhild's eyes flashed and her fist clenched, causing Ashilde's heart to lurch as her entire body tightened, preparing against an attack. She wasn't sure what she would do if the younger warrior decided to *actually* hit her. Brynhild, as if realizing her intent after the fact, recoiled and stood quickly, shoving between the others as she sped across the wall and then down the ladder, breaking into a run as she disappeared into the village.

Ashilde didn't realize that she, too, shook, now weighed down by the stares of the other warriors who still remained.

"I'll finish this watch," she said quietly. "If someone could go check on Brynhild after they finish eating, I'd appreciate it."

She wasn't ready to face her. Not yet.

Nods answered her, followed by the gathering of

plates and weapons as the warriors broke and began to file out from atop the wall. Once, if a fight like that had broken out, at least one of them would have stopped to talk to her, either offering comfort or gossiping about what had just transpired and picking her side with a laugh.

This time, each warrior disappeared until there were none left, marking those times as long past.

Standing, Ashilde clutched her coat closer to her shoulders, feeling a cold seep into her that wasn't from the night's chill. Leaving her own meal unfinished at her feet, she turned to face the woods, looking into the darkness and seeing nothing. Instead, she could only feel the wetness, as tears streaked down her cheeks.

She'd never felt more alone.

***

A week passed, and Ashilde's world continued to change.

Multiple times, Ashilde had tried to make peace with Brynhild, using every tool she could: from calm silence and giving her space to loud shouting matches that had to be broken up by the other warriors present to witness it. Ashilde wasn't proud of it, but Brynhild's silence and cold rejection grated on her nerves in a way nothing else could—except, perhaps, the silence of her Seidsian, who rejected her request for guidance with her new promise: "When I am ready, I will come to you."

Her interactions with her warriors were strained, at best. Among others in her clan, awkward—even with Dagfinn, whose advice was simply to be patient and let the gods reveal their intentions in time, not to act in haste. It made her skin itch with impatience and fear.

The only constant she had was Davyn warming her bed each night, even if he clutched her tighter than she once remembered. And Freydis, who, upon learning of Ashilde's failure to get the information and vengeance she promised, simply embraced her as they cried at the unfairness of it all.

So it wasn't a surprise that, the morning Ashilde felt the gods' promise of her failure coming true, she turned to her lover and her friend for support, before all others.

"Have you seen Davyn?" she asked, standing outside of his hut. One of Freydis's children, Sod, was inside instead, her work of identifying and cataloging plants as part of her apprenticeship with Davyn spread out on a table before her.

The youth shook her head. "Seidsian called 'im," she said quietly. "Saids it 'as important."

No.

"Your mother?"

"At the kennels, o' course."

Ashilde was running before Sod even finished her sentence.

She ignored the looks of surprise as she ran past, but she couldn't ignore what else she felt. The intense gazes of those who watched her, not in surprise, but concern, with narrowed eyes and taut lips. Like they had already guessed the reasons behind her panic, already judged her for it.

Worse, they were most likely right.

She skidded into the animal pens, slipping on a patch of ice she hadn't seen, colliding against the barn's wall. Freydis let out a yelp of surprise, dropping her pitchfork filled with manure and hay onto the ground with a wet slap. She barely dodged it before it landed on her feet. The mare she tended whinnied, but Ashilde didn't bother to listen. Instead, she met Freydis's exasperated stare with a wide-eyed gaze.

"Ash! What's got you in a huff?"

How was it not obvious? Though, perhaps she was too quick to believe the clan had already guessed at her worst fears, seeing judgment where there wasn't any. But the prediction had lingered in her mind for a fortnight, now. The timing was too right, as evident by many of her fellow warriors—her fellow *sangrild*—taking to their beds throughout the week, as the pain of their *dolorsandri* was too much.

"I'm late," Ash whispered.

Freydis's eyes widened, and she gestured Ashilde further inside the barn, as if the animal pens were the place of privacy. But, given that most of the clan would avoid her if what she feared was true, she didn't press to flee back to the false comforts of Freydis's home.

Instead, Freydis picked up the pitchfork and rested it against the wall. Speaking with the horse quickly, Freydis took her hand and pulled her around the mare, so they both were hidden in the back of the stall. Her friend didn't let go of her hand, bringing both of them together in hers.

"How can you be certain?"

Ash swallowed. It felt as taboo as the very idea, speaking it, allowed. As if speaking would bring the fact into existence; that the gods had taken her *dolorsandri* away, making her unable to bleed. Without the ability to bleed, she couldn't protect her clan. Yet she wasn't old enough to deem her price paid.

"You and Davyn haven't...?" Freydis continued when Ashilde didn't speak.

She shook her head. "Never. You know that."

Worse, everyone else in the village knew, too.

Pulling her hands out of Freydis's grip, Ashilde began to pace in the back of the stall. "It's what the Seidsian predicted, Frey," she said, not able to raise her voice above a whisper. "*This failure won't be your greatest one.*" Her eyes snapped back to meet hers, as Freydis shook her head. "What is a greater failure than the gods deeming me *tainted*?"

Freydis *tsked*, but her voice shook as she spoke. "You

never believed it before. Why would you believe it now?"

Freydis wasn't wrong. Ashilde learned the same rules, the same tales, as Freydis had, growing up as children. The lesson that had cemented Ashilde's doubt in her gods started in the lesson of the tainted *sangrild*. A legend more than truth, a warning more than expectation, for no one living, nor any in the Slátra's history, had ever done anything to become tainted; to have their ability to bleed, declared *sangrild*, given, but then taken away by an unnatural means, one not through conception, old age or death. To have it taken by the gods was deemed an omen, a sign of horrible things to come and displeasure from the gods.

Ashilde hadn't believed it. Instead, she'd questioned it. How could one be labeled tainted when anyone who was *sangrendi* since birth never had—and never would—bleed? Including those who had bodies like the Ravenmothers', capable of doing so, but never chosen for the burden?

She'd deemed the answer as insufficient then as she recalled now. *A mystery of the gods, but one we must trust. To never be given the gift of the blood price removes any chance of having it taken by the gods. To have it taken means only one thing: banishment, named Rhuanic, for the good of the clan.*

Freydis's hand touched her cheek, lifting Ashilde face to hers. "You are no more tainted than I am."

The words echoed a conversation they'd had once before, when they were both mere girls. Everyone their age—Ashilde included—had experienced their Wyrdan Day, bleeding for the first time. Freydis was the only one with the Ravenmother's body who hadn't. The Seidsian had named her *sangrendi*. Ashilde had held her as she cried, sobbing her questions of worth, declaring herself tainted. And Ash had spoken those exact words to her, in comfort.

Did they ring as hollow to Freydis then as they did

for Ashilde now?

Her panic must have remained in her eyes, for Freydis clutched her shoulder with her other hand. "Who else knows?"

"The warriors, of course," Ashilde said. "By observance, rather than my admission. Moria announced just this morning that her linens had come up clean already."

Ash's spoon had fallen in her bowl at that confession—spoken quietly, but all too loud in her ears. She'd run out to find Davyn moments later, food abandoned, appetite gone.

"Have you gone to see the Seidsian?"

She shook her head violently. "She won't speak to me. She's avoided me since I returned." Ash choked back a sob. "What if she knew? What if the gods told her this would happen? What if—"

"Ash." Freydis gripped her firmly. "You can't know that. Not without speaking to her first."

"Mama?" a voice called, just outside. Arnvid, Freydis's son.

"Coming, dove!" Freydis called, pulling Ashilde into a hug. "Please. Go and speak to her. I will meet you there. I *promise* you will be all right."

Ashilde attempted to swallow and found her throat dry. She struggled to promise Freydis she'd do just that, before her friend slipped away and out of the stall, going toward the needs of her son—while also protecting Ashilde from having to explain her panic, giving her an ounce of privacy.

Ashilde leaned against the wall, her hands shaking. She had to check, just one more time, before she spoke with her Seidsian. She had to know, for sure.

You already do.

No one knew a woman's body better than herself.

But Ashilde couldn't accept that.

Not with this.

Ash didn't care that she could be caught, unable to focus on anything else. In a rage, she ripped at her pants, shoving them away, as if they burned her. They got tangled at her ankles, her usual lithe movements out of control in near, fearful hysteria. Ashilde left them there as she checked the linen she had lined within; a linen that should have been used, stained red.

It wasn't.

Her breath hitching, she shoved her hand below her stomach, searching in-between her thighs for any sign of wetness, praying that her fingers would come away sticky with blood. She even slipped one finger completely inside her, knowing that she'd find traces, if she was due to start soon.

Blinking back tears, she pulled her hand away, clean.

Strength failing her, she collapsed onto the floor, hay tickling her bare legs, as her pants remained bunched up at her ankles, her clean linen mocking. She had skipped her *dolorsandri*, for the first time since being declared *sangrild*.

Relentless, the Dreyma's Seidsian's words echoed in her mind.

It will not be your greatest one.

Pulling her pants up, she ran to meet with her Seidsian.

CHAPTER TWELVE

Ashilde wasn't sure what scared her more: the way that everyone who'd been gathered in the Mess Hall fled as soon as she stepped through the doors; how Davyn turned and looked at her, his face tear stricken; or the fact that her Seidsian sat upon a throne that, before that moment, Ash would have thought was decoration only, a relic of the past, where the Seidsian sat only when dealing out judgment. She had never seen the Seidsian sit there, let alone have the need to. Until now.

Before the weight of that realization could hit her, Ashilde collided into Davyn, who clutched at her arms like a man drowning grasped at the surface, desperate for air.

"Ashilde," he whispered, his own panic causing hers to settle as she embraced him. "I don't believe it. I *won't*. I—"

"Heed our discussion, healer," the Seidsian called, her voice sharper than steel. "Shut the doors behind you."

His body went slack, slumping in defeat.

Ash's heart hammered.

"Davyn?" she whispered.

He kissed her with the ferocity of a desperate man. "I promise I will find you," he whispered back, before pulling away and striding between the long tables and benches between them. The large, arched doors behind him hadn't even shut fully when the Seidsian demanded her full attention with a single sentence.

"You've been declared tainted."

Ashilde stared at the Seidsian, as she sat on her throne. Two torches were lit on either side of her, illuminating the Seidsian's face with an eerie glow.

"That's impossible," Ash whispered.

"I have been in prayer for weeks, asking for guidance, ever since the attack," the Seidsian said, musing even as her iron voice remained unrelenting. "Róta has asked for her price. She asked for you. The Slátra will pay it."

"Why? I've done nothing wrong!"

Her eyes softened, but barely. "It is not for us to question the gods, child. You were marked."

She gestured at Ashilde's chest, at the broken mark tattooed there, the day Ash was named Faethegnar. Surely a ruined rune wasn't enough to deem *her* the proper payment?

Ashilde couldn't believe she was actually having this conversation; that she was really trying to convince the Seidsian of some mistake. In her heart, Ashilde knew she was in the right with a certainty that scared her. Especially when she almost never felt a confidence as strong as this when the topic of conversion was herself.

She'd worshiped the gods throughout her entire life, even if she questioned them privately. She bore her price every month. Pit, she'd *killed* for them. She was no different from the woman her people hailed a few weeks ago, as she risked her life to seek aid among the other clans. But because her legs were dry, suddenly *she* was unnatural, wrong, *tainted*? The word made her want to vomit.

A woman's worth wasn't defined by what her body could and could not do.

"The gods are wrong in this."

The Seidsian's gaze hardened. "You know our rules, Ashilde. For the sake of our clan, you must do this."

Ashilde stood rigidly. "Is that what you command of me, Seidsian? Speak plainly."

Her eyes narrowed dangerously, but Ashilde couldn't bring herself to care. She knew exactly what the Seidsian was about to say.

She just couldn't believe she was allowing it to happen.

"You must leave," the Seidsian said, using a tone she'd reserved for the clan's children, during a reprimand. "And not return, until you've made the journey to Skírrdrauin and back, and atoned, on behalf of the clan."

"I have done *nothing* wrong," Ashilde hissed, her heart pounding loud in her chest, even though it felt like it'd been lodged into her throat. "And neither has the clan! Surely you must know this is unjust. We made our sacrifice! We met their demands! The gods cannot—"

"They can and they have, child."

"Why? It ... it makes NO SENSE!" Ashilde screamed, throwing her balled-fists into the air, her entire body shaking.

Unphased by her emotional display, the Seidsian stared at her, hands folded in her lap. Her face remained passive, stoic. Emotionless. "We met their demands of sacrifice for now, but our gods recognize we cannot in the future. I prayed to them for guidance, for a solution, for help. The Ravenmother answered. She demanded one of our *sangrild* to become tainted and attempt atonement. As long as they remain alive, the gods will allow us to miss sacrifices without tainting more of our number. She chose you."

Ashilde rocked back, stunned. The gods—Róta,

specifically—had damned her? She would rip away everything Ashilde fought for, everything she loved, and force her to embark upon a death sentence? *That* was the solution to the Slátra's problems? Her banishment, unasked for and undeserved?

"Why me?" Ashilde whispered.

Finally, the Seidsian stumbled. "Her reasons were ... unclear."

Lying. "Tell me."

"Ashilde—"

"I have given *everything*," Ashilde said, the weight of her new reality bearing down on her, her insides curling and twisting, crushing her, making it hard to breathe, hard to think. She blinked furiously, holding onto the little focus she still had. "The least you could do is tell me what I have done to displease the gods; why I must carry the burden of our survival."

The Seidsian surprised her by relenting. So she *did* know Róta's rationale. "Your own choices, child. All the choices of your life have led to this moment. Your mistake that cost the lives of our hunters, your failure in gathering aid, putting the clan at greater risk."

"You all *agreed*. The clan—"

"Your constant questioning of the gods," the Seidsian continued, speaking without recognizing that Ashilde had interrupted her. It seemed, with the chance to lay out her failures before her, the Seidsian was unable to stop. "How you refuse to help in the ways we need the most, replenishing our numbers. Not to mention the role in your mother's death—"

Recoiling, Ashilde spat on the ground. "How *dare* you."

Was it not enough that she'd spent the past twenty years living in guilt over her mother's death? Was it not enough that she'd lost her sister over it, that she'd dedicated her life to becoming the best warrior the Slátra had ever known, so she'd never be powerless to prevent a death; so she'd be prepared to save a life? Was that not enough penance in Róta's eyes that now, she would take everything that Ashilde had left? Her clan, her home, her people, her purpose, her—

Oh, gods.

Oh gods, *no*.

Davyn.

His tears made sense now. The Seidsian had told him her fate before Ashilde had found her. Now declared tainted, any who were in her presence risked the same fate: to be outcast.

Ashilde had thought she sacrificed everything, for her clan.

She quickly realized how much she had left for them to take, her sacrifices not even scratching the surface of what was possible.

Now, her gods demanded it all.

"Be gone by sunrise, Ashilde. Go alone. Not even a horse travels with you," the Seidsian said, as if Ashilde hadn't spoken; as if her mouth didn't hang agape in horror, her eyes weren't wide in shock. "When the sun rises, you will no longer be Faethegnar. You will no longer be Slátra. Return to us once the gods allow, and not a moment sooner."

She left no more room for argument, her voice solidifying the conversation's end.

Stumbling and numb, Ashilde exited the Mess Hall, her entire sense of reality shaken to the core, as every aspect of her life unraveled before her.

The clan already knew, of course. If she had any doubt, then the sudden transformation of their village into a graveyard, with how suddenly everyone had become scarce—to the point not even their voices could be heard—was confirmation. She was no longer welcome there, no longer Slátra. The gods had spoken, robbing her of her *dolorsandri* and her ability to atone for the very deeds they demanded she do. And thievery it was.

Damn Róta, she thought, blinking away tears as she made her way back to her home by habit alone, unaware of her surroundings. *Damn Waldemar. Damn their rules and their contradictions. When I get there, I'll—*

The thought left her stumbling as she slipped inside familiar walls. Her mind raced, already making her choice without her evening thinking about it. For she *did* have a choice, even if the Seidsian had conveniently forgotten to offer her another. She could live out the rest of her life alone, in exile, for as short as that would last. If her soul was truly as tainted as the gods cursed it to become—Ashilde spit again at her thought of *that*—then she was a walking death sentence.

Or, she could go. She could travel to their home, Skírrdrauin—a place no one had ever reached, considering it was a home reserved only for souls that had passed on. To do so, it would require traveling across the entirety of Armadin: through the Flatrí and across Hafleden, places from their histories that had become monstrous. Finally, she'd have to reach Falos, a place that was only a blank space on her map, for no one knew what it had become, only that it existed.

All of this, she had to do within a month.

Or else her body would kill her.

A month without the ability to hunt, as her heavy price denied her that right. Without the option to kill, lest she speed up her own self destruction—for the more souls she carried, the quicker her body was poisoned from within. A month traveling in the heart of winter, without a horse to aid her or another soul to accompany her.

The price she paid as she was suddenly, publicly, deemed unworthy to bear her blood price.

And the price one of her warriors would inherit, if she died before reaching Skírrdrauin. For, no matter how personal the price was, it didn't change the fact that her clan's fate was explicitly tied with hers.

Ashilde continued to walk forward, but her body no longer shook. Her hands were clenched into fists and her back was straight, rigid to the point of pain. Ashilde didn't have to think to know her choice. She'd be going to Skírrdrauin, but not for absolution, not for cleansing.

In her heart, she knew she needed neither.

No, she would go to Skírrdrauin and demand answers.

Even if she had to kill the gods to get them.

CHAPTER THIRTEEN

Though her decision had been made hours ago, Ashilde waited until night descended upon the Slátra village before she prepared to depart—feeling only slightly shameful that her delay was not due to fear, but the desire to leave unwitnessed.

Most of what she had gathered for the trip visiting the clans was still collected in the corner of her home: flint, a map of what little had been scouted throughout Armadin, some leftover rations, rope and a blanket. She gathered it together, before forcing all of it to fit into a pack.

Then, she collected her weapons, laying them out onto her bed: a pair of throwing axes, a trio of knives, her bow and quiver. She faltered when she reached her spear, gifted from Davyn and Freydis, one fit for a Faethegnar. Her hand shook, knowing she no longer deserved to carry such a weapon. Yet the idea of leaving it behind made her insides twist. She laid it beside the others, determined to bring her full arsenal with her.

You can't use any of these weapons, you know, she realized, stilling at the thought. Not *without killing yourself even faster.*

Ashilde didn't believe that she was tainted. But, with the only evidence supporting the contrary—she didn't bleed between her legs—acting against what she'd been taught would only put her at greater risk.

So, try not to kill anyone, between here and Skírrdrauin, she thought, as she turned away from her weapons and walked over to her clothes rack. She wasn't sure how she'd avoid it—leaving her weapons behind *would* help. But the thought made her shiver more than the prospect of the journey head. She'd travel armed.

She'd deal with the consequences of that choice if it came to it.

Ashilde quickly stripped, changing her outfit for a layer of underclothes, black in color: a thin pair of pants and a sleeveless top. She slipped wraps around her feet, to help keep them warm within her boots against the cold, before she also pulled on a pair of thin, elongated fingerless gloves, reaching all the way up to the base of her elbow. Her fingers remained exposed. She had to keep the gloves thin, despite the chill, if she were to wear her mother's armor—now hers.

Returning to kneel beside her bed, Ashilde pulled a large, wooden chest out from underneath it. It had a delicate array of swirling shapes carved into the top, but otherwise, it was plain and covered in dust from neglect. She pulled the lid open before she could hesitate and convince herself otherwise, hinges creaking as her hands shook at seeing the armor within: a legendary set, made of the now non-existent dragonscale that was woven so expertly into the fabric, that it not only surpassed the strength akin to the sturdiest of armors, but also remained lightweight to wear and flexible to move in.

Dragons were but a story now, killed off by the Banishing, but this armor came from a much earlier time, passed down through her mother's family for generations—a one-of-a-kind set of scaled-pants and shirt, as dragon slaying was told not to have been common, nor an easy feat, especially amid battling a war. Her mother had given it to her as a gift on her Wyrdan Day. She'd never had a reason to wear it.

Now, her thudding heart told her she had no right. This was a relic of the Slátra as much as it was an heirloom of her family's line. By rights, it should be left behind, for Brynhild to inherit. But the thought of her sister taking this armor and donning it—no doubt making her bid as Faethegnar she'd threatened before in earnest—this time, made Ashilde's body sweat; the thought of being replaced so easily.

With shaking hands, Ashilde put it on anyway. She was about to embark on a journey with unknown threats and minimal resources and no help. She wouldn't leave behind the armor that could very well save her life, even if her clan hated her for wearing it.

Even if she hated herself.

The pants fit her form perfectly, while still allowing her to stretch and bend. The long-sleeved jerkin was also form-fitting, sticking to her curves and her muscles as if it had been hand-sewn for her body alone—the magic of dragon scale, considering her mother had been both taller and wider than her. The scales that adorned it, hardening it into armor, layered down the entire set, starting from her neck and blossoming out down her torso, to her shoulders, arms and legs, the scales stacking atop one another. In the sunlight, her mother said the scales could be a range of colors, depending on how one stood against the sun's rays. Yet nothing would blend into the darkness better than what she wore—and she feared she'd need such protection, in the days to come.

Before she could talk herself out of it, she gathered

her mother's necklace, as well, hiding it under her armor. Even if she had no right to her mother's things, she couldn't bear to leave them for Brynhild. It felt too much like a goodbye, instead of the promise that she'd return to hear her sister's wrath at the insult.

Ashilde didn't pause to look in the mirror. Instead, she gathered her weapons and the various sheaths and holsters and belts: axes on her waist, a pair of knives around her ankles and the third upon her wrist, bow and quiver on her back, alongside her pack, completing it all with her spear in hand.

Without anything else to prepare, she walked across her hut with purpose, not allowing herself to look at anything with longing, nor try to memorize any details of her home. She refused to accept this would be the last time she'd be there. Ash set her jaw, as if that motion and the hardening of her resolve would make it so, almost to her door.

She stopped herself just shy from leaving when she heard the hushed grunts of a struggle just outside.

The door shoved open.

She felt like throwing up all over again.

Davyn.

He wasn't alone. He had shoved past Bodil, who entered quickly after him, hissing, "Keep her steady," to someone outside. Ashilde couldn't make out what was happening outside her home—and, upon meeting her gaze, her fellow warrior quickly dropped her eyes to the ground. But Ashilde couldn't care much what was happening out there, not when Davyn stood right in front of her. Seeing him dressed in traveling leathers, Ashilde's heart sank into her stomach. He intended to abandon the clan to be with her.

"Ashilde—" he said, stepping toward her, but Bodil stepped in-between them, seemingly incomplete without an animal to keep her company.

"If you speak with her, you risk becoming as damned as she is," Bodil said, gently.

"You mean as damned as we all are, if you truly believe such nonsense," he spat, struggling to get past.

"Saying goodbye won't damn him anymore than looking at me will, Bodil," Ashilde said, her voice softer than the sharp anger stirring inside her suggested; softer than the pain she knew was about to come. "Any respect you once had for me, please, remember it now. Let me say goodbye to my partner."

Her fellow warrior didn't turn, didn't look at her. It pierced Ashilde's heart. Surely, she had to know that everything was not only out of Ashilde's control, but also undeserved? She didn't bother pleading and trying to make her understand. If Bodil—or any of the warriors, for that matter—needed convincing of that, then she feared losing something she'd never truly had.

Finally, the warrior stepped aside. "Don't take too long," she whispered to Davyn, before slipping past him and walking out the door, harsh whispering cut off only after the door shut. Ashilde didn't waste a second focusing on that, however, as Davyn crashed into her.

"Ash," he cried into her ear, his tears already slipping onto her neck. She gripped him tighter, inhaling his scent, stealing his warmth, committing every part and feel of him to memory. Her home, she could ignore and not regret, if she never returned. But Davyn? She shuddered against him. No amount of preparation could have helped her for this.

He spoke quickly, his words and confessions coming out in panicked gasps. "I tried to come as soon as I could, but they posted guards at your door. Freydis tried, too. Neither of us believe a word of it. I told the Seidsian as much and she threatened to lock me away. But I can't, Ash. I can't—"

"Oh Davyn, my love," she said, pulling away to touch

his cheek, unashamed that her own eyes were bristling, wet. Her warriors might believe the lie placed upon her, but they also did everything they could to protect the one person she cherished most, based on what they believed, because they knew it would be what she wanted.

Perhaps they still loved her, after all.

"They did what they had to do in order to protect you and keep you with the Slátra. I would thank them, if I could. Is Freydis safe?"

He frowned, but answered her question. "Yes. She was as determined to see you as I was. But ... she has her children to think about, too. So I ... may have drugged her ale at dinner. It is not her fault she isn't here to say goodbye."

Shock caused her mouth to drop open, but it all made sense. The warriors guarded her doors to prevent this very thing from happening—to protect Davyn from himself. He'd taken similar measures with Freydis. But between his presence here now and his attire, she knew he intended to damn himself so she would be forced to bring him along. Despite doing so ripping at the very fabrics of his faith, the one thing that tore them apart.

Ashilde choked on her sob, wishing there was more time. Wishing there was any other way. But there couldn't be. There *wasn't*. "I travel alone, my love. If you come with me, you'll exile yourself. And I cannot ask that of you."

"You do not have to. My life is pledged with yours."

"Which is exactly why I must protect *yours*, even if it means severing myself from you."

Davyn shook his head. "You can't mean that. You—"

She kissed him fiercely, threading her fingers into his hair. His words disappeared against her lips, his moan caught against her own. Never had she kissed him so passionately, with abandon. And never had he kissed her so desperately, in return. She didn't pull away until she felt slightly dizzy and she needed to hold onto him for support, her fingers clutched into the front of his shirt. His forehead remained pressed against hers, his breath coming out shaky, his eyes still squeezed closed, as if keeping them shut would prevent what would happen next.

Damn him for knowing her so well.

She leaned in and brushed his lips with a whisper to haunt them both. "I love you, Davyn," she said. "Do you believe me?"

His eyes shot open. "Of course I do."

"I'll come back for you," she continued, rushing her words before her resolve crumbled. "You don't have to wait, but I promise I'll come back. I love you, Davyn. I love you."

"Ashilde—"

His words were cut off as her hand snaked around his neck, finding the pressure point that as she pressed it just so, caused his body to go limp, falling immediately unconscious.

Ashilde collapsed onto the ground with a soft cry, barely catching Davyn before he fell, feeling worse than wretched. Instead, she lowered him down slowly, crying fully, now. The last thing she wanted was to trick him, but as well as he knew her, she knew him. The same way he knew Freydis would not stop, either. Nothing would stop him from going with her. Not while he was conscious.

She kissed him a final time, whispering apologies and love that he couldn't hear. He would be so angry with himself he woke up—the same way her friend would be angry at him, and they'd *both* be livid at her.

Because she would be gone.

And it would be too late to follow.

If she left now, they wouldn't risk trailing behind, trying to catch up with her. Neither could track, not well.

If either of them left, they'd be banished from the Slátra, forever. With winter upon them and their inability to kill, both her lover and her friend being *sangrendi*, chasing after her would put them at risk of being slain—by a foe, a creature or the elements, almost guaranteed. Leaving behind children who would become orphans and a clan without a well trained healer. Sacrifices that, upon seeing her leave, they'd both be willing to make. But how soon would it take before the guilt set in? The regret?

She would not let them take on that burden. Not for her.

Stepping over Davyn's unconscious body, she slipped out her door, not bothering to clean up her face as she forced down her sobs. Bodil stood guard outside, eyes downcast, while the source of the commotion struggled between Ingrit and Torunn: Brynhild. Upon seeing Ash emerge, her sister finally broke out of their hold, closing the distance between them quickly, eyes alight with something worse than anger.

Hatred.

She spat on the ground in front of Ashilde. "I see right through you, sister. I know the truth, and I couldn't let you leave without you realizing that."

Ashilde went stock still. "The truth?"

"The Seidsian announced at dinner what happened; how Róta promised forgiveness, and patience, as we work out a new way to collect sacrifices, in exchange for your banishment, becoming the first tainted of our clan—a life for a life, she called it. She painted you like a savior. The clan spent the afternoon gathering flowers, to decorate your home with. Learning new prayers, asking for your safe return." Brynhild shook her head, rolling her eyes, her disbelief plain. "But I know this is your punishment, for killing our mother, long overdue from the gods. And now, you *dare* to wear her armor, as if you have any claim? As if you have a right?" She stepped closer and Ashilde could smell the ale on her breath—the source of her courage to speak so plainly, perhaps, but certainly not the culprit of the emotions behind her words. "I don't care how many of the others mourn for your loss or whisper your name in praise. Because you *deserve* this. And if you die out there? Well … perhaps you deserve that, too."

Torunn grabbed Brynhild and pulled her back. "Brynhild, that's *enough*."

Ashilde let out a soft sound, releasing the intense bubbling of emotions she felt within her, created from a vortex she couldn't possibly understand: rage that her sister placed so much blame on her shoulders; awe that the Seidsian painted her in such a light to her people; sorrow that Brynhild could truly hate her so totally. But she'd spend all of her tears on Davyn and now, her eyes were dry.

Especially when, deep down, Ashilde feared Brynhild was right.

She glanced at Bodil, ignoring her sister. "All I ask is that you continue to protect him, especially from himself," she said, acknowledging what the warriors had already done for her by, essentially, keeping him hostage. But her voice held no thanks, instead going cold. "I will return."

Pushing past them all at a fast pace, her well of emotions dried up, much quicker than she'd expected. The gate to the village opened without Ashilde seeing who was stationed by the wheel, but she wasted no searching glance, unable to help remembering how, only a month prior, she'd walked out the same path to cheers and tearful partings, her warriors saluting as they prayed for her success.

How different this send off was, leaving her feeling empty, instead of full and fulfilled.

How … permanent.

Tightening one hand firmly around her spear, her left hand clenched into a fist at her side, Ashilde stepped through the gates of her home, outcast and alone, and hoped it wouldn't be the last time she did so. Instead, her prayer was a whispered promise, spoken in haste, threaded with vile.

"Róta, Waldemar. I'm coming for you."

CHAPTER FOURTEEN

Rummaging, Ashilde scraped against the very bottom of her pack, her fingers roughly searching for anything to eat, only to come up against empty edges. She threw her pack on the ground, frustration hissing out of her mouth as she suppressed the urge to yell.

Only three days into her journey and Ashilde was already out of food.

Completely.

Sighing, dirtying her armor as she knelt against the frozen ground, Ashilde retrieved her supplies, scattered around her from where she threw them moments before in frustration. Her stomach rumbled, and she bit her lip to keep herself from cursing, skin already flaking off her chapped lips against the cold. Winter had come in full force overnight. Though only the lightest dusting of snow and ice had invaded the ground so far, she already felt the bite of winter's air deep in her bones; wishing, more than anything, that she was back home, beside a warm fire and with a belly full of food.

You should have taken more before you left. Her choice to remain hidden within her home instead of braving the judgment of her clan had been a mistake. Yet, she couldn't deny the guilt that crept into her stomach and complicated her hunger pains anytime she thought about taking food from the Slátra, despite them rejecting her publicly, even if they praised her in private. They were going to be struggling on their own as it was.

The thought left a sour taste in her mouth. She slung the pack back over her shoulder and pulled out her waterskin, taking a deep drink.

Ashilde glanced up at the sun, peeking through a spattering of gray clouds. She'd reached the outskirts of what was considered Hvass territory that morning, though she'd chosen not to head directly toward their tree-top homes. Instead, she stuck to the middle of the forest—a more barren place, now that the green leaves had fallen, creating a beautiful array of dying foliage among the ground, compared to the lifeless black branches that patterned against the graying sky overhead. Her rationale was to avoid running into as many clans as possible, all while heading *toward* the Dreyma village, since they were bordered alongside the only known opening to the Flatrí. Her thoughts remained her only company, aside from the echoing bird calls off in the distance, more aggravating than peaceful.

Leaves crunched underneath her feet as she walked—near impossible to avoid, so she pushed forward, stepping as light as she could without sacrificing speed. Though not ideal, she hoped to find plants or berries that she could harvest. She *could* try to sneak into another clan's village and steal food, but she dismissed that notion as soon as she considered it. That would be a quicker death sentence than dying from starvation. Even if it wasn't, she'd put her own clan at risk, if she were caught.

Despite how they'd treated her, she couldn't bring herself to do that to them.

Of course, her people wouldn't have made her banishing public, though the truth would travel and find curious ears soon enough, the way it always did. If she was caught—whether stealing food or simply moving through another clan's territory, fully armed and wearing legendary armor—at best, she'd be killed, branded as a Rhuanic for her outcast status. At worst, whoever caught her would be unaware of her current cut ties from the Slátra and take her presence as a declaration of war, mistaking her for a scout who threatened to break an already too-fragile peace. In retaliation, they'd attack the Slátra.

Her banishing to "protect" her people would end up having the opposite effect.

Ashilde rounded and punched her anger out on a nearby tree, her fist grazing against the bark so her knuckles came away splintered. Worse, her anger remained, the punch doing nothing but fueling her frustrations still further, leaving her hand a throbbing mess. The past three days had been difficult, between fighting against her hunger and the cold—not to mention already having a scare when she almost stumbled into Hvass hunters, forcing her to hide for a few hours, before she found her courage to continue forward.

But none of it compared to the battle raging inside her own head.

She paused and stood still, allowing her thoughts a moment to process, even if only to give her anger a chance to cool, despite the throbbing in her hand staying to remind her of her foolishness, attempting to add fuel to an already dangerous flame.

One moment, determination motivated her, her

desperation for answers making every step sure and solid, the sunlight warm against her exposed face and the hardship she already felt not so acute, compared to its warmth. Her confidence felt unshakable, the black thoughts poisoning her mind a distant memory, a brief misstep against a brisk pace and constant progress toward the promise of answers.

It never seemed to last long enough.

Like the transition from day to night, her mind would turn against itself, quick to point out every mistake she'd made, every obstacle remaining in her way. Though she fought to keep it at bay, her pace would begin to slow, her focus and awareness of her surroundings less than sharp. Instead, she let blame bounce around inside her head, so rarely falling upon the gods or her clan, so often landing on herself.

Ashilde had experienced such swaying emotions before, but she always combated the darker ones that didn't deserve the light with a handful of things, back home: her training with her warriors, her daily tasks and chores, patrols with Dagfinn, sitting by a warm fire with Freydis, pulling Davyn tighter against her as she slept.

Alone, it was an entirely different experience.

Every moment, she had to decide, consciously, whether she would be driven by determination or despair.

It scared her how often she chose the latter.

"So, what are you going to choose now?"

She glanced around at the empty woods, having not moved since she'd taken her anger out on an unsuspecting tree. Closing her eyes for just a moment, she inhaled deeply through her nose, holding it until she had no option but release. She repeated the exercise a few more times until her heart stopped hammering, her pulse slowed and her mind felt less foggy.

Opening her eyes, she nodded once. "To fight," she whispered. "You will always choose to fight."

Tucking the spear underneath her arm, she began to walk again, pulling splinters out of her hand as she did so, wincing with every successful pull. She was distracted, finally tending to her hand that she didn't notice she wasn't alone until it was too late.

They already saw her.

Three men gathered around a small fire. The smell of the smoke alone should have warned her of their presence well before practically stumbling directly into their camp; or their voices, even quiet in normal conversation, only silenced when they noticed her. She didn't bother berating herself, knowing she would have plenty of time for that later. Instead, her eyes widened as she took in the one detail that made her heart pound and her body tense.

They bore no clan markings, faces clean.

Just like the Rhuanics who attacked her people.

A coincidence?

Ashilde dropped her spear and slipped her pack off to lay on the ground beside her, before pulling out her hunting knife from its sheath at her wrist.

She doubted it, swallowing.

The men stood, eerily in sync. Her abandoned spear was deadlier, but she couldn't kill them. She had no idea what would happen if she killed now that she couldn't bleed, but she knew it was just as forbidden as these men themselves, if they were in any way similar to the ones who attacked her people. But that didn't mean she couldn't leave them unconscious and incapable of following her, once they woke up.

For a split second, when none of them moved after standing, she considered the possibility that they weren't connected to the Rhuanics at all and, perhaps, the gods had blessed her with a stroke of luck. She let her eyes flicker, for a moment, over toward their makeshift firepit and the animal cooking over it.

She licked her lips at the thought of just one bite.

Perhaps she'd misjudged them. Perhaps she could ask to share in their meal and—

The flash of metal suddenly in their hands and the dark gleam mirrored between their expressions ruined any hopes of *that*. She doubted they had any intentions to let her pass in peace. Even if they did, she wasn't sure she'd be able to leave.

Not with that meat sitting there, waiting for her to take it.

You should run.

"Slátra," one man said, his long beard a stark red against the empty forest backdrop, many of the trees already as absent of their leaves as the top of his head was of hair. He stepped over a log toward her. "We were just on our way to collect you." He smiled, two of his teeth missing. "Thanks for saving us the journey."

Before she could respond, another—the smallest of the three, bones with some skin clinging on—spoke up. "But what do we bring to our god, as a sign of our devotion? Your head on a spike?" He laughed, a raspy sound, yet the new glint in his eyes made her inside twists, especially as the third continued the taunt.

"Or each of your limbs, severed, delivered one by one in separate bags," he said, bow in hand, staring at both of his companions before looking over at Ashilde, his eyes, startlingly, the same piercing blue color as Davyn's. "Another one of Róta's bitches delivered."

Ashilde lost all ability to respond, her mind struggling to keep up with the taunts the men spoke before her. By the Pit, what were they talking about? Loyalty to ... Waldemar? Hatred of Róta? Suggestions that they've done this before? Armed with weapons that bore no marks, yet holding them as if they had any experience with them—something none of them, as *sangrendi*, should have learned how to do.

"What kind of monsters are you?"

The bearded one didn't respond with words, but grinned. He slipped his knife back into its sheath and charged, feeling a cockiness bolstered by outnumbering her. She locked her knees, bracing herself for the assault, before sidestepping at the last moment, swiping her right hand in an arc in front of her, cutting the man in the chest. He adjusted, seemingly unfazed by the thin cut of her blade, still taunting her as he charged.

The other two remained by their fire, laughing at his game, the slow teasing of hunters and their prey.

They stopped when they realized their companion would never touch her.

She ducked underneath one arm, slamming her elbow backward. It caught him in the shoulder and didn't even knock him off balance, though he stumbled past her, surprised. She took no mercy, twisting around to slam into his back, forcing him into the trunk of a tree with speed. His head ricocheted off with a dangerous force, but without the distinct snapping sound, she knew it wasn't enough. Blinded by rage, her previously-calculated plans to only incapacitate her foes were forgotten. She kicked in both his knees, one after the other in quick succession before they could turn around, and the man collapsed forward.

Grabbing the back of his head, she slammed his face into the tree again, burying his nose into the bark. He choked on his own breath and she felt the fight leave him. Releasing his head, he collapsed onto the ground in front of her, unconscious, with a bruise forming on his forehead and trails of blood slipping from his nostrils.

Before she could land a killing blow, an arrow buried itself into her shoulder, startling her as the marksmen found a rare weak spot in her armor.

She'd been so focused on her main attacker that she'd completely forgotten to keep an eye on the other two. She hadn't even thought to keep track of them all.

Usually, her back was guarded by her warriors.

Foolish, she thought with a gasp as she turned to face them. The straggly one stared at his unconscious companion wide-eyed, his own shock freezing him. The bowman had been the one to move, yet he hadn't nocked a second arrow yet. She judged him for the mistake, but she was grateful for it.

It gave her time to retaliate.

Snapping the shaft in half and wincing against the arrowhead still buried within her, she ran towards the pair straight on, her injury calming her down and forcing her to focus on her two remaining attackers.

Even charging at full speed, she wasn't quick enough to dodge the second arrow.

Lucky for her, the bowman wasn't used to a target rushing him, either.

As it flew, she still flinched, but the arrow went wide, making a dull thud as it found a tree's trunk to bury into. Her attacker didn't have time to fire a third time, as she slammed into him, knocking the bow to the ground. She kicked him hard in the groin, letting his face catch her knee as he buckled forward, before she slammed the hilt of her knife against the back of his skull. He collapsed just as his companion finally got over his shock, grabbing her from behind.

Ash threw her head backward, colliding with his forehead. Spots blurred her vision, and his hold around her waist tightened instead of loosening. No alcohol reeked from them, as it had the other two. For taking the longest to attack her, this one might be the most coherent to do so.

Holding her waist secure, he reached up and tried to disarm her. She threw her head back again, unable to slip out of his grasp. Ashilde's vision grew blurrier, but his grip finally faltered, just enough for her to twist around, knife raised, and slam it into his side. The blade buried cleanly through his clothes—as none of them had thought to wear armor, despite supposedly hunting her—and beneath his ribs, before she realized her mistake. Her heart stilled in fear. She'd reacted with practiced skill instead of conscious hesitation.

Her stab was precise. The bulging of eyes and stunned stillness was proof of that. Though he wouldn't die immediately, he'd bleed out before he was able to get help. That much was certain.

Eyes dropped to meet hers. "You bitch," he muttered.

She ripped the knife back before taking a step away from his wobbling form. If he were going to die regardless, no point in dragging it out.

With a single, fluid motion, she snapped his neck.

Ashilde pushed him backward and he collapsed onto the ground. She didn't blink, no sorrow at the life lost. As his eyes froze over with that forever stare she still wasn't used to seeing, she cleaned her knife on his pants before touching her throat, checking her own pulse; accelerated, but normal, given the circumstances. She swallowed before inhaling and exhaling three times, slowly, calming herself down, trying to slow the too-quick beating of her heart, a mix of adrenaline from the fight and the fear of the aftermath. She flexed her fingers and blinked repeatedly. They were definitely dead. There was no doubt she was the cause. Yet she felt no different. No corruption, no ill feeling, no sudden choking on poisoned souls from the inside.

What, did you expect any corruption to be instantaneous?

That's the problem, isn't it? she thought back sourly. She didn't know *what* happened when a person couldn't cleanse their soul. She didn't know how she would become corrupted, how she would be able to tell or how long it would take to kill her—only that it would kill her, *if* it proved to be true.

Sheathing her knife, she took inventory of their camp. It wasn't hastily made, but it was no way near complete in what she'd hoped it would contain—namely provisions, aside from the meat burning on the spit. But, she did find rope, which saved her from abandoning her own.

Wrapping it around her uninjured shoulder, she went to the archer. She shook off the pain in her hand as she picked him up, noting the need to take care of that, on top of her shoulder, before she abandoned the camp and moved on.

Finally getting a good grip, she dragged his body, taking the incompetent archer to the tree she'd used to bash the bearded man's face in. She propped both of them on opposite sides of the trunk, the dried blood on the leader's face and chin cracking as she re-positioned them. Cutting the rope into strips, she bound each of their hands and feet separately, before using what remained to tie them all together, knotting the rope on the only side of the tree a body wasn't occupying.

Staring down at her handiwork, she realized that, if they didn't wake up soon, the remaining pair would probably die from exposure to the cold during the night, if another predator didn't find them first. Would their souls be absorbed by her, even if their deaths were delayed?

Ashilde frowned, unsure. But, she didn't waste much time debating that unknown, instead turning around to go back to take inventory of their camp. She'd already made a decision, albeit unconsciously. Now that she'd killed again after being robbed of her *dolorsandri* and was still fully functioning, she would no longer fear killing, *if* it was necessary. She wouldn't go searching to become a deliverer of death, but she couldn't afford to hesitate to kill. Her own body, it seemed, wouldn't also become her enemy.

No, that honor belonged to the gods and time.

She sat down on the log, picking up an abandoned plate of meat, scarfing it down without hesitation, not caring how her stomach cramped at finally getting filled. As Ashilde reached over and ripped off another piece from the spit, she glanced over at the head. It was still attached to the body and they hadn't used the time to properly skin it like they had the rest, so it was a charred, blackened thing, the ears and face distorted to the point that she couldn't pinpoint exactly *what* she was eating. Instead, she found the singular eyeball staring back at her, dripping liquid slowly onto the ground.

Ashilde stared back as she took a bite. "What?" she asked the dead creature, savoring the meat, this time. "You'd do this, too, if you hadn't eaten. I'm not used to it."

The creature didn't answer.

Well, of course it's not going to answer, her mind retorted. She could talk to animals, but only if they were still among the living.

Still, it was nice to have *something* to talk to, no matter how strange.

She glanced over at the tree, where she'd left the Rhuanics to rot, before glancing back at the dead creature. "Do you think I should interrogate them?" She frowned. "I *do* have a lot of questions, some they might be able to answer."

Too many questions: Why weren't they marked and identifiable by a clan? What spurred their rhuanical actions and thoughts? What purpose did their actions serve? Where did they come from? What interest did they have in the Slátra ... or was it her, specifically, now, since they mentioned they were hunting her, somehow? How did they worship Waldemar? Why did they hate Róta? How many of them were there? Surely, it was no coincidence that a group of Rhuanics had attacked her clan, only to be hunted by *another* group of Rhuanics now?

"It is odd, isn't it?" she continued, speaking through bites of the creature's flank. "But ... no, you bring up a good point. How could I trust anything they said? Questioning one would only delay my progress."

She finished her plate, licking her fingers clean and dry, before cocking her head to the side in thought. *Your Seidsian did chide you for not getting answers when you could. Can you risk making the mistake again?* Ashilde didn't fear them escaping to attack her. She'd just knock them unconscious, if need be.

Perhaps you can finally honor your promise to Freydis.

That thought gave her pause.

"I'll think on it for a moment," she told the animal, as if it could listen to her own deliberations. "I'll patch up my wounds, restock supplies and ... think."

She stole one of the Rhuanic's waterskins and sniffed it, only drinking it after she realized it was water and not whatever drink the bearded one had been swallowing. She felt more revitalized than she had in recent memory. Her body was slick from sweat after the exertion of fighting, killing and then trapping the bodies. The fire kept her warm. Her belly was full and her head clear. The hatred and confusion driving her so passionately since she left the Slátra was buried under these false comforts, and her mood, as much as it could be in her situation, brightened.

Perhaps she could do this, after all.

It didn't take long for guilt to slip to the surface to ruin it all.

You eat meat while your clan goes without. What justice is there in that?

You were shoved out as if diseased, she countered. *Why concern yourself with them?*

Ashilde shut away those thoughts as she began stripping the rest of the carcass, wrapping the meat in linens she created from her attackers' spare clothing as she went. "The mind's unfair, you know. It twists and contorts everything you've thought until you don't know how you're supposed to feel. Is it horrible, for me to still want to help them? To even consider if I *can*?"

The eyeball finally plopped from its socket, falling onto the ground with a wet *smack*.

Ashilde sighed and stood. "Yeah, some help you are. Thanks for the chat. I think."

Meat packed and shoved into her pack, adding back the extra weight she'd been missing, Ashilde used the rest of the water from the waterskin to clean her hands, before dabbing the back of her neck and splashing her face with two handfuls of it. Her shoulder winced as she did so, reminding her that she couldn't put that off any longer. She twisted around so she could see her armor better, surprised when she saw the archer had managed to find the one weak spot, where the scales didn't cover: just where her shoulder connected to her body. The arrow had ripped through the armor, barely missing the scales on either side of it, leaving a messy hole in its place.

Ashilde sighed again. She'd have to patch that up at some point, but she didn't really have the supplies for that. Instead, she pulled her armor off and laid it beside her on the ground, retrieving her knife and warming it over the fire's flame, cleaning the blade. Careful, she focused on remaining still, despite shivering against the cold wearing nothing but a sleeveless undershirt. Then, she dug out what remained from the arrow from her shoulder, hissing when it was finally removed. The cut wasn't as deep as she feared, but deep enough it merited extra attention.

She used the rest of the cloth stolen from the Rhuanics to wrap her shoulder, hoping to staunch the blood flow during the night and then wrap it up in something cleaner the next morning. She didn't bother wrapping the cut on her hand, wanting to save the other shirt she hadn't cut up yet as a fresh binding in the morning. She did use the last bit of their water supply to clean it, however, the small cuts stinging as she worked. Finally, both wounds taken care of, she pulled her armor back on, ignoring the discomfort of the pressure against her shoulder.

The process of cleaning her wounds allowed her to put things into perspective, enough to make a decision. Some things could only be answered by her gods, but she owed it not only to her people, but also to herself, to find out the truth behind these Rhuanics. There were too many unknowns about them and their purpose. If they were a further risk to her people, she needed to know.

One source of answers was tied up on a tree behind her.

Digging around their discarded packs, she finally found the waterskin filled with ale—stale and pungent, by its smell. She walked over to the tree and, unscrewing the top, she poured the contents onto the leader's face, kneeling in front of him as the brown liquid caressed down his sharp angles, burning the skin as it mixed with their blood and tried to slip under his closed eyes and into his open mouth.

He awoke with a start, spurting out spit, blood and ale as he choked on the mixture. Ashilde leaned back to avoid anything landing on her and the movement caught his attention, causing him to look up at her, eyes wide and teeth bared, like a predator.

It took only a flick of her eyes, guiding his own to discover bound wrists, feet and torso, to remind him he was prey.

He snarled, but before he could add any voice to his thoughts, she dropped the waterskin and cupped her palm over his lips, pressing her knife against his exposed throat. "You have answers for me, Rhuanic," she said, meeting his glare. "Give them to me and I'll only knock you out again, instead, and be on my way." She pressed the blade slightly harder against his throat, punctuating what 'instead' meant.

Ashilde waited a few more seconds before she pulled her hand away, leaving her knife where it was. "What do you want with me?"

"Nothing I need to confess to you," he said, grinning.

She sliced his throat, a thin cut.

"Bitch!"

"You won't bleed out … this time. Try again."

"You think you hold any sway over me?"

"Your life is in my hands," Ashilde said. "Why have you forsaken the gods? Which clan cast you out? Why do you hunt the Slátra?"

The man grinned wider. "You waste the little precious time you have, Slátra. I go to my god and will find welcome, knowing satisfaction that my last act was defying your curiosity."

Ashilde barely stopped herself from cutting his throat open fully right there, but her arm remained rigid, her muscles flexed to keep her grounded. *Don't kill unless your hand is forced. Nothing is certain.*

It didn't matter. After his declaration, the man had begun to grind his teeth, creating a grating sound Ashilde had assumed was just to spite her further, perhaps aggravate her enough to accidentally kill him and rob her of her questioning. It wasn't until she heard a sharp *crack* and the man inhaled sharply that she stood and backed away, as his mouth began to foam and a putrid stench escaped as he laughed, a hollow sound.

Within seconds, his head rolled and the Rhuanic was dead.

"Gods breath," Ashilde whispered.

Before she had a chance to process what had just

happened, Ashilde heard a sharp cry. She looked up and, amid the graying clouds, flew a raven, large wings outstretched as it circled slowly above the trees, before disappearing behind the remaining leaves.

When it cawed a second time, Ashilde fell to the ground in pain, the source coming from her stomach as cramps assaulted her. Her throat tightened, her head swam as if she'd just suffered a direct blow and her vision blurred, as she grit her teeth to keep herself from screaming, her entire body already drenched in sweat in a matter of seconds.

Gods, what is happening?

She twisted and writhed against the ground beside the dead man's body, her knife discarded as she rolled onto her back, her neck slicing against a dead branch as it snapped beneath her. Ashilde finally inhaled, her arms clenched around her stomach as she choked for breath, her chest on fire as her broken rune burned, as if alive. Blinking vision back into her eyes, she lifted her neck up to look, trying to see if something had attacked her and caught her unawares, expecting to see an axe jutting out of her torso.

Instead, she froze as she discovered something stranger.

Her hands were missing.

Ignoring the flaring cramps within her and the burning sensations against her chest as best she could, Ashilde sat up, blinking furiously, as if it was the fault of her shaky vision that caused her to mistake reality. Widening her eyes fully before looking back at her hands, she blanched while she watched both of her hands—at least, where her hands *should* have been— flicker, first appearing solid like she'd always known them, the cuts on her knuckles glaring; the next, her hands shimmered and faded, her fingers, knuckles and palms disappearing until it looked like she had nothing but stumps, with a faint outline of where her fingers should be remaining in a soft, eerie golden glow.

Ashilde's heart stopped.

Was *this* the price she paid when she could no longer pay in blood?

Before she could even begin to process that question, she cried out as a sharp cramp hit within her and she fell to the ground, curled up into a tight ball. The raven, Róta's creature, still circled above her, cawing once more, a strident sound. Ashilde watched as her hands flickered in and out of existence, until her entire world went dark.

CHAPTER FIFTEEN

In the days that followed, Ashilde found nothing she searched for: no new signs of any additional Rhuanics, nor answers to what had happened to her body in the clearing.

She also failed to locate the source of who watched her, though she felt their eyes ever since the Rhuanic had killed themself and she lost her hands for the first time.

Ashilde walked slowly through the trees as the mid-morning sun warmed the air around her, yet not warm enough to clear all the ice and light snow that fell from the night before, lingering in random patches upon the ground. Almost instinctively now, she flexed her hands, first her left, stretching it out as far as her fingers could go, focusing intently on each one, before moving onto her right, clenching it tightly into a fist until her knuckles turned white. Glancing down, she breathed a sigh of relief when both of her hands were fully visible, still intact and functioning.

That wasn't what she always discovered, each time she tested them.

Ducking under a low hanging branch, Ashilde knew it was impossible to be certain exactly *what* was happening to her—especially since no cramps had returned since that first assault, days earlier.

But, you haven't killed anyone since then, either.

The only solution she could come up with was that the supposed taint the gods had put on her was real and that, with each death, her body would revolt. Before, her price had been shedding blood monthly.

Now, it seemed, her price was risking losing the body *itself.*

Whether it was her entire body or just parts of it; whether permanently or just in flashes, it was impossible to know. Ashilde could only conclude that she'd have to be more careful, from now on, to avoid taking a life when confronted with the choice. She hoped she wouldn't run into anyone else on her way to Skírrdrauin, but there was no way to be certain.

And a tall order to ask, besides, with danger lurking all around you.

In the days that followed, Ashilde had continued her journey north, cutting as straight a path as she could toward the Flatrí. She'd made good time, only two days out from Dreyma territory, faster than when she and Davyn had first traveled through the Segan almost two months ago. Despite not having a horse, she took a more direct route, where before, they'd often skirted and backtracked, to ensure they spent as little time on each clan's land as possible. She also slept less and less each night, arguing with herself it was because she was fighting against time, *not* because she awoke to nightmares that her body had vanished, while she somehow remained trapped within its nothingness.

Yet, as she focused on moving ahead, she remained determined on looking for signs of the Rhuanics, searching the ground for any sign of footprints, checking the low-hanging branches for any recent cuts or missing limbs gathered for firewood; anything that might alert her to where the others were or had been. She had little to be confident over, but she was certain, now, of two things.

There were more than just a few rogue Rhuanics, outcast from a clan. There was a group, somewhere.

And they hunted her.

Why was beyond her mind to understand, the few fragments she'd caught more confusing than having no context at all. Just another thing to add to her endless list of questions.

Ashilde shivered, though no wind blew.

There it was again: the distinct feeling of someone watching her.

Or were they hunting?

No longer able to ignore it and feign ignorance while being so alert that her muscles had begun to cramp, Ashilde readied her spear and held it across her chest, visibly scanning her surroundings. This part of the forest wasn't as dense as her destination would be, making it hard for anything to sneak up on her or hide—at least, she hoped. It was quiet, not even the wind interrupting the morning's peace. Yet her spine tingled and sweat laced her palms. Surely she wasn't being—

A sharp *caw* broke the silence above her.

Her head snapped up to watch as a raven swooped across the sky, breaking free from its perch among the branches with speed, causing the limbs to shudder as it flapped its wings, carrying it higher. Ashilde cursed as she lowered her spear, her muscles not relaxing, but uncoiling ever so slightly.

"Is that what's spooked you these past few days, Ash? A bloody *bird*?"

Not any bird though, her mind retorted. *You're watched by Róta's creature.*

The same kind of bird who had appeared just before she'd lost her hands. *But surely not the exact same bird?* she wondered as her eyes traced it as it crossed the sky, before it circled back to fly directly overhead.

Ahead, much closer to her, something growled.

Ashilde whipped around to discover the real source of her nerves: a wolf, larger than any had the natural right to be. Coarse, black fur covered a stocky frame, with eyes a bright blue that surprised her, the left eye sporting a jagged scar that cut across the wolf's face and ended at the tip of its nose. Its lips curled up in a snarl and Ashilde had the sense to lower herself to the ground, laying her spear against the frozen dirt. White fangs disappeared, but the wolf did not move.

Above, the raven called, sending shivers down her spine.

The Ravenmother. The Wolffather. A pair of chosen creatures of her gods, meant to represent them and be used as symbols of the people's worship of them. Creatures that were in abundance within their home in decoration, but rare out in the wilds. Now, both of them were here, watching her?

They must be here for a reason.

The wolf stared at her, waiting.

But were they here to help her or to kill her?

Only one way to find out.

Keeping her eyes fixed on the wolf's, Ashilde stood, which earned a growl, yet she left her spear behind—and the wolf noticed, as it flicked its eyes toward the abandoned weapened before meeting her gaze once more. Moving slowly, Ashilde approached it, ignoring the warning growl vibrating in the creature's throat.

Ashilde had rejected Davyn's offer to come with her because she couldn't risk him; his help, though she could have sorely used it, was too high a price for her to pay. Yet, since leaving her borders, she'd gone hungry, lost sleep, suffered from the cold and began to, *literally*, start losing parts of her body, even if only for a moment; all before even reaching the Flatrí, the first of her destinations. What she was unwilling to take, before, was impossible to deny, now.

If she were to survive, she'd need help.

Perhaps the gods were kind enough to provide her some.

Ashilde refused to flinch as she approached, even as the wolf snapped at her. Instead, just in front of it, she lowered herself—slowly—onto her knees, before pressing her hands into the dirt, leaving her weapons secured on her person, her spear abandoned too far behind her to be of any use. She looked into the wolf's eyes before she bared her neck in surrender.

If you want to kill me, then do it.

Seconds passed, long enough for a singular bead of sweat to slip down her neck and onto her hand below. Swallowing, she moved to look at the wolf again, this time baring her teeth at it as she offered a growl of her own, deep-throated and raw. She might be willing to ask for its help, but she would not have it mistaken for submission.

Between the two of them, only one could be in charge, and she intended it to be her.

The wolf's lip curled, sending her heart into her throat as her body tensed, ready to experience the killing blow. Instead, the wolf leaned forward, sniffing her mouth. Before she could determine if it accepted her challenge, it sneezed.

Ashilde rocked backward as droplets of the wolf's snot hit her teeth. Wiping at her mouth, she spit onto the ground twice, the tension in the air—which, moments before, held the entire forest in its grasp, seeming unshakable—broken.

The wolf cocked its head at her as it sat down, sitting taller than her as she remained on her knees.

A moment later, the raven landed behind it on a low-hanging branch, fluttering its feathers before settling onto the branch, before turning to point its tiny red eyes at her, head cocked to the side, as if studying her.

Ashilde let out a breath, trying to get her heart to settle, as she focused her mind to create a link between her and the creatures in front of her. Since they hadn't attacked, she assumed they would be open to speaking with her. For once, it seemed Waldemar's gift would come in great use to her.

Yet, as she tried to speak to them with her mind, it was like she had run straight into a wall at full speed. Her entire body shuddered as if she'd physically been hit, causing her to gasp and her eyes—which she'd closed on instinct, to help her focus—shot open. Both creatures continued to stare at her, almost expectantly.

It was true that she hadn't used her gift, but she'd trained on how to use it. Surely the lack of use over the years hadn't made it impossible to use now?

You not being part of Slátra anymore might.

Ashilde blanched and it was the wolf's turn to cock its head, confused as to why she refused to speak with it.

"I ... can't," she whispered, tears stinging her eyes in shame, as her reality sunk in further, creating breaks in her heart. "I can't speak. It's ... gone."

The wolf's head cocked to the right side, now, its ears perched up.

"Can you ... still understand me?"

The wolf nodded.

Well, that was a start, at least. Though it did nothing to help ease the pain within her, the ... finality of her own tainted status still felt in every part of her core.

"Did your masters send you?"

The raven cawed, its feathers shaking, as if laughing.

More somber, the wolf shook its head.

"I need to reach Skírrdrauin. Can you ... *will* you

help me?"

The wolf turned its head to look back at its companion, who took off to the sky in response, cawing loudly to announce its departure. The wolf looked back at her and stood, stretching out its long limbs and huge paws slowly, before turning around and walking away, towards the Flatrí. Despair tried to worm its way within her at their rejection, but before it could take root, the wolf turned back and looked at her, one eyebrow raised.

Moving to retrieve her bow, not allowing herself to think too long about the strangeness of the day's events, Ashilde followed.

CHAPTER SIXTEEN

The trio quickly formed a routine and, in two days' time, made it to the outskirts of Dreyma territory, the Flatrí's border just beyond; a looming dark abyss of the unknown, waiting for her to gather enough courage to enter it.

So far, Ashilde had remained on the outskirts, keeping away as far as she could while still keeping the Flatrí's border in view. Currently, she sat on the ground as she leaned against a tree, taking a short break to massage her calf, which had cramped up after keeping up an intense pace, barely pausing to breathe. The raven perched in a tree above her, picking under its wings as it cleaned them. The wolf had left earlier that morning—presumably hunting—but hadn't returned, absent longer than usual. So, she allowed herself a moment's pause, waiting for the creature to return and let herself be lost in thought, if only to distract herself from the tightness in her legs.

The routine they'd followed for the past few days was minimal, focused only on the essentials: sleeping (barely), eating (minimally) and walking (mostly). Both raven and wolf kept her company as she traveled and didn't seem bothered by her talking quietly to them most of the day, until her voice went hoarse from overuse, instead of the croaking of not using it at all. She spoke to them about anything *other* than her journey and its purpose, her mind, for the first time since she'd left home, quiet.

When she'd ask for their help, she hadn't been certain what help she was asking *for*. What she wanted most was answers, but without the ability to hear their thoughts, she couldn't gain that—and that was assuming either of them knew the specifics of her plight and had any guidance from the gods they'd be willing to share, had she the chance to ask. Nor did she think they could take away whatever poisoned her from within, though her body had remained solid and intact since meeting them.

Yet, even only traveling with them for the two past sunrises, both had already proven themselves tenfold. The raven offered snared rabbits for her to eat, both companions ignoring her proffered pieces after she cooked her meal on a crudely-made spit from whatever sticks she could find laying around at the time; allowing her own meager rations—even after replenishing her stock from the meat she'd stolen from the Rhuanics—to remain untouched, which alone was enough to make her grateful. Then, the second night, she'd awoken in a panic when she felt something press against her as she'd slept, only to discover the wolf had decided to curl into her, sharing its warmth. She hadn't pushed it away, surprised by its generosity. She'd surprised herself still further when she found herself near tears as she pressed a little harder against the wolf.

Perhaps their greatest help would be making her feel, for the first time since she'd been banished, less alone.

Once, she would have considered such acts as

small gestures. Yet her gut warned her their aid could possibly be the difference between her waking up to face another day or her death, resulting in another from her clan to suffer the same challenge. Perhaps, if they grew to respect her enough, they might even come to her aid in a fight and save her soul in the process.

Now, with the wolf gone and the raven busy, her thoughts were quick to return, and the precision of returning her in a state of fear and confusion was harrowing. *It's too good to be true, their help. It must have a cost.*

Ashilde bit her lip, considering, before she ignored the bait, refusing to go down that toxic line of thought. Though she'd definitely experienced her share of challenges since departing from Slátra soil, all things considering, she felt quite lucky. A week she'd been traveling across Armadin and yet she hadn't run into any clans and only one set of Rhuanics—the latter frustrating in her quest for answers, but a blessing in her journey for survival. The weather had chilled, but the snow remained light. So many things *could* have gone wrong, yet hadn't. She needed to recognize that and be grateful for what she *did* have.

A shout ahead of her refocused her attention to her surroundings, causing her to still as she located its source.

Just as she'd appreciated her luck, it seemed to have run out.

A group of Dreyma hunters had just entered the clearing Ashilde paused to rest in.

Moving slowly, she positioned herself behind the trunk she'd leaned against moments before, lowering herself a little closer to the ground.

There were only four of them, each one dressed thickly in furs. Two carried spears and shields, the third a pair of axes, while the final hunter carried a bow, each of their weapons decorated in hues of blue and purple, their clan's colors. Together, all of them mimicked the same movements: staying crouched, low to the ground and moving slow, obviously in the middle of tracking their current prey.

A small number and she doubted that was their entire hunting force. Probably nothing more than a routine hunting trip—

No.

She blinked and then leaned forward, as if the slight increase in distance would help her see any better. But no, looking more intently, she knew her eyes weren't deceiving her.

Strapped on the back of one of the hunters carrying a spear and shield, was a child.

Bundled up just as thick, she couldn't see their face, but she knew the design the mother used to carry her child securely against her, the wrap enveloping the child as it hung snug over one shoulder and around her back and torso. The mothers of the Slátra used similar designs, though Ashilde had never heard of taking one's child out to *hunt*. At least, she assumed they were young, to still be carried by their parent, most likely a babe. But the chance the child could die was great, no matter what prey their mother tracked. What were the rest of the Dreyma doing—or that hunter's partner, for that matter?—to be unavailable to watch her child while she hunted for the clan's food?

The group paused, one of them pointing a spear. Another pointed in the opposite direction. They huddled closer together, arguing over where they thought the prey had gone, most likely. She couldn't see or hear any animals nearby. Ashilde hoped, for their sake, they rediscovered their prey quickly. She couldn't imagine they had much time to hunt, not when they were already far enough away from their clan that the borders of their walls were nowhere to be seen. And carrying a child, in the cold...

Ashilde flinched when the raven landed on her arm, nipping her hand through her glove.

Suddenly, a shout rose from the hunters.

Ashilde whipped around. One of the hunters pointed toward the last bit of the forest that was still wide enough to see through, before it darkened into Flatrí's border. A flash of dark fur against the trees was enough for Ashilde to confirm that her missing companion had finally showed up. Potentially becoming the Dreyma's prey—if they were desperate enough to attack one of the gods' creatures, a certain death wish. Yet could they even tell it was a wolf, with how quickly it moved between the trees?

She turned to look and see if they noticed her companion, but she discovered something much worse.

The mother wasn't looking at their rediscovered target. She'd looked away.

Staring directly at Ash.

Before she could decide whether to announce herself, she watched as the archer lifted her bow and took aim at the wolf. She couldn't let them hurt it.

Pit.

"Stop!" Ashilde cried, standing.

The arrow flew to the sound of startled cries of the hunters, who hadn't noticed Ashilde when the mother amongst them tried to point her out. The arrow buried itself into the trunk just before the distinct form of a wolf darted between a pair of bushes, disappearing out of sight.

Not bothering to be quiet anymore, Ash heard the archer curse. "You! How dare you try and steal our kill from us! On our own land, no less."

The hunter took a step toward her, but another held her back. "What business do you have trespassing here, Slátra?" the hunter—and Ashilde assumed their leader, perhaps even their Faethegnar—asked, after moving in front of the rest of the group. "You did not send word of your need to travel through here. And you just cost us our dinner."

Ashilde stepped out from between the bushes, raising one hand. The other still held her own spear, but she wasn't going to let it go. Not when she feared she might need it soon, especially since the Dreyma had two points against her. Not only did she rob them of their kill—even if she wanted to point out that she just stopped them from accidentally killing Waldemar's chosen animal—she *was* trespassing. She hadn't thought to announce her travels to the eastern clans, though that was an expectation, a condition of peace.

Failure to do so was never read as a peaceful intention.

"Look at their face, Asanti," one of the axe-wielders whispered.

The leader's eyebrows lowered as her face grew tight. "Your Seidsian dares send a warrior to scout our borders? In full arms, wearing armor of legend?"

Ashilde resisted the urge to touch her face, knowing exactly what alerted them to which clan she belonged to and what role she used to serve there. Her markings. There had never been an occasion to let anyone see her *without* her markings proudly painted upon her face. Markings she'd reapplied every morning, not even realizing she did it, so ingrained a practice it was.

She hadn't even considered washing her face clean.

As an outcast would have.

Shocked at her own foolishness, she failed to respond in time. The leader glanced back toward the hunter directly behind her. "Go to the Seidsian. Tell her that the Slátra have declared war."

"No!"

The hunter, who turned to leave, paused.

Asanti raised her eyebrow. "Speak, then, if you think we'll believe that you're anything more than a war-intentioned scout, sneaking along our border unannounced and well armed."

Ashilde took a step forward, raising one hand higher. Weapons were lowered in her direction and she froze. "Please," she said, unsure of how much to tell them and how to explain her situation without putting the Slátra in danger. First, their hunters were gone and now, one of their warriors was outcast, *after* Rhuanics targeted her clan specifically? It was almost too tempting of an invitation, a declaration of growing weakness. But that risk depended on whether they believed she'd truly been cast out and were willing to take her at her word. Yet, if they *didn't* believe her, they might go through with their threat, believing one of the Slátra had broken the peace, thus making the entire clan responsible.

She couldn't let that happen.

"Please," she repeated, finally lowering her spear to the ground, trying to prove her non-lethal intentions. "My name is Ashilde. I visited with you a month ago. Our healer ... he helped your Seidsian's grandchild!"

Ashilde couldn't believe she'd forgotten about that. So focused she'd been on the Dreyma's rejection, cementing her quest as a failure, she hadn't even asked Davyn what had been wrong with the child and what he had done, and hadn't given it a moment's thought afterward. That knowledge would have been a great help now. *You fool.*

As murmurs broke out among the hunters, she hoped that good deed would be enough to spare her people now, as lacking as her knowledge was.

"I see," Asanti said. "So why—"

A sharp whistling in the air cut off her words, as the all too familiar breeze of an arrow whipped by her face.

Ashilde's eyes widened in shock as the arrow lodged itself into the throat of one of the hunters standing off to Asanti's left.

Shouts suddenly rang out from behind her as a group of six men burst out of the bushes, all of them with unpainted faces, brandishing weapons and charging without hesitation.

Ashilde met Asanti's glare as their hunter fell to the ground, bleeding out. "You *dare* lead Rhuanics here?"

"No! I—"

She snapped her attention away from Ashilde, looking back at her hunters. "Go gather reinforcements," she commanded. "We'll take out this Slátra and then kill the Rhuanics, buy you some time."

Ashilde stole a precious glance behind her. The men were gaining and would be on top of them in seconds, arrows flying as they ran, but so far, none had yet to hit its mark, now that surprise was no longer on their side. She had to help the Dreyma hunters fight them off, despite her shock that all of them appeared willing to sacrifice their souls to kill other humans for the first time, without a moment's hesitation. Perhaps her aid would make them realize she hadn't led them there at all, even if her heart feared she somehow did exactly that.

Yet she couldn't let the scout escape, even to bring reinforcements they might need.

For if Ashilde was killed, they'd bring devastation upon the Slátra next.

She couldn't risk it.

She dove onto the ground just as an arrow flew from the Dreyma hunter, barely missing her. As she moved, Ashilde dropped her spear and pulled her own bow off of her back, already nocking an arrow. Without wasting another moment to think, she fired after the sprinting hunter, not realizing until she let the arrow fly that the one Asanti had sent back to their clan was the mother, with the child still strapped to her back.

Ashilde didn't—*couldn't*—let herself see the arrow fall, instead turning and running directly towards the

Rhuanics that charged them, picking up her spear as she moved.

She pretended she couldn't hear the shrill cry of her arrow finding its target.

She screamed herself as soon as she heard a second, younger cry, echoing it.

Her insides twisted, fighting an emotional battle just as deadly within as the one she'd just thrown herself into, both the physical and emotional warring over which got her full attention. As she ran at their attackers, her head was filled with the echo of the child's wails, strident even amid the fray. Not stopping, she charged into one of the Rhuanics at full force, using the weight of her entire body as she knocked the thrust of his spear away, barrelling into him, propelling his body backward while the rest of his companions continued forward. Yet even as she drove her knees into his torso, before lowering one and jerking it into his groin—her stomach threatening to throw up her meal from that morning—a single sentence suddenly took the forefront of her thoughts.

You always leave orphans behind you.

Her sister's voice.

Ashilde screamed, slashing the tip of her spear against the throat of the Rhuanic pinned below her. A dirty gash was left in its wake and he shoved at her, trying to push her off his dirty hands wrapped around his throat, attempting to stop the damage she'd done. But they both knew the effort was futile. The Rhuanic would bleed out well before he could staunch the wound closed.

Similar to how her guilt would try and suffocate her before she'd learn to allow herself a breath of forgiveness.

But some things simply didn't deserve it.

Turning around once more, she found the fight, which had progressed to the center of clearing she'd run from moments before. One Rhuanic was down, an arrow sticking out of his forehead where clan markings should be. Another fought the axe-wielder, one-on-one.

Two fought Asanti.

Leaving one Rhuanic missing.

And she knew with distinct certainty she hadn't heard any more cries from the scout she'd downed.

Glancing up, she noticed the raven flying directly above her, circling slowly, observing. "Help us!" she cried out to it, before she ran up and attacked the man on Asanti's left, driving her spear through the bend of his knee from behind.

Just as the attacker on Asanti's right jabbed his sword up into the Dreyma Faethegnar's torso, eliciting a startled gasp from Asanti that was quickly gurgled by blood.

Ashilde grabbed the man's face who she'd crippled through the knee and quickly snapped his neck, not wanting to waste time switching between weapons when her hands did the job just fine. As he dropped, she turned to face the other as he pulled his sword out from Asanti's stomach. The lead hunter clutched at her waist, her coat already darkening from the blood stain. Considering her downed as she dropped to her knees, the Rhuanic turned his back on Asanti and smiled at Ashilde, one of his front teeth missing. He *enjoyed* this. Swallowing bile, Ashilde crouched, steeling her legs as she lifted her spear, ready to engage. The man laughed, but didn't bother speaking to her, obviously not impressed that she'd already killed half of his number.

As he lowered to match her stance, Ashilde unintentionally glanced over his shoulder.

Forcing her surprise to not show on her face, Ashilde dove to the ground, making the Rhuanic's own lips frown in confusion.

A second later, the wolf collided into him from behind, digging its claws into his back as it snapped its jaws around his ear, burying into his neck, before ripping his ear and part of his scalp off his body.

The Rhuanic, screaming, tried to twist around and pull the massive creature off, but he was no match for a creature that size, exposed fangs already stained red as it went in for the next bite.

Pushing herself up onto her arms, still laying on her side, Ashilde glanced around what remained of the battlefield, searching for her next target. Another Rhuanic was being distracted by the raven as it flitted around his face, slicing its talons at his head while he attempted—and failed—to hit it out of the air with his spear.

Ashilde re-equipped her bow and took aim, shooting the Rhuanic three times in the back.

She winced as he fell on top of the Dreyma hunter, already dead by their feet, axes lying abandoned between them.

Looking back behind her, Ash rushed to stand, bow still in hand, her heart hammering.

The mother was still alive.

She pushed herself backward on the ground, one arm wrapped back around the bundle she'd twisted to position on her back. Ashilde's arrow stuck out of her left leg, maiming it to the point of uselessness. She hadn't wanted to kill the hunter, only stop them from reaching the Dreyma until Ashilde had a chance to clear her clan's name. Yet her choice might have doomed the hunter to death.

The last Rhuanic stalked her slowly, toying with his kill.

Reaching her, the man unsheathed his knife.

Ashilde shot her bow just as his arm lowered.

The man stumbled for a few moments before he finally fell forward, dead.

Running over, Ash's stomach twisted in knots that, if the woman had died, would never become unclenched.

As she reached the pair, she shoved the rhunaic's

corpse off the hunter, falling to her knees.

The woman lay in the ground beneath her, struggling to breathe. The knife had fallen from the man's grasp as she'd shot him, straight into the waist of the woman Ashilde had tried to save; a hunter in danger only because of her in the first place.

She met the eyes of the scout, surprised to see forgiveness reflected there. "You weren't … with them…" she said, choking out the words. "You were … protecting your … people."

Ashilde, curse her, didn't have the voice to respond. She swallowed, her eyes filled with tears. She could only nod, not even taking the woman's hand as she died.

"Now…" The woman coughed, before she tried again. "Now … you can protect … mine."

Spitting blood, the woman's eyes glazed over and her head rolled to the side, to rest on the frozen ground.

A second later, the sharp wail of a child began to sound.

CHAPTER SEVENTEEN

Ashilde frowned in confusion, staring at the mother's dead body.

The wailing—high pitched and broken—came from behind her. She looked around, trying to find the source, yet she saw nothing but dead corpses littered among the barren trees. Returning her focus to the slain hunter, she knelt and gently moved her, checking on the child the mother had pinned behind her for protection.

Ashilde choked, covering her mouth with her free hand, before she lowered the mother's body, to rest with the gods forevermore with her slain babe, their neck snapped.

Before she could fully process the tragedy, something crashed into her from behind with a high-pitched scream, as a stick slapped against her side.

Turning, ready to use her own fists as a weapon, she discovered another child, their face tear-stricken as they whacked at her again with the stick, hitting the back of her kneecap with a pointed precision.

"What—"

"Leave them alone!" the child cried, pushing past

Ashilde to drop beside the body. As she regained her balance, she stared down at the new arrival, whose hair was the same black shade of the slain hunter, clutching the mother's chest, pulling at the strap, trying to unearth the slain babe.

Without thinking, Ashilde swept the youth into her arms. Despite reaching up to her waist in height, the child was thin and bony, light in her arms. She spun around and returned them to the ground as they began to scream, punching at her chest, her arms, at anything they could swing and hit. She quickly grasped the child firmly by the shoulders, steadying them and forcing them to meet her eyes, their own blue eyes widening as they saw her.

"I'm sorry, child," she said, guessing the fallen hunter was their mother. "But you needn't look. It ... it won't help."

Immediately, the child began shaking their head, the mess of black waves tangled and framing their face shaking with the motion. Ashilde leaned closer, so she could barely make out the soft matra the child had begun, muttering the same three words, in near hysteria.

"It's all true. It's all true, it's all true, it's all true, itsalltrueitsalltrue..."

Ashilde had no idea what to do.

She wanted to comfort them, but how did you comfort someone so young who had to witness the death of not only their parent, but also their young sibling? Especially without scaring them into doing something foolish, like running away from her? They didn't know her. They couldn't know that she wasn't the murderer, anymore than they could know that, in some ways, she actually was.

But they also couldn't stay there, alone. There were way more Rhuanics than she imagined. She couldn't leave the child alone, to be slaughtered and added to the

Dreyma's fallen body count. She had to get them home.

It'll cost time. Time and—

Going to leave more orphans behind you.

She swallowed her guilt, wiping sweaty, shaky palms against her armor as her heart sank into her stomach. She couldn't leave them alone. She certainly couldn't take them with her. No, she knew. No matter how one looked at it, they lost their family because of her.

She owed this to them, no matter what personal cost she had to pay.

Ashilde prayed her clan would forgive her.

"Hey," she said. They had squeezed their eyes closed and were shaking their head, holding their mother's necklace she hadn't seen them take clutched into a tiny, white-knuckled fist. They didn't open their eyes and Ashilde heard snippets of their whispering, catching, "it's not fair," and "this wasn't how it was supposed to happen." Her curiosity piqued at that, but that was the least of her focus, right now.

"Hey," Ashilde repeated, making her voice gentler still. "I'm not going to hurt you. Please, open your eyes."

The child did. Large, dark blue eyes stared at her, tears already drying up even though their face was streaked with them, creating pale streaks against their white face, while snot had started to slip down onto their lip. They wiped it away stubbornly with the back of their sleeve. Their facepaint—a line through their eyes and small circles above it—was painted green, a nice complement to their brown and light green breeches, tunic and cloak.

"How may I address you, child?"

They stared at the ground, before glancing back up. "Anóra. I am she."

"Anóra, I'm Ashilde and she is me," Ashilde said, unsure of where to begin, but knowing she had to do something. "There is nothing I can say that will take away the pain from today. Nothing—"

Before Ashilde could finish her thought, her body spasmed, her throat catching on her words. She fell forward, leaning on one arm against the ground as she gasped, barely making out when Anóra spoke to her, the quiver in the young girl's voice betraying her sudden fear.

"Why ... why is your arm disappearing?"

Blinking her eyes open, Ashilde saw her left arm—which she'd cradled against her stomach as a silent plea for the torrent of torment within her to cease—begin to fade, shimmering in and out of view. Her heart hammered at the sight, especially as it wasn't just her hand that disappeared this time, but her entire forearm, from elbow to fingertip. It disappeared entirely, leaving a faint outline of what *should* have been there behind. Her chest heaved.

Before she could process what was happening to her or try in vain to comfort the child, a sharp howl came from behind them. Twisting her body, she turned to see the wolf staring at them from across the clearing, its maw red and dripping blood. From behind her, the child screamed—but whether because of the wolf's appearance or the trio of Rhuanics screaming in the distance, appearing as if out of nowhere, Ashilde didn't know.

And she couldn't have time to care. The wolf growled and took off, heading toward the Rhuanics, while the raven called ahead, showing the path that Ashilde needed to follow—and quickly, before the Rhuanics gained on them.

The raven flew toward the Flatrí.

Ashilde gasped, struggling to breathe, as she looked at the young girl, who had frozen in fear. *Gods help us*, Ashilde thought as she forced herself to stand. Using her only good arm, not trusting her left as it flickered between ethereal and solid forms, she picked up the child, commanding her to wrap her arms and legs around her and hold on tight. The girl screamed, but Ashilde cupped the back of her head with her hand, burying her face into her shoulder as the girl latched onto her.

"I'm so sorry," she whispered, before taking off across the clearing at a sprint.

Ashilde wanted to vomit at the thought of entering the Flatrí, especially rushed like this, taking off at a sprint, with the whoops and calls becoming clearer now. But, as she shook and stumbled multiple times, her body still trying to revolt against her, she had to set aside her fears of the unknown to make room for her fears of the present, praying the Rhuanics wouldn't follow her. She had no idea how she'd fight them off while also battling her body, all while protecting the child.

The girl clutched tighter as a deep-throated scream echoed.

The Rhuanics had found them.

"We're almost there," Ashilde whispered. "We're almost safe."

She hoped more than anything that she wasn't lying.

Without slowing down, she ran into the Flatrí.

Two things happened at once.

Ashilde immediately felt blinded, unable to see anything in the paralyzing darkness; a sensation only made worse when she felt something catch on her foot, causing her to trip. Only air met her and she barely pivoted to land on her side, though Anóra still cried out into her chest as they collided with the ground. Together, they rolled down a sloped decline for a few moments, before Ashilde crashed against what felt like the trunk of a very large tree, finally settling in a pile of wet leaves, the girl landing on top of her. Her injured shoulder rang out in pain, but she ignored it, quickly clutching Anóra closer to her, her good arm wrapping around the back of her head.

"We're okay," she whispered as the girl gasped,

crying softly, now. "Just stay quiet, okay? Sshh, sshh." She began to pet her hair, hoping that she would calm down before the Rhuanics reached the edge of the Flatrí, where they had entered.

But she could no longer see it.

Craning her neck, Ashilde could make out the light from outside, slightly above and away from them, yet everywhere else she looked was nothing but darkness, blacker than any starless night. She could hear the soft flow of a small river still beside them, but the rest of the Flatrí was eerily silent. She had no idea where the raven had gone and she hoped the wolf hadn't gotten itself killed on her account. But she couldn't check, not daring to move until she could be certain the Rhuanics wouldn't find them.

All the while, her body shook and Ashilde had to fight to keep herself conscious, as her head swam. She puked inside her mouth, forcing herself to swallow it, lest she cover the child in the evidence of her body's curse.

Moments passed before shadows infiltrated the little light source above them. She tried to move to get a better view, but she'd landed awkwardly on her side and didn't want to roll over and risk snapping her bow. So she remained frozen, holding Anóra in her arms, who had thankfully gone quiet, her thin body too rigid, frozen in fear. The shadows remained and she could make out some voices, though not what they said.

Suddenly, a sharp bark interrupted their conversation and someone let out a startled curse.

Ashilde held her breath.

Years didn't feel long enough to describe how much time passed before the shadows wavered and grew smaller, before finally disappearing. As they did, Anóra squirmed in her arms, but Ashilde gripped her tighter.

"Not yet," she whispered. "I have to be certain—"

"They're gone," she replied, Anóra's tone adopting

a surprising confidence Ashilde certainly didn't feel. "Your wolf is coming back."

Only moments after the girl spoke, she heard the soft crunching against the leaves before she felt a wet tongue lick the side of her face. Anóra had been right.

Before she could ask her how she had possibly known that, she shivered and her vision blurred. She bit through her lip to keep from screaming out as a sharp sensation shot through her left arm.

"Anóra... I..."

But before Ashilde could finish her sentence, her body screamed from within and she passed out.

***

Though she wasn't sure what had happened or how much time had passed, somehow, Ashilde knew she was dreaming. It happened so infrequently that, any time she did, she was aware of it, even if she couldn't pull herself out of the dream enough to stop or alter where her mind took her, let alone wake herself from it.

This time, however, she didn't want to. For she was back home, with her people, where she belonged.

Standing inside her house, Magnhild sat on the ground, yanking at her hair stubbornly with a brush. It was strange to see Magnhild so young, only 10, at the time—not even a warrior yet, though she knew now the shy girl would become one, even though she'd never wanted to. Stranger still to be watching from the outside and able to see herself, without the lines of worry on her face, she herself a good ten years younger, too. She was clean, warm.

Accepted.

Past-Ashilde laughed, walking over to Magnhild and taking the brush out of her hand. Though she had repressed it then, she could feel it now, even as an outsider in the dream: the guilt that had wormed its way into her core, how she shared more sisterly-acts with Magnhild than she had in years with Brynhild; the questioning of where it had all gone wrong.

"Here, let me," she said. "No reason to get yourself up in a fuss about it."

"But everyone *will* be there!"

"*It's a wedding,*" Ashilde responded dryly. "*Where else would we all be?*"

Magnhild threw her hands up in the air, frustrated that Ashilde couldn't understand. Leaning forward, Ashilde whispered in her ear, "I hear Hannin plans to arrive early. Will you?"

The young girl shot up from where she'd squatted on the ground, the brush almost slipping out of Ashilde's hands as the unruly hair she'd been working to untangle disappeared from underneath her fingertips. "I don't care that he's there! I want to look good for Ingrit and Torunn."

"Oh, is that all?"

Crossing her arms, she nodded sharply once. "Of course it is!"

She had been able to see right through Magnhild's lies, but Ashilde couldn't help but smile. Of course the girl was nervous and wanted to look her best, oblivious to how the young boy already adored her.

"Here," Ashilde said, handing the brush back. "Go finish getting ready. I need to wish the brides well before the ceremony, and we're obviously not making any progress here."

Magnhild ignored the slight, instead becoming wide-eyed. "You're on guard duty? During a wedding?"

Ashilde nodded, masking the little sorrow she felt at missing the ceremony between two of her dearest friends. Instead, she said, "You might have to yourself, one day. The times you shouldn't have to be on guard—a wedding, a birth, on your dolorsandri—is the time you must be most alert of all."

Her expression switched to wary. "During our price? No one would attack then. By gods, no one could."

Ashilde walked over and kissed her on the forehead. "May that always be so. Now, go."

Ashilde felt herself slipping in and out of the memory, the initial good feeling of being back home and reliving such a joyous occasion turned sour by the foreshadowing she never could have guessed would come to pass. The memory—her dream—continued in flashes as she tossed and turned on the ground, witnesses glimpses from the rest of that day: Ingrit and Torunn both dressed in vibrant colors, laughing and wiping tears of joy away after the wives shared a kiss, bonded together for the rest of their lives; Ashilde staring at the night sky up on the ramparts while echoes of music and good cheer continued from behind her, everything quiet beyond; Davyn sneaking up and bringing her a cup of warm cider and sitting with her throughout the rest of the evening, with her head on his shoulder.

Simpler times.

Happier times.

Ashilde felt the dream leave her as her heart contracted, in pain at the reality she was stuck in, but didn't wake up, like she fought to, instead slipping back into an even deeper, uninterrupted sleep.

CHAPTER EIGHTEEN

When Ashilde woke up, she couldn't see.

Worse, the child was missing.

She jerked up, in a panic, the pleasant memories of a rare dream immediately forgotten and discarded, after discovering the girl was no longer in her arms and remembering, foggily, that she had passed out. But then, she heard her moan softly, complaining against being moved. Poking around gently, she discovered the child had laid beside her and hadn't run off after all. Reaching a little further, she found the wolf curled up beside the child, helping her to stay warm against the chill. A pause, and then its tongue licked the back of her hand, confirming her relief: they were okay.

Ashilde sighed, grateful that nothing happened during the night—or, what she had assumed was the night. Her stomach rumbled and her throat was dry, her cracked lips protesting as she ran her tongue across them, while her entire body ached, weakened by the aftereffects of her killing. She quickly went through her hand exercises, confirming that both felt solid, so at least she hadn't lost them. Yet.

She swallowed, trying to clear her mind and slow the panicked beating of her heart. Ashilde knew she needed to wake the girl up, get some food in them and then decide what to do next. Finally locating it, she found the light of the sun was faint above them—a barely noticeable reminder of the outside world she wanted nothing more than to return to. Yet she didn't make her way out there. She couldn't risk it, in case the Rhuanics had set up nearby, waiting them out.

Flashes of yesterday's events penetrated her mind, making her feel sick beyond hunger pains.

It also reminded her of something she had to do; something she could no longer put off.

"I'll be right back," she told the wolf, who growled softly in acknowledgement.

Standing, Ashilde walked slowly, discovering stray tree limbs or uprooted branches littered the ground, waiting to catch her unawares. Even still, it only took a few moments for her to reach the river, one foot stumbling into the water to let her know she'd found it.

Ashilde knelt down, feeling numb. Twice since she'd left, someone had recognized her as part of the Slátra, thanks to the markings on her face. The first time, with the trio of Rhuanics, she hadn't thought twice. She was too focused on stealing their food, distracted by hunger. The second time, however, it put her people at risk, almost starting a war with the Dreyma clan.

A war only avoided because they all died, instead.

She couldn't risk it happening again.

Unable to see her reflection, she was thankful for the unrelenting darkness of the Flatrí for the first time. Ashilde could feel the dirt on her face, the dried stickiness of blood—both a mixture of her own from a cut she discovered on her lip and remnants from the Rhuanics she'd killed. She could imagine how disheveled she looked, but her appearance reflecting the difficulties of the journey didn't bother her.

Ashilde reached down and began splashing water on her face, before bending over to scrub.

No, she just didn't want to see her face completely clean, knowing she had no intentions—and no right—to wear the markings of her people.

She was no longer Slátra.

Who will you see, now that you've left the lands you know? Why put yourself through this pain?

It didn't matter. There was too much unknown, too much risk to associate herself with a clan she had suffered to protect. She had to do this, no matter how much it hurt.

Ash didn't stop until her face was sore from rubbing it so fiercely. Standing, she moved away from the river, but only made it far enough to lean her face against the trunk of a nearby tree before she finally let herself sob, feeling the pain: of losing her people; of becoming an outcast, no matter how temporarily; of losing Davyn, Freydis, Dagfinn and her warriors; of the pain she'd brought to the Dreyma and the questions she still couldn't solve.

Ashilde cried until her fingers began to feel numb against the chill and the back of her mind yelled at her to return and make sure nothing had happened to the girl. She wanted to take the time to wash completely, but she had spent too much time away from her companions already. And she knew, deep down, she was avoiding what had to come next.

If the girl was going to stay with her—and her gut told her she was, for what other choice did they have?—she deserved to know the truth of her destination and why Ashilde traveled there in the first place.

Stumbling back, she managed to find where she'd left her companions and hadn't even had a chance to sit back down before Anóra asked, "Why's your face blank?"

She stilled, but quickly recovered. Too many thoughts ran through her head at once: wondering how Anóra was feeling, how she was holding up, how long she'd been awake, what she'd thought of her passing out. Even deeper, she felt fear, confessing what the gods had deemed her guilty of.

For, to fully explain it to her, she'd have to confess a crime she wasn't ready to face, even now.

Yet, instead of voicing any of those thoughts or questions, she went with a more immediate surprise. "You can see that?"

The girl snorted. "Of course I can," she said, her tone a mixture of pride and belittlement, as if she couldn't believe Ashilde was unaware of that talent.

Just then, Ashilde remembered who she was talking to.

"Wait a moment," she said. "Anóra. Can you *see* in here? Within the Flatrí?"

"Uh ... yes?" she replied, confidence faltering, as if being asked a trick question.

Because of course she could see, Ashilde realized. She could see everything as clear as day. *She's a member of the Dreyma clan.* The Dreyma had the gift of *sight*.

They could, essentially, see in the dark.

Even one, apparently, as warped as the Flatrí.

"That's ... that's incredible," Ashilde admitted, finally sitting down where she thought was across from the girl and her things. "I promise to explain everything, but could you ... would you mind describing to me what's around us?"

"Trees," she said. "Lots and lots of trees."

"Is there a path that you can see? Anything to follow?"

"No," she said, her voice trembling.

Ashilde sucked in a breath. Letting Anóra know her nerves wouldn't help her keep her own intact and she needed to make sure the girl's emotions didn't get the better of her. In fact, she was surprised that she was doing as well as she was, given … everything. She didn't deserve Ashilde's irritation of wanting more details than those she could already guess on her own.

Suddenly, she had an idea, something she'd seen Davyn do when trying to keep a younger child calm as he treated them. "Who is your closest friend back home, Anóra?"

"Taya."

"Taya. They sound like a good friend."

"She is," Anóra confirmed, sounding more sure of herself.

"When you get home, you'll need to tell Taya everything, right? You want to describe it in so much detail, she'll be able to picture everything. Almost like she was here with you."

She made a humming noise, albeit faint, still unsure.

"So practice with me. Tell me everything you see, so that when you tell Taya all about your adventures, you know exactly what you're going to say."

A pause. "You want me to come with you?"

Ashilde glanced down at her hands, her heart stilling when she couldn't even see those. "I believe you might have to, Anóra. But not without … not without knowing exactly what I'm going to do. It's your choice."

"Okay."

She didn't sound excited, but she didn't sound upset, either. More curious, than anything else.

"Would you mind handing me my pack, Anóra? I think some food is necessary for this kind of talk."

"Okay!"

The girl's tone brightening at the thought of food, Ashilde felt the weight of her pack being put into her hands a few moments later. She was able to open it and find some of the meat she'd stolen. She handed a few pieces to Anóra, who took them quickly, before she ripped off a bite of her own.

"I'm going to travel through Flatrí," she said. "I'm heading to Skírrdrauin."

"I know," Anóra said.

"The gods—what?"

"I, uh ... I know," the girl said again, more sheepishly, this time. "I ... saw it. In a dream."

Ashilde had heard of many different talents and skills, but she'd never heard of something like this. "You saw what, exactly?"

"Flashes, mostly," she admitted, sounding much older than her appearance suggested—only ten, perhaps eleven, most likely not having experienced her Wyrdan day yet, if the gods chose her to become *sangrild*. Was that because she was simply a smart child or because she'd been forced to grow up too quickly?

She did *watch her family die yesterday.*

Ashilde swallowed.

"Grandma said none of it was real, but my mom ... I saw..."

Slowly, she pieced together what Anóra couldn't say. The girl had visions, of some sort. Prophetic visions that told her of the future. She somehow saw *her* and knew of her quest. But what purpose did her visions have, and why had the gods deemed to give her such a blessing?

Or was it a curse?

"How long have you had these dreams?"

She mumbled, not giving her a clear answer.

Ashilde didn't press it. "Are they ... unpleasant?"

"Yes," Anóra whispered, barely loud enough for her to hear. "They have always been scary. But now they are coming true and ... it's worse. I ... no one was supposed to die."

Ashilde wasn't sure how to respond to that. She wanted to comfort the girl, though comfort had never been her strength, as Brynhild loved to remind her. She also had so many questions and she wanted nothing more than to spend the morning learning more about Anóra and her gift. But she couldn't deny how suffocated she felt in the Flatrí, the growing unease within her at sitting still, even on the outskirts, with Rhuanics lurking outside to kill them and unknown terrors waiting within.

They couldn't afford to delay much longer, especially with her own people fighting against Róta's mood. Who was to say the god wouldn't care that Ashilde still lived and curse another of their warriors as tainted anyway? Or worse, destroy the entire clan for her failures?

She took another bite, her hand coming up to brush her mother's necklace on reflex, seeking comfort. "You saw me, before? In the Flatrí?"

"Not you," she said. "Just the Flatrí. And a voice ... telling me to help. I want to help," Anóra said, her confidence growing.

"A voice," Ashilde wondered, her thoughts slipping out. "Who spoke to you?"

"No one, if you ask grandma, my mom. Even Taya."

"What do you believe?"

"My dad," Anóra whispered. "It's my dad. He was killed, too. Not by men, though. Men aren't supposed to do that."

"No, they're not," Ashilde agreed, her heart breaking. A girl so young, yet she'd already experienced so much loss.

"The dreams ... I don't really remember having them," she said, her voice shaking. "At first, I only knew because mother said I talked in my sleep, about the Flatrí, even though I was only three," Anóra explained. "I remember, now. It repeats."

She went quiet for a moment—lost in thought or caught up in emotion, Ashilde couldn't tell. Finally, she continued, "Flatrí—it looked like nighttime, always nighttime—and a woman, lost, I think?" Her voice dropped to a whisper.

"And he told me I had to help. If I help, then … then I might get to see him again." She paused for a moment, sounding sheepish. "You're her, right?"

"I believe I am," Ashilde said, stunned. She had no idea what to make of Anóra's claims, but she couldn't help but believe her. She already accepted help from a wolf and a raven. She couldn't deny that she needed Anóra's help, too, especially thanks to her gift. She was one of the only people alive who could see through the Flatrí. Ashilde couldn't even see her own feet.

She had to accept.

"Then, I *have* to help. It's the only way … please."

Ashilde swallowed, trying to find the voice to speak. While she wasn't sure she believed the girl's dead father could speak to her from beyond the afterlife, who was she to deny her that hope, without proof?

"I admit, I need it," she said. "But Anóra … I've been outcast. From the Slátra, by the gods' will. I don't think you'll be tainted, since you're not Slátra yourself, but you deserve to know that."

A pause. "Why?"

So she *didn't* know that part. Interesting.

Ashilde wrapped her hands together, her knuckles turning white. "Because our hunters are dead and we can't make the sacrifices required by the Ravenmother, so the gods decided to sacrifice one of us. And, because I killed my mother, I was chosen to pay for the failings of both myself and my people."

She said it.

She finally actually *said* it.

Ashilde had lived with the guilt for the past twenty years; with the shame, with the sorrow at losing her best friend in her mother, when she was only thirteen years old. Brynhild had reminded her often enough how much she hated Ashilde for taking their mother away—especially after their father had disappeared, only a few years prior, never returning and never heard from again, a mystery unlike any the Slátra had experienced before, forever unsolved. But almost everyone else didn't bring it up, never forced her to speak of it. So, even though she felt the guilt, she'd never spoken it aloud, except once, when she was drunk, with Davyn.

"Oh," Anóra said. "What happened? With your mother, I mean?"

Well, she didn't run away immediately. That was something.

"I was with her, exploring the borders of our lands. It was the one year anniversary of my Wyrdan Day, and my mother thought it important for me, as a still-new warrior, to know every part of the land I would be protecting." Her voice began to shake, but she forced herself to continue. "I was excited and overconfident. I pushed my mother, begging to go farther, explore farther. Irritated at my insistence, we went beyond our borders. We ... we weren't the only ones to do so, that day."

Ashilde's fists tightened, her fingers throbbing within her palm. "We were walking along the coastal edge, me atop our horse we'd brought. My legs were tired, and my mother walked ahead. She had paused to explain how I could predict upcoming weather patterns based off what kinds of birds flew in the sky, before she was interrupted by a pair of Fundi warriors attacking us from behind; still bitter at the Slátra's involvement of wiping out many of their number from my great-grandmother's time, I later learned, so when they discovered two lone warriors outside of our borders, they didn't care about peace.

"One went after the horse, attempting to slice its legs at the knees, but our horse panicked and bucked, fending the attacker off. The other went after her. She evaded the first attack, but she had no weapon, not thinking to bring one. But, before she engaged fully, she commanded the horse to flee, before the warrior attacked me again. I was barely able to hold on and my mare was too spooked to listen to me as I tried to turn her around. By the time I managed to get her to calm down and return, my mother—"

Ashilde shook her head, the memory she'd repressed trying to resurface and take over everything inside her head.

Thankfully, Anóra spoke, drawing her back to the present—even if her mother's voice, screaming, "Go!" continued to echo in the back of her mind. "But ... why are you in trouble for that? You didn't kill anyone."

"Exactly. That's the problem," Ashilde said, with more bite than she meant to. She sighed. "I wasn't strong enough to protect my mother that day and I couldn't seek revenge without bringing all of the clans into another war we couldn't survive. It's because of me that she died; my selfishness, my cowardness, my carelessness." She looked over at Anóra, where she believed the child to be sitting, anyway, based on where her voice sounded. "The gods noticed and now ask for atonement, for both myself and my clan."

And you deserve it, her mind berated, thinking back to her hunters, murdered in cold blood by the Rhuanics. The Dreyma scouting party she'd discovered. Anóra's mother and the baby.

She'd failed them all.

"That's dumb," Anóra said. "You're not tainted *or* a murderer. You saved my life!"

But I killed your mother, too.

Ashilde looked away.

That was enough confessions for one day.

"You still want to come with me, knowing where I have to go?"

Anóra didn't pause this time. "Yes. I need to go there, too."

Ashilde popped her knuckles as she sighed, resolved. "All right. If we're going to make any progress, I need to know where I'm going," she said, trying to push forward, ignoring the tightness of her chest from her memories and the constricting in her throat at her role in Anóra's mother's death—only made worse by her choice to not reveal that to her, not yet.

Her mother's necklace felt heavy.

"Do you mind describing what you can see to me, now?"

The girl paused. "Um ... can I ask a question, first?"

Ashilde swallowed, ignoring her own impatience. "Of course, child."

"Are you ... uh ... what happened to your arm, yesterday? Do I ... um..."

Oh pit. That's a pretty big thing to forget to mention, Ash.

"Um, yeah, about that..." Ashilde said, unsure exactly how to explain what she herself didn't understand. "To be honest, I don't really know what is happening to me, when that happens. When I was outcast by Róta, I became *sangrendi*, but unnaturally so. As such, my body revolts when I kill, when it once could handle it as any *sangrild* could." Ashilde wished she could see the child's expressions to know what she was thinking. She glanced at what she assumed was the ground, but it was just as dark as everything else. "When I kill, I start to ... lose myself. Physically. I fear that, if I kill too many people before we reach Skírrdrauin, my body may disappear entirely."

"That's not good."

Ashilde couldn't help it as she snorted at the child's candidness. "No, it is not. I hope that I won't be put in that position again. I'm ... sorry you had to see that."

"It's okay," Anóra said, though Ashilde could tell she was lying by the sudden lift in her voice. "I mean, it was scary, but I wish ... I just want to help, next time."

"Let's hope there is no next time," Ashilde said,

not sure how to respond to the child's kindness. "Any other questions?"

"Uh … not yet."

Ashilde nodded and, when she didn't respond right away, gently reminded her, "What can you see?"

"Oh, right!" Anóra said, more animated, this time. "So … in front of us … *directly* in front of us, are trees. But they aren't like the trees that we usually—oh, well, Taya and I…"

"No, go ahead," Ashilde encouraged, happy that she chose to still talk to her as she would with her friend. "You can pretend I know what Taya knows. Keep talking."

"Okay. Well, the trees we play in? Those are *normal* trees. These aren't. They are *tall*, higher than any I have ever seen," she finally said, her voice growing in confidence the more she spoke, taking on a more childlike demeanor. It surprised Ash how much her heart was gladdened by it. "I can't even see the tops of them, and they don't have any leaves. The ground does, though. Lots of them. Which is weird. If there are no leaves, why is it so dark?"

Why indeed?

"Those definitely are unlike any trees I've seen," Ashilde agreed. "How much room is there to move around?"

"Um … well, there isn't much space around the trees. All the trees are really, really close together. And there are a *lot* of trees."

Ashilde frowned. It explained why she felt so claustrophobic. "Do you see any animals?"

"No."

"Plants?"

"Um … no."

"But you can see the river?"

"Yeah, I can see it. We should probably follow it, right?"

"Exactly right," Ashilde agreed, instinctually looking around, trying to follow what Anóra described with her eyes, yet all that filled her vision was darkness.

Her imagination tried to fill in the gaps while her mind raced, processing everything Anóra had told her. *Can't see the tree tops? How tall are these trees?* Surely they couldn't be any taller than the ones she was used to, within the Segan. Otherwise, wouldn't she have been able to see the tops of the trees towering from a distance, outside the Flatrí?

She didn't think Anóra was wrong, though, even if it didn't seem plausible. The darkness alone was enough to prove this part of Armadin was different from the rest, the taint of Róta's wrath still present here. The way the air felt constricted, and how no noises—no chirps, no cries, no whispers, no whines—interrupted the silence, it was obvious this was an unnatural place.

Just as obvious as how getting lost within it was a death sentence.

"Okay. Did you eat everything I gave you?"

Silence answered her.

"Anóra?"

"What? I—oh, you can't see me when I nod, can you?"

Ashilde chuckled, surprising herself when the sound escaped her lips. "No, little one, I can't."

"That's okay," Anóra said. "I can be your eyes."

Her heart swelled. "I'm going to need that," she said. "Where's the wolf? And can you spot the raven anywhere?"

"You mean your friends? Yeah, they're both here. Wait!" she exclaimed. "Are they going with us?"

"If they'd like."

"Oh wow. What are their names?"

"Names? They don't have any."

"You didn't *ask* them?"

At that moment, the wolf made a loud huffing sound, followed by another, gentler version. Was it ... was it *laughing* at her, in agreement with Anóra's disbelief at her apparent rude manners?

"I can't speak with them, actually," she confessed.

"Oh. I thought Slátra—"

"*Slátra* can," Ashilde said. "I'm no longer Slátra. Remember?"

"Oh. Right."

Ashilde cursed inwardly. *Stop snapping. She's done nothing to deserve your anger.*

"Why don't you do the honors, Anóra? They seem to have taken a liking to you."

Though she couldn't see it, she liked to imagine that the child grinned. "Really?"

"Go ahead."

"Okay, wolf, come sit in front of me," Anóra said, before she added, "I'm saying what I'm doing so you can see it, too."

"That's ... very kind of you. Thank you."

Ashilde could picture it, now that Anóra said something. She'd been traveling with the wolf long enough to imagine what it looked like. Even sitting down, the wolf was taller than Anóra. She was glad the girl was no longer scared of the creature, but she couldn't have blamed her first instinct.

She had felt the same, when she first met it.

"Your name is obvious," she said. "Funakiin." Her voice dropped to a whisper, even though Ashilde could still hear her clearly. "It means 'protector,' but it's a secret language! Only Taya, me and our friends know it. No adults. So don't tell anyone, okay?"

The wolf barked his assent.

Ashilde began feeling through her bag, pretending she couldn't hear and hiding her smile by turning away.

"Look, the—er, well, the raven is flying down." Anóra squealed slightly. "She landed on my shoulder!"

"What are you going to name her?" Ashilde asked, knowing the raven was a female thanks to her size and finally dawning to think of her as such, instead of the defaulted "it" she'd chosen for both creatures.

"Ieka."

She raised an eyebrow. "Does that name have any significance?"

"Well, isn't that what ravens sound like?" Anóra asked, before choosing to demonstrate herself. "*Eeeeekkkkkaaaaa.*"

Based on the noise the raven made, she was less pleased than her companion at her new name.

Ashilde winced against the loud noise, but she forced herself to smile, instead of scolding the girl. If the Rhuanics remained outside, they'd either come after them or they wouldn't. She'd have to be prepared for either option.

"Well, that settles it, then. Thank you, Anóra. Help me keep an eye on them?"

"Okay!"

"And you two," Ashilde said, "help me keep an eye on Anóra."

"Hey!"

Ashilde stood up, slinging her pack back over her shoulder. "I'm only teasing. Mostly," she muttered. "But, we can delay no longer. Anóra, our journey is not going to be easy. I only have three more weeks—maybe less—before I must reach Skírrdrauin. We'll need to make a steady pace. But I want you to let me know if you need any breaks, okay?"

She hummed his agreement, sounding less than thrilled.

By feel, she found her rope and pulled it out of her pack.

"Where are Funakiin and Ieka?"

"Funakiin is right beside you. You can reach down and be able to pet him."

Ashilde did, stroking Funakiin's head with her left hand. The wolf licked her hand in response.

"Ieka is floating above our heads. I don't think she likes it here." Anóra's voice switched to a tone of questioning wonder. "I bet it's hard, trying to fly when there are all these twisty branches in the sky."

Ashilde bit her lip, an idea forming. Removing her hand from Funakiin's head, she knelt down, facing Anóra.

"I'm, ah, actually behind you."

Ashilde sighed.

"Grab my hand so I can actually know where you are. I have an idea."

A few moments later, she felt Anóra's tiny hand slip into hers.

In her other hand, she held up the rope she'd pulled out. "I have this. I want you to tie it around your waist and then I'll tie it around mine. Funakiin, touch my leg if you can hear me."

A second later, a large, pointed nose deliberately pressed into her thigh.

"I'd like to tie the rope around your waist, as well," she said, not surprised when the wolf growled his dislike a moment later. "I don't want to lose you to the darkness, either. Ieka, can you find my staff? Perch there, and don't leave it; you should be safe, too."

A fluttering of wings behind her head confirmed the bird had been listening. She hardly noticed the bird's weight as she settled onto the staff she'd strapped against her back, but a soft caw confirmed that she was ready.

"I won't use the rope on you if you're not willing, Funakiin."

The wolf sighed.

"He's moved in front of you," Anóra said, taking one of her hands and moving it so it rested on Funakiin's back.

"Thank you."

Ashilde pulled the rest of the rope out of her pack before she closed and tied it up. Finding the end of the rope, she knelt back down. Petting him gently, she reached around the edge of the rope and wrapped it around his middle, tying it tight enough that he couldn't slip out, but loose enough that it only sat on top of his fur, instead of biting into it.

"How does that feel?"

Funakiin moved and walked away from her, the rope slipping gently out of her hand, but only after he rubbed his head against her leg. She assumed that meant he was comfortable and at least partly okay with it.

"You next, Anóra."

"I can do it!"

"Okay," she assented. "But let me check it when you're done."

Anóra reached up and took the rope from her hand.

"Don't forget to leave some slack for Funakiin to walk."

"I already did, silly!"

Smart girl.

Ashilde couldn't see what Anóra did, but she could hear rustling beside her. She resisted the urge to turn around and look back outside, toward the light. She didn't know if it was possible for her eyes to adjust to the unnatural darkness that shrouded the Flatrí, but she didn't want to ruin her chances by looking back at the little light behind them. The more she could stay focused on the darkness now, the better chance her eyes would adjust before they got too far in.

"I'm finished," Anóra said.

The rope was gently pushed back into her hands.

"Guide my hands back toward your rope," Ash said. "I want to make sure you won't slip out."

"I won't!" the girl protested, as Ashilde felt her hands be guided toward the rope. Feeling gently, she followed the rope around Anóra's waist, slipping a finger in-between the rope and her clothes to make sure it wasn't wrapped too tightly. Then, she pulled on the rope, hard, ensuring it also wasn't too loose, like she had with Funakiin. Ieka had squawked once in protest to her continual movement, but the bird had remained thankfully silent since as Ashilde continued to work.

"You did good, Anóra."

She hoped she smiled at the compliment.

"Can you hand me the rest of the rope, placing my hand where I can start wrapping myself up, so you have enough slack, too?"

Humming in response, Anóra did what she asked. Ashilde quickly wrapped the rope around her own torso, wrapping it higher, just underneath her breasts, to help avoid her pack and the various weapons she had strapped to her. As she tied off her bit, there was barely enough rope to tie her knot twice over. She'd been lucky to have enough to wrap around the three of them and still give them room to walk without stepping over one another.

Well, as much room as the Flatrí would allow, at any rate.

Ashilde sighed, double checking once more that her pack was closed. "Okay. Anóra, I want you to stay on my left, walking just ahead of me, but always keeping the river on our right." Now that she focused, she could faintly hear the water moving, but not loud enough that she could relocate it if she got turned around. "Funakiin, you're going to walk just ahead of her, in the lead. Ieka, I want you to stay perched, if you can, and help me guard the rear."

With the soft crunching on fallen branches alerting her, everyone moved into position, according to Ashilde's instructions.

"Anóra, I'm not going to hold your hand so I can keep my own free, to feel around." *And to quickly arm myself, if I have to.* "Is that okay with you?"

"Y-yes."

Reaching out, she found her shoulders and squeezed once. "You can do this. I want you to keep telling me what you see, especially if you see something new, talking as if I were Taya. I bet Funakiin can see already, but I don't think he'd mind if you helped him out as he leads us. Can you do that?"

"I can," she said, her voice stronger.

"I know you can. Let's walk until you get hungry again, okay?"

Anóra paused for a moment. "And if I'm already hungry?"

Ashilde suppressed a sigh, but quickly pulled out another piece of meat and offered it to her, before closing her pack once more. "When you get hungry a second time, then."

"Okay!" she said, more brightly this time, before she added, "Alright, if you were Taya and I was telling you about my adventures *step by step*, I'd tell you ahead of us are trees. And then, behind those? More trees."

A few moments after Anóra began her narration, the rope against her chest pulled gently and Ashilde started walking forward.

Their journey through the Flatrí had finally begun.

CHAPTER NINETEEN

They lost the river before they stopped to eat.

Ashilde's legs were sore, her feet already starting to blister. Though she couldn't be certain, at least most of the morning was gone, if not some of the afternoon. But two weeks could have passed and it wouldn't have mattered.

It was still much too early to be lost.

But that wasn't Ashilde's greatest worry.

"One more time, Anóra," she said, as they paused to rest. "The river did *what*?"

If Anóra was a little bit older, Ashilde imagined the girl would have sighed at her request to repeat herself, having already lost count how many times she had asked Anóra to tell her what she saw and describe it in intricate detail. However, by the soft sniffling Ashilde could barely make out, she thought Anóra was too busy struggling not to cry to be annoyed with her, feeling guilty at losing the one lifeline they couldn't lose. Though, if what she claimed was accurate, Ashilde couldn't really blame the child for getting lost. She couldn't blame anything.

It was ... unnatural.

Anóra sniffled. "It was there! A tiny river, so it was hard to keep track of, all the time—there are just so many *trees*—but it disappeared, even though I told it not to."

"Into a tree?"

"Yes! It slipped around a tree and then it disappeared! That's why I ran for a second, because you told me not to lose it and I didn't ... I didn't mean to..."

Ashilde squeezed her shoulder. "It's okay, Anóra. It's okay. It's not your fault and I'm not upset. I'm just ... trying to understand why we can't go around to follow the river."

This time, Anóra did huff. "I *told* you. There *is* no way around. We can only go *up*."

Ashilde rubbed her temple, before holding out her waterskin. It disappeared from her hand a moment later. She wished, more than anything, that she could see. But even time spent within the Flatrí wasn't enough to let her eyes adjust and instead, it was like her eyes were never open. It didn't matter that they felt strained—from the lack of vision or with how often she'd widened them as far as they could go, just to remind herself that they *were* open, she couldn't differentiate. Foolishly, she'd hoped she might get used to it, but she'd never been more on edge in her life, and she had no idea how long the Flatrí lasted.

"I'm sorry, Anóra. I just want to understand. It's hard to wrap my head around, but I'll have to, if we're to figure out what to do next."

"But I'm not making it up!" she protested, mistaking Ash's irritation for disbelief. "I wouldn't lie. I—"

Ashilde held her hands up. "I know! I *know* that, Anóra. I'm just trying to ... picture what you're seeing and figure out how to get around it."

"We *can't*," Anóra said, exasperated. "We. Go. Up."

"Because the trees are no longer individual trees,

but have formed a wall that we must climb?"

There was a pause—a longer pause than usual—and Ashilde guessed that Anóra nodded to her, as she muttered, "Oh, you couldn't see that," before her voice grew louder and she said, "Yes, exactly like a wall! Except, the wall isn't straight up and down, like ... well, like walls usually are. The trunks ... lean a lot."

"So, they're slanted, like an incline?"

"I think so."

Ashilde frowned. "If I were to walk one of these ... trunks, would I fall off the side?"

"No. Funakiin could walk beside us, too. But only on the trees right here, ah, in front of me. The other trees don't lean, but go straight up, like normal trees. Except there is no space between them, like ... *unnormal trees.*"

Aside from wishing she could see so she could stop feeling so helpless—a feeling she knew to be a lie, for it wasn't her sight that gave her power, it was simply something she was used to being able to rely on— Ashilde wished she could see what Anóra described. It had to be an incredible sight, even if it were unnatural. Of course, she couldn't focus on it from a natural beauty standpoint, even in her imagination.

No, her focus narrowed on why the gods made a wall that also served as an apparent path, if one was willing to climb it. What was the point of a wall that could be climbed?

And what is it meant to keep away—or seal in?

"How far across does this wall travel?"

"Forever," Anóra said. "I didn't want to go look and lose the river even more than I've already lost it."

The girl had a point. If they tried to find a way around the wall, they had no idea if they could find the river again on the other side. Ashilde wondered if perhaps that was the point: forcing those within to choose whether to find another route or risk climbing up the trees when they couldn't see if they were going to fall off or not. Of course, without Anóra, she wouldn't be able to discover this barrier aside from running straight into it. Did that mean she'd already disproven her latest train of thought?

You're giving yourself a headache, is what you're doing.

Ashilde sighed quietly, not wanting Anóra to think she was directing it at her. No matter the whys or the hows that she could internally debate for as long as she lived, she knew they had to climb, as odd an idea as it was.

"Ieka," she said, glancing up to the top of her spear—the raven's impromptu perch, at her suggestion. "Is there an opening for you to fly up and see just how high we'll have to climb?"

Her back felt a little lighter as a soft *whoosh* of air hit the back of her head, as Róta's creature went to do her bidding.

Thinking of the raven like that, chills escaped down her body, reminding her that she still had no idea why Ieka and Funakiin helped her ... nor what price they would ask for their assistance in return; let alone what Anóra's dreams meant, and if the child's father was truly helping them from somewhere in Skírrdrauin, again for some unknown purpose.

Thoughts and problems she would let future Ashilde worry about.

"How will you understand her answer, if you can't talk to her?" Anóra asked, as they waited for the bird's return.

"There are many different ways to communicate, even if you can't speak," Ashilde said. Anóra seemed to accept her answer, which she was thankful for. Ash believed what she said, but mostly, she was just buying herself a little bit of time to figure out the exact answer to Anóra's question herself.

No need for the girl to know that, though.

She felt around for the knots of her pack and began

trying to undo them just from feel. "You said you were hungry, right?"

"Oh, yes, I'm starving!" Anóra said, before she quickly added, "I mean, yes, something to eat would be nice. Please."

Ashilde smiled. "Come help me find my food, then, and we can eat before we figure out how to climb this thing."

With Anóra's help, they pulled out more dried meat. It was enough to be meager portions for the four of them, but considering she'd asked Anóra to stay on the lookout for food within Flatrí, as well, and she hadn't found anything so far, Ashilde wanted to make sure and ration what they did have, praying they'd find a source of food along the way. Otherwise, it wouldn't matter if they found the river or not. Starvation would be a slow killer, but in the end, did it matter? Dead was dead.

Anóra fed Funakiin, who laid beside Ashilde after she sat down, leaning against one of the large tree trunks that made up the wall, she assumed, the rough bark scratching against her armor, as she fidgeted. She chewed on her meat slowly, the days it was stored in her pack hardening it to the point of a stubborn toughness, making her mouth work even to bite a piece off. They ate quietly for a few moments, focusing on their food while letting their already sore legs rest, waiting for Ieka to return. Funakiin began to snore softly beside her.

Ashilde tried hard to not wonder what was taking so long.

"You're not afraid of heights, are you?" Ashilde asked.

"No. Are you?"

"No."

Ashilde wondered if either of them believed the other. Based on their tones, she certainly didn't.

"I think I'd be more scared if I couldn't see," Anóra said, confirming her suspicion that she didn't believe her, either.

Thanks for the reminder.

"But you won't fall," she added. "I'll protect you."

She hummed in response to that. Ashilde hadn't thought about it like that. But she couldn't deny that she didn't mind the sound of it, even if logically, she had no idea what a small child would do if Ash tripped and slipped off the edge of a giant tree. Still, she didn't care how old Anóra was or what clan she came from. It was nice to know that someone else was watching her back, without having any ulterior motives for doing so, but instead, simply because it was the right thing to do.

Or because she's been guided to do so.

But by a dead father? Or ... could the gods have something to do with it?

"May I ask you something, Anóra?"

As she waited for her response, Ashilde took the waterskin back when Anóra pressed it gently into her hand and took another drink. They had refilled it just before the river had dipped below the trees. They'd have to ration that, too.

"You want to know about my dreams," she said. "About my father."

She didn't say it like a question.

"Um ... well..."

"It's okay. If I wasn't me and I *met* me, I'd ask, too."

Ashilde felt as if the entire forest took the awkwardness growing between them—or perhaps just enveloping her—and amplified it tenfold, until it tainted the very air around them. "Actually, it's okay, Anóra. You don't have to—"

"I broke both my legs three years ago."

She inhaled sharply, unsure of how this tied into her questions, but engrossed nonetheless. "It's amazing you can still walk."

"Our healers never left me alone. Grandma made sure of it," she said. "Taya—you remember Taya, right?—

and me, we used to climb a lot of trees. *Normal* trees, we did. When he brought me back, everyone thought it was an accident."

Ashilde swallowed, not liking where this was going. She actually hadn't planned to ask the child about her dreams or her father, though she'd been very curious about both. She'd just wanted to ask her ... *something*, and try to get to know the little girl who she entrusted her life with—all while Ashilde was endangering hers. She wasn't expecting Anóra to open up to her so soon.

"It wasn't," she whispered, barely loud enough for her to catch it.

"Why don't you tell me your version of it," Ash suggested, careful to keep her voice and face neutral, remembering Anóra could see her clearly.

"Why?" she asked, raising her voice. "Why would you listen? Would you believe me? No one else did, not even grandma! Well..." she added, after a moment. "Mother did. She always did."

She heard her begin to cry, softly, beside her.

Ashilde waited a moment, looking away, staring at what she hoped was the ground. "May I put my arm around you, Anóra?"

She mumbled, before leaning into her. Ashilde wrapped her arm around her, petting her hair gently, the same way her mother used to do to her, when she was upset.

"I know you miss her," she said. "I miss my mother, too."

She cried for a little while longer and Ashilde held her as she did, not wanting to rush her. Ieka still hadn't returned, and though she felt enough time had passed that they should start climbing, regardless of where the raven went, she felt it more important, in that moment, to let Anóra grieve. She couldn't really give her any space, but she could give her a little time.

Eventually, she heard soft sobs turn into stubborn

sniffles. Finally, she whispered, "Do you want to hear the rest of the story?"

"Only if you want to tell me," she said, squeezing her shoulders. "But know this: I will believe you because you asked me to. Because I trust ... I trust you not to lie to me."

"Oh," Anóra said. She went silent for a moment, allowing Ashilde to sit and stew in her own guilt.

Here you are, preaching truth and trust when you haven't even confessed your own sins; haven't confessed your role in her mother's death, instead holding her as she grieves for the woman you killed. Some example you are.

Swallowing hard once more, Ashilde decided, once Anóra was finished telling her this story, she would share her own confession. The girl deserved it. If it gave her conscience one less thing to make her feel guilty about, all the better.

"Most don't know," Anóra amended, as if being caught in the middle of a lie. "From my clan. I told mother, and *she* believed me. But she told me not to tell. Grandma ... she would have been mad. It's not good when grandma gets mad."

Frowning, she asked, "What couldn't you tell, Anóra?"

"Taya and I were *playing*," she said defensively. "She had climbed so high, higher than me, higher than *ever*! The leaves hid her and I tried to follow, but Taya was *fast*. Plus, I ... don't like heights all that much."

Ashilde could picture her blushing as she accidentally confessed that she lied to her earlier about not being afraid of heights.

But Anóra quickly pushed on. "I was only halfway up when father came. He shouted, told me to come down. He didn't like it when we climbed trees. He didn't like it when I did much of anything." Her voice lowered until it wasn't much more than a whisper. "I don't think he ever liked me at all."

"Don't say that, Anóra," Ashilde said, her heart

breaking. She never wanted the responsibility and the work of raising a child herself. But what Anóra described... What parent could ever hate their child? "I'm sure your father loved you. He may have just had a hard time showing it."

"He didn't."

"Anóra—"

"He *didn't*, okay?" Anóra cried, her shout echoing through the demanding silence, sending chills down her spine—chills that didn't have to do with fear of them being overheard, though she swallowed the desire to shush her, all the same, her instincts to protect fighting against the needs of comfort. "I didn't fall. I climbed down, telling Taya to do the same. When I reached the bottom, Father grabbed me and shook me, telling me it was dangerous to climb trees so close to the cliff's edge. He pulled me close and then ... and then ... he whispered, 'What if you *slip*?'"

Ashilde knew how this ended.

And there was no way it was true.

No father could—

"I don't remember leaving his arms," Anóra said, her voice small. "I don't even remember screaming. But I remember hitting the ground and ... and feeling my legs break, hearing that loud *snapping* sound. I remember..."

She began to choke up and Ashilde could hear the tears in her voice, but could only focus on the sickness growing in her stomach, no longer wanting to eat the little meat left between her fingers. She forced it down anyway, looking in the direction of Anóra's voice, hoping she was meeting the child's eyes, trying to let her know she was here, she was listening. She believed her.

"He carried me back to the village," Anóra said. "Taya and I both cried. I'd never seen Taya cry before. But father ... he pretended it was all an accident."

"Why didn't your mother expose him?" Ashilde

couldn't withhold the incredulousness from her voice.

Gods breath, she was a *child*.

She sniffed again. "Mother always said it was her fault, always promising to protect me better. She said ... she used to say ... no one would believe her anyway. I overheard—I mean, I wasn't *supposed* to, but mother is loud when she gets angry." Ashilde felt the girl shrug against her arm. "She kept bringing up Tevyn, during a hunt, when talking to Taya's mom. I don't know why. He's another man from my clan. Father used to use his name a lot, when he yelled at my mother, saying I looked too much like him. I don't know why he said that," Anóra continued, her voice growing quieter with each passing word. "I look just like her."

Understanding started to blossom, obvious to Ashilde what Anóra was too young to fully grasp, yet. But regardless of the truth of it—no matter how faithful her mother was, who Anóra's birth father had been—how could that be enough to, what? *Murder* Anóra?

"Your mother couldn't tell your Seidsian?"

Anóra snorted. "Of course not, silly. Grandma loves me and mother, but of course she loved father the best."

It took a moment before Ashilde was able to connect what Anóra said with what she knew. She had assumed, when Anóra spoke of her grandmother, that she was simply another member of her clan; most likely an honored member, to live to become an elder.

She hadn't realized her grandmother was the Dreyma's *Seidsian*.

Not only had Ashilde killed the Seidsian's son's wife, but she had brought her grandchild into the Flatrí.

The realization should have hit Ashilde more, sending fear at the consequences of these connections; fear for her clan, of the Dreyma's potential retaliation if they found out, of their Seidsian's wrath if she didn't bring Anóra back safely. Instead, all she felt was broken, that

Anóra had expected so much heartbreak at so young an age; moreso even than Ashilde herself, something she hadn't considered possible, before that moment.

"Anóra, I am so sorry."

She shrugged against Ashilde once more. "The worst part is the night terrors. I just want them to go away. But no one ... no one could ever help."

Ashilde bit her lip, not sure how to offer comfort there. Instead, her mind went a different direction and though she felt like she shouldn't ignore what Anóra just told her, her curiosity won. "Anóra, why do you believe it's your father speaking to you, in your dreams?"

"Well ... they didn't happen, before he died," Anóra said. "He was killed a year after my ... *accident*. Mother said it was a raid of some kind." Her voice didn't carry the same sadness talking about her father as when she spoke of her mother, though Ashilde couldn't imagine it was still easy to lose him. She also swallowed her questions about the babe Anóra's mother had carried, who also died in that clearing; also a child of Tevyn's, perhaps?

Not your place, she reminded herself. Anóra had already shared so much with her and she hadn't spoken about her dead sibling. Ashilde had pried enough already.

"I thought ... maybe, I'm supposed to help you so I can reach him," Anóra continued. "So, I can finally say I'm sorry. Maybe ... maybe he won't be mad at me, anymore, after that."

"Why do you think he's mad?"

"Because the dreams ... they hurt. They hurt my head, and I can't see, and my legs hurt *really* badly. Sometimes, I scream." She shuddered. "They scare me and it's hard to ... come back, sometimes. Sometimes, I forget it isn't real."

"These are the night terrors you mentioned?"

The girl whimpered.

"Is there ... anything I can do to help?"

"I don't know," she whispered.

"Did you have a dream recently? Perhaps only a few weeks ago?"

"I..." Anóra stopped herself. "How did you know that?"

"Because I think I was there. Did a healer come to help you? From another clan?"

"Mmhmm."

"That was Davyn. My partner."

"I remember!" Anóra perked up at that. "Did he tell you about me? He was really, really nice."

Ashilde actually found herself blushing. "He mentioned how brave you were and how happy he was, being able to help you," she lied. *You ever going to stop lying to her?*

"He helped," Anóra said. "I don't know how, but he made the pain go away. Mother cried when she told him thank you."

She distinctly heard the girl sniff again, before feeling her tuck herself further against her. Ashilde wrapped her arm more tightly in response.

Your turn, her mind told her, relentless.

But still, a promise was a promise.

And Anóra deserved to know.

Ashilde sucked in a breath. "Thank you, Anóra. For telling me." She waited a moment for her to respond, but when she heard nothing but her sniffling, she pressed on. "Listen, I—"

Anóra said something, interrupting her, but she didn't make it out.

"What?"

She spoke again, this time at a whisper. "Who's going to protect me now?" Her voice cracked and Ashilde could tell she was sobbing, now. "Those men ... they took my mother ... away," she cried, between hiccups. "I ... I have no family ... left. I hate them!"

Then, suddenly, she felt Anóra collide into her chest,

wrapping her arms around her as best she could as she climbed into her lap. Ashilde immediately froze, but quickly pushed back her discomfort or surprise, instead wrapping her arms around Anóra as she cried into her chest, her shoulders shaking as she sobbed.

"Who will protect me now?" she whispered again.

Ashilde reached one hand up and stroked her hair, her own confession dying on her lips at her outburst, screaming her hate at the people who stole her mother, the only person who protected her from an abusive father, away from her.

Selfishly, she wasn't ready for that hate to be directed at her.

Even if she deserved it.

"I will, child," she whispered back instead, rocking her gently as she'd seen other mothers from the clan do when their children cried, determined more than anything else, to keep this promise—even if it was exactly the promise she'd never been able to keep with those she loved. Not her mother, not her hunters, not her clan. Was she promising something she was incapable of doing?

Ashilde shook her head, determination hardening her.

"I will."

CHAPTER TWENTY

Ashilde stirred in her sleep, surprised when she awoke. Anóra was curled up against her chest, while she felt Funakiin against her thigh, breathing slowly and deeply. Ashilde blinked, but it didn't matter—no amount of blinking cleared her vision. She didn't remember falling asleep, but she remembered holding Anóra as she cried.

She remembered being a coward.

Ashilde flinched. But, before she could allow herself the mental lashing she believed she deserved, she felt Funakiin stiffen beside her, suddenly alert. In response, her own body went rigid as she strained, desperate for her ears to make up for what she'd lost through her sight.

"Funakiin, what—"

Then, she heard it.

A chirping call, unlike any she'd ever heard before.

Her heart stilled as Funakiin growled.

"Anóra," Ashilde said, shaking her body. "Get up. We have to move. *Now.*"

"Whhhattt," Anóra mumbled, coming back to

consciousness. She quickly complained as Ashilde stood, the rope that was still tied around their waists pulling her up with her, but Ashilde cut her off quickly.

"We're being hunted, Anóra," she said, looking around on reflex, before cursing when she realized how much of a waste it was.

"What?" Anóra cried, almost in a panic. "How? We—"

The chirp called again, louder this time.

A second one answered it.

Ashilde felt herself blanch as Anóra whispered beside her, "Raptors. But ... they aren't real!"

Ashilde knelt down. "Can you see?"

"Yes," she replied, her voice trembling.

"Good. Climb into my arms and tell me where to climb. And pray they can't climb, too."

Quickly, Anóra did what she was told, and Ashilde scooped her up in her arms. The child told her to run to the right, as they had perched up against a solid section of the wall, nearby where the incline was—the only place they could climb. Ashilde barked at Funakiin to move and the wolf quickly followed orders, the rope tugging tightly against her chest. Nearby, the chirps became strident screeches that ripped through the unnatural silence in the air, reverberating off the trees themselves to echo throughout the jungled-forest, making it impossible for her to pin down where the creatures were coming from.

The crashing of leaves to the left, however, made it much more apparent.

"Ashilde!" Anóra screamed in her ear.

The raptors were here.

Instantly, Ashilde felt the rope jerk upward. She shouted at Anóra, "Is the tree in front of us?"

"Yes! I can't climb up—it's too tall!"

Ashilde made a split decision. "Funakiin, catch!"

She threw Anóra up, praying to the gods to give her

mercy just this once and allow her to reach what was hopeful safety, atop the incline. She wanted to turn and pull a weapon, giving her companions time to escape, but Ashilde wasn't a fool. She wasn't trained to defeat creatures she couldn't see—and, even if she had been, raptors were a creature of legend, rumored to have been wiped out during the Banishing.

Instead, they'd simply been trapped here.

"Ashilde, behind you!"

Wasting no time, Ashilde launched herself forward, crashing into the tree's curve, misjudging the height slightly. She heard a crash of scales and claws against the wood below her foot that shook the trunk as she pulled herself up. A screech of protest deafened her for a moment as she found her footing, standing once more.

"Anóra!" she called.

"I'm here," she said, grabbing hold of her hand.

"Go, Anóra. Go, *go*."

They began to run up the trunk as fast as they could move, Anóra trying to warn her each time before they stumbled across a new twig or vine that were layered across the trunk's floor. Ashilde tripped a few times, but never stopped pushing the pace; not until Anóra finally confirmed they had escaped, the raptors unable to climb up the trunk and give pursuit.

Ashilde gasped as she called a halt, her calves burning. Even now, as she knelt over her knees to catch her breath, she had to position her feet to keep her steady, lest she slip and fall back down the slowly—but certainly—still rising incline.

She reached out and managed to find Anóra's face, caressing it gently. "Are you okay?"

"Yeah," she said, in a shaking voice.

"Funakiin?"

"He's fine," Anóra confirmed. "He caught me after I almost slipped off the edge of the trunk, after you threw me."

Praise Waldemar.

"Sorry about that," she said, before she sighed. "Where's Ieka?"

"I don't know."

Ashilde frowned. Ultimately, however, there wasn't anything she could do about their missing raven, except hope it wasn't still searching for the top. "Are you good to keep walking? I'd like to keep moving away from those creatures. We'll rest once we get to the top."

"Okay," Anóra said, though she let out a little huff, as if she was preparing for the journey.

They continued forward, and silence slipped back over them like a shroud, thickening the darkness, only interrupted when Anóra warned her of a dangerous area where she might lose her footing. Ashilde was thankful for the quiet, especially after that surprise attack left her heart thundering, her face and neck still dripping with sweat. Ashilde struggled to accept that the raptors she'd only heard tales about had survived in such a dark place, yet she couldn't deny what she'd just experienced. But what did they eat, to sustain them enough to hide within an impossible environment?

They aren't the only thing to surprise you, of late.

Ashilde bit her lip, attempting to steady her breathing as they climbed. Though she'd gotten more questions than answers in regards to the Rhuanics, their sudden appearance—not to mention their number and their singular interest in not only her clan, but her specifically—left a taste in her mouth that almost had her choking. Could they ... no, it wasn't possible. Was it?

"Anóra," she said quietly, hoping to not scare the girl and cause her to fall. A soft humming noise answered her. "In your dreams. How long have you been having them?"

"For years," the girl answered, threads of wariness coming through the obvious weariness she felt.

"And not with me in particular, correct?"

"No," she said. "At least, not always. The faces ...they were always changing, but coming into the Flatrí and making their way to Skírrdrauin. That was always the same."

Ashilde didn't like the discomfort growing within her, as if she'd swallowed the rope instead of having it secured around her waist, her insides becoming entangled in its knots. "Did you ... ever dream of Rhuanics?"

The girl paused, considering. "No, I don't think so. I ... I don't want to think about them."

Ashilde flinched at her own insincerity, already forgetting her conversation with Anóra earlier. Worse, now she was about to purposefully ignore it, as she pushed on. "I know and I'm sorry. It's just ... well, I think we might have bigger problems than finding the river again."

"What kind of problems?" Anóra asked, whimpering.

Ashilde cursed. "Nothing. Nothing, child. I'm sorry, I didn't mean to alarm you—"

"I'm not scared."

"No, I didn't think you were," Ashilde lied. "It's just ... well, our clan was taught that the raptors, and predators like them, were wiped out during the Banishing. Yet here they are. We were also taught that you became a Rhuanic singularly, after being outcast from your clan." Ashilde's voice caught. *Like you?* She ignored it and pressed on, hoping Anóra didn't notice. "Yet over the past few days, I've encountered small groups of them. It suggests..."

Moments passed as Ashilde struggled to process her thoughts. Anóra didn't speak, either disinterested, confused or distracted by her own thoughts, leaving Ashilde to process alone internally. The idea of a *purposeful* group of Rhuanics working together seemed impossible to fathom. Where in the Segan would they live, with all the clans already grouped together too close for comfort? Yet, if other creatures could survive within the Flatrí, who could deny the possibility that the Rhuanics somehow survived *here*, as well?

But where did they come from? What is their purpose? And why do they hunt you?

Ashilde knew these questions were answers she couldn't gain alone. Unconsciously, she'd given up searching for signs of their whereabouts after entering the Flatrí, believing that no one had ever traveled through here and survived. Yet, perhaps she shouldn't be so quick to trust what she believed she knew.

"I'm not sure of anything anymore, Anóra," Ashilde said, the admission feeling like a weight had been lifted off her shoulders. "But ... well, I want to find out more about these Rhuanics who hunt me, who threaten our clans. Would you mind looking for any signs of them, ah, living here?"

Anóra gasped. "No one can live within the Flatrí. Even *babies* know that."

Ashilde bit her lip. "I know. Or, at least, I thought I did. Just ... look for any signs of life, any signs of disturbance within the forest, and let me know. Okay?"

Anóra went quiet long enough that Ashilde was about to ask if she'd heard her when the girl whispered, "And if we find them, you'll kill them, right? For my mother?"

Heart breaking, the shattering punctured more precisely by her own guilt, Ashilde made her second promise in as many days. "Yes, child. I'll kill them all."

***

Time passed. Too much time. She didn't think night had fallen, marking their first full day within the dark jungle, but her body was certainly sore enough for it to be nearing time for them to take a break. She could only imagine how Anóra felt, but the girl had gone silent after Ashilde spoke her promise and she hadn't known what to bring up to get her to speak again.

Her hand lazily swayed her spear back and forth against the bark, not having run into any roots for a while, yet her body pushed forward on reflex rather than need. She couldn't pin her finger on it, but something about the air felt … different; more restrictive, almost. She had no idea when it had changed—her mind had wandered, often thinking about home, about those who she'd left behind, before she'd quickly force it to think of nothing, if only to avoid the pain of missing them. But blinking herself into more alertness, she definitely noticed it now.

"Anóra," she half-whispered.

She felt the rope tug just a little harder after the girl let out a gasp. "Whoa! I forgot what your voice sounded like."

"I didn't mean to startle you. How are you feeling?"

"Like I could sleep forever."

Ashilde chuckled. "You and me both. Do you mind being my eyes, once again?"

"Sure. Though, we *are* still walking up the same tree."

"And nothing's changed?"

"It's dark. Well, dark*er*," she admitted, making a new lump form in Ashilde's stomach. "I can see my feet, but it's hard to see ahead."

"Can you see Funakiin?"

"His tail. Barely."

Ashilde cursed. That wasn't good. "How long has it been like this? What else can you see?"

"Most of the climb," she answered. "Before, I could see lots of branches—the twisty, pointy kind. They wrapped around the trees beside ours, before crawling above us and wrapping around everywhere but below our feet."

Ashilde considered that, for a moment. Vines and thorns, then, wrapping them up in some sort of cocoon. Could explain how it got darker for Anóra, though her gift being hindered scared Ashilde.

"Has our walkway gotten ... smaller, at all? More constrictive?"

"Umm..." Anóra paused, probably looking around. "I don't—"

The rope snapped taut.

Funakiin howled, startled.

The rope jerked, pulling her forward with a ridiculous amount of force.

"Ashilde!" Anóra screamed, terrified.

They'd found the top of the tree trunk. And its edge.

By her companions falling over it.

And they were currently trying to drag Ashilde down with them.

She tried to jab her spear down, to slow her scuffling feet, attempting to stay upright. Instead, her right foot slipped as Anóra screamed her name again, and the rope pulled harder against her chest, constricting her ability to breathe. She fell backward, landing on her back. Still the rope pulled her, pieces of wood ripping up and flicking off her armor with soft *clinks*.

Forcing herself to remain calm, she pictured the thorny arch enclosing them that Anóra had just described. It was a chance, but it was her only option. She lifted her spear up and flipped it horizontally, slamming each edge into what she hoped would be the sides.

She felt one edge catch, then the second.

Lifting herself up, she hugged the spear, her chest slamming into it as she collided, the force of the impact choking her breath out of her. The rope grew stressed, tightening its hold against her, as she pushed her knees as hard as she could into the ground, her feet pulled back and pinned underneath her.

For a moment, everything remained still.

And silent.

Struggling to breathe, she called out, "Anóra! Anóra,

can you hear me?"

Silence answered her, for too long.

Until, finally, came a response.

From below.

"Yy—eess."

She was crying, reliving her worst nightmare. And Ashilde couldn't see her.

Ashilde adjusted her grip on the spear, praying it held. "Where are you? What happened?"

"I was looking ... around..." She inhaled heavily, speaking between shuddering sobs. "To help. But then ... I ... I..."

"It's okay, Anóra, it's okay," Ashilde said, struggling to breathe herself. She could feel the rope moving against her chest, gently back and forth, tightening with every pass, forcing the scales of her armor to dig into her, compressing her chest. Her companions swung below her.

"Funakiin just disappeared! One moment, he was ... he was right there ... and then he dropped. Then, the rope pulled me forward and I couldn't ... I couldn't stop it. There was nothing to ... to ... to hold onto!"

"Anóra, listen to me. You are not going to fall. I am going to pull you back up. I promised to protect you and I will. Okay?"

Ashilde struggled, readjusting and pulling herself up higher against her spear as she pressed her knees more sharply into the bark, trying not to let her feet slip from underneath her. "Be my eyes so I can help you. Are you hanging in midair?"

A moment passed. Then another. "Yes," she said, her voice sounding stronger, without the interruption of hiccups and tears.

"How far to the bottom? Can you see it?"

"Nn—no."

Inwardly, she cursed. Her mind raced, trying to

think of a way to pull them back up. It had to be an immediate drop, for Funakiin to be caught unawares so suddenly and slip over the edge. How they were meant to get down it originally was no one's guess, but she couldn't worry about that now.

"Just hang tight, Anóra. I just need to check something." Holding the spear in a deathgrip, she began pulling one leg slowly out from underneath her. "Is Funakiin still with you?"

"Yes! He's below me. He's ... he's whining."

"It's okay, it's okay," Ashilde kept repeating, fear trying to convince her it was anything but as her mind raced.

She managed to get one leg free and she stretched it forward, slowly. With one leg still bent, she extended the other until it was fully stretched. Her foot suddenly had no tree underneath it, but instead, found open air. She pulled it back quickly.

She was mere paces from the drop.

Ashilde swallowed. Her spear was wedged steadily. But with no place to use as a foothold—she checked, as she once again pushed one leg out to search, swinging it wide across the path ahead, not running into anything besides open air and the smooth wood underneath her; and without the ability to let go of the spear without falling over, too, she had no idea how to pull them back up.

"What else can you see, Anóra? Keep talking to me!"

She was silent for a moment. "You can't pull us up, can you?"

Her heart broke at the way her inflection pitched, slipping higher than normal.

"I'm working on it, Anóra. I promise."

She felt a new weight land on the spear. A familiar peck quickly tapped her hand, almost startling her into letting go of her lifeline. Ieka had finally returned. Instead, she re-tightened her grip, now fighting against slippery sweat from her palms and the waning strength in her arms. Ieka must have landed beside her. Ashilde glanced over to where she thought the bird was, her cheek resting against her spear. "Ieka, what do I do?" she whispered, struggling to keep her composure, as the idea of losing Anóra sent her into a near hysteria. "You're Róta's creature. Tell me what to do."

The raven didn't answer her.

Or, if she did, Ashilde couldn't hear her.

Her arms began to shake.

Her entire body shifted just a fraction closer to the edge she couldn't see.

"Anóra, are you sure you can't see the bottom?"

"No ... I can't. Ashilde, please, don't drop me!" she cried, panic rising as her voice became shrill. "Don't let me fall again!"

Again.

That word triggered her. She'd not only fallen before, but had been *thrown* off a cliff. Even knowing this, Ashilde had asked her to face this lifelong fear.

After she'd promised to keep her safe.

And here she was, considering cutting the child loose, hoping the fall wasn't too far so she could climb down and find Anóra, forcing her to relive one of the worst memories of her young life so far, and completely breaking any faith or trust she had in her.

Below, she could hear Anóra begin to chant, "Don't, don't, don't," as she started crying more fully.

The rope began to swing more dangerously.

"Anóra. Anóra, listen to me!" she called, trying to get her to calm down. "You're going to be fine. You're going to be okay."

Her crying only got louder.

"Please," she whispered, which Ash could barely hear. "Please, please, please..."

Ashilde squeezed her eyes shut, tears streaming down her own face at what she was about to do. What other choice did she have? She couldn't get a foothold to pull the girl up and she couldn't hold onto them forever. If she lost her hold, they'd all fall down together. And if it *was* dangerously far down, there would be no one to help them, if they all fell. But if she cut Anóra and Funakiin loose, then she could follow them down, unharmed, so if they *did* get hurt, she would actually be in a position to help them.

That was if they didn't die during the fall.

And if she could find a way down, *without* being able to see.

Without getting herself killed, in the process.

And being able to find them, once she lost them.

And.

And.

And.

Her grip continued to slip even further.

Anóra was dangerously quiet.

"Anóra! Are you still with me?"

"I am," came a small reply.

She sounded defeated, resolute.

Curse you, Ashilde. Tactical or not, she couldn't condemn that child to the possible physical harm and certain psychological damage of cutting her loose. She couldn't believe she even considered it for so long, even if that meant the odds of her surviving were better, if she did.

"I'm sorry," she said. "I'm trying to figure out a way—"

"Will you find me?"

Ashilde stilled. "What?"

"Will you come after me and find me? And Funakiin?" Anóra asked again.

"I'm not going to drop you," Ashilde said, her voice firm.

"But you can't pull me up."

"I'm ... working on that."

"Promise me you'll come after me. Promise you won't leave me alone, no matter what."

What was she going on about? Aahilde wasn't going to leave her. Now that her decision was made, it was most likely that she was going to fall alongside her, if only a few moments later.

She just had to pray they all survived it.

"I promise, Anóra. No matter what we endure in our journey to Skírrdrauin, I will never abandon you."

Silence answered her for a moment.

Then, a soft, scared voice finally responded.

"Please hurry."

Suddenly, a sharp *snap* followed and the weight that had been constantly pulling Ashilde toward the edge was no longer there, as Anóra screamed below, the scream shrinking away from her with every second. Instead of resting against the spear, Ashilde pushed herself underneath it and felt her way to the edge, poking her head out over it, as if she could see anything but darkness below.

"Anóra!"

Only her fading scream answered.

CHAPTER TWENTY-ONE

Ashilde stared at everything and saw nothing, disbelieving.

The girl's scream still echoed in her ears. Ash quickly pulled the rope up, her mind not wanting to believe the only conclusion she could come up with. But she found the edge of the rope too quickly, her fingers brushing against the frayed edges, hurriedly cut. She hadn't even thought to check a child so young for a weapon, but she quite obviously had a knife hidden on her.

Anóra couldn't have cut herself loose, otherwise.

Ashilde ran her fingers through her hair, her fingers getting caught up in tangles and knots as she shook her head. She couldn't believe she'd done it. She'd never met a braver child—no, a braver *person*, in all her life; braver, or more selfless. Not only did she face her greatest fear, but she saved Ashilde the guilt of cutting her loose. All she asked in return was for her to come and find him, after she fell.

Ash helped no one by sitting there, staring.

Pushing herself up, Ashilde scooted backward until

her back hit the spear. Dipping beneath it, she kept her weapon between her and the edge, keeping one hand on the spear to keep herself oriented. She had no intention of leaving Anóra alone, at the bottom of the other side of this twisted tree.

But she had no idea how she could possibly help her, either.

To her right, she heard a squawk.

Ieka.

The bird had been quiet since their other companions fell, hardly making any sounds. That, or Ashilde had been too busy to notice her. But the raven squawked again, right before she pecked Ashilde's hand rapidly, repeatedly.

Pulling her hand away, Ashilde snapped, "What?"

The bird didn't help her when she asked for it, which meant Róta hadn't, either. If that didn't mean she was truly on her own, the chosen creatures of her gods as her companions or not, she wasn't sure what better sign she could get. She didn't think Ieka could help her now, especially since she couldn't understand what the bird was saying or see what she was doing.

Something prickly was shoved against her fist.

Opening her palm, a plant was placed firmly onto it.

Ashilde frowned, closing her hand over it. The prickles were more ticklish than painful, not breaking through her skin. It was slightly sticky, as well, and oblong in shape, almost like a natural rope—

A vine.

Closing her fist more firmly, now, she found the end of the vine that Ieka gave her. She began pulling the vine toward her, dropping it onto her lap as she continued to follow it. And it just kept going. And going. And going, until eventually, Ashilde forced herself to stop, the pile in her lap heavy.

"Ieka, did you untangle this from the archway's edges?"

A sharp caw confirmed her guess.

"Would have been helpful a couple minutes earlier," she muttered, before biting her lip. Taking her anger out on her companion solved nothing, especially now that Ieka was offering her a solution to a problem where she had none moments before. "Is it ... still attached, at the other end?"

A sharper caw, before she felt the raven land on her lap and start digging through her pile. The end of the vine was placed once again in her hand, as Ieka then tugged against the frayed rope currently tied against her waist. Ashilde didn't need her Gift to guess what the creature was trying to tell her and she almost thanked the gods for the luck, before she swallowed such praise.

The gods didn't deserve it.

But Ieka did.

"Thank you," she told Ieka, momentarily awed by the fact that, without the help of her companions, she would have never made it this far. Then, she got to work.

Moving slowly, Ashilde pulled the knife sheathed on her wrist. Slower still, she slid the blade underneath the rope she'd tied around her upper torso, sawing it loose, the tight, constricting feeling releasing like a breath held too long as it came undone. Fuck, it hurt. An injury to check, if she survived what came next. *When you survive.*

Ash winced as she replaced the rope with the vine, whatever cuts or bruises it'd inflicted under her armor, not happy she was putting fresh pressure there. She could've simply held the vine, instead of wrapping it around her, but she'd rather use the vine as a second lifeline, if she slipped, rather than only having her own reflexes to catch her.

Of course, you could always jump down.

She stilled at the thought. After Ieka gave her the vine

and she discovered the length she had to work with felt endless, she had planned to propel herself slowly down the other side of the tree, climbing down the side—and that was assuming there would be hand-and foot-holds for her to use, to do just that. She didn't think of another alternative, like simply running and jumping off the side of the tree and letting the rope catch her fall.

It would *get you down there faster.*

And the faster she got down there, the faster she could find Anóra.

Yet her gut disagreed with her, as evident with her suddenly sweaty palms as she tightened the vine around her chest. There were too many flaws with that idea to make it worth trying, even if she gained more speed by doing so. The vine could snap. Her body could jerk too much as the vine stopped her fall, causing her *body* to snap. She had no idea if it was a clear drop or if she'd be falling through branches and trees—and potentially getting caught in one. No, she had to climb down, using the tree's edge and hoping that, blind and unfamiliar with the terrain, she could still find a way down without killing herself in the process.

She double checked the knot and then gathered the loose vine in her hands. Ducking underneath the spear, Ashilde placed the pile of the untangled vine on the edge. She followed it to where it climbed back into the arched vines tangled within the branches above her and gave a sharp tug. The hold was strong. She tugged as hard as she could, trying to pull the vine all the way loose. It didn't budge.

Leaning back, she dislodged her spear from where it had saved her and placed it back into her sling. "Ieka, are you still there?"

The raven responded with a soft squawk.

"Do you think you can follow me down and ... well, try to warn me if I'm about to misstep?"

A second passed without an answer.

Then, she felt Ieka rub the top of her head against the back of her hand. A quick flutter of wings and a small gust of air, and Ieka was gone. She squawked again, farther away from Ashilde.

Over the edge.

She swallowed and rubbed her sweaty palms against her armor, her hand slipping off the embedded scales thanks to the added moisture of her nerves. Trying not to take that as a bad sign, Ashilde checked that her weapons were all secured—including replacing her knife in her sheath, after dropping it twice in the attempt to do just that. Finally, Ashilde began to crawl toward the drop, reaching it much faster than she wanted.

Please hurry.

Without letting her own fears keep her from lingering any longer, she turned around and, keeping herself steady, pushed herself backward, until she was hovering just over the side of the tree.

Breathe.

Ashilde lowered herself down, her feet frantically trying to find a foothold. After a second of hanging by her arms, with nothing but the vine wrapped around her chest to secure her in any way if she fell, Ashilde found a jagged root that stuck out from the tree. She quickly dug her foot into it, giving her shaking arms a rest, as her other foot found its own hold, slightly lower.

Keeping one hold firm on the edge above her, Ashilde lowered her other arm to grab onto a solid root that poked into her shoulder.

Finally, she let go, grabbing onto a larger branch just above her, judging by the roundness of it.

Ashilde exhaled loudly, her grip so tight onto the various branches, roots and twigs that stuck out from the tree's cliff-like side that her muscles started to cramp. But she'd made it over the side and, if the rest of the way down was as covered in extended limbs as this was so far, she might—just might—make it down.

How long that would take, however, she had no idea.

This isn't hurrying, she thought.

Anóra could be in trouble.

But rushing and killing yourself by slipping isn't going to help her, either.

Forcing herself to stay calm and move steadily, Ashilde tightened her grip as she lowered one leg, searching for a new foothold until she found it, before lowering the other, her top half inching down as she went. She kept her pace slow, purposeful, but she forced herself to keep moving, not pausing unless her muscles needed a moment to relax and stretch, as much as she was able, before she continued on. Ashilde found a rhythm, growing more confident in her descent. Which gave her mind permission to wonder.

And worry.

She worried about how long it would take her to climb down. It'd taken most of the day to make the climb up. What if her body didn't last long enough, before her muscles gave way to exhaustion? She worried that Anóra and Funakiin didn't survive the fall. She worried about what she would do if one of them was hurt, without supplies to help them.

She worried one of them was dead.

Her body went rigid at the thought. Ash forced herself to breathe and continue.

Just one foot after the other. You can do this, Ashilde. You can.

Something beneath her foot snapped.

Ieka squawked from behind her.

Her body gave way beneath her.

And then, she was falling.

Resisting the urge to flail and panic, she grabbed the vine, making sure it was tightly wound around her chest.

She pulled against the vine, hoping it would catch and allow her to pull herself upward, to attempt and grab hold of the tree once more. But she couldn't get herself righted, instead falling head first toward the ground.

Both too quickly and too long, the vine suddenly vent taut, causing her entire body to snap to a stop. She froze, hanging horizontally, her hands white-knuckling the vine as she began to sway, ever so gently, against a breeze. Her lungs hurt and her entire torso felt like she had trained for hours without blocking a single hit against her, but she was alive and nothing felt broken. Yet.

Inhaling sharply, Ashilde couldn't mistake the smell the breeze carried.

Water.

She couldn't hear it, but the river had to be nearby.

And the ground...?

She was hesitant to move around too much, lest she cause the vine to snap and lose the only thing that kept her from crushing into the ground below. But she couldn't just hang there, either. Choosing to take a risk, she pulled on the vine, hard.

The hold didn't break.

Breathing through her nostrils, she counted to three before she started climbing the rope, pulling herself up to a sitting position. It still held, though she could feel it start to shake.

"Ieka, am I facing the direction of the wall? Make noise if I am."

Ieka squawked immediately.

Extending her legs, she pulled them tight together as she thrust her entire body forward, barely swinging at all after the first thrust, but once she started to build momentum, it only took her a couple of times, swinging back and forth, before she collided to the wall with an *oof*.

Quickly, she secured a sturdy hold with one hand before lodging her feet on two more branches, her left hand still wrapped tightly around the vine.

A vine that, now that it saved her life, she had to cut loose.

As soon as she had the thought, Ashilde knew it was her only option. The vine no longer had any give, so she couldn't continue climbing down the side while the vine was still wrapped around her. It would only stop her progress. Keeping one hand tightly wrapped around her new hold, she found her knife once more. She cut the vine free. Her entire torso exploded with a mixture of pain and relief.

"Ieka," she called, resheathing her knife and finding a hold for her left hand. "Are you still with me?"

The bird responded, a few feet away from her right side.

"Thank you for staying. Let's hope I can make it to the bottom."

Ieka squawked again, in what Ashilde hoped might be encouragement. Bracing herself, her arms already shaking—like they knew what she was about to do next and were protesting her decision—she put all of her weight into her arms as she lowered one foot, slowly, searching for a new foothold.

Her hold almost slipped in surprise when her foot found something solid.

Much more solid than a tree branch.

Steadying herself and tightening her grip on the branches, she settled her outstretched foot and then lowered her other foot until it was even, once again finding a completely solid surface. She moved her foot a few inches to the left, not lifting it, yet everything she touched below her was solid.

She'd finally found the ground.

Letting go, Ashilde stood, completely free from the wall she'd just descended to get there. She took a few steps back, waving her arms out in front of her.

She'd made it. Ieka landed on her shoulder and rubbed against her cheek with her head, giving her the only confirmation she could get, in a place shrouded in permanent darkness.

Ashilde collapsed on her knees and cried.

***

After she let all of her pent up stress, fear and uncertainty release through silent tears, Ashilde checked herself, as much as she could, via touch. Nothing seemed broken or too badly bruised, though her torso, from the rope and vine burns, worried her. Her shoulder, too, was sore, having not been cleaned in almost two days. In fact, her entire body ached, making her want nothing more than to collapse onto the ground, curl up into a ball and sleep the pain away.

But doing so served no one.

So instead, Ashilde squared her shoulders, wincing as she did, and drank the little water she had left out of her waterskin. The breeze, blowing through again, was strong enough to send strands of hair across her face.

There hadn't been a breeze after they first entered the Flatrí.

If there was one now, did that mean she was close to finding her way out?

It doesn't matter, she thought.

She had something much more important to find than the exit, right now.

"Ieka, do you see them?"

The bird didn't answer her. So, a no, then?

"Can you see the river?"

Ieka chirped.

"Lead me there."

It was the logical choice. After Anóra and Funakiin fell, they'd head toward the water. That had been their goal in the first place and, since they had to have fallen near where she stood now, Anóra would have been able to see it, too.

Assuming the fall didn't kill them.

She hated herself, if only for a moment, when her gut tried to agree, telling her that, by all logic, there was no way either of them could survive a fall that far down—even if, somehow, it wasn't nearly as far down as it should have been, based on how long it took them to climb up, and how her own descent and subsequent fall had taken a much shorter time than that. But Ashilde refused to believe that either of them were dead, no matter what her brain, gut or logic tried to tell her. The Flatrí was the most unnatural place she'd ever encountered. If at any place a miracle could happen, it was here.

She wasn't sure if her heart could take it, if proven otherwise.

Ieka leaped off her shoulder and took flight above her, squawking a few feet away loudly, until Ashilde started walking toward her. The duration of the noise made Ashilde nervous. What if Ieka accidentally brought predators and their attention to them, especially more raptors? Yet as Ashilde kept walking, spear outstretched, she held onto hope they wouldn't be discovered again. Aside from the raptor scare, since entering the Flatrí, she hadn't seen—well, *heard*—any other animals. Anóra never called attention to any, either, during her narration, so she trusted the idea that, perhaps, there *were* none.

That didn't help her nerves like she wished it would.

She walked long enough to trip over two branches and get turned around so badly from where Ieka tried to lead her, that the raven had to fly down and poke at her hand until she turned back around, before she could finally hear what the wind helped her smell. It was soft, but in the surrounding silence, it sounded practically deafening.

Yet it couldn't mask the sound of a very soft whimper.

"Funakiin?"

A sharp bark answered her, just ahead.

"Ieka, take me to him!" Ashilde commanded, breaking into a sprint even though she still couldn't see anything ahead of her. "Anóra! Anóra!"

She received no answer from the child.

Ashilde wished, not for the first time, that her ability to speak with her animal companions hadn't been stripped. Ieka could easily have been describing what she saw and where Anóra was now, what Funakiin's condition was, why he was whimpering, instead of Ashilde being clueless in almost every regard. She almost relished the chance to visit the gods, if only so she could give them a sharp, relentless lashing of exactly how she felt about their robbing of so many aspects of her personality.

Even those she had chosen to reject.

The butt of her spear slipped, no longer landing on solid ground. Ashilde stopped and flipped her spear over, touching the end. Her fingers came back wet. She made it to the river.

Just to her right, Funakiin issues a warning growl.

"Funakiin! Funakiin, where's Anóra?"

Another small gust of air hit her face as Ieka hovered inches in front of her face. Ashilde forced herself to remain still, as a sharp trio of talons wrapped around her wrist and *pulled*, hard. She let herself be led by the bird, blinking against the small current of wind Ieka's wings blew back into her face, as Ieka kept herself aloft while she guided Ashilde along the riverbed.

She walked only momentarily before Ieka let go of her hand with a squawk.

A small voice spoke.

"You ... you came for me."

"Anóra!"

Dropping her spear, she knelt on the ground, one hand outstretched. "Anóra, you brave, brave young heart. Are you okay? Where are you? Does anything hurt? How—"

Suddenly, after a few moments of stumbling into the open air, Ashilde found the girl's hand. Trailing her fingers up her arm, she found one shoulder and then the other. Quickly, she wrapped herself around her, burying the girl in a crushing hug as relief crashed over her, a force stronger than any ocean wave.

She was alive.

And she was drenched.

Ashilde pulled back. "You're soaking. What happened?"

"Magic, of course!" Anóra responded, teeth chattering. "But ... it's a little cold in the river and my foot is stuck between some sticky rocks. Can you pull me out?"

Ashilde moved over so she could put her arms underneath her shoulders. She hesitated to ask her next question, but she ignored her potential guilt and asked, "Is anything broken?"

"Not me," Anóra said. "But Funakiin's leg, it ... it shouldn't bend that way."

She shook her head, cursing again under her breath. She wasn't sure what exactly she could do about *that*. But she'd have to do something. *One problem at a time, Slátra.*

She flinched at her own thought, referring to herself out of habit to what she once was.

What she could no longer be.

Gently, she pulled Anóra out of the water, after discovering the log and rocks she'd got pinned against. Her small frame shivered against her and she felt even lighter than before.

"What's behind me?"

"It looks like home. Normal trees!" Anóra said. "You *are* about to walk straight into a big tree, though.

Right behind you."

With a little more prompting and guiding, Anóra guided her away from running into anything until they finally stopped at a large tree, and she set the girl up beside it. After she was comfortable, Ashilde took off her weapons and pack, and laid them beside her, pulling out her blanket she'd bundled up in the bottom of her pack.

"Anóra, take off your wet clothes and lay them out to dry beside you. The blanket's thin, but at least it'll dry you off."

"But..."

"Hush. I'm not going to lose you to the river's chill."

"Okay."

"I'm going to go and get Funakiin and bring him over here. I'll need your help mending his leg, but after that, I'll get you food and water. Okay?"

"Y-yes."

"Good. Wrap yourself up in that as best you can. I'll be right back."

Ashilde turned and made her way back to the water, before she called out, "Funakiin? Can you let me know where you are?"

The wolf responded with a bark. Ashilde followed the noise and knelt down roughly where she thought the wolf was, stretching out her hands. Fingertips brushed fur as she grazed Funakiin's ear. She scratched the back of his head.

"I'm so sorry," she whispered. She meant it. The wolf had shown up and helped her more than almost anyone else, since she'd been outcast. He deserved better than to be injured because she hadn't been able to protect him. "Can you walk?"

The wolf growled, though she didn't think he was actually mad at her, but the situation itself. He was both lone wolf and leader, not used to relying on anyone but himself. And, in order to move him over to Anóra, he was going to need Ashilde's help to do so. She wouldn't like that helpless feeling, either.

He also wasn't going to like how she planned to do so.

"I need to get you over to Anóra," she told him. "It's not far, so I'm going to carry you in my arms. It's going to hurt, though. Try your best not to bite me."

He nuzzled her hand. Ashilde slipped her arms underneath his torso. He growled as her arm brushed his front legs, but she couldn't feel anything broken as she secured her hold on his other side. Pushing herself up from her squatted position, she stood, the large wolf cradled in her arms like a pup. Ashilde hadn't even taken a step before she started breathing heavily.

"Perhaps eat less rabbits next time," she muttered, her back straining against carrying something so large, even over such a short distance.

Funakiin snapped at her, though without any bite to it.

She made her way over to their "camp," Anóra calling out directions as she got closer. She put the wolf down beside the girl, earning a howl of pain as she didn't put him down nearly as gently as she should have, but the wolf was *heavy*—lighter than his large frame suggested, but still heavy enough to push her to her limits. She winced as she offered an apology, before she knelt down, in-between child and wolf.

"Are you warmer?"

"Much. Thank you," Anóra said quietly, as if she'd suddenly become shy.

"Did you lay your clothes out on the ground to dry?"

"Yes."

"Good. Let's rest a bit." She paused. "How bad is his leg?"

"It's ... bent at a wrong angle. His front left paw."

"Any exposed bone?"

"No."

She bit her lip, thinking. This was much more Freydis's speciality than hers. It took all of her willpower not to follow the pains of her heart as her chest spasmed at the thought of her abandoned friend—a woman she hadn't thought much about, hadn't even said *goodbye* to; a realization that only complicated her guilt still further. She shook her head. There was no winning, not within her own mind and not within her heart.

But perhaps she could save Funakiin's leg.

"Any chance you were studying to be a healer, Anóra?"

The young girl snorted. "Of course not. I'm going to become *sangrild*, same as you!"

Ash nodded, a bit absentmindedly. Of course the girl had no plans to learn any other trades. It was a rare thing, for anyone with the Ravenmother's body, to ever have a different fate. *Good thing Freydis liked to talk about those she helped. In detail.*

"I've … never personally done this," Ashilde admitted, "but I think I know how."

"Really?"

"Mostly," she said. "I'll guide you through what you need to do, to the best of my knowledge."

"What, *me*? Why do I have to do it?"

"I'm not the most confident about this to begin with," Ashilde said. "I'm *definitely* not confident I can do this blind."

"Oh, right." She paused, considering. "I can try."

"I know Funakiin would be happy if you did." *And I'd rather not leave him behind if we're unable to fix that leg,* she didn't bother to add aloud. She wasn't even sure if she could consider the idea. But could she risk all of their lives, after the gods killed her, if she didn't reach Skírrdrauin in time, in order to not abandon the wolf?

Best it doesn't come to that. Focus.

"Okay," Anóra said, though her tone told her the girl wasn't exactly happy about it.

"I'm sorry you can't rest just quite yet, Anóra. But I need you. More importantly, so does Funakiin."

That seemed to motivate her more. Her voice regained a little strength and no longer gave any weight to the whiny tone she carried a few moments earlier. "Tell me what to do."

With her instruction, Anóra got to work. She ripped up a corner of the blanket and cut it into thin strips. Then, she found a few different pieces of wood and used the flat of the blade to smooth out any potential splinters or rough edges on each piece, measuring the wood to the length of Funakiin's leg and cutting them down to size, with Ashilde's verbal guidance. Funakiin napped in-between them.

As she worked, Ashilde asked Ieka if any of the trees contained leaves with sap on them. Before she could add any more detail, Ieka disappeared, returning quickly with a beakful of sticky leaves, Anóra confirmed. It made her heart beat faster, to find something familiar from home in the strangeness of the Flatrí; a reminder of what the land once was, before the Ravenmother's wrath ruined it.

Commanding Anóra to gather the leaves, wood and wool together, Ashilde explained to Funakiin what they were going to do.

"He looks nervous, but he nodded at you," Anóra told her, after she finished. "I think he's okay with it."

"I'll hold him down as I explain how to wrap his leg up, step-by-step, to help steady him, okay?"

"Okay."

With minimal struggle on the wolf's part, Ashilde guided Anóra to use the rest of the water from the waterskin to clean off Funakiin's broken leg, before wrapping two of the five strips around it. They placed a piece of wood on either side of the leg and one underneath the paw, wrapping more cloth around the wood. To make sure the bandages and the wood didn't come apart as Funakiin walked—*if* the wolf would be able to walk much, until the bone healed—Ashilde instructed Anóra to use the leaves, which had sticky sap on one side, to stick the cloth and wood together.

The entire process took much longer than Ashilde might have guessed. Once Anóra announced that they were done, she heard the girl sigh loudly and lean back onto the tree. Ash let her rest as she went and refilled their water, before she returned and sat back beside Funakiin—no longer whimpering, but panting gently beside her. Ashilde passed the water around, giving some to Funakiin as well, before she passed Anóra her pack and asked her to get out what was left and see how much they had, before determining their shares.

Anóra pulled out the last of her stolen meat, but it was enough for each of them—including both animals—to eat a full share.

Rationing be damned, Ashilde thought. After the day they had, they deserved full stomachs.

"Ieka also brought back a stalk of berries," Anóra told her, putting dried meat and a heavy, berry-ladened twig in her hand.

"Now we'll truly feast," she said with a smile. After recognizing the plant she needed to properly bind the wolf's leg, Ashilde didn't fear that the raven couldn't tell the difference between a poisonous berry or a safe one—even if this was the first sign of any food found in the Flatrí. She should have held onto that and studied that new discovery more, but Ashilde couldn't. She was too thankful to have a moment to rest, allow her body to relax, surrounded by companions who were alive. The sheer amount of relief and gratitude that had welled up within her surprised Ashilde. While she hadn't anticipated companions on this journey, she certainly hadn't expected to grow so attached to them so quickly.

Ashilde popped a berry in her mouth, the sharp sweetness of the juice sent a jolt through her, energizing her for the conversation they needed to have.

"I'm glad you're okay, Anóra. Really, really glad," she said, staring at where her feet were, even if she couldn't actually see them. "I'm sorry ... I'm sorry that I couldn't save you from experiencing that again."

Anóra took a moment before she responded. "It's okay," she lied, for both of them. "You kept your promise. How did you get down?"

"I used a vine that Ieka gave me and climbed some of the way ... and fell the rest of it," she said.

"Wow. The gods are *definitely* looking after us, then. Both of us!"

Ashilde frowned, remembering her plea to Róta through Ieka, begging her for guidance on how to save Anóra, yet getting no answer. Or the fact that she was only stuck out in the Flatrí to begin with, thanks to the gods' demands. "Why do you say that?"

"I..." Anóra sniffed, still processing. "I thought we were going to die. I was scared and mother ... she told me, if I was ever scared, that I should pray. The gods, they love me, she said. They won't let anything else bad happen to me."

Anything else.

"I am glad they listened," Ashilde said, unsure of how to respond, shoving her own personal opinions about their gods aside for the moment.

"I told them I was sorry if I was ever bad. I didn't mean to be bad, if I was," Anóra continued, ignoring her. "I asked if I—and Funakiin—could go to Skírrdrauin. I ... wanted to see my mother again." Her voice dropped to almost a whisper. "I also asked them to help you reach Skírrdrauin, too, but alive. I ... I told them I didn't think you deserved being an outcast and they should forgive you."

Ashilde's eyes welled up, but she didn't dare speak.

Realizing she wasn't going to interrupt again, Anóra continued. "They didn't answer. Even my father didn't..." She choked up. "But then, suddenly, the wind grabbed us and shoved us sideways! We landed in the water. Well, I did. Funakiin landed halfway in, halfway out. I think that's how he broke his leg."

Anóra started sniffling again and Ashilde moved over to wrap one arm around her, an act so unfamiliar just days ago, now occurring without a second thought. She was just so relieved that the girl was alive.

"It's okay, Anóra," she whispered, kissing her on the forehead on reflex, before she realized she did it, blushing. "You're okay. And you did great." She squeezed her arm. "Curl up and get some rest."

"What about you?"

"Oh, I'll be getting some, too. I think we both need it."

At the thought of closing her eyes, Ashilde felt a rush of relief. Exhaustion was becoming a dangerous companion that she needed to stop allowing to sneak up on her. Her entire body felt like it would collapse, even with her already resting on the ground.

As the girl nuzzled up beside her, Ashilde whispered, "Thank you."

"For what?"

She pressed the other half of her body against Funakiin, stealing some of the wolf's warmth, while he gave the rest of it to Anóra, who needed it more than she. She kept her arm wrapped around Anóra's tiny frame, glad to find she no longer shook. It startled Ashilde to realize that, in the less than three days since she had known this child, she had grown a fierce attachment to her; greater than what was rational, but that didn't make it any less real.

"For everything," she said.

CHAPTER TWENTY-TWO

For the second time, Ashilde dreamed, and was aware of doing so. But this time, she was certain she witnessed something she shouldn't be present to see.

Dream-Ashilde stood behind a small wooden fence erected in the back right corner of Slátra territory, with the half of the pit encircled by the larger, towering wooden wall making up their outer border. It was the designated training area, where they ripped up all the grass inside the small circle and kept the dirt padded down, in attempts to keep the dust and slipping feet to a minimum.

"But not too much," Ashilde watched as Brynhild explained to a young Magnhild. "You won't always get to choose your battleground, nor the conditions you'll be fighting in. You'll need to learn how to fight harder battles than blocking a thrust while you're blinded by dust."

Outside the dream, Ashilde floated unseen, watching the discussion unfold like an outsider. Though she hadn't been there for Magnhild's first training, she knew Dagfinn had asked the warriors to introduce the newest *of their number.*

She had no idea that her sister had volunteered.

Watching now, she could see the wide-eyed stare of Magnhild, terrified. If that wasn't enough of a giveaway, the fact that she shook like she suffered from the worst chills in winter during a warm, spring summer day confirmed it. Ash had always assumed those nerves had been because Magnhild was one of the few of her age and the only one to experience a Wyrdan Day, going through the training process alone.

Now, however, it appeared she'd been wrong.

Magnhild's eyes flickered. "I, um... I'm not sure..."

"Mags," Brynhild said, her tone softening. She reached up and wiped a tear from the girl's eyes. "Do you want to know why I volunteered to be your partner, instead of Dagfinn assigning you one?"

She shook her head, biting her lip to keep herself from breaking, her crossed arms shaking ever so slightly.

"Us warriors, we are a tight knit group, close in age. We grew up with our grandmothers' stories of battle, with their desperate fight for survival and the heartbreak of ending a war only because our numbers had grown too few to fight any longer; our mothers taught us the importance of vigilance, of sacrifice. All of us, here..." She waved her hand around her, gesturing toward the other warriors already sparring under the morning sun. "We wanted this. We knew of nothing else, despite being the first generation to truly experience peace. That isn't the same for you."

"No! It's not that. It's just..."

"There is no shame in wanting a different life for yourself, Mags," Brynhild said softly. "I wished for it myself, many times."

The girl's eyes widened. "You didn't want to become a warrior? But, you're so skilled!"

Brynhild laughed at that. "No, a warrior's life always

called to me. But … well, there are other things I wish I could change, but the gods deemed it otherwise. Yet for you, we can work with this. For the clan."

Magnhild swallowed, but then nodded, resolute. "For the clan."

Brynhild kissed her forehead, before gesturing for her to follow, handing her a blunted blade. Together, they walked into the ring, Magnhild no longer shaking.

Dream-Ashilde frowned—and not because she couldn't remember what had called her away, that day, to miss Magnhild's first day of training. No, she frowned for too many other reasons. Because she had never realized the true source of Magnhild's fears; had never even considered that anyone in the clan wouldn't dream of experiencing their Wyrdan Day, hopeful for the chance to give themselves entirely to the preservation of the Slátra. Seeing Magnhild's fears revealed, it felt so obvious. Yet it also served another purpose: an additional reminder of how the gods did as they pleased, not caring about the individual wishes of their people, when Magnhild never wanted to become a warrior and Freydis never wanted to be sangrendi—yet it mattered not, for either.

Her frown deepened at her final thought: surprise, as she saw a side of Brynhild that was hidden while in her presence, something she almost didn't believe, despite how well loved her sister could be; wondering what it'd feel like, to experience that herself.

"Ashilde!"

A little girl stood behind her, her face veiled, excitedly whispering her name as she stood just outside the ring, dirt covering her boots. A little girl? There shouldn't have been a child there. Was this the sister she once had, before she'd pushed her away by killing their mother?

"Ashilde!"

She groggily felt a hand shake her. "Ashilde," Anóra whispered, directly in her ear.

Ashilde bolted up, startling Anóra away from her, immediately reaching for her weapons. "Anóra! What's happening? What's—"

"It's okay!" she squeaked, somewhere off to her left. "We're not dead! Nothing's wrong!"

"Pit," she breathed. "What's so urgent to wake me up like that? I thought someone was trying to hurt you!"

"I'm sorry," Anóra said. "But ... don't you see it?"

She didn't bother trying to hide her scowl in irritation, feeling the emotion prickle up underneath her skin. She hadn't been able to see for, what, two days now? Three? Anóra bloody well knew that.

Ashilde felt her tiny hand touch her on the shoulder. "Turn around."

Humoring the girl, she did.

And her heart stopped.

"You *can* see it, can't you?"

Gods breath, but she *could*.

Ashilde stared. In the distance, still a day's walk away, she could see it: light. It was only a sliver, as far as she could tell. It was so bright against the unwavering darkness that she couldn't make out anything other than the fact that there was a white brightness, tinged with yellow, finally breaking through.

"Do you think it's—"

"It is," Anóra said excitedly. "I can see it. It's the edge of the Flatrí."

Ashilde forced herself to remain still, instead of standing up and rushing toward it.

She could hear Anóra's confusion in her voice; hear her sudden disappointment as Ashilde didn't move. "You ... aren't excited? Ashilde, we found a way out!"

"Words aren't enough," she said, offering her a genuine smile, before delivering the blunt truth. "But we can't go rushing out, no matter how much I want to. I still can't see directly in front of me and breaking an ankle running to open ground won't help us." Not to mention she still needed to figure out what to do about Funakiin's leg. But first, she asked, "How are you feeling?"

"Much better. I'm ... I'm sorry about yesterday. I—"

"There's nothing to apologize for," Ashilde said and she meant it. The fact that Anóra still spoke to her after she'd made the girl relive her worst memory and nightmare meant more to her than she'd expected. Gods, Ashilde was beginning to believe that *she* meant more to her than she wanted to admit. Her dream shoved its way back to the surface of her mind, sharp and fierce.

Like a replacement for Brynhild?

Just as quickly as her heart soared at the prospect of escaping the Flatrí, it plummeted to the bottom of her stomach, carrying darker thoughts than the Flatrí could ever be.

"Ashilde ... are you okay?"

"Yes," she said, much too quickly, refusing to unleash her inner turmoil out on Anóra. She let out a breath. "Yes. Can you guide us out of here?"

"Absolutely," Anóra said. "Hold out your hands."

As she did, Anóra placed the blanket into her hands, one edge missing, instead wrapped as a makeshift bandage around Funakiin's leg.

Ashilde took her pack and slipped the blanket back inside. With Anóra's help, handing her each weapon, Ashilde re-equipped herself. "Is Ieka nearby?"

"She's up above us."

Ashilde was about to ask the raven how she felt about doing some scouting on their behalf, before she remembered that, even if Ieka found anything worth noting, she wouldn't be able to communicate back. It wasn't worth the risk of losing her, within the final stretch of the Flatrí—though Ashilde would have given much to have *any* sort of information about their next destination. As excited as she was to leave this wretched place, she had no idea what layed beyond it, except for the name her ancestors had given, after the Banishing.

The Hafleden.

The god's remains.

A blank spot on her map, as no one living had ever traveled there.

Kneeling down, she reached out until she found Funakiin's head. Accidentally poking his nose, she quickly lifted her hand up to the top of his head, scratching behind his ears before he could snap at her.

"Think you'll be able to walk?"

Standing, she took a step back, giving Funakiin some room. She couldn't help staring out at the light, even though it hurt her eyes, as she waited for the wolf to stand and test out their handiwork.

Funakiin whimpered.

"I ... I don't think he can stand on it. Not yet," Anóra said.

She feared as much. The splint they'd made should help, but she was no healer. She wasn't sure if it truly enabled him to walk or would only help the bones heal correctly; if it would even help at all.

Ashilde knew what she *should* do. She should leave Funakiin behind. They'd make better time and, if something tried to attack them, she wouldn't have to worry about protecting a wounded wolf or watching as he was killed, unable to defend himself.

She turned and faced the opening. "Do we have everything, Anóra?"

"What? Ashilde, what about—"

"Do we have everything?"

"Y-yes."

Slipping her spear out of her sling and onto the ground, she squatted down, putting her hand on Funakiin's side. "You're not going to like this," she said. "But I don't see another option."

And neither am I, going against my better judgment.

Ashilde couldn't abandon him, even if it was the smarter option. The wolf had saved her life and killed on her behalf, given her warmth when she lacked it and companionship after being rejected. Most of all, he'd given her hope.

After that, she couldn't leave him.

No matter what.

Tucking her arms underneath the wolf, she picked him up and lifted him up over her shoulders, almost falling forward flat on her face as she did so. She wasn't used to lifting that much weight and putting it over her head. Yet she caught herself as she stumbled before settling in a crouched position, then lifting herself up fully and standing, Funakiin's belly pressed into her neck and back. Her arms, meanwhile, were wrapped back behind his shoulders and his hind legs, keeping both sets of paws hanging off her shoulders.

It was a strain, but she could manage.

Years of training and building muscle were the only reason she could lift and carry a wolf this size, but that didn't mean it was easy; it wouldn't come without a cost, the longer she bore the burden.

Funakiin panted, but he didn't growl or bite her.

"You're … you're not going to leave him behind?"

"Not as long as I have strength left. Grab my spear, Anóra. Then, lead on and tell me where to go. I'll follow the sound of your voice."

Suddenly more animated than the girl was a few moments ago—*most likely because she thought you were going to kill or abandon Funakiin,* Ash realized, as an afterthought—Anóra once again began her narration of what she saw around them. Ashilde walked at her slowest pace since they'd entered the Flatrí, without her spear as a safeguard or her hands to catch her if she tripped. With the additional weight slung across her shoulders, she felt she'd fall at any moment, but she pushed forward all the same.

Anóra didn't seem to mind the pace, telling her about the new details she could make out, thanks to the additional sunlight slipping through in the distance, the sound of the spear dragging against the roots and rocks accompanying her narration. It was still too far away for Ashilde to make out anything more than the beacon of light amidst the darkness, but for Anóra, even the sunlight in the distance now seemed like sunlight directly above her, thanks to her gift.

Anóra described how the trees behind them towered higher than any she'd ever seen, the tops still unreachable by gaze alone, creating that menacing wall they had spent the better part of the day climbing— and apparently a good portion of the night falling from. Looking ahead, the trees scattered once more and were slowly shrinking in size and height, until, just along Flatrí's edge, they returned to familiar size. The river remained on their left and, though she didn't see any fish or frogs, Anóra reported the water to be clear enough to see the bottom, where silver rocks and bronze sand collected. The river itself had grown in size, doubling the length it was when they'd originally found it.

Anóra also told her that "it was deep enough to fit two of her stacked on top of each other under the water," which made Ashilde snort.

What she enjoyed listening about the most, however, was her newfound discovery of the plants.

They varied in bright hues of violet, blue and gold, completely covering the ground in a myriad of colors. She had no idea how plants were able to grow here. The new addition of bright, bold colors had a hard time fitting into the image she'd created inside her head as the child spoke. Before, her imaginations of the Flatrí certainly hadn't been an image with room for any active life—only composed of the dead corpses and remnants of life that *tried* to flourish, but failed. Now, as Anóra continued speaking, Ashilde started to imagine this place in a different way. Was it finally fighting back against Róta's wrath?

Could it win?

Trusting her own feet to not betray her and gaining heart from Ieka's occasional, encouraging cry, Ashilde distracted herself with Anóra's new tale, instead of focusing on the burning sensation of her shoulders or how heavy Funakiin grew with every step, his panting in her ear a new constant. They could take a break once they got outside the Flatrí. They just had to make it there, first.

At least, that's what she told herself.

Step after grueling step.

CHAPTER TWENTY-THREE

It took too long for them to reach the edge, but upon finally stepping out of the cursed forest, Ashilde immediately forgot her irritation as she discovered two things at once. The change from the maze-like jungle to the Hafleden was just as drastic as changing from mapped-out territory to the complete unknown.

The Hafleden was, apparently, Armadin's desert.

Worse, however, were the footprints that traveled out of the Flatrí, walking ahead of them and out into the endless sand ahead.

The trio stood, momentarily stunned, Funakiin's panting quietly in her ear.

Anóra reached up, trying to grab onto her hand that currently held Funakiin in place on her shoulders, which had begun to shake as they paused. "How did those get here?" she whispered.

"I ... I don't know," Ashilde replied as Ieka took off into the skies, most likely just as desperate to stretch her wings as Ashilde had been to see again. "Here's, let's pause a moment here. I need a break."

"Okay."

They moved to sit underneath one of the trees along Flatrí's edge, slipping into the shade that was provided more by the large trunk than the leaves, which swayed and moved against the wind, creating reflections that flickered against the sand. Ashilde was eager to move forward, her mind never forgetting she battled against the passing days.

Yet the appearance of footprints—even as blurred as they were, unable to judge the length of time that had passed since they were printed—made her pause. She wanted a moment to think through what that could possibly mean, while she allowed her body a chance to recover from carrying Funakiin; not to mention that her eyes burned against the sudden brightness, staring out into a terrain she'd never encountered before.

As much as she wanted to continue forward, they needed a plan.

The first thing she needed to deal with was this heat.

While in the Flatrí, she wasn't freezing as she had been in the Segan. But, it'd been cold enough that her muscles groaned against movement and her body shook when she'd slept. She didn't think she'd have that problem within the heat of the Hafleden.

Funakiin already panted hard, laying down halfway still inside the Flatrí, his broken paw stretched out awkwardly in front of him. The sun wasn't high enough in the sky for it to be the height of midday yet, but it certainly was well past the morning. She glanced over at Anóra. "You warm?"

The girl nodded. It was good to be able to see her face again, not nearly as covered in dirt as she would have guessed. Instead, Anóra had thin cuts across her cheek, but otherwise looked unharmed, her runes still painted stubbornly onto her forehead, albeit smeared by sweat and neglect.

"More than I've ever been," she complained.

"Take off your coat, then," Ash said, frowning at the obviousness of it, while wishing she had such a luxury. She wore her armor over a set of tight underclothes and hadn't been expecting to deal with such a drastic change in temperature. She slipped off her gloves, but otherwise, she couldn't leave her armor behind. She'd have to wear it, and bear whatever weather came their way.

But, she could have a little relief, at least for the moment.

Gingerly, she unladed herself from her armor and laid it out onto the sand, leaving her wearing only her second layer: a sleeveless shirt and pants that cut off at her mid-calf. She'd also slipped off her heavy boots and placed them beside her pile, her feet now wrapped only in a thinner linen. She didn't think the wrapping alone would be able to withstand walking across the sand, if it proved to be as hot as the air was. But for now, the shade provided enough protection that she could afford to let her feet breathe for a while.

Anóra dumped her coat beside Ashilde's gloves and armor, rolling up her shirt sleeves. Ash noticed the girl still wore her mother's necklace, the small green beads glinting against the sunlight. Ashilde didn't make a comment on it, however. She was glad the girl had it.

"The gods really *are* mad at you, huh?"

Ashilde stilled. "What do you mean?"

"Your mark. It's broken."

Ashilde glazed down at her chest. Her shirt had been pulled down lower thanks to being compressed under her armor, allowing some of the runes from her Faethegnar ceremony to show. The jagged line that slashed through the runes at Dagfinn's reaction to the Rhuanics attack glared red against her chest.

She forced herself to meet the girl's eyes. "You're right," she admitted. "It's why I intend to have words with them. Very soon."

Anóra shrugged, as if it didn't matter to her either way. Her nonchalance sent a surprising amount of relief through Ashilde, and she wished she could be as accepting of herself as this child seemed to be.

Anóra glanced over at her armor. "I've never seen that before. Is it special? Only for Slá—er, your clan?"

Ashilde shook her head, offering her a small smile, happy to move on, adjusting her shirt so the broken rune was fully covered once more. "No, it's rare, even for my people. It was my mother's and hers before her. It's been passed down by generations, until eventually, it came to me."

Her fingers twitched. "What's it made of?"

"Dragon scales."

"What!" Anóra's mouth dropped open and Ashilde couldn't help but laugh; a strange sound, having become unfamiliar in the past months.

"You can touch it, if you want."

The words were barely out of her mouth before Anóra rushed over to sit beside the armor, her tiny fingers brushing against the scales interwoven with the fabric. Anóra made soft "oo-ing" sounds as she slipped a finger down the smooth metal, before making a fist and knocking it against the armor.

"So dragons *were* real," she whispered.

Ashilde nodded, stretching out her back and wincing slightly against the pain. "Many things were, before the Banishing." *And could be still, if the Flatrí is any indication.*

Anóra didn't respond, instead mesmerized by something so new, now that they didn't have Rhuanics breathing down their necks or the Flatrí to distract her. Ashilde took the moment to glance down at her thin gloves and the small pile of Anóra's outer layers she'd removed, before glancing out into the desert. *Would they even need any of it anymore, in this heat?* She doubted it. They had no idea how long the desert stretched or what the ominous name describing the region of Falos—the god's descent—implied. If it was anything as drastically different as the Flatrí and now Hafleden proved to be from one another—and especially from where she'd grown up within the Segan—she could only assume another change in scenery was coming.

Was it a change they could survive, if they abandoned the layers?

But can you survive the journey carrying them?

Ashilde cursed, glancing back at the footprints she'd begun to ignore, distracting herself with other logistics. *One problem at a time.*

"Do you still have your knife on you?"

Anóra blushed. "Yes," she muttered.

"Would you mind cutting my gloves into strips?" she asked. "I'm going to go over to the river and clean up a bit. I may need them."

"Are you hurt?"

"We're about to find out, aren't we?" She offered the girl a wry grin to mask her nerves, silently fearing to discover a wound she couldn't treat. "Let me get cleaned up. Then, we'll figure out our next steps. Okay?"

Anóra nodded, glancing at the armor longingly, as if she didn't want to stop messing with it. Perhaps she didn't want to, but she listened to Ashilde's request, taking her knife and the gloves, before moving to sit by Funakiin. The giant wolf put his head on Anóra's knee after she sat, while Anóra began talking to him.

Moving her spear, bow and quiver over to lean against a different trunk, Ashilde carried her pack with her and walked the short distance to the river. It was wider than it had been in the Flatrí, based on Anóra's descriptions, but she feared that wouldn't last. She could only hope it continued to run through the desert; give them something to follow, perhaps, on top of being a constant water source.

She paused, staring at the river as it twisted away, into the desert and disappearing beyond the horizon. Aside from the river, there didn't seem to be much else, though she thought she could make out ... hills? They were too far away to make out for certain, and the distance had a shimmering effect she had never seen before. She wiggled her toes against the sand, still not too hot to burn them, and was once again amazed by where she was, that something like this existed within Armadin.

She wondered how her ancestors had lived here, once.

And who had recently traveled out into the vastness—and *how*; not to mention where they were headed and how they planned to survive it.

Ashilde dropped her pack by her legs, kneeling down to unstrap her knives and sheaths, before undoing her wrappings. The water was deep enough for her to wade in, so she rolled her pants up to above her knee and slipped in. As the sun hit her directly on her back, she regretted her choice of wearing her entirely black set as her bottom layer of clothes, which seemed to soak in the heat and keep it there. *Should have worn your tan set.*

So many questions tried to pop into her head, but she shut them all down, keeping her mind as empty as she could. She could marvel about making it this far and worry about the rest of her journey in a moment.

Now, she needed to assess the toll the Flatrí had taken on her.

She took off her shirt, already wincing as she was forced to actually *pull* it off of her torso, coming away sticky and crusted. Ashilde flipped the shirt inside out, dipping it in the water and washing it quickly, before hanging it on a nearby tree limb to dry. She then peeled the makeshift bandage she'd wrapped around her shoulder off, sucking in a breath as she did so, and threw it on the ground.

As she undressed, she purposefully avoided glancing into the water. She could feel how dirty her face was; eager didn't begin to describe how ready she was to clean it. But that didn't mean she needed to see her reflection and the missing pieces that should have been there for the first time.

Ashilde ... wasn't sure if she was ready for that. Not yet.

Instead, she glanced down at her left side, wrapping her arms around her breasts and pulling them up and to the side, so she could get a better view of her torso. Like she'd expected, both the rope and the vine had bitten into her skin, creating a circle of chafed skin that wrapped around her entire upper torso, just underneath the wrap she used to bind her breasts. She couldn't decide which was worse: the chafed skin of her torso or how irritated between her thighs were, rubbed raw from so much constant movement over the past few weeks, the skin feeling wrinkled and sensitive to the touch as her fingers trailed there. Yet her torso might have won out, once she noticed, mixed into the irritated skin, were various bruises where the rope had rubbed too much or bit too tightly, suffocating her even through her armor. In a few places, it cut deep enough to draw thin lines of blood, already dried over. An irritating injury, but not a debilitating one.

Letting go of her chest, she moved on to look over her shoulder. It was stained with dried blood, with flakes of dead and dried skin sprinkled throughout, adding new freckles to her already spotted shoulder. Yet the cut itself had completely scabbed over. She touched it gingerly and was confident that, after cleaning it and bandaging it once more, it would heal completely. A rare lucky break.

At what cost, later?

Ashilde shook her head and continued to distract herself, taking her time with her own personal inventory.

Next, she checked both her hands, which she'd torn up when Anóra and Funakiin fell. They were slightly bloodied, after trying to catch herself, but she could still make a fist and extend all of her fingers without much effort—though, she did find a splinter stuck in the side of her left palm that she hadn't noticed before. Ashilde picked it out and threw it in the water absentmindedly, even more thankful that both hands were whole and intact.

Perhaps, as long as she didn't kill again, she wouldn't find out what it would be like if one of them disappeared permanently.

Kneeling in the water, she proceeded to clean each wound, accompanying each area with a series of inhales and winces that made the process slow, creating a small pool of red grime to be washed away down the river beneath her. A part of her, deep in the back of her mind, tried to point out that she bathed and bleed in the only source of water she could use to quench her thirst. Ashilde almost laughed at the thought. A few weeks ago, she might have had such luxury to be picky.

But that, like so much else, was something stuck in the past.

She cleaned her face and hair last, keeping her eyes closed throughout the entire process. Once her face felt significantly rubbed raw, she swallowed her fear and opened her eyes, staring down at her reflection. Clean, even despite the cut through her chapped lips and her swollen eyes making her look a little worse than usual. But she hardly noticed either, instead seeing how well of a job she'd done blind in the Flatrí, wiping the markings of the Slátra clean off. The skin around her eyes was a stark white, absent of the red paint usually painted over them; her face empty, her throat bare. Nothing to link her back to the Slátra, the clan she used to call her people.

Even standing knee-deep in the water, she felt her

palms become sweaty as her shoulders shook. For a moment, she struggled to inhale as her vision blurred, her clean face and the broken rune on her chest filling her mind.

No longer Faethegnar.

No longer Slátra.

Simply Ashilde.

Her heart constricted, agreeing with her mind.

It wasn't enough.

Ashilde stumbled out of the water, unsteady as her emotions tried to take hold. Shaking her thoughts away, droplets of water from her hair that felt like blessed rain after a long drought fell on her shoulders. She wiped her hands dry on her pants and picked up her shirt, surprised to find it already dry. She didn't put it on yet, walking back over to Anóra, who was still talking away to the wolf, a line of newly made bandages lying neatly beside her.

Ashilde rung her hair out on Funakiin's head, earning a growl that turned into almost a purr. She could only imagine how hot the wolf was. Perhaps she'd offer to take him down to the river, before they set off.

Upon noticing her return, Anóra asked, "Feel better?" without looking up, grinning as she turned to her and said, "You smell—"

Her smile faltered as the girl looked upon her, her eyes scanning over to her shoulder and hands, narrowing in onto the wounds around her chest, before her eyes widened at old scars crisscrossing down her back, as Ashilde bent down to retrieve the strips.

"Ashilde..."

"I'm happy to be out of Flatrí. I feel like a new woman," she said, wincing as her mind whispered, *but you are.* "Those strips will be very useful. Thank you."

The girl nodded, as if suddenly unsure how to act around her, upon seeing a warrior's cost—both from this journey and her past.

Ashilde offered her a hand, pulling the girl up with ease. "Your turn."

Immediately, her mood switched as Anóra pouted, the shock at her injuries forgotten by her demand. "Do I have to? I'm not nearly as dirty as you were."

"Wash up," Ashilde said. "Your face, at least. Your paint is smeared."

Anóra's eyes widened in a panic. "What? I didn't know! I haven't—"

"You're not in trouble, Anóra," she said, cheeks flushing at having no paint at all on her face, yet being bold enough to mention a smudge on her companion's. She focused on pinning her hair back up behind her head instead. "But you should clean it up, especially since we're on our way to meet the gods. That way, at least *one* of us won't earn their ire."

She looked down at her feet, suddenly ashamed. "I ... I can't."

"Why not?"

"I ... I didn't think to bring my paints with me. I ... um, well, I wasn't supposed to follow the hunt, since I haven't had my Wyrdan Day."

Ashilde glanced over at her. "It's okay," she said quietly. "You can use mine."

"Will you help me?" Anóra asked, a little too quickly. "I'm ... still not great at making the circles look good."

Ashilde almost rejected the request outright. Not only was the girl from another clan, but helping someone paint their face was a very private matter. Only the ones closest to you should do that—almost always a parent to a child or siblings together. She wasn't Anóra's mother, nor her older sister. And she didn't want to be either, no matter if her dreams were trying to tell her. Yet who else did the girl have to turn to?

"It's okay," Anóra said. "I didn't—"

"No, no, Anóra," Ashilde responded, reaching out and wrapping her hand around hers. "I'd love to help you. But I'm not touching your face if there is any dirt left on it."

Anóra smiled at her then, bashful, before heading toward the river.

"And stay where I can see you!" Ashilde called after her as she settled down beside Funakiin. The wolf looked up at her, giving her a look that almost looked smug; as if the wolf could have told her he knew she'd start caring for Anóra, after she'd spent enough time with the child.

"Don't give me that," she muttered.

Within her, her emotions warred in a battle of intensity—on one side, the growing attachment and love she felt for Anóra blossoming naturally; on the other, her guilt at her hand of the child's birth mother's death. Ashilde wasn't surprised she was good with the girl. She'd often watched Freydis's children, helping raise them as all in the clan did. But, watching Anóra in the river—splashing water into her face and laughing, enjoying herself in a rare moment of reprieve—Ashilde felt new emotions grow into the tangle of knots inside her heart.

She hadn't thought about, if they survived, what would happen to Anóra. Thinking upon it now, she assumed the girl would return to the Dreyma, to live with her grandmother and her clan, where she belonged. Ash was surprised when her heart hurt at the thought.

As if you could ask her to return home with you.

Ashilde stilled. Did she even want her to? How could she, even the idea of raising her throughout the rest of her life—as a mother or a sister, it didn't matter; the age difference would make both roles feel the same. Her legs twitched, as if eager to run from the thought.

Yet the idea of not seeing Anóra grow up—of not

knowing the type of woman she'd become, of her fate as a *sangrild* or a *sangrendi* unfolded, of who she chose to love—filled her with a sadness she wasn't sure how to place; especially knowing that her return from this journey would not be to a world where a visit to the Dreyma to visit Anóra would be welcomed. In fact, her theft of the Seidsian's grandchild would likely renew the war.

Let's not forget she still doesn't know what you did to her mother; to her unspoken sibling, one she refuses to acknowledge, even now. And even if she did, she's the daughter of a different clan. Would the Slátra even accept her?

Will they even accept you?

Ashilde's heart hammered and she dropped a few of the makeshift bandages back on the ground, fumbling them. "One thing at a time, Ashilde," she whispered. "One thing at a time."

Funakiin leaned over and licked her hand, as if he could sense where her thoughts had gone, too.

Pit, perhaps he had.

While Anóra finished bathing, Ashilde wrapped up her final preparations: bangaging her wounds, before going through her pack and taking inventory of their remaining stock. They were out of food—a fact she'd forgotten.

There's some plants by the river.

She needed to take a closer look at them. Perhaps they might provide something to put in their bellies, at least. She could have Ieka help identify which were safe, after she returned.

Even if the plants proved edible, she worried they wouldn't be enough. A quick glance at her surroundings didn't strengthen her hopes, either. Everything ahead of them looked the same: hot, dry and full of nothing.

"Pit," she muttered as she pulled her paints out. "You didn't see any animals in the Flatrí, did you, that we could hunt?"

Funakiin shook his head.

"Pit."

With no food source behind and potentially no food source ahead, this was going to be a problem.

Her stomach rumbled, punctuating the issue.

Anóra returned, fully clothed but with a clean face and her hair a soaking mess, water dripping down past her ears. Ashilde plastered on a smile, not wanting to burden her with too many problems. Not yet. "Feel better, don't you?"

"Nooo," Anóra said, but she grinned.

"Alright, wipe your face dry with your shirt or we'll be here all afternoon," she said. "Then sit in front of me."

The girl did as she was bid, sitting on her knees and resting her hands on top of them. "Have you ever painted someone else before?"

Ashilde nodded, thinking of a time when she'd helped Brynhild; memories she'd all forgotten. "A long time ago. But I think I can still manage."

Anóra didn't pry and Ashilde was grateful, as she pulled out black and white paint she usually used to accentuate the red she used to paint her own.

"I don't have your clan's colors, but I can use these. In this instance, I think the gods will be forgiving."

The girl nodded, satisfied.

Ashilde licked the tip of her brush, the bristles having hardened after so long without use. She dipped it into the white paint, planning to paint the lines between Anóra's eyes and the circles above in white, while doing a thin black border around each one, to help them stand out against her pale white face. "Now hold still and try not to fidget too much."

Anóra stilled, and Ashilde gently cupped one side of her face. The girl closed her eyes, but Ashilde's hand was steady, despite her nerves slipping through her body like they hadn't since she showed up for her first day of training. This felt too personal, too intimate, pulling memories of her time with Brynhild back that hurt too much to remember.

To distract herself, she asked, "Do you know anything about the Hafleden? Did your Seidsian tell you any stories you can remember?"

"Almost nothing," she admitted. "Only about the Banishing. We can't make Róta mad or she'll ... we can't make her mad."

Anóra began to move her head and Ashilde gripped her chin to still her, giving her a look. The girl smiled sheepishly, peeking her eyes open before rushing to close them once more, while Ashilde's thoughts returned to the footsteps that had stunned them both; footsteps that, according to their histories, shouldn't exist.

"What did your Seidsian tell you?" Anóra asked, curious.

"Not much more than your grandmother has, I believe," Ashilde guessed. "Flatrí, Hafleden, Falos; they were once all places where our ancestors lived, many generations ago. The Skalda killed ravens, thinking it would impress the Wolffather and show their devotion to him and *only* him. Róta, in a rare fit of jealous rage, wiped out not only the Skalda, but made these lands completely inhabitable, forcing the rest of the clans to live crowded together in the region we now call the Segan—the god's blessing—leaving us with the new decree to worship them both as equals as our only defense against another disaster."

Ashilde felt Anóra shiver under her palm and she paused before she began tracing one of the circles with careful, steady strokes. She couldn't blame her fear. It was a part of their shared history that scared all the clans—or should have, though her earlier journey through the Segan showed her not all of the clans had taken the new decree to heart; nor had they been punished for it. *Just another question to pose to the gods.*

"Then ... why were there footprints? I thought no one lived out here."

Smart girl.

Ashilde paused to look at her and Anóra, sensing the change, opened her eyes. "I thought so, too. And yet, you saw no signs of anything living within the Flatrí?"

"Nope," Anóra confirmed.

Sighing, Ashilde said, "I don't mean to alarm you, Anóra, but we may need to move both cautiously and quickly through this desert. My gut tells me the Rhuanics suddenly showing up to attack my clan—and yours—while also finding proof of people living within places we once thought impossible, to not be a coincidence."

"But ... how? It doesn't make sense. I thought you became a Rhuanic by being cast out of your clan?"

Ashilde's mouth felt dry as she responded, "Yes, that's true."

"We've never cast out anybody," Anóra said. "How many Rhuanics have you seen?"

Mentally calculating, Ashilde paused to confirm in her head, before she replied. "Eleven, I think, in the past two months."

"Wow. That's a lot of people who upset the gods. I wonder what clan they came from."

Ashilde frowned. *I wonder, indeed.*

Touching her chin, Ashilde tilted Anóra's head up just a tad as she finished outlining. She breathed out a heavy sigh. "I'm not sure what to think, Anóra. We'll just ... need to be careful, on our way to Skírrdrauin."

"With you to protect us, I know we can conquer anything!" Anóra said with a confidence that Ashilde didn't feel, the ghosts of those she'd failed to protect so far haunting her, filling up her mind like relentless dark clouds.

"I ... ah, can I ask a question?"

"Of course you can," Ashilde said, grateful for the distraction, before her mind overtook her once more.

"I thought Skírrdrauin was in the clouds, somewhere. It's where we all go when we die. Where ... my mother and sibling are. And ... my father." The girl was quiet for a moment, before she asked, "Are we even *allowed* to go to Skírrdrauin? We're not dead."

Ashilde paused, brushing off some specks of sand from the girl's face. The girl had a point; one she hadn't thought she'd live long enough to truly need to consider. "I'm not sure, to be honest."

"Oh." Anóra paused, lost in thought. "If we make it ... er, *once* we make it, can we stop to see my family? Or at least my mother?"

Ashilde froze. She hadn't even considered who she might see, once they reached Skírrdrauin. She'd been too focused on staying determined to *make* it there. Being confronted by the dead of her past... She reached down and took the girl's hand. "I promise we will."

"Okay. I'd like that."

"Me too," Ashilde lied, nowhere near ready to confront the ghosts of her ancestors, on top of confronting her gods. Instead, she followed the other trail of thoughts Anóra's questions inspired, this one lined with curiosity, instead of guilt. "Anóra. You ... haven't had any visions since we've met, have you?"

The girl shook her head. "Not one. My head has been quiet. Well, unless I'm thinking. And I do that a lot. Think, that is."

Oh, you precious thing. "I know you do," she said. "Is that ... normal, for you? To not experience them?"

"Nope," Anóra said matter-of-factly. "But I'm not worried about it."

"You're not?"

"Nope," she said again, shaking her head while wearing a grin. "I'm doing exactly what my father said to do, in my dreams: help you! Why would he need to tell me anything else? Are you done yet?" Ashilde nodded as the girl took the brushes out of her hand. "Want me to go wash these for you?"

"That'd be helpful, Anóra. Thank you."

Before she left, Anóra looked down at the ground, blushing as she asked, "Will you help me practice? My painting, I mean."

"Of course, child," Ashilde said, her stomach shifting to see the happiness in Anóra's eyes.

Ashilde watched her run off back toward the river, before glancing out into the desert. A girl who had a terrible "accident" that might have caused visions of their journey, yet the visions stopped as soon as the journey started? Ash felt like she was missing something, something *important*. But, she'd never met anyone who'd experienced something like that before, so she had no idea what it meant, if anything.

Add the question to the list for your gods. You need to get moving, she told herself.

You need to push harder, her mind replied, ever relentless. *You let your growing love for the girl and the wolf's injuries distract you.*

Ashilde reached over and scruffed behind Funakiin's ears, causing the wolf to grin in his sleep. Her body already ached and the idea that she'd have to carry him through the uncertain footing across the sand made her shoulders sag. Could she really afford to carry him?

You must. You will not abandon him now; none of them. And you will make it, no matter what.

Her eyes returned to the horizon and, surprisingly, she thought of Davyn. Her entire body ached with longing as she moved to put on her armor, preparing to take even more steps further away from the very person who's mere essence propelled her forward.

You must make it.

***

"I'm hungry," Anóra complained. "Are you *truly* sure we don't have any food? Like, *truly*, truly?"

Ashilde almost stopped walking to turn and address Anóra's latest complaint, but she couldn't afford to. The weight of Funakiin was stark against her back. If she stopped moving, she knew she'd put him down. And he'd just finished his turn of walking unaided by her, limping all the way. She couldn't shortchange her turn just because Anóra had taken it upon herself to restart her complaining.

Yet another aspect to make this new leg of the journey miserable, she dared to think, blinking sweat out of her eyes.

They'd been walking long enough that the sun was high in the sky, only just now beginning its slow descent back toward the horizon. By the time they had begun their journey into the desert, the footprints they saw had vanished completely, wiped away by the soft, yet occasionally harsh, winds. Since they saw no other signs of life—no camps, no fires, no noises or traces of any existence other than their small party—Ashilde almost convinced herself she made up the existence of footprints in the first place. Even still, she stubbornly scanned the horizon for any clues, her search becoming less and less diligent the longer she found nothing.

At first, it hadn't felt too bad. Anóra had been in high spirits, and Ashilde had helped distract her mind by asking her questions, which she'd answered eagerly, telling her more about her adventures with Taya—a girl that, based on Anóra's stories, Ashilde couldn't help but hope became her partner, one day. The pair wouldn't keep one another out of trouble, that much was clear, but they clearly made one another happy.

The world could use some more of that.

But now, with their bodies coated in sweat and the Flatrí a glistening memory behind them on the opposite end of the horizon, the conversation had dropped from the upbeat trading of tales. Ashilde's replies had become shorter and shorter before Anóra finally stopped telling her stories altogether, instead speaking what was on her mind.

Her complaints.

"I'm hot."

"I'm tired."

"My feet hurt."

"Are we *there* yet?"

Ashilde had answered, at first, by trying to assuage the girl's complaints, letting her know not only did she understand, but she shared many of her ailments. But with every repetition of a complaint she'd already addressed, eventually, she'd had enough, turning to snap at her without thinking. Anóra had dropped into silence after that, and Ashilde had been too tired to feel guilt.

Until now.

She glanced over at the girl, who must have been starving something fierce to risk inciting her sharp tongue again by starting to complain once more. Ash wished, not for the first time, she could confidently identify the plants that grew sparingly along the river's edge. Yet they were unfamiliar to her, thin and brittle to the touch, leaving a sticky residue against her fingers. Without Ieka to confirm—the bird still hadn't returned—she didn't think their hunger levels were desperate enough to risk being poisoned, especially when Funakiin had offered her no answer when she'd ask if the plant was safe.

At least, she told herself that, but the rumbling of her stomach suggested otherwise.

She finally shook her head, Funakiin's fur tickling

the back of her neck as she did so. "I don't," she said. "Trust me, I wish I did."

Anóra looked toward the ground, her small shoulders slumping.

"I'm sorry, Anóra," she said. "I know this isn't easy. If we keep pushing, we should reach those hills by nightfall. Once we do that, I promise I'll let you and Funakiin rest while I go hunting, okay?"

"But what can you possibly find out here?" she whined.

Ashilde looked away, if only to keep herself from snapping at the youth once more. She didn't ask for this. *And she's only here because of you.* "I'm not sure," Ashilde said, pausing for a second to catch her breath. "Do you trust me?"

Anóra looked surprised by her question. "Of course I do!"

"Are you still with me? Until we reach Skírrdrauin?"

"Yesss," Anóra said, though she drew out the word, her brows knitted together as she warily agreed, trying to sense a trap.

"Then help me reach those hills," Ashilde said, gesturing by pointing her chin downward out in front of them. "Every step we take is one step closer."

Anóra didn't seem to like her answer very much. But, she did roll her shoulders forward before stepping with more purpose, forcing Ashilde to do the same. She couldn't help but feel a certain sense of pride, at how much she pushed herself, no matter what Ashilde asked of her.

Ravenmother and Wolffather, if you're watching and waiting for me to arrive, you could offer a little help, she prayed. *For her sake. Please.*

As always, the gods didn't answer her. But Funakiin did take that moment to lick her hand that held onto one of his unbroken paws as they walked, which she was desperate enough to take as a promising sign.

***

Her feet had blistered and Anóra had cried twice before they reached what she'd called the hills, but upon reaching them, she felt the name wasn't enough to do the spectacle justice. Up until that point, the land around them had been flat and seemingly endless, while the river continued to slim down more and more—though never disappearing entirely, the only spot of luck they'd had so far. Now, they paused to stare at the landscape before them and her stomach dropped in a mixture of dread and wonder.

They stood upon the edge of flat land, before it stooped and dropped into the bottom curve of a hill. Just ahead of them, the sand rose, following the curve of the hill as it climbed up to its peak, level to where they stood now, before dipping again, disappearing back down the other side, beyond what she could see. But what she *could* see were hills stretching for leagues upon leagues, the river twisting and turning throughout them.

Scattered through the hills were the remains of a destroyed village.

"Wow," Anóra whispered. "Have you ever seen anything like that?"

"No, I haven't," Ashilde said. "Have you?"

"Nope."

"I think … I think we've found the remnants of the Skalda."

A few moments passed before she reached up and took Ashilde's hand. "No one at home is going to believe me."

"You have an incredible story to tell Taya, that's for certain." Ashilde squeezed her hand gently, thankful that the sun had almost disappeared from the horizon. "Let's at least go to the bottom there. I want to get a closer look. Then, I promise, I'll go hunting and find us some food."

Carefully, Funakiin following behind a little more slowly, they made their way down the first slope. Ashilde asked Anóra to refill their waterskin by the river as she approached the structure, moving warily, as if the ghosts of the wiped-out clan still haunted the ruins.

At the bottom of the hill was a collection of broken wood, with larger pieces, still intact, sticking out of the ground and into the air. Ashilde reached out and touched one of the intact pieces, still sturdy and strong, appearing to be made from ash trees, like the ones her people used back home. Yet, the scattered pieces of the wood on the ground were in less of a whole state, scattered holes of rot breaking the pieces apart.

There was too little left to confirm what this structure once was, but the chance that this *could* be part of the Skalda ruins—that the clan none alive had ever known currently lay buried beneath their feet— brought tears to her eyes while her throat constricted in fear. *This* was what was left, as a result of Róta's wrath? *This* was the power of the god she was on her way to challenge?

Ashilde shook her head. *What have you gotten yourself into, Ash?*

A small tug on her hand brought her attention back, as she looked down to find Anóra beside her, waterskin in hand. The girl offered it and Ashilde gladly took it, as the girl's wide-eyed wonder took away her darker musings, for a moment.

"What's that?" the child asked.

Ashilde shrugged. "It's hard to say for certain, with so little left. But, I'd guess it's—"

"No, not this," Anóra said, gesturing to the ruins around them. "That!"

Turning swiftly, Ashilde saw immediately what had caught the girl's attention: a spec up high in the sky, slowly coming toward them. Her heart sped up as she tightened her grip on her bow, though her mind had a guess that this was no threat to them. She watched and waited as the spec slowly grew bigger and bigger, before finally becoming something recognizable.

"It's Ieka," Anóra said, pulling on her arm and pointing.

"So it is," she said without looking away from the bird. She grinned as she noticed something was clutched in her claws. "And I don't think she's alone."

Ieka finally came down into a dive, flying directly over them before she dropped two dead rabbits onto the ground behind them. Ashilde held up one arm for the bird to land on as Anóra actually squealed her delight, running over to where their food had been dropped. Ashilde waited for the bird to land, nuzzling her face with one finger.

"So that's where you've been all day, little huntress," she whispered to the bird, who cawed softly in greeting. Not for the first time, Ashilde was grateful she'd asked for their help, when she'd found them; or they had found her, she wasn't sure which. Either way, she remained grateful, letting the bird know as much as she caressed her feathers gently.

Anóra spoke from behind her. "Huh," she muttered. "I didn't know birds knew how to cook."

"What?" Ashilde asked, chuckling. "Anóra, what are you—"

As she turned, she cut herself off.

Sitting on the ground beside her feet were two whole rabbits, already cleaned of skin and gutted, their outsides charred like they had spent hours hanging off a spit. Her earlier elation vanished in an instant.

"They don't," she whispered, as Anóra ripped off a leg and began chewing on it.

"It's cold, but it's good. It's *so* good. This is the best thing I've ever eaten!" Anóra reported, shaking her rabbit leg up at the sky in triumph. "Wait, did you say something?"

"Birds don't know how to cook."

"Ieka does, *obviously*," Anóra said confidently, missing her point and the connection that Ashilde immediately drew upon, in her mind.

They were not alone.

CHAPTER TWENTY-FOUR

It took six days for them to find another sign of life.

Prior, they found nothing but sand, hills and more hills between the moment they woke up and the moment they collapsed to sleep, only occasionally stumbling upon the scattered remains and ruins of a time when the land wasn't swallowed by sand. They never found anything whole enough to shelter against the elements. They stuck close to the river, unwilling to lose the water source, but always on alert for signs of the others who somehow inhabited this desert, especially as Ieka was able to deliver them one meager, stolen meal each day.

Wiping sweat off her brow, Ashilde glanced over at her companions. Anóra looked miserable, with her slumped shoulders, burnt arms and trudging walk, as if her feet were too heavy to continue lifting fully off the ground. She walked beside Funakiin through the river, if only to attempt to create some relief for them amidst the heat. Ashilde didn't have the heart to complain to them about dirtying up their drinking water. They hadn't spoken in three days, for what was there to talk about? At this point, she was content that Funakiin could walk for longer spurts without needing her to carry him, limping or not, and she allowed the child her silence, as it allowed her to continue to look for signs of life, while also trying to keep up the will to continue forward.

They followed another rise, tracking the water as it climbed. Her calves began burning halfway up, but she grunted against the effort and forced herself to keep climbing, reaching the top of the hill a few seconds ahead of her companions.

Ashilde paused to catch her breath, before looking out ahead of her, only to discover something worthy of taking her breath away.

"Please tell me my eyes are playing tricks on me."

Anóra shook her head. "Those are definitely footprints."

Ashilde followed them with her eyes. Just across the river, leading away from them and across a different hill, in the opposite direction. Judging by what she could see, whomever the prints had belonged to had walked up to the river, gotten a drink—for how long or how long ago, it was impossible to know—and then left again, leaving prints behind that definitely appeared to be human, before retreating back the way they came, disappearing over a different hill's edge.

"Who could be out here?"

Ashilde sighed. "A part of me really wants to follow those," she muttered, talking to herself.

"You are considering *not* following? Ashilde, those could be the Rhuanics!"

"You're right, Anóra, they could be. But, to discover who made those tracks, we'd have to leave the river, trusting ourselves to know how to find it once again." She glanced down at her companion. "I'm not sure that's a risk I want to take."

Anóra bit her lip, considering. "But if we don't search for them … what if they find us?"

It was a fair point. It was also the one that made her stomach drop when she considered it.

"*That's* the only reason I'm considering searching for them in the first place. Despite the risk." She took a long drink out of her waterskin, before handing it to Anóra. "What do you think?"

"You're asking *me*?"

She hummed her agreement.

"Mother told me my curiosity would get me killed, one day."

"So you want to follow the tracks, then, and see where they lead?"

She nodded, sheepishly.

"Funakiin, could you handle walking that much? Even if we track down this mysterious outsider, we'll have to eventually double back and reconnect with the river." To do anything else, regardless of what she decided to do next, was not an option. The river was too important a resource to lose. "If we run into trouble, I may not be able to carry you back out."

For the first time since coming into the desert, Funakiin had walked on his own power the entire day— still hobbling and obviously in a ton of pain, but each time Ashilde had offered to carry him, he'd growled his disapproval, picking up his pace to prove he had no desire for her to continue helping him anymore. Whether he still needed it or not was another issue altogether, but the wolf was smart. Certainly smart enough to make his own decision, regarding his own injury.

"If you can't," Ashilde said, "then we'll press on. I'm not leaving you behind—and it might not be such a bad thing, if we didn't falter." She glanced over at the horizon, wondering if they'd ever make it there. Who knew how far off Skírrdrauin still was, let alone if they could even reach the realm of the gods, as living mortals. Was it truly worth investigating the strange footsteps, with what they risked losing and the time they'd waste to do so?

Funakiin met her eyes before looking over at the footprints. Ieka, for what it was worth, had already taken off in that direction, never staying with them long enough for them to truly include her in any of their discussions, unless it was to settle in for the evening.

"So we go?" Anóra asked.

Ashilde hesitated. She was running out of time.

Anóra tugged on her arm.

"Yes?" she asked her.

"Perhaps, if we find them, we might be able to steal more than just one rabbit."

Ashilde stared at the youth with a new appreciation in her eyes. Her stomach rumbled and Anóra's own echoed hers even louder, making her guilt clench up within her.

"Alright," she said. "Today only. If we don't find them by the time the sun goes down, we return and find the river, not resting until we do. Agreed?"

Anóra nodded and Funakiin barked once.

Taking a deep breath, Ashilde crossed the river and began following the footprints.

***

They found their target much quicker than Ashilde expected.

Upon reaching the top of one of the larger hills they'd encountered—the incline difficult to overcome, causing her calves to burn as she pushed past tired legs and slippery sand—Ashilde immediately dropped onto the ground, commanding Anóra and Funakiin to do so, as well.

Below them, nestled in a pit created by the downward slope of many tall hills, was an entire hidden village.

An *occupied* village.

She wasn't sure which was harder to believe: that anyone was living out in the middle of this massive desert or that anyone could live in a village of that condition. It was a ruin, but the most complete structure she'd found so far to survive the Banishing. The buildings—massive in size, yet still easily hidden among the tall sand dunes—were in various states of destruction, not a single one completely standing, fully intact. Most were hollowed shells of what they must have once been, this time made of stone and brick—a surprising find, when her people usually used wood structures. Piles of rubble stacked near the buildings' skeletons, and even more jagged corners stuck out from beneath the sand. Yet in the center of the ruins, there were people—both men and women. As her eyes darted and scanned, Ashilde noticed something immediately that made her blood run cold.

None of them had markings on their faces.

They had found not only a *group* of Rhuanics, but their home.

Anóra nestled close beside her, pressing her head close to her ear. "What are they doing out here?"

The impossible. "Living."

As she spoke, she saw signs that they hadn't just set up camp recently. Tapestries were hung on walls still high enough to hold them. A fire pit sat in the center of a building that had no roof on it, currently unlit, but the stones beneath it were stained dark from use. Weapons—spears, knives, bows, swords and axes—littered every corner, while baskets filled with supplies balanced on cracked window ledges. Throughout their entire camp—though the label felt too meager a term to truly describe what they lived in, yet 'village' felt too familiar, too *established*—people worked, the sounds of their laughter and discussion too faint from above for

Ashilde to make out. But the more she watched, the more individuals she discovered.

Dozens of them.

But she also couldn't help but notice another element, helping reaffirm her growing belief they had been here for quite some time. There were also multiple carvings erected and placed between the ruins of buildings; perhaps even made out of pieces from the ruins themselves, signifying their worship.

Carvings of wolves.

But none, she noticed, of ravens.

Could they truly be worshippers of Waldemar, like those I've slain have claimed? How could our god allow such an act, allow them to exist, after what they've done? How could Róta not smite them down?

"How is this possible?" Anóra asked.

"I can't know for certain. I've never heard of a group of Rhuanics like this before," Ashilde said, spitting on the ground, thinking back to her various encounters she'd had so far with them, the memories tasting foul. The fact that there were enough of them to create their own clan made her insides twist and even more questions blossom inside her head.

And here they were, all gathered together in one spot.

She wanted to kill them all.

Anóra's voice dropped. "Is this the group who killed my mother?"

Ashilde didn't look at her. "Most likely, though we can't know for certain."

"But why? Why would they do that?" She joined Ash in staring down below, watching a pair of men wrap thread around arrowheads as they attached them to widdled wood, sitting on large, broken pieces of stone as they worked. Just behind them, a woman and a man fought one another, the woman taking him down with ease, her axe placed dangerously close to his exposed neck after he hit the ground, before she extended a hand and helped him up. Then, they began again, the man attacking first, this time.

"Their souls will never reach Skírrdrauin. Are they stupid? Don't they know that? That they will be cursed to live in the Pit forever?" Anóra went silent for a moment, before she continued her whispered train of thought, rambling now. "*How* can those men kill and still survive? Without their *dolorsandri*, they cannot purge the souls they steal. But they fight! I'm watching them fight, right now!"

"I don't know what makes them do what they do," Ashilde said, her mind reliving the memory of the Rhuanics attacking her village, killing her hunters; killing Hildrid right in front of her eyes. It surprised her to find women among them, especially when she'd only encountered men, so far; surprised her and broke her heart. What woman could condone these actions, let alone *partake* in them?

"So, what are we going to do?"

"What?"

"We can't just leave them here. We have to ... to do something!"

"Anóra, there are dozens of them and only four of us—and one of us isn't exactly healthy enough to fight."

Funakiin whimpered softly, but didn't try to argue her point. The wolf shook. This was the most he had walked on his own and their pace certainly hadn't been kind or slow. She couldn't count on him in a fight, even though she considered him the most dangerous of them, after her. She was being generous, including Ieka or Anóra into her total number at all. Funakiin could do some damage, fully healthy. She'd seen it. Ieka had her tactics, as well, and could do well in a small fight, as they had before.

But Anóra?

Even if she was older and stronger, asking her to fight before knowing if the gods would let her experience a Wyrdan Day or not would be asking her to become the very thing they were trying to destroy.

It was too high a price to pay.

"I'm a good warrior, Anóra," she said. "A good warrior knows when she's beaten."

"But you're not even going to try?" Tears brimmed on her eyes, stubbornly refusing to fall past her eyelashes.

"Anóra—"

"They killed my *mother*. My ... my baby sibling!"

She closed her eyes for a moment, before putting her hand on Anóra's shoulder. "I know. But they are not our problem. They cannot be. Not yet. We—"

The girl shoved at her. "You have to do something. You *have* to. We can't just leave!"

Ashilde's eyes narrowed. "We *must* leave, Anóra. We can't—"

"You're being selfish!" she yelled, her voice becoming dangerously loud, though the distance should have been far enough away that no one would hear them. Yet. "You promised! Don't you listen? They *killed* her. They killed my family! They—"

Finally, Ashilde snapped, her patience broken. "They didn't kill your mother, Anóra! I did!"

The girl recoiled away from her worse than if a physical blow had landed on her.

Ashilde's heart broke, her confession slipping out unintended thanks to exhaustion, frustration or just pure idiocy, she couldn't pinpoint which. But now the girl knew the truth—with much less tact than she wished, seeing the way her eyes widened, looking at her like she was a monster; like the entire time as Anóra had known Ashilde had just crumbled from underneath her.

Honestly, it probably had.

Pit.

"What?" she whispered, eyes threatening tears.

Ashilde knelt down so she could look her in the eye, her throat conflicting when she flinched away from her. "When the Dreyma hunters first stumbled upon me, they thought I was with the Rhuanics. They sent your mother, carrying your brother, to warn your clan. But they were mistaken. I would never align with the Rhuanics. But when I saw her running ... I couldn't let her spread that lie to your people; couldn't let the Dreyma seek revenge against *my* people, who'd done nothing wrong."

"But she did nothing wrong," Anóra whimpered. "She didn't know."

"I know. That's why I shot—"

"How could you?" She slammed her fists against Ashilde's shoulders, hard. Ash was so surprised at her sudden anger, she slipped, falling backward and landing on the sand.

Staring at Anóra, tears poured down the girl's face.

"I ... I *hate* you," she whispered.

Anóra turned and ran, sliding down the hill they'd just climbed, taking away Ashilde's chance to explain how she hadn't landed the killing blow, not personally. It was the injury she'd inflicted that led to her mother's death. Of course, she'd taken responsibility, since her mother hadn't been able to fight back *or* escape when the Rhuanic stuck a sword into her stomach, slaying her and causing her to fall atop of the babe and slay them, too. She didn't get the chance to break it to her easily, didn't get a chance to explain herself, a chance to ask forgiveness. Ashilde didn't even get to tell her how she planned to wipe out every single Rhuanic that lived below in the hidden village, with an army at her back.

Instead, she watched as Anóra made it down the hill and began climbing up the next, Funakiin following in tow.

While she sat on her ass, in shock and slowly breaking.

You didn't even purposely confess, her mind taunted, trying to add more guilt where too much already weighed her down.

But at least she knows now. Finally, she snapped back, before shoving herself back up, moving to follow. Ashilde had no idea what to say and how to repair the relationships she'd just broken. She wasn't even sure she deserved for it to *be* repaired.

Fighting the urge to vomit, she quickly used her spear to erase their tracks, hoping that, by following slightly slower behind Anóra—but never losing the girl in her sights—she might come up with what to say, giving her time to grieve and process the trust she'd broken.

Anóra didn't look up at her, after Ashilde finally caught up, continuing her rushed pace back toward the river. Even though Ashilde understood how she felt, she had no idea what to say, how to make it better—just like she'd never known how to comfort Brynhild, until it'd been too late, her sister's hatred run too deep.

So she did what she'd done with Bryn: kept her mouth shut, not wanting to do any more damage than had already been done.

When they found the river once more, their silence still remained unbroken.

Anóra found a small patch of shade at the bottom of the hill, just beyond the river. She sat down against it.

"You know, I was thinking, we could push on for a little—"

But the girl didn't answer her, instead laying down on the sand, turning to offer Ashilde her back.

Ashilde swallowed, her throat thick.

The sun *was* setting and they'd already pushed on longer that day than they had since they entered the Hafleden. Still, she had hoped to put more distance between themselves and the Rhuanics, even if they were already a good distance away from their village;

hoped that pushing forward might provide inspiration of what she should do, what she should say. '*I'm sorry*' just didn't seem like enough.

She opened her mouth, ready to explain to Anóra how they needed to do just that, for their own safety.

I hate you.

Ashilde choked back her own sob as she stared at the girl's back, watching as she shuddered, crying herself to sleep. After a moment, Funakiin moved and laid beside her. The girl wrapped an arm around the wolf's torso as best she could, her fingers curling into his fur as she pressed closer, burying her face into the wolf's chest.

Funakiin's bright yellow eyes moved to stare at her, unblinking.

She turned away, not wanting to see the blame written there.

With a sigh, she looked up at the stars and hoped tomorrow would fare better for all of them. Perhaps sleep and rest was what they needed, a little time to process everything, before figuring out how to move forward together, despite this latest revelation. She cocked her head to the side, looking more intently above. She couldn't believe she hadn't noticed before, but these stars were unfamiliar to her. The stars she knew were nowhere to be found.

Her body shook slightly at that revelation as her heart sank.

She'd never felt so alone.

Swallowing her discomfort, Ashilde took off her weapons and pulled out the thin blanket, laying it over the girl and the wolf. The gesture was met with silence. She curled up across from them, tucking her arms underneath her head as she let sleep take her, experiencing a dreamless sleep for the first time since she'd left her home.

***

Ashilde awoke to find herself alone.

She didn't panic, though her gut response was to jump up at a run, screaming their names. Instead, she pushed herself up from where she slept in the sand, cleaned herself off and glanced around, purposefully keeping her movements slow and calculated, lest her panic take hold of her and steal her the ability to reason—a skill she couldn't afford to lose, especially now.

Anóra was gone, but Ashilde's pack and weapons remained. Funakiin and Ieka were missing, too, but she hadn't seen the bird at all the day before and they'd gone to sleep before they usually did. Ieka was most likely out hunting ... unless she'd joined the others in leaving. With everything of hers undisturbed, Ashilde had no reason to believe that Funakiin and Anóra had done anything but leave on their own accord. They couldn't have been taken by the Rhuanics. If they had been, Ashilde would have heard it and stopped them. And that was only if they had been trying to steal them without her noticing. More likely, she would have been taken or killed, as well. No, her companions left on their own. But to do what, she had no idea.

Well, that wasn't entirely true.

Pit.

"What do you plan to do?" she whispered, as if Anóra could hear her. Even if the child managed to find their home again, without getting lost within the desert, Anóra couldn't kill the Rhuanics—not unless she wanted to risk her own soul in the process. Even if that didn't bother her and she was willing to pay that price, she was only one person against an entire clan of killers, albeit small. Sure, she might have the gods' chosen with her, but that suddenly didn't feel like enough, where

Anóra's safety was concerned.

What could they possibly do besides get themselves killed?

How could either Funakiin or Ieka think it was a good idea to let Anóra go sneaking off and damning her own soul to avenge her family?

Even if she hates me, Anóra knows better, she thought, gathering her things and forcing herself to move normally, to remain calm, to ignore the stabbing pain in her heart or the panic growing in her stomach. *Why didn't she listen?*

Ashilde knew the answer to that, though.

She'd been caught trying to sneak off Slátra lands *three* different times, attempting to go off on her own to take on the entire Fundi clan by herself. Even after the Seidsian punished her by making someone stay with her at all times, it had taken time for her to realize why even her solitary response could be disastrous for her people; how she had to put the clan's well-being before her own desires for the first time, even above her own vengeance.

They killed my mother.

If their places had been reversed, Ashilde had no doubt what she would have done.

She wouldn't have been much smarter than Anóra.

A new thought hit her, freezing her in a crouch as she gripped her pack.

Anóra knew the truth, now. What if vengeance wasn't her only motive, any more? What if she just needed to get away from *her*, her mother's murderer; a woman she had grown to trust, even like, who betrayed her by failing to protect the one person she loved more than anything?

Brynhild's face flashed before her eyes, the situation too familiar by far.

"You stupid, stupid woman," Ashilde muttered,

wanting to puke, as her heart shattered inside her. Though she hadn't wanted to admit it fully to herself, in their few weeks together, she had grown to love Anóra like a sister.

And now she'd lost her just like she'd lost her own blood, failing not because of her lack of physical strength, but because of the strength of her heart; her fear her adopted sister would hate her just as much as her real one.

Instead, she'd only repeated her mistakes and caused more pain.

You leave nothing but orphans behind you.

Brynhild's words shook inside her brain. Ashilde shivered against them, unable to bear the truth behind them, now.

It took a few moments for her to unfreeze herself and continue moving. Ashilde drank the rest of her waterskin before refilling it once more, securing it on a sling on her waist while ignoring the hunger pains in her stomach. Blinded by her desire to sneak away, Anóra had forgotten to cover her tracks; easy to spot, now that Ashilde was ready to look for them. They'd be easy to follow, too, small beside the giant paw prints paired alongside them.

So you're going after them, then?

The thought surprised her into stillness for the second time. She hadn't considered there to be any other option, other than to follow Anóra and see her vengeance through, to save her from not only herself and the Rhuanics, if she was still alive, but also from what Ashilde had gotten her into; for the chance, selfishly, to apologize and beg her to let her help her get back to the Segan, where Anóra would never have to see her again, but at least would be *safe*.

But there was another option.

She could continue on her own quest.

Alone.

To go chasing after Anóra instead of continuing on

her way would waste precious time.

And she wasn't the only one who might pay the price for it.

She had to think about her people.

Ashilde hadn't thought about them much, since she'd left, especially after meeting Anóra and leaving the world she was familiar with. One could believe it was because it was too painful to think about, leaving them, but that wasn't the whole truth. She missed them, of course. And there was still a part of her—a dark part—deep down, that resented them, for casting her out when she needed them most. But, she truly avoided thinking about them because she was afraid for them.

She was afraid she'd come home and find them all gone. Dead.

Their chances weren't great, when she left. All their hunters, gone. Their Faethegnar, banished by their own decree. With no aid coming from other clans, yet knowledge of their vulnerability already spread, they risked war just as much as the Ravenmother's wrath— for Ashilde wasn't certain she trusted the god to keep her word; that her own banishment was enough.

She was only one person, but the Slátra were a small enough clan as it was. After losing all of the hunters, losing another could prove detrimental. She *had* to return. Could she really afford to delay in pursuit of an endeavor that could very well cost her own life, when that time could be spent reaching Skírrdrauin, before returning home to her clan that much sooner?

To see Davyn again?

Her heart panged and she took a half step forward, turning to follow the river, instead of crossing it and following the footsteps of her missing companions. But she stopped herself, squeezing her eyes closed.

Anóra stood with her, even more than her people did. By their logic, the child was as damned as she, for not shunning her once she learned of her "taint." Even being from a different clan, it didn't matter. That belief was universal.

Could she really abandon her now, even if for the sake of her own people?

The way Brynhild claimed she'd abandoned her during her childhood, guilt-ridden at being unable to save their mother?

You ruined your relationship with your sister because you couldn't handle the consequences of what you'd done. You shoved her away and let her hate you, regretting it every day since. You won't do that to Anóra, too.

Ashilde sighed.

Anóra deserved better.

And truly? So did she.

Turning away, Ashilde crossed the river once more and began following Anóra's footsteps, leaving a trail purposefully behind. She hoped she could use it to find the river again, once they were reunited—if they could even return that quickly, before the wind wiped it all away.

The pit in her stomach, growing larger with each step, gave her little confidence to believe in such a false hope. Instead, she could only hope she'd find them again.

Perhaps, this time, she wouldn't be too late.

CHAPTER TWENTY-FIVE

Ashilde followed the tracks for most of the morning, before she discovered a second set that made her body run cold. The new tracks—from two different people, walking side by side—came from a different direction, intercepting the ones she'd been tracking, ending in a scuffle in the dirt that erased any signs of tracks at all, becoming an untraceable mess. She had to walk a little farther onward before she rediscovered any semblance of a footstep's whisper, two more pairs of tracks continuing on in the direction she originally followed.

But *only* two sets of tracks.

Neither of which belonged to a small girl or a wolf.

She knelt on the ground, brushing her fingers over the sand. There was no sign of blood, though some altercation had obviously taken place. She assumed Anóra and Funakiin were ambushed by Rhuanics and—hopefully—taken to their camp, rather than killed outright. She saw no signs pointing to either of their deaths, unless they were killed cleanly and their bodies taken to the camp anyway.

Ashilde shook her head, forcing the thought away, though her body still shook at the very idea that Anóra could be—

No.

She refused to consider it.

At least until she could be sure.

I will not fail someone I love again.

Taking another rationed drink from her waterskin, Ashilde pushed forward, spear in hand, trying her best to keep her theorizing to a minimum, but failing to do so, fixated on how Anóra let herself be ambushed in a place like this, where nothing spanned in any direction as far as the eye could see.

She understood the girl's error a little better when the same thing almost happened to her.

Ashilde had just finished climbing yet *another* hill when she stopped herself at the top and immediately dropped to the ground, pushing herself backward back onto the other side, waiting to hear shouts of alarm after being seen. When she didn't hear any after managing to regulate her breathing to a slower rate, Ashilde crawled back up slowly to peer over the top of the hill, into the crevasse between the hills down below.

A small camp was set up, with a firepit—over which a piece of unfamiliar looking meat roasted—and a tent.

With a pair of feet sticking out of it.

Unmoving.

Ashilde exhaled. She'd almost stumbled into a Rhuanic's camp and practically alerted them of her whereabouts without them having to do any of the work of catching her. Her eyes relocated the footprints she'd been following, not moving from her hiding place just yet, until she understood exactly what had happened here.

The footprints she'd tracked didn't lead to the tent, instead curving along the side before traveling up and across another peak. After searching for a moment, she found other tracks leading down into the camp.

There was only one set.

So did Anóra's captors stop here or did they move on? And where are her tracks? Or Funakiin's? Surely they—

Her stomach growled as the smell of the meat finally hit her. It was unfamiliar, poignant, but not necessarily bad. It reminded her that she hadn't eaten in over a day, after missing their usual meal they ate before bed. And with Ieka missing—*watching over Anóra,* she hoped—so too did her food supply.

Perhaps she could do more here than learn answers from a lone Rhuanic.

She wasn't sure which she desired more.

Keeping her spear out and close to her, she crawled over the top of the hill, before she began slipping down the side. She kept her eyes fixed on the Rhuanic's feet as she slid down into their camp, waiting to see if her arrival would awaken them, despite trying to stay silent. As the dust cloud cleared, she untensed ever so slightly.

The sleeping soul hadn't moved at all.

Ashilde slipped off her pack and set it gently down beside the unattended fire pit. She scanned for any weapons left lying around, assuming they didn't sleep with them on their person. If they were paranoid enough to do that, they wouldn't have trusted this environment enough to sleep without a proper watch in the first place. She didn't see any weapons left out in the open, and it wasn't like there were a lot of options to hide them, unless the weapons had been buried. A great tactic against thieves, but she wasn't planning on stealing much.

Their meal and life, besides.

Ashilde snuck around the fire pit until she was at the base of the tent. A man slept on his stomach, atop a pile of thick furs, with bare feet sticking out of the edge of the tent. The mouth of the tent was wide—

easy enough for her to slip into without touching him. Ashilde crept along the edge, her plan forming as she moved. She needed answers and she couldn't have the man following her after she got them. But she *had* to avoid killing him. She couldn't be slowed down by her limbs disappearing before she could find Anóra.

In position, she raised her spear, almost sorry for what she was about to do, especially to someone who couldn't defend against it. But as the memory of watching Hildrid's throat being sliced open came into her mind, any sympathy vanished as she drove her spear through the back of the man's kneecap, not stopping until the entire blade was lost, buried deep within the sand.

Ashilde jumped on top of the man as he woke up screaming, pinning him to the ground, one arm wrapped around his throat, choking him quiet, while she pointed the knife she'd pulled out at the side of his face, filling his peripherals with a readied blade.

"Give me the answers I seek and I'll let you live to crawl back from whatever hole you came from," she hissed into his ear. "Lie to me, and this bed will become your grave."

Ashilde expected a lot of different reactions from a self-chosen Rhuanic who she'd just awoken by shattering their kneecap: aggression, anger, pain, perhaps even fear, if he was smart enough to realize he had everything to fear from her. But she wasn't sure she was willing to give him that much credit.

What she hadn't expected was for him to go completely rigid and then begin to chuckle, if only for a moment, before he spoke, his words coming as wheezed-gasps in the midst of excruciating pain.

"So you're the ... latest victim. Bitch."

She blinked.

"You'd better elaborate on that," she growled, pointing her knife for emphasis. Yet the man beneath her appeared to be unfazed, even if his body had begun to shake from both her weight on top of him and his injury. He hissed, tears slipping down the sides of his face against the pain.

"Go ahead … and kill me, huntress," he said, slowly regaining his strength to speak. "Doing so serves my cause just as well, even if I'd rather live."

She leaned back and jerked him up, his greasy hair fisted in her dirty fingers, so her knife could sit just below his throat. "What cause?"

"Only what our Wolffather asks of us," he said, his tone sincere.

This nonsense again.

"You lie," she said, her spit landing unnoticed on his shoulder.

"Believe what you must," the man said. "Your own ignorance will kill you, if your own heresy doesn't do so first."

Her shock almost caused her to drop her weapon. Almost. Instead, she tightened her grip and pressed the point against the thin flesh of his jugular, pricking enough to release blood. "I am no Rhuanic."

"You certainly aren't as clean as your judgment of my brothers and sisters exalts you to believe," he said, unphased by the blood running from his throat, dropping onto his blanket below in small, unhurried drips. "You've killed *sangrendi*, when traditionally, the gods expect and allow you to only kill fellow *sangrild*, as part of war."

"To protect my clan. To—"

"And you expect me to believe you're still clean, despite how dry you are between your legs? Tell me: how many souls are you harboring inside you right now, unable to cleanse?" He actually made a *tsking* sound, though he avoided shaking his head, after the barest movement caused her knife to cut a little deeper.

The puddle of blood on his blanket began to grow.

Ashilde stared at the back of the man's head. "How

do you know all this?"

"Because there is only one reason for a woman of the clans to be out here, amid the Hafleden, but away from our camp: you're Róta's latest chosen one. But *we* will never allow you to succeed. And, if you continue to chase after your friends, then you make our job that much simpler."

Her mind swam, but she couldn't allow herself to chase after all of the threads. Nor waste much more time asking her captive questions, especially now that she knew Anóra was alive. "What do you plan to do with them?"

"Do with them? Foolish outcast. It's already *done*."

Ashilde wanted to slam the man's head down and knock the riddles out of him, if only so he'd speak plainly. But before she could even consider that, the man spoke once more.

"May Waldemar have mercy on your soul. He's already pardoned mine."

Then, he did the only thing her instincts weren't prepared for.

He slammed his own head down, lodging her poised knife deep through his own throat.

Ashilde stumbled backward, letting go of her knife in surprise, but not before she felt the warmth of blood splatter across the side of her hand, making fingers sticky. She stood at the edge of the tent, listening to the man's choking gasps before blood finally gurgled from his throat and he spit out his last, the spray hitting the tent's wall before his head collapsed onto the furs and his entire body stilled.

Her own hands shook, but not because the man had just died in front of her. Not even because he had killed himself with her blade, sparing her the decision of whether or not to do it herself, instead damning himself even further to spending eternity in the Pit.

They shook because she ambushed him seeking

answers and she'd only gotten more questions, this new set much more dangerous than the last.

"Fuck!" she screamed, her mind whirling.

The Rhuanics who first attacked her. The Rhuanics she'd stumbled upon in the middle of the Segan. This one, alone. *All* of them had pointed in the same direction: that they not only worshiped Waldemar, but that they *served* him, under direct orders *from* the Wolffather. Pit, the presence of the wolf statues at their home within the Hafleden gave strength to such an idea—a home they surely couldn't survive within, without some sort of direct aid from the gods.

She couldn't believe it. It wasn't *possible*.

But she also couldn't deny what she was discovering, what every new discovery pointed toward. Why? What purpose could a group of Rhuanics have to serve Waldemar, when their very existence was an affront to him by his own decree?

And that was only the beginning. How did she play into all of this? She could convince herself about the dead Rhuanic's ability to deduce she was condemned and robbed of her *dolorsandri*, because he was right: there was no reason for her to be out among the Hafleden otherwise. But, what was this about her being Róta's chosen one—and her latest one, at that? A contradiction in and of itself, but Ashilde couldn't care less about such trivial distinctions. No, she was more focused on the idea that Róta was somehow ... *using* her, for some other purpose aside from personal penance and protection for her clan, like her own Seidsian confessed.

It was becoming too complicated, too complex.

And none of it helped her rescue Anóra.

Ashilde worked quickly. Ducking back into the tent, she lifted the body so she could pull her knife out, letting the Rhuanic fall back down with a thud, before she ripped her spear back out of his knee. She wiped her blade and her hand clean as much as she was able on the back of his shirt, before searching quickly through his person, finding a waterskin buried beneath the furs.

She gasped for air when she left the tent, the putrid smell of his quickly warming corpse filling her nostrils. Gagging, she drank the rest of his water, saving her own precious supply. Then, she walked over to the spit and took the meat off to cool, knowing she couldn't waste too much time waiting, but also not able to force herself to leave the meal behind.

She may need the strength the food would provide to infiltrate the rhuanic's base alone.

With effort, her mind remained empty, despite wanting to travel off into various dark thoughts and unanswerable questions. Instead, she placed her spear in the sand—blade first, to clean some of the blood off— and sat beside it, a thin layer of sweat covering her as she inspected her hands, and then her arms.

All remained fully intact.

So far.

Breathing in relief, Ashilde took the thin blanket the Rhuanic had tossed to the side, too warm to use for a midday nap amid the desert heat, even with the shade. Taking her blood-stained knife, she ripped it in half and then cut it into strips to wrap the leftover meat up in, once again storing it in her pack, finally able to replenish their supply. It wasn't the cleanest way to store her meat, but she hoped to reach the camp before dark. Anóra and the others would easily be as hungry as she was now, especially if they hadn't been fed.

That's assuming they are even still alive, once you get there.

Ashilde checked on the meat, finally cool enough for her to eat. She started cutting it into thin strips, too, the meat a lot tougher than she was used to. She tore off a piece with her teeth, chewing dedicatedly, surprised by the toughness and bitterness of the taste. Had the Rhuanic not seasoned it at all? Whatever meat this was—and she was positive she'd never tasted the like in her life—it desperately needed some attention from a skilled cook. If only she knew what kind—

You're ignoring me.

Ashilde bit her lip, finally swallowing her first bite of food for the day. Why her own mind wouldn't allow her to brush past the thought of Anóra dying by the Rhuanics' hand was an unusual cruelty.

I don't want to think about it, she replied sourly.

She'd much rather try and figure out what kind of meat she was eating and where the animal had come from; had to be in the desert somewhere, though what could survive out here among so much nothingness was beyond her knowledge.

Yet, she'd called herself out and she wasn't wrong.

The possibility that Anóra and Funakiin had been killed already was very, very real.

She forced another bite down, knowing she couldn't afford not to eat, not with how little food her body had gotten since she'd left home. No matter how queasy her stomach felt.

If they're dead, what are you going to do?

She had no response to that.

Please, not Anóra. Not her.

Ashilde ate until she was full. Leaving the rest of the meager camp undisturbed, hoping a rare predator of some sort would find the Rhuanic before another of his ilk did, she climbed up the other side of the hill, finding that the footsteps in the sand she'd been following had started to fade and shift, thanks to a new, steadily growing wind. At first, she worried how she'd find the camp, if the tracks faded before she found it.

Then, she noticed large plumes of black smoke

rising into the dying day's sky, just ahead.

Ashilde made her way toward it, begging whomever had the mercy to listen she wasn't too late.

***

Ashilde arrived at the outskirts of the Rhuanics' camp within the ruined city just as the sun was setting. Her feet were sore, while her entire body ached. Her skin cracked on the back of her exposed neck, pieces of skin peeling off every time she moved.

Yet all of that pain was forgotten as she crawled up the hill and, laying hidden on her stomach once more, finally discovered the source of the flames.

Just outside the ruined village they'd claimed as their own, a newly constructed massive fire pit had been raised—the largest one she'd ever seen. While impressive, that wasn't what held her attention.

Instead, it was the creature cooking on top of it.

Easily the biggest creature she'd ever laid eyes upon—let alone ever thought could possibly exist; it was propped stationary over the fire pit, belly exposed to the flames. She couldn't make out any of the finer details from such a distance, but it had eight legs, four on each side and a large, rotund body that easily matched the size of one of the broken buildings.

The most impressive—and unfamiliar—parts were its claws and tail. Two claws framed where its face might be, sticking out from arms as thick as tree trunks. Most massive was its tail, curved upward so it came around the backside of its body, stuck upright in that position by how the Rhuanics had positioned it over the fire.

Four Rhuanics approached the massive beast and it took all four of them to turn the crank of the spit to flip it on its side.

Ashilde had no idea what it was, how the Rhuanics

had managed to kill it, let alone *move* it or how they knew how to cook it. Its black shell shone against the fire's blaze and it looked as hard as stone. How would they pry it off to reach the meat underneath, if there was anything under it at all? Why wouldn't they strip it first?

Not really relevant right now, is it, Ashilde?

Especially when she noticed how many had gathered around the pit, watching their spoils cook.

Ashilde double checked her pack was fashioned tight against her waist, touching the hilt of her knife on her wrist to ensure it was exactly where it needed to be: quickly accessible. Leaving her spear on her back, she slipped her bow off and cradled it against her side, fingering her fletchings as she did a quick count. Two dozen arrows and at least twice as many Rhuanics, if it came down to it.

She'd have to ensure it didn't.

No one could know she was there.

Keeping low, she half-walked, half-slid down the side of the hill, reaching the side of the ruins before she finally stopped moving, crouched low against the smooth stone.

Inhaling through her nose, the aroma of whatever creature they'd killed hit her like a well-placed punch, almost knocking her backward with how strong it was—a smoky mixture between charred and bittersweet. Her stomach growled even though it'd only been a few hours since she'd eaten and she wrapped one hand around it, praying it would stay quiet.

Pressing her body as flat as she could against the stone, Ashilde glanced around it, looking into the ruins properly. Sconces encompassing candles had been wedged into the cracks of each building that still remained taller than she was, providing small patches of light that failed to give her a good sense of her surroundings, letting too many shadows out to play. Across the way, on the other edge of the ruins, a torch moved on its own, the darkness hiding the Rhuanic who held it.

Plenty of shadows for her to hide in.

Plenty more for others to do the same.

With her bow in her hand, clutched close to her chest, she moved along the wall at a crouch, keeping to the shadows as best she could, as she slipped through the Rhuanics' camp. Now that she was so close, she could hear the laughter of the individuals just below, where most had gathered around the enormous fire from the front of the camp. How could they sit and laugh after everything they'd done, after everyone they'd killed? How could they be so cheerful, knowing their very existence corrupted the natural balance of life and damned each and every one of them to the Pit? Could they truly be so careless of what their actions had caused or where their souls would spend eternity?

Ignoring them and her unanswered questions, she ran at a crouch across the ruins, dodging broken structure pieces and small piles of stone until she reached the next spot completely shrouded in shadow. Aside from items she'd already noticed earlier, when they first discovered the campsite—baskets, blankets, weapons and the like—she didn't see anything that would be out of the ordinary for any long-term home. She was surprised to notice, glancing at a pile of blankets in a basket beside her, that the top blanket had designs incorporating the colors and runes of the Fundi. Could the Rhuanics truly have branched off from her rival clan? Or worse, still be associated with them, despite their faces scrubbed clean?

As if you needed another reason to hate them more.

Taking a risk, she knelt down and lifted the top blanket up, expecting to see another black and purple blanket beneath it, the same runes woven into the fabric. Instead, she found a blanket of light blue and gold. *That doesn't make sense,* she thought. *That's the sign of the Dirheil...*

Since discovering there were Rhuanics among them, she'd always expected them to be rogue members from a single clan, even though every clan she'd spoken to denied any and all accusations of such heresy. Finding their presence in the Hafleden had made her question how they lived there or if this was where they originated; perhaps remnants of a clan who somehow had survived the Banishing and thrived here, instead? But that theory gave too much credit to the impossibilities the Rhuanics she'd already slain lied about earlier, because no clan could have survived out here without the blessing of the gods, especially for generations. And the camp around her was too shoddy to have lasted that long.

But now, these blankets not only suggested these Rhuanics came from the Segan, but that they came from multiple clans.

She couldn't imagine how anyone would respond if such an accusation proved true.

Ashilde wanted to stay crouched in the dark, thinking about all the people in her clan and if any of them had gone missing recently, with bodies never recovered. But she'd already spent too long crouched in one spot and she couldn't afford to worry about that now. What was done was done. No matter who they were or where they once came from—even her own people—she wouldn't hesitate to kill them all. Especially if any harm had come to Anóra.

Pushing forward, she made her way around another half-standing building before Ashilde threw herself backward against the stone. Just around the corner, stood a scene she had never expected to see out here— as if she could have dreamed any group would have survived out within the desert wasteland.

But a *family*?

She peeked around once more. A father, mother and son were gathered on top of one of the stone structures. The father sat across from the mother and child, weaving together threads for a basket. The mother knelt against the stone, her fingers stained as she used a wet cloth, stubbornly wiping at the child's face, who fidgeted in response. For half a breath, Ashilde hoped it was Anóra, but the child was too tall, a young boy.

"Hold still," the mother murmured, her voice sweet, sending waves of emotions jabbing into Ashilde's heart. If she were caught here, was she expected to be able to kill a *child*? Or, leaving them alive, robbing another of their parents?

You leave nothing but orphans behind.

"You hover over them too much," the father said, not looking up from his work. "Look at where we live. The child is going to get dirty."

She *tsked.* "He's going to be part of the first generation who will know *true* peace," she replied, her tone hinting that they'd had this conversation numerous times before. "But that doesn't excuse them from learning the basics of cleanliness."

"*Mother—*"

"Listen to her, child," the father snapped, stopping the boy's complaints as their mother began to clean behind their ears. A few more moments passed before she gripped their chin, raising their face up to her inspection. "There," she said gently. "Was that so hard?"

"Can I go play now? *Please?*"

"Yes, fine," she said. "But be back in time for food!"

The child scurried off, forcing Ashilde back into the shadows, even though they ran in the complete opposite direction of where she hid. Waiting a breath, she slipped around the broken rock, listening as the parents shared a laugh, before their voices faded. She snuck a look around the corner again, seeing the father carrying the basket at the hip, following his wife across the stone both toward the front of the ruined village.

Ashilde's heart pounded. How could a family be part of the Rhuanics who lived here, who were aware of what sort of havoc their own members had caused throughout the Segan? Based on her experience with these Rhuanics so far, she would have guessed they all shared the same qualities: twisted, corrupted souls who abandoned the rules of the gods, cast off the clans they once knew and lost their humanity.

The presence of anything *but* made this so much harder.

Tightening her grip on her bow, she pushed off the stone and doubled back in the shadows, following a torch's bouncing glow as it walked the perimeter ahead of her, hoping that perhaps a sentry would be the key to finding her missing companions she sought. Her desire for stealth suddenly became that much more important. As long as she wasn't caught, then she wouldn't have to decide what to do about the complexities of the Rhuanics who hunted her.

Keeping to the shadows, Ashilde continued her search.

***

It took her almost over an hour of searching and hiding before she finally not only caught up to the torchbearer, but found what she was looking for.

Well, one of them, anyway.

On the complete opposite side of the ruins—which she had to climb between two smaller hills to reach, discovering this village was much larger than she had anticipated, larger than any clan's holdings within the Segan—was Funakiin.

This far away from the main throng of the camp made the Rhuanics' home almost seem non-existent, the surrounding area was so quiet. Aside from a few broken pieces of stone, out ahead was nothing but more rolling hills within the desert, the flattened land of the horizon closer than ever before.

Funakiin, meanwhile, was locked in a stone cage, a rope around his neck tied to a stake within—or, at least, it had been. The wolf had pulled the rope free and it now trailed behind him as he paced within the small enclosure, creating a line in the sand. For those who claimed to worship Waldemar, the disrespect they showed his creature was telling.

Even more confusing, his broken leg had straightened, his brace gone. Had they treated the wolf, or somehow even healed it? Why help Funakiin with an injury, only to lock him up afterward?

Not important, Ash. *Not right now.*

Ashilde glanced around from her cover. Above and behind her loomed the ruin's edge, more dark than light, the smoke from the Rhuanics' kill no longer showing up in the night sky. There were no torches lining the perimeter, save for the single one ahead of her. The torchbearer had his back to her and was using a stick to push a thick piece of meat toward Funakiin in the cage. The wolf ignored it, instead pacing along the opposite side, growling all the while.

Ashilde didn't hesitate.

Moving swiftly, she crept up from behind the Rhuanic until she breathed down their neck, grabbing at the throat and holding them in a chokehold. They began to flail as she squeezed away the access of air into their lungs, but Ashilde, even in her weakened state, was stronger. Eventually, their form went limp in her arm as Funakiin let out a warning growl.

From behind, nothing stirred.

Funakiin's growl stopped as she dropped the body, allowing the wolf to finally recognize her against the shadows. She heard him tear into the meat a second later, as she finally reached the cage.

Kneeling down, she reached her hand in.

Funakiin licked her fingers, before nuzzling his head against her palm, eyes wide in surprise.

"It's good to see you again," she whispered.

Her eyes adjusting quickly, she searched the unconscious form of the man she'd suffocated, thankful she found the key with ease. Locating the lock, she opened the cage, slipping the door open slowly. It creaked, but Funakiin bolted out the moment the opening was large enough to do so. Holding the door ajar, she dragged the man's body inside. Logic told her to hide it, but Funakiin's absence would be sign enough to not bother with trying to hide anything. She only hoped the man remained passed out long enough for them to escape, silently cursing her inability to kill.

Might as well leave a warning for the rest of the Rhuanics, if any of them dared to try and follow her.

She locked the cage door before throwing the key on top of the body inside, buying herself as much time as she could.

Funakiin waited for her at another ruined building. Keeping her bow out, just in case, she made her way over to the wolf, who clawed at his own neck, until the rope wrapped around it pulled free, falling to the ground in a tangle.

"Funakiin, where is Anóra?"

Funakiin jerked his head in the opposite direction of the camp. Did he know where the girl was being kept?

She motioned for Funakiin to lead on. Together, they snaked through the other side of the Rhuanics' camp, often stopping when a torch's light got too close or the sudden sound of voices froze them in their tracks. They remained undetected, however, until they were skirting alongside the front of the camp, the magnificent dead creature and the pit it burned over now in front of her, instead of to her right. The fire continued to burn and only a few Rhuanics remained to guard it, but as the night continued to grow darker, most of the camp had drifted off into slumber.

As they moved, Ashilde glanced around, trying to find any place where Anóra could be hiding or kept, but there was nothing amongst the rubble for her to hide, the living quarters the Rhuanics had set up on the complete opposite side of the ruins.

But Funakiin kept going.

Where was he going?

"Funakiin!" she hissed, her heart hammering as the wolf slipped around another broken stump of a pillar, noticing their escape into the open desert lay just ahead. She caught up to the creature and grabbed him by the neck, causing him to growl in warning. But she didn't let go, leaning close to his face. "Funakiin, *where* is Anóra?"

The wolf's expression changed and a lump formed in her throat.

She caught the direction of his eyes as they flickered.

Ahead was a smaller fire pit, smoldering still, the ashes filling the circular base made of stones. Sticking out of the center was a long metal rod, with a circular hoop hanging down from the top, moving gently every time the breeze picked up, creating a soft *clink* that she hadn't noticed before, too focused on moving forward.

Noticing now, the noise was deafening.

Funakiin whined as she moved toward it.

Ashilde took a few steps closer, despite the wolf's soft protests. Standing directly over the pit, she knelt in front of it and dug her hands into the ashes, able to bury her arms up to her elbows. Her mind tried to warn her that she was too exposed, but her focus had narrowed, her breath laboring as she worked. She discovered two more items, buried within the ashes. Bones, obviously human, even without close inspection; and something glittering, just along the edge. Swallowing bile, she reached down and pulled it out, ashes slipping off the ruined necklace. She'd known before seeing it what it was, but holding it in the palm of her hand now made her want to scream, even as within, she became numb.

It was the necklace Anóra had pulled off her mother, before they left. It was so big on her, it often slipped underneath her shirt and coat, making it easily forgotten. She'd last seen it when they'd washed, just leaving the Flatrí. She was certain the girl had never taken it off.

Instead, it died with her.

Her head snapped over to Funakiin, who had snuck closer to her. "They *burned* her?" she hissed, her voice cracking against the cruelty. "She was just a fucking *child*."

Funakiin whined.

Her vision flashed red. Ashilde moved without thought, responded without reason, stalking back toward the heart of the ruins, her bow suddenly strung as she no longer snuck, staying close to the ground, but strode boldly, ready to kill. She didn't care that she had a quest to fulfill, that her people depended on her to make it home. She didn't care what questions she had, whether the gods wanted to use her or kill her. She didn't care how many Rhuanics filled that ruin, what lives they lived, what motivated them, *who they loved*. She hoped to find every single one, every person foolish enough to join their little cult.

She would kill them all.

Her vision didn't clear until she felt Funakiin bit down on her wrist, *hard*, as he pulled her in the other direction. She realized her purpose as soon as she noticed him, but she shook her head. "No," she told him. "You will not deny me this."

She left the rest unsaid.

I loved her. I loved her and they took her from me. I

failed to protect her, just like I fail to protect all who I love.

"They will pay," she whispered, meeting the wolf's eyes. "They will pay with their lives for daring to touch her. Then, I will pay for the rest of mine. It's what we all deserve."

She took another step towards the camp before collapsing against the ground, her cramps returning in a force she had never felt before. *Pit, not now!*

Ashilde struggled to breathe, the pain blinding her from her senses. It was all she could do to lie paralyzed in the sand, hidden from view, until the wave subsided a moment later. A warning, that her body would kill her, if the Rhuanics did not, as she took her vengeance?

Funakiin pulled her away from the camp once more, his tugging more insistent.

Ashilde felt tears spring to the corner of her eyes. "But they *burned* her, Funakiin. And it's all *my fault.* They—"

She cried out as her body revolted once more, her hands fading, a flickering threat. Shouts from the fair side of the ruins answered her and Ashilde spat a string of curses as cramps assaulted her from within, accompanying her fading form as her left hand disappeared entirely, an eerie glow left in its wake, the glow slowly climbing up her wrist, her physical body disappearing in its wake.

Her anger switched to despair, while fear made her throat catch. "Funakiin. What's happening to me?"

The wolf whined.

"Please ... help me."

Allowing Funakiin to help pull her along, she half-stumbled and half-crawled between the stone pillars, Anóra's necklace clutched in a death grip in her good hand, her own mother's necklace swaying gently as she moved; both a stark reminder of her failures and the lives who paid the price for it. They reached the open hills by the time the ruins were alight with torches and worried shouts were carried by the night's wind.

Gaining the strength to stand, Ashilde pushed forward at a run, Funakiin following beside her. With no idea how long it would be before the next wave of cramps hit—or if her body was truly going to disappear, this time—she needed to keep moving. And, if she couldn't kill to release emotions too powerful for her to shove away, running was the next best thing, even if she slipped and slid against the sand.

They made it well into the desert, even finding the river sometime during the night, to help them get back on course. They continued on, even when weariness started to kick in, eventually slowing back to a walk, each step still not far enough from where the Rhuanics hid.

Ashilde didn't stop until forced to, her unrelenting cramps finally causing her to buckle to her knees, biting her lip to keep herself from screaming.

It didn't take long for her to pass out.

CHAPTER TWENTY-SIX

When she awoke, Ashilde discovered her left arm was gone.

From her wrist to her fingers, there was nothing there. Where flesh and bone and muscle once were, it had become translucent, a faint outline with a soft golden glow outlining each finger and the curves of her palm. The absence of any flesh, muscle and bone continued up into her forearm, encompassed her elbow and ran up the length of her arm, ending at her shoulder, allowing her to see the sand below; only a faint outline remained to remind her it had been there at all, for there was no pain. Stranger still, in some ways, it still functioned. When she squeezed it into a fist, the outline of what should have been there moved to complete the motion. Yet, when she tried to pick up a pile of sand, the particles passed straight through her fingers. She could grab onto nothing, touch nothing.

Ashilde swallowed hard, her voice still hoarse from screaming her frustrations after she woke. The signs had all pointed to this outcome, that this was the price she paid when she could no longer pay in blood. But avoiding it for so long since she'd first lost parts of her hands—only to lose an entire *arm*—had shaken her.

If you don't get moving soon, your legs might disappear, before you can reach Skírrdrauin.

Ashilde blinked.

Was she truly considering continuing trying?

With how much the thought surprised her, her mind caught up with what her heart had already decided.

She'd given up.

And why shouldn't she? Her body had given up on *her*, knowing she wouldn't make it and gain the answers she sought. She'd failed in her quest. She couldn't even keep a young girl alive, who deserved so much better than her broken promise of protection and lies. All the training she had dedicated herself to, the sacrifices she had made after she'd failed to save her mother, had been for nothing.

Anóra was dead.

No amount of suffering, no amount of love, could bring her back.

The Slátra were most likely starving and cold, if they had survived the winter at all. Davyn, cursing her name and wishing she had never abandoned them to suffer alone; Brynhild, smug in the confirmation of her hatred, her fear of being asked to give too much for the clan twisting into anger at Ashilde's failure; Freydis, collapsed and crying, with no answers gained from the one she trusted as to why she had to raise her children alone; Dagfinn, questioning his decision to ever name her Faethegnar; her Seidsian, gathering everyone to announce her death, her failure, while the gods prepared to punish another of her warriors, thanks to her inability to reach their realm in time—if they hadn't wiped out her clan already, ever fickle, always angry.

Ashilde took a shuddering breath, her entire body

shaking as she squeezed her eyes shut.

She was a failure. She'd been proven wrong. Her body was tainted with the souls she took, so no one else would have to make that sacrifice, and now, she was dying because of it. Because her clan needed her to. Because it was asked of her, to protect them. Because her heavy blood flow during her *dolorsandri* had destined her to become a warrior and carry that burden, even reaching the rank of Faethegnar, dedicating herself that much further to her clan's survival.

Because the gods demanded it.

She opened her eyes, blinking as she swallowed, her throat tight with a sudden rage.

Ashilde was right.

She had given *everything*.

What right did the gods have, in taking it all away? What justification could they have for condemning her, costing her her people, her identity, her love and her way of life? And now, they had the gall to expect to be able to take her *life*, without giving any answers in return? Without any consequences on their part? They had given her nothing except questions her entire life, always taking from her without answers.

"No," she whispered as she stood, her transparent left arm hanging uselessly by her side, her heart hardening.

She turned and looked at Funakiin. "They have no right."

But that didn't matter.

She was running out of time.

Ashilde took off at a sprint, running as hard as she could against the sandy terrain. Keeping the river to her left, she pushed forward. A moment later, Funakiin ran up alongside her, his tongue hanging lopsided out of his mouth—not grinning, but no longer sulking away from her, either. The gods could rob her of everything she'd given them and more, but they would not take away the answers she deserved. To give up just because they had stacked everything against her would be an insult to her very life.

No, they couldn't stop her, not now.

They'd have to kill her, first.

***

Traveling through the same barren landscape at a breakneck pace for most of the day had proven uneventful—a thankful reprieve, as the rest of her body remained intact. For now.

So, of course, when that decided to change, everything happened at once.

Ashilde had been forced to slow her pace to a walk. Though her legs were tired and her feet blistered and sore, she could've kept up the pace. She felt like she needed to, as she wasn't any closer to finding Skírrdrauin. But her cramps had a different idea, hitting her so fiercely that she counted herself lucky to be moving forward at all, her spear one of the only things keeping her upright.

Pausing, she hunched over, her left arm positioned to be wrapped around her stomach, yet she felt nothing there, the outline of where her arm should be—now missing up to her shoulder—flickering against the consistent breeze.

The sand had slowly receded until she walked across solid, cracked yellow ground. Much better conditions to run on, if her cramps ever stopped long enough for her to pick up the pace. The change in environment gave Ashilde hope—a feeling she thought robbed from her. They had to be getting closer to Falos, closer to Skírrdrauin. They just *had* to.

Ashilde stood back up and inhaled deeply, holding her breath as her cramps hit again, while squinting at the horizon. Something seemed off about it, though she couldn't tell what it was. A slight discoloration ahead of her, the usual golden-brown haze—a constant companion through the Hafleden—darkening along it. Her cramps lessening, she released her breath with a loud sigh. Ashilde went to wipe her brow with her left hand, sweat dripping in her eye before she thought to lean her spear against her chest and repeat the motion with her right—the sweat wetting her hand, this time.

Putting one foot in front of the other, she continued. Her stomach rumbled, but she ignored it, just as she ignored the aching of her body, the thirst of her throat and strived to ignore the pain of her cramps. She'd been too slow and now, she was paying the price for it. She couldn't—

The ground shook.

Cracks exploded, surrounding her.

Ashilde froze, spreading her arm out wide to steady her, before slamming her spear butt down to help her from falling over. She met Funakiin's gaze.

"What was that?"

The wolf's eyes grew wide as everything shook again, but this time, it didn't stop. Little pieces of broken rock shook on top of the ground. Ashilde knelt, using her spear as an anchor, as she waited to see what test the gods decided to throw at her next.

Funakiin knocked her down before landing behind her and quickly bit her arm, pulling her backward.

"Funakiin, what—"

Seconds later, a creature exploded out from underneath the hard ground in front of them.

Landing on eight legs, the massive creature—the same as the one the Rhuanics had slain—spun around, searching for its prey, the large stinger arched over its wide frame. The dark black sheen of its hardened body blinded Ashilde for a moment, but she shoved herself up and back onto her feet. Funakiin came up from behind her and pushed her away, hard.

Toward the horizon.

She glanced down at the wolf, opening her mouth to speak, before a shadow raised over their heads. She dove away on the ground, as a claw slammed into the space they'd preoccupied moments before.

It found them.

Ashilde turned to face it, whipping her spear around to grip the bottom half with her left hand. Instead, she whacked herself with the bottom of the spear. Her heart sank into her gut. She couldn't grip the spear correctly. She definitely couldn't use a bow. How was she meant to defend herself against a creature of this magnitude with one arm missing?

She jumped again out of the way as the creature swiped at her, fear transitioning into focus—one of the first lessons her mother taught her. Holding onto the center of her spear tightly with her right hand, she stood back up. The beast's attention, momentarily, was on Funakiin, who had lunged at it from behind while it had attacked her. She'd already lost Ieka and Anóra. She wouldn't let this creature take away Funakiin, too.

Ashilde calculated, sweat already trying to loosen her death grip on her weapon. Perhaps, if they stayed on opposite sides of it, they could slowly wear the beast down, while she figured out how to land a killing blow.

With a racing heart and suppressed nerves, she approached it from the side. Ashilde jabbed her spear at it, grunting with effort, the thrust awkward and lacking the proper guiding force behind it. Still, she managed to make contact with the creatures's flank...

...Only to watch her spearhead spin off as the top third of her spear shattered into splinters against the creature's shell.

Ashilde pulled the weapon back, staring at her

broken spear with wide, surprised eyes. She had no idea what this creature was—no fireside stories had ever spoken of something like this—but no shell should have been able to shatter her weapon so easily.

Breaking the last thing you have that Davyn and Freydis gave you; when they loved you.

Ashilde didn't have time to break under that realization, though she did scream, a guttural, desperate sound as she ducked, the beast's tail whipping toward her; still using both claws to try and catch the quick, dodging wolf in front of it.

Apparently, it could fight on both fronts at the same time, too.

Throwing her broken spear on the ground, Ashilde continued to dodge the creature's attacks, the thrusts and swipes from its massive tail, the pointed stinger at the end coming much too close for her own comfort. She was quickly becoming exhausted, dodging one blow with barely enough time to collect herself before another assault was directed toward her, twisting to ensure she landed on her right side when she fell, so she could use her remaining arm to push herself back up. Funakiin circled around the beast, jumping up to attack where she imagined its face was—she hadn't gotten a good enough look at it to tell. It gave her a moment to breathe and a moment to think, as the creature let out a ground-shaking hiss at being assaulted so directly.

Glancing around for anything she could use against this beast one-handed, she noticed they had moved far along toward the horizon, in their dance of dodges. The whispering trail of the river was behind her, running along the ground until it—

She gasped, the battle between beasts forgotten, for a moment.

The river continued to run until it fell off the side, disappearing to the unknown below. They could only be at one place.

She had found Falos, the god's descent.

It was, apparently, the end of the world.

It stretched endlessly on either side. Beyond it were bright blue skies, but in the distance, she saw nothing: no land, no water, nothing save a darkness that grew the farther down you looked.

Funakiin howled from behind her.

Her mind snapped back to the battle ongoing as she cursed. "*Pit*. Funakiin!"

Ashilde turned back around to look, only to see the wolf wasn't the one in danger.

She was.

A large claw swung its way toward her and she didn't have time to duck.

Suddenly, something hit her square in the head, pushing her backward and out of the way of the claw, which landed exactly where she had been standing only moments before. But Ashilde barely registered what happened, as she landed on her back, staring up into the sky.

And saw a raven circling back around.

"Ieka?" she whispered, before her body curled inward, as cramps hit her once again—but this time, stronger than she'd ever felt before.

Ashilde screamed.

Blinking her eyes open past tears, she looked down at her body and watched, in horror, as it slowly disappeared in front of her eyes. Starting at her feet, then her ankles, crawling up past her knees, her entire body was quickly becoming ethereal.

"No, no, no!"

She was so close. She'd found Falos. Skírrdrauin had to be nearby, somewhere. She couldn't die yet. She couldn't—

Forcing herself up despite the pain, she screamed again, but the sound was cut off as her mouth disappeared. She raised a hand to touch her face but she didn't feel the touch, even though the faint, glowing outline showed her fingers—from her right hand, this time—hovered just in front of where her lips should be. On the ground below her, her stuff laid in a pile: her bow, arrows, her pack, even her armor and clothes, all lying discarded, no longer having a body to cling onto.

Her mother's necklace.

Anóra's.

She was still able to see and hear—Funakiin's yelp of pain strident, echoing throughout the air. She watched the wolf's body as it was flung away from the creature. He collapsed onto the ground, limp.

The creature turned and focused on her.

Whatever was happening, she wasn't dead yet.

And it could still see her.

The massive creature charged.

Looking around, Ashilde knew she couldn't defend herself against it, not when she no longer had a body she could use. Instinctually, she began pedaling backward and discovered that, even though her legs were gone, she was still able to move. Thankful she could at least do *that*, she heard a raven caw from above. Risking a glance, she spotted who she impossibly believed to be Ieka flying just above the river, before shooting out over the edge, flying into the open air. Ashilde caught the raven's meaning and couldn't believe she was considering listening to her. That fall would kill her!

But could it, now that she didn't have a body to break?

If that doesn't, that creature is certainly going to try!

Knowing which death she'd rather risk, Ashilde turned around and began sprinting toward the river, dodging to the left at the last second, thanks to the warning of a shadow, as the stinger came overhead and crashed into the ground beside her, sending her off balance as it buried itself into the ground. She righted herself and ran beside the river, ignoring every instinct that told her to stop running as she approached the edge.

Reaching it, she jumped.

Ashilde felt the wind not only guide her, but pass *through* her. Looking ahead, she watched as the empty blue sky in front of her slowly darkened until there was nothing ahead of her to see. Flipping around, she could barely make out the stone rockwall behind her, especially as the sun became further and further away, until she saw nothing around her except for a darkness only akin to the blindness she felt in the Flatrí—except she could see herself glowing in the midst of it; an *outline* of herself, at least.

Flipping her body back around so that she was hovering with her stomach facing the ground, she spread her arms out wide, staring at her ethereal body and wondering what in the gods' name she was meant to do next; wondering why Ieka had instructed her to jump; wondering if the drop ever ended and what she would find at the bottom.

When she finally reached the bottom, she didn't see it. Ashilde didn't even feel it, when she hit. Instead, one moment, she was falling in darkness, touching nothing, seeing nothing, aside from her new, glowing form. The next, she collided with a large body of water. Yet there was no crash, no splash of water, that should have accompanied such a fall.

She closed her eyes once she realized she made an impact, not opening them for a few seconds.

Once she did, all her fear and confusion slipped away—if only for a moment—to make room for wonder.

She hovered in water so vast, she couldn't see anything else. Ashilde was surprised she could see anything at all, but her surroundings were clear and easy to make out, as if the sun shone directly overhead. But darkness continued to loom above her, keeping her light source a mystery.

Instead of searching for it, she looked around, awed by the life surrounding her. She'd swam in the ocean before—hard to avoid it, living her entire life just off its coast. But, she'd never seen water so clear as this, and was lucky if she saw a few dozen fish, during an afternoon swim, since the Dirheil usually got to them first.

But here, surrounding her?

There were thousands.

All the creatures gave her a wide berth, but they were still close enough for her to notice some finer details. There were fish as tiny as her palm and she saw at least one bigger than her, with a large, pointed fin protruding from the middle of its back in the distance. She saw flashes of every color, sometimes all the colors she knew of painted on just one creature alone. Some swam in circles around her, curiously inspecting her, while others ducked between the various growths of plants and seaweed, content to ignore her completely. She turned in circles, trying to take in all of the details.

Eventually, she realized that she hadn't gone up for air for quite some time and she wasn't actively holding her breath, either. Considering she was completely transparent now, Ashilde shouldn't have been surprised that she now breathed underwater. Or perhaps she wasn't breathing at all? Is this what the Dirheil felt like? Their gift of waterbreathing from Waldemar took on new, incredible meaning for her.

Seeing no other signs of what she should do—and receiving no further instruction from Ieka, who had once again disappeared, unable to follow her into the depths—Ashilde started to swim deeper into the water, her fears of drowning forgotten. She didn't bother to try and figure out why sometimes, her body worked as if she still had a physical form and others, it proved as translucent as it had become. It was just another question for the gods that, if she was going the right way, would be answered soon.

As she descended, she noticed the sea was not as never-ending as she assumed. On either side of her were solid rock formations, enclosing the water like an outer shell. The rocks were slowly coming closer together, until the only path in front of her was through a small, circular opening within the rock. An underwater cavern. The only other option was to turn around and see how far the water traveled on the other side, or to swim up to the surface and take a look. Yet above her was still dark and uninviting. Glancing behind, the fish had created a wall so thick, she'd have trouble actually making her way back through them, as they'd quickly filled any space she'd taken up only moments before.

You can always turn around if this leads to nowhere.

Reaching the opening, she put her hands along the edge, her fingertips passing through the rock. Frowning, she kicked with her invisible feet and propelled herself inside. Within, the cavern walls were covered with small specs of light, giving off a blue glow that was more beautiful than eerie. Small plants also grew out from the cracks in the rock, little silver mushrooms and purple weeds swaying against the flow of the current.

Despite the beauty surrounding her, her nerves were on edge from how narrow the passage was—and how it continued to shrink—encouraging her feet to continue to kick without a break. Even without pausing, Ashilde didn't feel tired. In fact, now that she thought about it, she didn't feel weak at all. Nor hungry.

Her cramps had completely disappeared.

Look at all the things you forget to notice while your body is becoming translucent and you have to jump off a cliff to avoid being killed by a monster.

Though that was the answer, wasn't it? She no longer had a body, unsure of what exactly she had become now and how she was able to move at all, having lost the ability to grab onto or hold anything, while still maintaining the ability to move. Yet, without a physical body, didn't it make sense that she wouldn't feel the aches and pains that body had carried with her? Though thankful for the relief, the realization didn't sit well with her. If she didn't die from this, Ashilde wasn't sure she could truly adjust to life as ... whatever she now was.

The path she followed turned, giving her no option but to follow. As she did, she noticed a bright light dawning in the distance.

Ashilde swam faster toward it, reaching the light in mere moments. Slipping out of the path, she was once again in clear, open water, but this time, there was no darkness above her. Instead, there was a welcoming brightness. More fish swam apathetically around her, but she hardly noticed them as she angled herself upward and began rising toward the surface. She hadn't realized how *deep* in the water she had dove into, as too much time passed before she finally broke the surface.

Ashilde gaped, the sway of the waves sending her back and forth over the same spot.

In front of her was land, unlike any she'd ever seen.

A small stretch of sandy beach sat beyond the shore, before immediately being interrupted by a scattering of large trees and dark green foliage. Just beyond that was a large rock formation. She traced her eyes up the rocks, continuing to climb until she realized that it wasn't plain rocks at all.

It was the base of a mountain.

Peeking out above white, fluffy clouds, she could see it, if she squinted: the top of the mountain, looming higher than anything she'd ever seen, its shadow blocking out the sun over the water she currently floated in, making it appear darker than it actually was. Ashilde found that she couldn't properly breathe—and imagined, if she still had a body, the feeling wouldn't've changed.

Skírrdrauin.

She'd found it.

She actually *found it*.

Ashilde twisted around, looking behind her. The ocean—at least, she thought it was an ocean—had an end. She could see the edge, where the water stopped, yet it didn't slip over the side, like the river had. Instead, the water just stilled, perfectly lined up with the edge.

Beyond it, she saw nothing but sky.

Ashilde quickly turned and swam toward the shore. Though she was confident this was Skírrdrauin, she was at a loss of how it came to be; how she'd reached something that seemed to float in the sky after falling *down* into the deepest depths. Yet, for now, that didn't matter, the last question for her to be concerned with. She had other answers to demand and now, she was finally going to get them.

The first mortal to enter the Skírrdrauin, the god's domain.

The weight of that accomplishment was not lost on Ashilde, as she climbed onto the shore. But she didn't let herself get distracted by it. She'd paid too much to get here and let her own emotions distract her.

Ashilde walked toward the center of the cliffside, lined with trees she'd never seen before. With trunks that curved, the leaves didn't start until almost at the top of the tree, the branches sprouting out in various directions, tiny blades of green and yellow leaves hanging tightly together from each branch. On the small beach, she saw no animals, which surprised her, considering how many fish she'd just encountered underwater. Bird calls *did* echo, but they were well in the distance—though where the birds could be hiding when all around her was nothing but empty sky, she had no idea.

She paused at the base of the mountain. The rock base was jagged, jutting out to provide plenty of hand holds and foot rests for her to utilize in her climb up to the top. After everything she'd gone through to get here, she wasn't surprised she'd have to put in more work to reach the top, where she assumed the god's dwelled.

When had the gods ever made anything easy for her?

Reaching up to the nearest potential handhold, Ashilde made a move to grab onto it and hoist herself up, despite expecting to smack her face against the stone as her hand passed right through the rock, not grabbing anything.

But instead of smacking her face, the rock passed through her forehead, too.

Ashilde took a step back, trying not to panic. She still couldn't grab onto anything. How in the Pit was she supposed to climb up to the top of the mountain if she couldn't actually climb?

For someone who forced me to be here and ruined my life in the process, you're not exactly being very accommodating, Ashilde thought.

Suddenly, a large gust of wind swept across the beach.

Ashilde found herself being carried with it.

She panicked, arms flailing as she tried to grab onto something, anything, as she became airborne. But everything within reach passed right through her and, without a physical body to catch onto anything, she was completely at the wind's mercy. She flailed for a few more seconds before she finally forced herself to still, calming down enough to realize that she wasn't just being swept off the island, to be dropped and abandoned into the abyss below. She was *climbing.*

Looking down, Ashilde saw the small stretch of beach she'd stood on moments before growing smaller and smaller. The mountainside remained in front of her. She passed by it with growing velocity, but she no longer worried about what was happening to her. This was no ordinary wind gust.

The gods were bringing her to them.

No, she no longer felt panic, even as she rose high enough to pass through clouds.

She was terrified.

Ashilde was about to meet the gods. Her *gods*. Beings that, as far as she understood, no living mortal had ever actually met, aside from those who died and lived honorable enough lives to earn spending eternity within Skírrdrauin. Though with how difficult—and seemingly impossible, with a physical body—it was to reach Skírrdrauin, she wasn't surprised no one had managed to do this before.

The only thing that surprised her more was that *she* had.

Ashilde felt her anger and her burning desire to demand answers to her questions—and even recompense for what she was undeservingly put through—trying to slip away. These were literal gods she wanted to confront! They were the entire reason she was here, alive, in this moment.

Well, alive was a newly debatable state.

But she still couldn't ignore the sudden fear and intimidation she felt, now that she'd finally made it.

Then, a single word entered into her brain, igniting a passion in her missing heart that not even the presence of her gods would diminish.

No.

Ashilde had lost everything. If she believed the Rhuanics, it was because Róta and Waldemar were fighting and, somehow, Róta wanted Ashilde to be her champion and do ... what, exactly? Fight Waldemar for her, in some lovers' quarrel? She didn't believe it herself, no matter what evidence pointed in that direction.

What she did know, however, was that her *dolorsandri* had been taken away from her, unnaturally, robbing her the ability to bleed and forcing her people to falsely condemn her as tainted—commanded by the gods, dictated by the teachings *they* passed down to her people. The gods *had* chosen to force her into this journey. It was her choice to begin it, her choices that led her to this moment and helped her survive as long as she had.

Her choices that led to many regrets.

Ashilde didn't care who or what the gods were. She would not tremble with terror at their presence nor be awed by their godliness. She would not cower before them in fear, nor become meek by their power.

She was Ashilde, once Faethegnar of the Slátra, daughter of Gunnvor.

She would have her answers.

Finally, she reached the top. The wind carried her and dropped her onto the ground. Standing, she looked back over the edge and saw nothing but clouds.

She wasn't brave enough to peek over it to see how far the ground was below her.

Instead, she turned around and took in the sight before her: the top of the mountain peak. Snow covered the tip, still towering even higher above her. More snow littered the ground around her, reminding her of home. Birds were nested in the few trees that grew this high, as if she was walking just outside the Slátra borders. But what drew her attention the most was what interrupted the mountain, just ahead of her.

An entryway.

It might have only been a cave, at one point, but the gods had fashioned it to their liking, claiming it— or perhaps even creating it—as their own. The mouth opened up wide into the heart of the mountain, with stone steps descending into it. Three carven statues made of stone framed the doorway. Ashilde walked toward them, taking a closer look.

On either side of the entryway stood two identical statues, easily thrice the size of her: a wolf, sitting down, looking more regal than any wolf she'd encountered—including Funakiin, who she could easily believe this statue was based off of. Her heart panged at the thought of her lost companion, who died to allow her to reach this moment. She bowed her head, taking a moment to honor him, before she returned to look at the statues that bore his likeness. With ears pointed up, mouth closed and eyes staring straight ahead, both wolves looked attentive, poised and calm, comfortable in the role of guardian of this sacred realm.

Directly above her, covering the top of the entrance, was a raven. Only half of the raven's torso protruded from the rock, as if the raven was flying directly out of it. Snow covered the tops of the feathers while icicles hung off of her wings, like a row of sharp front teeth, while the outstretched wings covered each wolf's head, protecting their heads from the elements.

Ashilde swallowed, wanting to reach out and touch one of the statues, wishing she still had fingers so she could *feel* them. This was it. This was Skírrdrauin, the realm where only the dead should have been able to go. Ashilde paused as if struck. Anóra's request came back into her mind, unbidden, reminding her that it wasn't only the gods she'd be confronting here, within these sacred walls.

My mother?

Ashilde hadn't even thought about what it would be like, seeing the souls of the dead. Could she interact with them? Would they be able to see her? Would she have the chance of speaking to her mother again? To apologize and beg forgiveness?

Did she even deserve to ask?

Anóra will be here, too.

Pit.

Meeting the gods suddenly didn't seem so nerve wracking, in comparison.

But it didn't matter. It *couldn't* matter. She'd made it this far and she refused to give up now, no matter what awaited her within.

Glancing at the stone guardians one last time, Ashilde began her descent down the frozen steps leading into Skírrdrauin.

CHAPTER TWENTY-SEVEN

Ashilde walked into the cavern at first with slow, timid steps, unsure of what to expect. Yet nothing prepared her for the emptiness that greeted her. Instead of walking into the promised afterlife and home of her gods, it felt like she'd walked into a tomb.

Walls of stone created a narrow hallway ahead of her, perfectly smooth yet so cold, even in her ethereal form, Ashilde could still feel the chill. Sconces lined both sides, spaced out evenly to illuminate the hallway—if they had been lit. Instead, darkness reigned, sending a wave of nervousness through her, as a dangerous thought entered her mind.

Ashilde shook her head, unwilling to believe it. Not here, finally, at the end of it all: the place she truly didn't believe she could reach, yet she did. But what did she find? Nothing but a hallway, appearing endless, adored with nothing but cobwebs, filled with a silence that was as deafening as it was dominating.

No. No, *no*, NO.

What if this isn't it? What if you've found the wrong

place? Or worse: what if the gods have abandoned Armadin?

Not liking where her thoughts were going, Ashilde ignored her mind and picked her pace, running as fast as she could.

"You cowards!" she screamed, her anger pouring out of her as her voice returned. "You want me to pay penance? You want me to prove my worth, so you could offer my clan forgiveness? Well, here I am! Come and welcome me, oh worshiped Ravenmother and cherished Wolffather. I will have words with you!"

Expecting equally to be killed immediately by her unfiltered demands or to remain stuck in the crushing silence, Ashilde stilled when a third option, instead, responded.

The strident call of a raven's cry.

Then, directly in front of her, an arched doorway shimmered into view.

Ashilde took off, running toward it. She didn't slow down as she passed through it, though she stumbled to a stop as she took in the drastic, sudden change in scenery.

Inside was a forest that shouldn't exist.

It appeared as if she'd stumbled out of a cave and straight into a deeply secluded forest, instead of still being buried deep within the heart of a mountain. The trees were large and gorgeous, with thick gold leaves hanging overhead, providing shade from the light of a sun she couldn't see. Flowers dotted between the leaves, two different kinds: the first, a small, six petaled white flower, barely bigger than her fist. The second type was larger, with nine petals, black and larger than her head, weighing down each branch it sprouted from.

Within the trees, flitting across overhead, pecking at the ground, were dozens and dozens of birds. A small pond sat in the center, among the grass that transformed the hard stone into something livable. At the center of the room—and it was still a room, encased in stone, with another arched entryway sat on the opposite side of where she stood, leading deeper into the mountain—were two identical trees. Taller than the rest, with black trunks and golden leaves, they were rooted on either side of the object their leaves came together overhead to hang over.

A throne.

A currently *empty* throne.

Except…

Ashilde walked into the room, moving around a tree to confirm what she thought she caught a glimpse of from behind it. She stilled again as she discovered two more creatures, one laying beside the wooden throne, the other, sitting atop the highest branch that made up its back.

"Funakiin?" Ashilde whispered. "Ieka?"

The wolf's head raised from sleeping, turning to look at her with large, familiar eyes. His expression didn't change and he didn't smile, but she didn't have a doubt. That was Funakiin, even though she'd watched as the wolf's body snapped in half, his whimpered cries as he died still fresh and echoing in her mind. Ieka raised her wings and squawked once, though she didn't approach Ashilde. She frowned. Their reception of her wasn't what she expected—not that she expected to see either of them at all.

It felt … cold.

"What interesting names you gave them," a voice said, startling Ashilde. "Would you like to know their real ones?"

Before she could respond, a soft glow began to fill the throne, creating an outline that looked … human. The throne didn't move, but from within it, a shape rose out, an ethereal body with golden edges, brighter than Ashilde, with curves that made Ashilde's breath catch and hair that flowed like a river from her head and down past her shoulders. Her face was aglow to the point where Ashilde couldn't make out her features, not yet. She wore nothing, but her entire body shimmered, making her appear more like a whisper of what she truly was; as if Ashilde was only catching a passing glance, despite the being sitting directly in front of her. The shape rose to a sitting position, arms draped over the throne's armrests, confidently claiming the throne as her own. Even without an introduction, Ashilde knew exactly who this was.

Róta, the Ravenmother.

She immediately dropped to the floor, bowing her head low. No matter how angry she was, this was her god. She would still show the proper respect.

For now.

She could hear the god's smile as she said, "Ah, I do miss this type of worship. If only the constant questioning and begging and *asking* hadn't ruined it." A pause. "Rise, champion."

Ashilde was standing before she realized she commanded her legs to lift her up. She met Róta's gaze. Now that she'd shown her respect, she would demand her answers. Especially as her nerves heightened after her god called her by the very same name the Rhuanics' teased.

And there was no sign of Waldemar anywhere.

The god spoke before she could begin, gesturing with one hand toward Funakiin. "This is Sokin, Waldemar's favored pet who has always liked me better—which proved to be a great benefit to you. And my own heart, Visindi."

Ieka flew down and landed on Róta's outstretched hand, not passing through it, but instead, sitting on it as if it were something solid. She rubbed her head against Róta's cheek, causing the god to smile. Róta settled back into her seat, Ie—*Visindi*—settled firmly on her hand, while Sokin lowered his head onto his paws and fell back asleep once more. Róta's eyes met Ashilde's once more, the clear gaze more intense than any she'd experienced before.

"Finally," the god breathed. "Someone did not fail me."

Ashilde's head swam. Already, so much information had been given to her, teased in offhand comments and explanations she hadn't asked for. Information that hinted at lies she refused to believe as truths.

"An explanation would be kind," Ashilde said.

"I need a champion. I chose you—but don't let that go to your head," the Ravenmother said, with a wave of her hand. "You're only the most recent of many I thought worthy candidates. But the first to actually succeed in proving their worth. *That* you should be proud of."

"A champion for what?"

"You have all the information you need to draw that conclusion," the god said. "Why is it so hard to believe I want you to kill Waldemar?"

Ashilde felt everything go still.

"He's your partner, our god," Ashilde said, still struggling to believe that Róta would want to *kill* Waldemar, proving the Rhuanics' ravings to be grounded in truth. The gods had built the entire world together. They had created one another to be the perfect complement. It was implausible—should have been impossible—for them to war with one another.

Pit, if the gods were at war, how else was her world about to change?

"Why would you want to kill him?"

"We had a minor disagreement." The god spoke plainly, almost as if she were ... bored.

"A disagreement worthy enough to kill him?" Ashilde didn't hide her own incredibility, or her judgment.

"Take a seat," Róta offered with a wave of her hand. Suddenly, Ashilde was forced into a chair made from vines, branches and leaves that grew up from the ground behind her. "Though you should simply do my bidding as you're told, I've become rather fond of you, watching over you in the past month. You have a fire within you that reminds me of myself. For a mortal."

Ashilde wasn't sure, but for a moment, it appeared that the glow over Róta's face faded, showing ethereal eyes that had become wreathed in flame as she glanced over.

"I'll share with you the story behind Waldemar's downfall, though much of it should be familiar to you." The goddess settled into her own seat, Visindi moving to return back on her perch above the throne. "Then, I will enjoy sending you to kill him."

Ashilde, for once, kept her mouth shut.

Róta's smirk suggested that was a good idea.

"It was the Skalda who first shed light on the fact that Waldemar was not the god I believed him to be; the god I *needed* him to be. You are familiar with the Banishing, are you not?"

Ashilde wasn't sure if that was a question Róta was seriously asking. The Banishing was only the singular most devastating event in all of Armadin's history. Of *course* she knew about it.

"You want Waldemar killed because the Skalda liked him better than you and sacrificed your birds in his name? Can you truly be so petty?"

She expected to see Róta's rage firsthand when she forgot to control her tongue. Ashilde was unable to hide her widened eyes at her shock when the Ravenmother turned and laughed with her pet.

"Don't act so shocked that I'm not angered at your fire," Róta said, turning back to her. "You think I don't *know* you, haven't watched you since you were a child? I know all about you. That's why you should do nicely."

"I still don't understand. You want me to kill a god because you're jealous—"

"I am *not jealous*," she hissed, her calm demeanor gone in an instant as she threw herself forward, arms still braced on her throne, as all the birds around them at once went silent. Ashilde flinched, but the vine chair she sat on kept a strong hold, latching her in place as if she had a physical form to hold onto. "If only it were so slight. No, child. I am *angry*. The Banishing happened because I believed it was the only solution, to teach our people how both of us must be worshiped in unison, together; how preference between one god over the other would result in more doom for the clans than what your own foolish wars did to yourselves."

Ashilde felt her own anger stirring within. "Wars *you* allowed to happen. Wars—"

Róta waved her hand—a favored gesture of hers, it seemed—and Ashilde went silent, her voice suddenly constricted. The birds took up their song around them once more, but the tension in the air remained. "Let's not waste time on the semantics of godhood, my dear. What you don't understand—what *no mortal* can possibly understand—is the price a god pays for her people. I killed many of my children in that disaster to teach a lesson, to try and divert what I saw as the inevitable consequence of unequal worship." Finally, she leaned back in her chair again and Ashilde felt the pressure on her throat cease. "But it didn't matter. Waldemar and his Rhuanics found a way to persevere, despite my best efforts. I realized death and destruction over what I held most dear wasn't enough. I had to destroy the source."

Trying to keep up with what her god confessed to her, Ashilde asked, "Waldemar created the Rhuanics? Why?"

"Something I have been trying to understand for quite some time, my child," Róta said. "But some minds you simply cannot understand, just like some actions you simply cannot tolerate. Rhuanics upsetting the natural balance—the very rules my husband and I made, *together*—cannot continue. You have experienced firsthand their destruction. Do you believe there is a place in the world for them?"

A flood of memories suddenly assaulted her like a wave. Her hunters, wiped out. Anóra crying on the chest of her dead mother, herself burned to death for simply being in the wrong place at the wrong time. The Rhuanics who hunted her—and other champions of Róta, most likely succeeding in killing them in cold blood without any of them realizing why they'd been chosen or hunted in the first place.

No, the goddess was right about that.

They didn't belong there at all.

But Ashilde wasn't sure if that was enough, her mind flashing to the family she'd stumbled upon there: the mother's kind voice, the child's desire to do nothing but play, expressing no ulterior desires than to experience a lasting peace. What had *they* done wrong?

"How will killing Waldemar stop the Rhuanics from spreading?"

"A body is worthless without its head, is it not? Without his direction, they will scramble, panic. They'll lose their source of food, their guiding hand traveling through the lands I had destroyed. No more will there be organized attacks on clans simply trying to live in peace. No more will there be children orphaned, as their parents are killed before them." Her voice lowered an octave. "No more will children be burned because it is asked of them."

Ashilde stiffened, trying not to lose control. "Waldemar *asked*? He asked the Rhuanics ... to kill ... he asked...Why?"

"*Why?* Keep *up*, child. To get to you! No warrior I claimed to become my champion has ever made it as far as you have, always failing to even make it out of the Segan. My husband grew nervous and needed to do everything he could to weaken you, to *break* you. Killing a child you loved like a sister, when your own rejected you? A trivial step, to him, to lure you to his followers and allow them to finish the job."

She felt like she was going to vomit.

Not only had one of her gods blessed the very Rhuanics that destroyed so much of her life, but he had *ordered* Anóra be killed? He threw away the child's life to try and get to her?

She would kill Waldemar herself, with or without the Ravenmother's prompting. But that didn't mean the god before her would escape her ire.

"You sat by and did nothing. Why not kill Waldemar yourself?"

"It is impossible for a god to kill another," Róta said. "A rule I have spent the past half millennium regretting ever agreeing to. But there is no rule saying a mortal can't kill a god, if she proves strong enough for the task."

"So that's why you robbed me of my *dolorsandri*? So I would come here and kill for you?"

Róta's lips pursed. "Well, naturally, child. You and dozens of women before you. Yet none of them could pass the tests I put in front of them, dying before they reached Skírrdrauin. Even *you* needed assistance. In desperation, I gave more than I usually do; more than I properly should. I'm tired of waiting for Waldemar to die so order can be restored."

"But ... the Seidsian ... why didn't you tell her? Why did you lie, saying—"

"That you were the price your clan needed to pay, to protect them from my wrath; chosen to atone for your mother's death? An unfortunate accident, that. The Fundi have always been a ruthless group." Róta waved her hand like it was miniscule, like she hadn't just brushed aside one of the most harrowing experiences in Ashilde's life like it was nothing. "How do you think the clans would respond if they knew their gods were at war with one another? Don't bother, I'll answer for you: *not well*. Not to mention I needed to keep my own council, my plans secret from him. And I succeeded to do so, for a time.

"Yet, as each of my chosen champions continued to die before reaching Skírrdrauin, it was only a matter of time." For the first time, Róta looked down at her with true appreciation. "The fact that you survived not only my tests, but his Rhuanics' attacks, too? You are truly the one designed for this task."

Ashilde blinked, too many emotions warring within her to give attention to any one of them. "So ... so why not just bring me here directly, if you wanted him killed so badly? What did I have to *prove*?"

"The strength of your soul. Only the mightiest of wills could make it across the uninhabitable lands without godly aid. Only the most stubborn of hearts could bear the taints of those they'd killed and still push on, even as their physical form left them with every new life taken. Only the greatest of souls could endure until they became nothing *but* that. Even in my omnipotence, there is knowledge denied to me. I had no idea if you were strong enough to endure, only that you had the promise and the drive to do so. Your quest to make it here was necessary to prove that I had chosen correctly."

Her head pounded, even in translucence. Everything was falling apart. The questions she had come to demand answers to were lying unspoken on her proverbial tongue, forcibly swallowed in favor of trying to gain clarity on the god's latest demands of her life. Everything she suffered, everything she'd *lost*, had just been some sort of test to prove her worth, as a pawn to assist in her gods' quarrels?

She'd kill both of them, if Róta wasn't careful.

"Well, congratulations, Ravenmother. Your champion has arrived," Ashilde spit, seething. "Say I agree to kill the Wolffather. How?"

"Oh, child, never fear. That's the easy part."

Róta smiled, filling Ashilde with unease that enveloped her as soon as her god opened her mouth to speak once more.

"All you have to do is die."

Ashilde stared at the Ravenmother in disbelief, the rest of her questions and curiosities momentarily forgotten. "What?"

"I've done most of the hard work for you. Waldemar is locked up in his own corner of our home. He has been for centuries now. His strength has waned considerably. I'll even gift you your physical form back, if that will make you more comfortable. Plus, any weapon you desire—or, the return of your old attire, if that will suffice. All you have to do is go to him and drive your weapon of choice through his heart. His soul will be taken and mixed with yours, killing him. But, by trying to harbor a soul of a god, yours, too, will perish." Róta smiled as if that *wouldn't* be an issue for Ashilde. "I cannot think of a more noble sacrifice."

Her god was wrong.

"I did not travel all this way to simply die at your command," she hissed.

Róta *tsked* to Visindi. "Such fire, this one. And such ignorance, to think she's ever had any choice at all."

Ashilde shook with rage, the glow around her form becoming brighter, causing Róta to raise an eyebrow in return. "I came here for answers. You took *everything* from me. My home, my people, my *life*. You expect me to just roll over and die, because you ask it? Because you're my god?" Ashilde shook her head almost hard enough to snap it. "You are sorely mistaken. I have not doubted you all of these years only to roll over now like a good pet and do your bidding. I am not your servant."

"But you are, *pet*," Róta cooed. "I didn't know the strength of your soul until now. I am confident you are strong enough to harbor the soul of a weakened god long enough to kill him. But I've always known your character. I've had an eye on you, throughout your life. One who curses at us so vehemently does not easily escape my notice—on your *dolorsandri* or not."

Ashilde couldn't believe it. The Seidsian had always told her that cursing the gods would do her no good. She'd never expected her Seidsian to be right. "So, you chose me out of pettiness? Because I offended you, lacking in my undying worship?"

Róta snorted. "Hardly. I brought you here because I know I can control you."

"You're wrong," Ashilde whispered, her rage boiling over to the point where she could barely speak.

Róta's hand moved in a graceful gesture, her palm opening to lay flat against the open air. "Watch," she commanded.

In midair, a circle formed, as if made by wisps of smoke. Within it were moving images. Images Ashilde could clearly make out. Though what magic Róta showed off now was unfamiliar, what she saw inside the circles wasn't. She saw her home. She'd recognize those walls and those trees anywhere; could almost smell the distinct tang of the ocean breeze that blew in each day with the morning sun.

The image began to pan, allowing her to see glimpses of individuals. Most of her warriors, fighting together in the training grounds. Brynhild, playing with one of her daughters while the Seidsian stood beside them, laughing. Dagfinn, relaxing with the other elders, drinking ale. Davyn and Freydis sitting together in the animal pens while Freydis's children ran around, chasing a new litter of puppies.

Emotions grew tight within her. Was this what they were doing now, in real time? *They were okay. They were all okay.* Her relief was so palpable, it hurt.

Suddenly, the image shifted, disappearing one moment only to be replaced by another, one of horror.

Everything caught fire.

Ashilde tried to recoil, but her body was frozen, rigid, the vines holding her firm, the heat from the flames hot against her translucent face. She was forced to watch as everyone she knew died.

Dagfinn stood brave against the flames, the bucket of water falling against the ground as flames licked up his arms, his tattoos melting out off his flesh in blank ink. The Seidsian, kneeling at the altar in prayer, the screams of the dying loud, unmoving as the flames licked up her fur coat and climbed onto her back. Freydis screaming, eyes wide, shoving her children forward as she rushed to get all the animal pens open, only to be trampled by the creatures she'd served all her life, her body twisting in unnatural angles as her bones snapped. Brynhild lying dead on the scorched earth, eyes unseeing, half her hair burned clean away, while her innards lie, dripping.

Davyn, his body burning from the legs up as he screamed, shouting her name, begging for her to save him once again—a strident sound that tore at her ears, making her insides bleed—before a falling tree collapsed on top of him, crushing his screams that continued to sound inside her head, even as the images went black.

The distinct feeling of tears streaming down her face overwhelmed her, choking on sobs she couldn't express. Ashilde felt her chest tighten, the phantom emotions strong enough to even overcome her lack of a physical form.

Worse, the images didn't stop.

Ashilde was forced to watch as, clan after clan, a different horror wiped them out: freezing ice, hunger, plague, famine, slaughtered by beasts, war. She even saw Anóra, a girl who already died gruesomely once, being offered a repeat performance, thanks to Róta's power—or perhaps her cruelty. The child was brought up in chains, climbing up steps that were hidden beneath the sand, as she was brought forth into the light. She was forced to her knees as an ax swept and wiped her head off of her shoulders.

After three strokes.

But before the first stroke fell, Ashilde could hear her screaming, repeating one word desperately, believing with her dying breath that it'd be enough to save her.

Ashilde!

With a wave of the god's hand, the images vanished and Ashilde could move again.

She collapsed onto the floor, gasping.

She felt Róta's shadow climb over her as the goddess leaned out from atop her throne, her ethereal form glowing brightly. "A future I can create with a snap of my fingers," she promised. "You can die peacefully, knowing you prevented such a future from happening, through fulfilling this final task I give to you: protecting your clan, like you set out to do. Or, you can die last, after watching all of that destruction come to life.

"I have destroyed life once before and it killed me inside to do it, Ashilde, you must know," the Ravenmother continued, leaning back into her throne. "But I cannot let the Rhuanics continue. They are an affront to everything we created, everything we stand for. I'd rather *not* start over completely to wipe them out, for it'd be a wasted effort. Their leader would remain and, from the ashes, more would rise, creating a cycle of suffering that will never end. Waldemar *must* be stopped."

Ashilde raised her eyes. She had never experienced true hatred until that moment. These were the types of gods they followed? Liars with fragility so great, they couldn't solve their own problems, instead threatening the entire world they'd created simply because they no longer lived in harmony with one another? It might have been Waldemar's pride that triggered Ashilde's fate, but it was Róta's vengeance which sealed it.

"Do not test my patience still further," the god said, after Ashilde answered her with silence. "Knife, axe, sword or spear?"

"Knife," she whispered.

If she was going to kill her god, she wanted to look him in the eyes as she did so.

Her god leaned back with a smile. "Quite a close and personal choice," she said. She snapped her fingers and Ashilde cried out, collapsing fully onto the ground as her entire body suddenly racked with pain, her cramps returning. She blinked back tears as she curled inward, her knees pressing into her chest as she tried to combat the sudden flow of pain.

Her eyes snapped open.

Her body was back.

And she felt horrible.

A knife appeared in front of her, laying on the ground. "It seems your body still doesn't take too kindly toward harboring souls you cannot cleanse. If you want to kill Waldemar before your body kills *you*, I suggest you hurry. The fate of all Armadin depends on it."

Shaking, Ashilde pushed herself up to her knees, snatching her knife in the process. She met Róta's eyes, not bothering to hide the hate she held there. The god was unphased as she gestured toward a new doorway, opening between trees in the opposite corner, pointing her towards where Waldemar's prison lay and her own death awaited.

"My armor?" Ashilde asked, noticing she only wore the outfit that she'd worn underneath her mother's sacred set.

"You won't need it, where you're going," the Ravenmother said, no longer looking at her.

Feeling queasy, Ashilde gripped the knife tightly as she

stood and began walking toward the door, moving slowly, her cramps intensifying with every step.

And with it, hope faded.

When she reached the doorway, Ashilde heard a voice inside her head. *Kill them. Kill them both.*

Whipping around, she turned to look back at Róta, who was no longer paying attention to her, but cooing at Visindi resting on her arm, giggling like a child at her pet. Instead, she found the sleeping wolf on the ground staring straight at her, eyes alert.

Without looking, Róta waved her hand absentmindedly.

The door closed, shutting Ashilde back into darkness.

CHAPTER TWENTY-EIGHT

Walking through the next labyrinth of empty stone hallways, following the only path ahead of her as each step took her closer to killing a god, Ashilde's mind whirled. But not about what Róta had revealed to her: her strife between her husband, how he was responsible for the Rhuanics, how Ashilde had been chosen to sacrifice herself to kill a *god*.

Sokin—or Funakiin—had just given her a message. It was the only possibility that made sense, even if after, when she tried to reach back out to the wolf, she was only answered with silence.

He wanted her to not only kill Waldemar, but Róta as well. Yet killing Waldemar would kill *her*. How was she supposed to stay alive long enough to kill Róta, too?

Even if she could somehow manage it before she died, *then* what happened? She wasn't sure how much of this worked, but she couldn't imagine a world without its gods wouldn't have consequences, a rippling effect that would leave its mark on everyone she hated just as much as it was felt among everyone she loved.

It was too much to wrap her head around.

It was *almost* a good enough distraction from what was about to happen next.

No matter what, she was about to die.

Though she was angry that everything she'd gone through in the past month led to this, despite it all, she felt ... calm. Ashilde moved slowly, but with unclenched fists, a straight spine, her stride purposeful.

Perhaps it was because she had no other option. She didn't doubt Róta's strength or her power. She'd walked through both the Flatrí and the Hafleden, places her ancestors lived, once, but had become ruined and practically uninhabitable, thanks to the Ravenmother's wrath. When the god threatened to kill not only the Slátra, but every single soul in Armadin if Ashilde didn't go and do what she commanded, Ashilde had no doubt it not only *could* happen, but it would.

She cursed the god for knowing her so well. Róta knew there was no reality in which she could sit by and let death consume them, not when she had the very real power to stop it.

She'd already given them everything.

What was asking for her life, as well, on top of the rest?

Ashilde closed her eyes for a brief moment, letting out a sigh that felt broken, despite her determination to see this through, before she continued on.

She didn't waste time planning how to kill a god. One could not plan for such an attack. What she *should* have done—what she wanted to do—was think back on her life and those she loved; those she would die for now, focusing on them and the good memories she shared, which made such a sacrifice worth it.

But Ashilde couldn't. Her brain had only two modes: over-analyzing the information she'd just been given or completely shutting down. She switched between the two as she forced herself to continue moving forward, albeit slowly. She was exhausted, her body sore and her cramps relentless, the true toll of the past month finally weighing down on her.

It would be a miracle if she actually made it to Waldemar's prison.

As she finally reached the end of the hallway, her mind was like a night sky during a new moon: dark, silent and uninterrupted. She walked through the doorway without hesitation, gripping the knife tightly in her right hand. Even with her missing armor, the familiarity of her old clothes returned to her brought her comfort in such a strange setting—even if her clothes were torn, muddy, bloody and smelled true to her journey, as someone who'd traveled across all of Armadin in a month and had only taken a handful of baths along the way.

Only her necklaces were missing.

She didn't expect the loss to hurt as much as it did.

Upon reaching Waldemar's prison, she paused, certain she'd found it even without having no other paths to take. It looked like one. It was a small room, made completely from stone and smelled distinctly like wet dog. In the center, the stone sunk down to create a large pool of water, the top of the water completely still. It took up almost the entire room, leaving hardly enough space for anything else. There was no furniture, no belongings, no signs that anyone lived there at all. The only surprising thing was the open archway, allowing whoever was meant to be stuck there the freedom to come and go as they chose; unless Róta had only just opened the doorway on her way here.

Water splashed as a figure swam up to the surface, breaking through and climbing out onto the rock in one smooth motion.

Ashilde jumped in surprise. The water was clear. She hadn't seen any shadows hinting at figures swimming down below. From the stillness of the surface, she hadn't believed it was possible anyone was down there. But she was in the home of the god, a fact she continually forgot, with how underwhelming the actual inside of it was and how overwhelmed *she* was from everything she'd learned since arriving. Anything was possible.

Perhaps like the fact that Waldemar looked like a man instead of a god.

As he turned to face her, she tried to summon forth the anger she'd felt only moments ago, after her discussion with Róta. She wanted to rage for what this man had done, for taking Anóra away from her.

But she was so, so tired.

The god looked at her, his stark blue eyes bright against the grayness of his surroundings, lacking the ethereal form or golden glow Ashilde had moments ago, a form Róta perfected and embraced. He snapped his fingers and a blanket appeared, wrapped around his waist within a blink of an eye.

"Didn't mean to startle you," Waldemar said, moving to sit on the bench he just created out of nothing, his tone gentle, his voice ancient, though he looked like a man in his early fifties, perhaps—not someone who was born with the beginning of time. Droplets of water continued to drip onto his muscular shoulders from his silver-flecked hair. He didn't appear to be nervous in the least. She hadn't bothered to hide the presence of her knife and she struggled to believe he wasn't aware of why she was here. Róta didn't seem the type to mince words or hide her intentions.

He leaned his head back against the stone, staring at Ashilde with an intensity that should have made her nervous. But she was on the brink of death, though her body felt well past that.

She just couldn't bring herself to care.

"So, Róta's chosen one has finally arrived," he said,

not bothering to hide his distaste. "You don't seem particularly eager to get the job done."

"I've never been particularly eager to die."

"Is that what she told you would happen, once you kill me?" He smirked, raising an eyebrow in consideration. "It's possible, I suppose."

Her eyes narrowed. "Are you suggesting she lied to me?" Ashilde frowned. "Next, you'll tell me this has all just been a big misunderstanding and you're actually just the victim here."

"Isn't that what you would do, in my situation?"

Ashilde blinked.

But Waldemar shook his head, water shaking off to patter against the stone. "But no, that's not my intention. My fate has been sealed for many years—and desired for far more. I'm just glad someone finally made it."

"You *want* to die?"

"It will be a relief. My power is all but gone. I'm stuck in my mortal form. Róta put events in motion I was too arrogant to notice, until it was too late." He sat back and closed his eyes. "No, no. My time here is done and I'm ready to finish it, answering for the supposed heresy I committed."

"*Supposed*? You claim that you *didn't* convince the Skalda clan to slaughter Róta's ravens in your name? You didn't open yourself up to worship by a band of Rhuanics who went against everything you taught us to believe?"

Waldemar's eyes snapped back open. "Oh no, I certainly did do that," he admitted, without hesitation or regret. "When we noticed the clans starting to pick favorites, Róta herself suggested we play a game and see how many followers we could each get. I was all for it. Even had fun with it, for quite some time. Róta's jealousy was..." Waldemar actually chuckled. "Well, let's just say I miss those times."

Ashilde felt her anger begin to build, pushing past

her exhaustion. "You don't regret what you caused them to do? What you're having the Rhuanics still do, *now*? You've damned them! What will happen to them and the souls they carry but cannot purge? How can you not care?"

"Nothing," Waldemar said.

"What?"

"Nothing will happen to their souls. They aren't tainted."

"But ... that's not possible. They've killed. When you kill—"

"...A life is taken, and their soul is released to the Greater Realm, to live an eternity in peace. But nothing happens to the killer. Not their soul, at any rate. Their own conscience and emotions toward the act they've committed? Well, they'll have to live with that the rest of their lives. So, you are right, in a sense. Still a heavy price to pay."

Ashilde stammered, confused. "That's ... that's not what we've learned, not what *you* taught us. *Dolorsandri's* are—"

"A natural, perfectly normal body function that some people go through, as part of the process of preparing, if they choose it, to become a mother. Normal, necessary and varied, just like the people who have them. That's it."

Her head ached. How was this *possible*? No, it couldn't be possible. It suggested that ... *everything* their culture was built around, the way they chose their warriors and hunters, the belief in purging and the role of tainted souls—pit, even her beliefs in the *afterlife*, was wrong.

"You're lying," she whispered.

"You're here to kill me and I'm going to let you. Lying now serves no purpose."

"And lying to all of us? To your people? What purpose did *that* serve?"

"Simple. The first mortals we created didn't understand why one person bleeds while another didn't. Or why someone hurt a lot, immobilized for days, while others could bleed and not notice, aside from soiling their clothes. Or how someone could bleed one month, but not the next, while another never bled at all, even if their body was fit for it. It scared them. They didn't see it as a natural bodily function, designed for life to be created and continue. Instead, some began to see it as wrong, as filthy, dirty, tainted; as *other*. Unnatural, of all the things!" Waldemar looked at her with an expression of pure shock, as if he still wasn't over the idea of how someone could think that way, despite having an eternity himself to consider it.

"A rift started to form, between the people who bled and those who did not, within the clans," he continued. "Those who did continually prayed to us, asking why we cursed them with such an infliction that would be met with such scorn, such revulsion, such judgment. It was, honestly, a reaction we had not anticipated. It made no sense. Such dynamics worked well enough before, without question.

"So, we gave it another purpose; a greater one that, we believed, might make those who judged not degrade those who bore those prices, but respect them." He opened his arms wide. "As you can see, it worked."

Ashilde wasn't sure what was harder to believe: that the foundation of their very existence was a lie or that someone would truly respond to something as simple as a person's *dolorsandri* with any form of revulsion. Could anyone really have been so small minded and unempathetic, even so long ago?

Yet look how they cast you out, simply because you didn't bleed as expected.

Yes, she realized.

People were still that small minded, now.

Her joy at realizing there was nothing wrong with her—that her personal, secret belief that an individual couldn't be tainted, no matter what happened to their body—was short lived. "It worked," she spat. "But not well enough. We outcast those whose blood price you've robbed too early! Those who don't bleed naturally feel lesser in comparison, less valued in society, denied a calling they might feel because we were led to believe *you* made it so. You've only traded one stigma for another."

Waldemar shrugged, apathetic. "We tried to right a wrong. It is not our fault it wasn't universally received."

Ashilde stared. "You could have told us the truth."

The god chuckled, a soft sound. A weak sound. "Ah, my child. The truth is a dangerous thing. Though, I suppose, if more knew of it, perhaps we wouldn't be in this situation we are today."

Narrowing her eyes, Ashilde asked, "What else have you hidden?"

"Unfortunately, we don't have time to go through a list as long as that. And I believe you have more specific questions?" The Wolffather waved an arm, offering her a seat beside him on the bench. "I will at least give you peace of mind, before you die. Or don't die. We don't know, yet."

Ashilde didn't take it, choosing to stand away from him. "How can you not know what will happen once I kill you?"

"Well, neither of us have ever died before, have we?"

The smallest flicker of hope that she could somehow survive this ignited. Ashilde grasped onto it with every ounce of strength she had. Though resolved to die, if nothing else but to save her people, Ashilde didn't *want* to. Not if there was another option.

"I have no souls within me?"

"None."

"So, when I kill you—"

"Mine should be transferred to you, yes; the first soul you will have ever truly carried. It's how gods were designed. A god cannot kill another god, but a mortal can. Will she die as a result or become a god herself?" He shrugged again, his favorite motion compared to the arm waving of his wife. "We won't find out until you decide to finally do something with that knife."

Ashilde bit her lip. She knew she shouldn't be taking so much time. She should kill him quickly, get it over with, not only because she didn't want to risk Róta's wrath, but because she wanted justice for those lives Waldemar stole through his Rhuanics. But now, talking with the god, her gut told her to wait. There was more to the story than Róta had told her and, if she killed him too quickly, she'd lose her chance at understanding.

So, what was she missing?

"If you lied to us, then why did I miss my *dolorsandri* this month? Why were my cramps worse than ever? Why did my body *disappear entirely*? I thought it was a result of ... tainted blood, of killing those I no longer bore the right to kill."

Waldemar gave her a look. "We both know you didn't believe that at all."

"It was what I was taught—and *expected*—to believe. Now you're telling me it's all a lie and everything this past month was a coincidence?"

"I think you know the answer to that, too, actually."

Of course she did.

Róta.

She was a god. The Ravenmother created lives and ended them as she saw fit. Was it so hard to believe that she could not only take Ashilde's *dolorsandri* away, but change her body into acting the way Ashilde believed it would, based on how she believed the world worked; teachings instructed by the god herself? Róta admitted as much when telling her she forced her to come here, by choosing her as her latest champion.

"Then ... the Rhuanics you have following you now.

They aren't Rhuanics at all."

He shook his head.

"Just really horrible people."

She was surprised when Waldemar flinched.

"You misunderstand them," he tried to say. "They are just searching for a better life. They—"

"Do you command them to act that way? To murder?" Her voice shook as she spoke, interrupting him. "To burn innocent children alive?"

"She's not dead."

Ashilde felt her breath get knocked out of her, as she became lightheaded.

"What?" she whispered.

"The girl, the one who helped lead you to me. Anóra. My chosen one. She's not dead," Waldemar said, his expression earnest.

She touched her neck, where the girl's necklace should have been. "But ... I saw—"

"You saw what I needed you to see. But I promise you, the girl is safe. Unhappy and confused, living among those she was raised to see as evil, but alive and well." Waldemar smirked. "She'll be taken care of."

Ashilde collapsed to the ground, falling on her knees. Tears fell free, streaking down her face silently, her relief at Anóra being alive tainted by her anger. She held Waldemar's stare through her tears, her own fury causing her arms to shake, the knife rattling in her hand.

She was so *tired* of being yanked around and lied to.

"You need to explain everything," she whispered. "*Now.*"

Waldemar nodded, folding his hands together in his lap, as if his words and confessions weren't on the verge of breaking her. "I think it best if I start back at the beginning. With the Rhuanics and how they came to be and ... where it all went wrong."

"Do that."

"Like you accused, I did praise the Skalda, who

sacrificed ravens in my honor, for showing their devotion. No one had ever shown such a strong preference before and I was ... flattered. Róta was jealous and, in her rage, destroyed the Skalda and most of the land that we allocated specifically to the clans."

"Land you allocated? There's more, beyond Armadin?"

Waldemar blinked. "But, of course there is. You think the entire world consists of a single continent?"

Ashilde frowned, not sure what he meant by that.

Her god ran his fingers through his hair. "Perhaps we shouldn't have kept you all in the dark as much as we did. Because if sailing across the ocean to discover more land surprises you, well, the existence of other worlds and gods would shatter society, I expect."

Ashilde threw her hands up in the air. "I came to learn the truth, not more lies and stories!"

"I do speak the truth," Waldemar snapped, a rare form of anger that took her aback. The god calmed immediately, leaving Ashilde on edge. Would he accidentally kill her, if she were to anger him enough?

"But, you're right," he continued, glancing at the entrance from where she'd come in. "Those sorts of revelations aren't important. What *is* important is that, soon after the Banishing, despite Róta's decrees—the new implementation of the animal sacrifice and the demand for equal worship—there were those who were still drawn to me and wanted to worship me alone. Róta had ... changed.

"So, I welcomed them and guided them to a new home, away from her prying eyes. I helped them reach Hafleden and there, I provided for them, promising a new life, a chance to start over, once ... once my wife settled down. Or, was dealt with."

Despite her head swimming with all of this new information, what Waldemar spoke of now *was* plausible. Her travels had confirmed that many clans were divided on matters of faith. And while she now believed they only escaped punishment because they gods were too focused on trying to kill the other by using the living as tools, she focused instead on a bigger concern: the idea of Anóra was stuck with a group of these Rhuanics leaving a bad taste in her mouth.

"Your Rhuanics weren't just some believers who were displeased with Róta's teachings. They killed in cold blood, with little regard to our core beliefs. You guided them to do that?"

For the first time, Waldemar actually looked ashamed. "At first … yes. But only after I realized the true intentions of my wife; realized how power hungry she had truly become. My initial intentions were to create a safe haven in the ashes of what she destroyed in her wrath. But, things quickly escalated and I had to take … precautions." He shook his head. "By the time I realized I could choose a different course, some of my people—*some*, not all, mind—had taken my teachings too far. It was all I could do to try and persuade them to stop. I can't help that they didn't listen."

Ashilde seethed. "You think that's an excuse? You're a *god*. How can you encourage followers and then abandon them to do what they want and let *us* suffer the consequences of your ineptitude? I—"

"You may be here to kill me, mortal, but that doesn't mean I'll allow you to waste my last moments alive berating me for things you can never understand," Waldemar snapped back, with a wrath to match her own. "A god cannot give their creations free will, as we have, and then be expected to be held responsible for what every individual chooses to do with that power. My followers are not the most worthy or good, but they *are* prepared. For me, that's enough." His voice dropped. "It has to be enough."

"Prepared for what?"

"The inevitable demise of their god and the abandonment of the other," he said. "I've prepared them for the truth: that soon, they will live in a world that is godless. And those will be dark days indeed."

Ashilde stared, blinking in confusion. But, she couldn't help thinking back to Funakiin's command.

Kill them both.

Did Waldemar somehow know what the wolf asked of her? Was he going to ... encourage it?

"My wife has drained me of much of my power," he continued, after she didn't speak. "I didn't realize she was even doing so until it was too late to stop it. In order for her to gain it all, I must die. You'll kill me and one of two things will happen: you'll steal my soul and carrying it will indeed kill you, as she's led you to believe it will. But then, my soul will be released, upon your death, and what remains of my power will be hers to collect.

"Or," the god continued, meeting her with a stare that sent chills into her bones, "you'll absorb it and be able to carry it. If she discovers this, she'll have no choice but to kill you and steal it for herself."

Ashilde felt every muscle in her body go rigid. "You're lying. Róta said..." But Ashilde cut herself off. Even her own protest felt weak in comparison to the god's words, the sinking feeling within her that the reality of her situation was much more complex—and darker—than she realized.

"I can see you're working it out for yourself," Waldemar said, leaning forward. "I'll speed up your process. Regardless of how she gets my soul and the rest of my power, Róta *will* leave Armadin and travel to the Greater Realm, where gods are made, the dead rest and *our* god lives. Róta is not content with the reign she has. She wants more. So, she made a plan to kill *them,* our creator. She wants the ultimate throne and the sovereignty that comes with ruling over the gods of *all* worlds." He looked over at her, his eyes wide. "It's a fate you could stop, if you so wished it."

Finally, she couldn't take it anymore.

Ashilde sat down on the floor, setting the knife down on the ground. She wrapped her arms around her legs, her head pounding more than it ever had in her life. He said it so casually. *It's a fate you could stop, if you so wished it.* As if he hadn't just spent the entire time they spoke together—a handful of moments—describing to her not only how both of her gods were corrupt, but somehow, they weren't the only gods to exist—which meant there were other worlds out there, too, with other *people* living on them. And all the gods served another higher power and Róta wanted to, what? Kill them and take their throne? To do that, she was willing to kill her husband and abandon the people *she* created, to rule over gods.

Because *that* was going to end well.

That was plenty enough to make her head pound and fuel her desire to pretend she knew none of it and go back home—ignorant, but at least happy and alive. But she had to include the fact that most of the foundations she'd built her life upon—that *all* the clans had built their lives upon—was a lie. Her *dolorsandri* was nothing more than a bodily function. Those who couldn't bleed could kill as easily as those who did—and apparently, the *sangrendi* once judged the *sangrild* for something that, biologically, they couldn't control. All souls were transferred directly to this … Greater Realm for eternity, not carried by the warriors who claimed them, not transported to Skírrdrauin or cursed to the Pit. Skírrdrauin was nothing more than a home where her gods lived.

And Anóra was alive.

It was the only thing the god had told her to give her any sort of comfort, even if it cemented her hatred toward him, for using the girl to get to her, for allowing her to believe in the farce that was the child's death. It also resolved her desire to make it out of here alive, somehow. She couldn't leave Anóra left in the hands of Rhuanics, even if they weren't going to kill her.

Everything he'd shared was breaking her. It was all too much.

But there was so much still she didn't understand, so much she was struggling to grasp.

Hurry, her mind begged. She had no idea how long she'd have before the Ravenmother questioned what was taking so long.

"What did you order the Rhuanics to do, once you realized what Róta wanted?"

"I knew Róta couldn't kill me, not completely. She needed a mortal champion to do it for her. She thought she covered her tracks well, but it wasn't hard, especially with my followers reporting to me, to figure out that Róta was contacting Seidsians from all different clans, picking out their strongest warriors and hunters, and declaring them tainted—a new consequence from the Banishing, she lied."

Inside, Ashilde seethed.

"And no Seidsian would think to fight it. Because why would we believe our gods would lie to us?" Ashilde glared.

Waldemar was unphased by her venom, no longer even looking at her. "Once I learned what she was doing, I ... ordered my followers to intercept any champion who got close."

Ashilde squeezed her eyes shut.

No. *Please, no.*

"And then I ordered them to kill the chosen ones."

Her eyes snapped open. "In cold blood. People who were simply trying to survive after being falsely condemned, doing their best to make amends when they did *nothing wrong.* You had your Rhuanics slaughter them like animals."

"I don't expect—or ask you—to understand my motivations," he said with a sigh, as if exasperated by their conversation.

"You have an entire group of Rhuanics sitting out in the desert right now. Why not bring them here, allow them to fight Róta for you?"

He shook his head. "I couldn't ask them—no. I *refused* to ask that of them."

"What? Why not?"

Glancing away, he said, "I love them. I will not sacrifice their lives, not when I promised them a future beyond my death; a *peaceful* future."

"But you're willing to risk me and countless other chosen warriors?"

He shrugged, apathetic that he was willing to sacrifice those who didn't worship him solely. He was no better than his wife.

"And yet ... you sent your Rhuanics after me. The attack on my village, where all of our hunters were wiped out." Ashilde struggled to breathe. "They weren't meant to die. The Rhuanics were after *me*."

"They were," Waldemar said, making her feel like an arrow had lodged into her gut. "But I didn't send them."

"Of course you did," Ashilde said. "You *just* said—"

"No!" Waldemar barked. "I said *at first*, I ordered Róta's supposed champions killed. Not until I realized there was no stopping Róta, not with how weakened I had become. The only way to stop her was to tell her champion the truth and convince them to not just kill me, but kill us both. So, I ordered my Rhuanics to stop, to assist the champions as Róta picked them out." Waldemar looked away. "They refused."

Ashilde blinked. She cursed her gods plenty in secret, but she'd never considered outright refusing them, always wary of the consequences and how it would reflect on her people. "They can do that? How could they deny you?"

"They are fanatics," Waldemar admitted, yet with a hint of pride in his voice. "Their love for me surpassed their desire to serve; said they couldn't risk my life on a champion who wouldn't listen to the truth, who might attempt to kill me before hearing my side of history. No amount of begging on my behalf could persuade them to take the risk, knowing that my life would be forfeit in the process. They loved me too much."

Ashilde snorted.

"So, I turned elsewhere."

"Funakiin and Ieka."

"No ... and yes," Waldemar said. "But I was actually referring to Anóra."

Knowing the god was willing to stoop low enough to use a *child* sickened her. "You. You're the one who sent the dreams."

Nodding, Waldemar said, "As I sent you yours, throughout the Flatrí. Dreams can be a powerful motivator, if you know how to manipulate them."

The knife continued to grow heavier in her palm the more they spoke. "I don't understand. Why would you pick a child? What was Anóra supposed to do against the Rhuanics, traveling a month through the Banished Lands to accompany me?"

"To serve the same purpose as the dreams I stole from your memories: to motivate you. To help encourage you to continue, to persevere."

So the dreams she experienced within the Flatrí were given by Waldemar. It did explain why she suddenly dreamed so consistently, after experiencing so many years never dreaming at all. But how were they meant to help motivate her? All they did was make her want to return home, to the life she once knew.

To the life she still missed.

"It didn't work."

"Did it not?" Waldemar asked, spreading his arms wide, to wave across the empty room. "You made it here, didn't you? By reminding you of your home, by giving you a charge to look after and care for, you suddenly had a stronger motivation to propel you than simple survival. And in all my years watching you, I knew that—a duty to protect others—to be stronger than any desire to serve yourself."

Ashilde frowned. "Anóra never dreamed. Not once, while she was with me."

"She didn't need to, anymore. She'd already found you. What more motivation did she need?"

"But it wasn't intended for me, specifically. It could have been any champion Róta chose, in her lifetime. I was just the first that Anóra met."

Waldemar nodded.

For some reason, that hurt, sending a sharp pang in her chest like a jabbing knife.

"You could have explained it directly to me. Why the secrecy?"

"Because I needed you here, to kill us both. Knowing the truth and being able to go where you please and do what you want with that knowledge didn't serve my purposes."

"Outside of your control, you mean."

"In a manner, yes."

Ashilde rubbed her fingers through her hair, letting out a breath. The god had given her so much to think about, so much to process. Her head throbbed with a new headache. At this rate, she would *never* be done asking questions, especially when every answer spawned two new ones she hadn't brought with her before.

She looked over at Waldemar, who stared at her with a straight face, not rushing her as she slipped momentarily into thought. She had two sides of the same story, from two gods she had worshiped equally all of her life, even if she hated both of them for the pain she'd *believed* they forced her to endure on a monthly basis.

Knowing the truth now; knowing her *dolorsandri* was nothing more than a bodily function that served a simple purpose, same as any other?

Well.

She found she hated both of them a little bit more.

Even now, with all the information swirling in her brain, Ashilde knew could only believe one of them. If Róta spoke true, then Waldemar was trying to trick her, somehow using her to kill his wife so he could lord over all of them, alone. Except, he'd be dead, killed already by her hand. And, if he were to be believed, then if she didn't kill Róta, too, she would abandon their world to try and ... overtake some sort of supreme god?

Her gut told her which she believed, just as much as the knot it had become reminded her that, no matter how this ended, she and all the people of Armadin would pay the price for it. But she felt, even godless, their problems would only multiply, if Róta gained more power than she already had.

Damn you both.

She swallowed, trying to settle her breathing. *You have no choice. For your people, you must do this. And hope with every ounce of your being we all figure out how to survive the aftermath.*

Ashilde met Waldemar's gaze, resolute. "How do I kill her?"

Waldemar smiled weakly. "With the assumption that consuming my power doesn't kill you, but instead, you harvest what remains of it? If you become her equal, you may have a chance to kill her in combat. Take my power away from her and bring her into a mortal form, like she has to me."

She scoffed. "And how am I supposed to do all of that?"

"You must kill those who protect her: Sokin and Visindi."

Her heart stopped.

Funakiin and Ieka.

"Why?"

"Sokin she took from me. All the power she has harvested from me, she siphons from him. He's never worked for her, only stayed by her side in hopes that he could protect me, by staying close. And he did, by protecting you and bringing you here." The god sighed, the weight of everything he'd dealt with and the nearness of his passing poured into it. They both felt the air in the room shifting, signaling it was almost time. "If you kill him, that power will be released—and hopefully transferred into you, giving you the power of a god."

"And Visindi?"

"Like Sokin was for me, Visindi is for her: a well for her power. Kill her precious pet. Róta will be stripped of her celestial form and forced into a mortal one, like I have been. Only in our mortal forms can we be killed. What powers she'll still have is ... unknowable. But it'll give you a chance."

"They are ... mortal, Visindi and Sokin?"

The god blinked. "But of course."

"Then how are they here? How are they *alive*? I saw Funakiin die, saw—"

He snorted. "Róta wouldn't let them die simply because she sent them out to bring her a champion."

"So how am I supposed to kill them, then, if she can just bring them back to life?"

"Quickly."

Ashilde wanted to spit the sour taste from her mouth. "This is impossible," she muttered. She came here searching for answers, not to be given a task so towering, it overshadowed any and all hardships she bore before it.

"Oh, I imagine you're quite right about that."

"What?"

"Personally, I don't believe you're actually strong

enough to harbor my soul at all. I've probably wasted the last moments of my life preparing you for a fight you'll never swing a blade in." Waldemar shrugged. "But still, there is a chance, however miniscule, that you might pull this off. So, like my followers, I wanted you to be prepared."

"Prepare me? You haven't done anything of the sort!"

"But I have. I've given you the greatest weapon you couldn't think to ask for: the truth. You know the truth of your gods and their character, the reality that there are more than just us in the universe and what will happen to your people if you fail. I've given you everything I can offer you, in my current state." He paused, snapping his fingers after a moment of consideration. Along the wall, appeared an array of weapons. "There. *Now* I have."

Ashilde stood, but hesitated before going to inspect the weapons he offered her. "But there is so much you've left unanswered. So much I don't understand."

Again, Waldemar shrugged, as if it were of no consequence to him. It probably wasn't, considering he would die as soon as their conversation was over. "We could sit here and discuss and debate for decades and you'd still respond to me with the same complaint. But, for the first time in my life, we simply don't have the time. Róta can only be distracted by life on Armadin for so long before she realizes your devotion to her is not as strong as her arrogance believed it to be."

"So she isn't ... watching over us, now?"

"You think you'd be able to have this discussion if she was?" He shook his head. "I don't have much power left, but shielding my chamber so she cannot scry into it? That much I can still manage." Before Ashilde could ask what exactly he meant by scrying, he gestured over to the weapon rack. "Now gather your weapons to prepare to fight my wife and let us get on with it."

Breathing slowly, Ashilde walked over to the rack,

certain to keep Waldemar in her peripheral vision at all times. Not that she thought the god would truly try to do anything to her—he seemed almost eager for death, for one who knew it approached him. But she refused to let her guard down, either.

That didn't mean she couldn't also admire the weapons before her.

They were the most elegant she'd ever seen. Each one was painted black, with gold accents, except for one: a bow, which had the reverse color scheme. She lifted it off the rack and raised it, testing the weight of the draw and the strength of the string. Never had a weapon been more balanced or felt more perfect in her hands.

And you're going to kill your friends with it.

Ashilde knew that's how it had to be done. Once she returned to Róta, she couldn't waste time getting close to Funakiin or Ieka to kill them with any close-range weapon. The chance of Róta realizing her intent to kill her before she robbed her of her ethereal shield was too great for Ashilde to waste any time. A bow was her only option.

That she wouldn't be able to see the life leave their eyes as they died was simply an ironic coincidence.

Ashilde slipped it over her back, adding the quiver of arrows with it. She picked the rest of her weapons quickly, replacing those she'd lost back on Falos. She leaned the spear against the wall and placed the knife Róta had given her on the weapon rack, inadequate in comparison to the blades Waldemar had provided her.

She held a new knife in her hand.

Waldemar stood.

Her fingers tightened around the hilt. Though she felt she had no choice in his death—and the fire at wanting to kill him had lessened, if only slightly—she wanted this moment burned into her memory for the rest of her life; to serve as a reminder, perhaps, of what she was capable of, to help prepare her for all the unknowns which awaited, if she managed to pull this off.

Waldemar raised his hands. "I'm not going to resist," he said. "I simply have no desire to die without being on my feet."

Ashilde turned to face him, letting Waldemar close the distance between them. She met his eyes squarely, despite the rest of her body shaking.

"I sincerely hope my soul doesn't kill you, Ashilde," he said, speaking her name for the first time. "It would be a waste."

In one, rapid motion, Ashilde plunged the knife into Waldemar's chest, her opposite hand resting on the back of the hilt, the extra force helping her bury the blade that much deeper into his flesh, past muscles and tendons, straight into his heart. Waldemar gasped, a very mortal sound as the air escaped between his lips, looking down at her with widened eyes, as if surprised that the moment he'd waited decades for had finally come.

Ashilde choked on her own bile, tears streaming down her face.

Releasing the handle, she stepped away, stumbling as her legs shook.

Her eyes couldn't leave the handle, the blade still embedded in his chest.

Waldemar closed his eyes, standing upright, albeit on wobbling legs. "Take me home," he whispered.

His body began to shimmer and fade, until his mortal form disappeared entirely, leaving only his ethereal shadow, his true form as a god, his soul. It glowed with a golden hue brighter than anything Ashilde had ever seen, forcing her arm up to shield her eyes, her own numbing shock that she had just plunged her knife into a *god* giving way to fear at what was about to happen next.

In the next moment, she would either die or gain the powers no mortal had a right to yield.

Immediately after she closed her eyes, the glow

vanished as a force swept into her like a gust of wind. She forced her eyes open to watch the knife she used to kill Waldemar fall onto the stone floor with a *clank*, rattling before it fell silent, the blade's sticky red sheen the only clue it'd just been used to kill anyone at all.

Ashilde clutched at her chest, inhaling deeply.

Her body was still intact. Waldemar's soul was nowhere to be seen and she felt no different, aside from an emptiness that threatened to consume her.

Waldemar, Wolffather and god of Armadin, was dead.

And she had killed him.

Ashilde stumbled, falling to her hands and knees, shaking fingers brushing against the bloodied knife lying on the stone floor. She had no love for the gods, any love for them dying after her own mother was slain. But that didn't stop her from breaking out into sobs, feeling the weight of what she had just done; what she had managed to *survive*.

She squeezed her eyes shut.

The ripple of this action would change Armadin forever.

Her eyes snapped open.

Now, it was time to make a wave.

Ashilde stood and left the empty chamber, leaving the bloodied knife behind.

CHAPTER TWENTY-NINE

Ashilde ran through the hallways, trusting them to lead her to the chamber where the remaining god resided. She had no idea what had just happened, exactly.

Aside from the fact that Waldemar was dead.

Whether his soul lived in her and gave her power was a mystery she couldn't solve. Whether it was inside her and slowly killing her was an answer only time could give. If that proved true, it was a time she couldn't let it reach, until her task was done.

She had to kill Róta. She couldn't allow the goddess to abandon Armadin in pursuit of obtaining ultimate power, going on her own godly killing spree.

And killing her won't result in the same outcome?

Ashilde skidded as the hallway quickly shifted, curving to the right where it was just straight moments ago. The corner caught her and she pushed off of it, picking her pace back up. It was the answer Waldemar didn't give her and the one she most desperately needed. She couldn't let Róta absorb Waldemar's power and then leave Armadin. She had no idea who—or what—this supreme god was, but she couldn't let Róta kill them and ruin whatever balance the universe, as Waldemar had called it, currently maintained.

But that still left the people of Armadin to pay the price, becoming godless in the span of one afternoon, leaving Waldemar's followers unchecked and the rest of Armadin ignorant of the truths; truths that Ashilde needed to live to pass on. Her Seidsian would know what to do. Ashilde simply had to live to—

She buckled, her cramps hitting her like an unexpected wave from the ocean crashing into her while her back was turned. She reached out, placing one steady hand on the stone wall, while she leaned her body into her spear to keep herself upright.

No.

Another wave hit, this one stronger than the last. Her entire body broke out in a feverish sweat, heating up to dangerous levels. She gagged before she vomited liquid onto her linen-wrapped feet, her stomach empty of anything more solid. Wiping her mouth with the back of her hand, she squeezed her eyes shut, her feet slipping against the slick stone as her body shook.

No, she thought again, this time with more force. She didn't care what Waldemar said or how this was supposed to work. She didn't care if her soul "wasn't strong enough" to mix with his. She didn't care if his soul was currently trying to kill her from the inside, or that Róta planned to finish the job if she withstood it.

She.

Didn't.

Care.

She was Ashilde, Faethegnar and protector of the Slátra, killer of a god. She was daughter of Gunnvor, partner of Davyn, friend of Freydis, sister of Brynhild and Anóra, protégé of Dagfinn.

She was *not done.*

Pulling herself up with the spear, Ash stood, wobbling like Waldemar had, before he died. She forced a foot forward, before her other foot followed. Breathing heavily, she continued along the path at a crawling pace, as wave after wave of cramps tried to deter her. Using every ounce of will she had left, she forced herself to never stop moving, no matter how painful her cramps became, no matter how tear-stricken her face was stained, no matter how much her body wanted to do nothing more but collapse onto the ground and never move again.

She kept moving until the cramps finally stopped.

Ashilde paused, breathing heavily. Everywhere was drenched in sweat and her body felt weary, exhausted, aching in every place imaginable.

If Waldemar—or his soul or whoever it was that forced these cramps upon her—thought that little display would be enough to stop her, they were about to be very rudely awakened.

Breaking off into a shaky run that gained momentum the more she moved, Ashilde continued along the hall, hoping to return to Róta and kill her before the next wave hit. For as much bravado as she fronted, she knew deep down, she'd never experienced pain like this before, so sudden, crippling and intense. There was only so far her own stubbornness could push her.

Ashilde skidded to a stop just before she reached the arched opening that led back into the chamber Róta resided in. Waiting until her breathing slowed, Ashilde peeked around the corner.

The last living god of Armadin still sat atop her wooden throne, her posture lax as she leaned against the branches that made up the back, the wayward pieces sticking through her ethereal form like spikes through her chest. In front of her were various glowing circles, similar to the one she'd created to show Ashilde her threatened destruction of the future. Ashilde couldn't make out what Róta watched from the dozens of smaller circles floating in front of her, though if the expression on the goddess's face was any indication, it wasn't anything interesting. Ieka perched on the arm of the throne, her head cocked to the side as she watched alongside Róta.

Funakiin, still sleeping curled up beside the chair, opened his eyes as soon as she peeked around the corner.

Ashilde stilled, but Funakiin didn't move. Instead, she heard his voice in her head once more. *You succeeded in killing him, then,* he said, his voice void of all emotion. *Did my master speak with you, before he died?*

Yes, she thought, pulling herself back behind the entryway.

Then you know what needs to be done. Do not hesitate, Slátra. Not even for me.

Ashilde swallowed, hard. *Funakiin—Sokin—there is so much I still don't know. Waldemar's soul—*

Is within you. I can feel it, now that you've arrived.

I think ... I think it's trying to kill me.

With Róta's encouragement, no doubt. The wolf's words were punctuated with a tone: disdain. *You're strong enough to survive this, Ashilde. You have to be.*

Waldemar said I had to harness his power to defeat Róta. How do I do that?

Killing me will give you what's been severed, Funakiin confirmed. *It'll recognize the energy you have within you. It'll come to you, instead of her—especially if you kill Visindi first. She doesn't see it as I do. She serves Róta without a doubt and with a loyalty that is unwavering. Neither of them expect your betrayal.*

Ashilde winced. She didn't see it as a betrayal, though she was confident the remaining god would disagree with her on that. Regardless of who called it what, her path was set, even if she still didn't understand how to pursue it.

Once I absorb the rest of his power, then—

It's unknown. No mortal has ever carried a piece of a god's soul within them. Once you carry it in its entirety... The wolf paused, making Ashilde feel uneasy. *Just trust that you'll recognize what to do and hope it's enough to kill her.*

Ashilde sighed silently, blowing the air gently through her nose as she leaned her head back against the stone and squeezed her eyes closed. Moving slowly, hoping to remain undetected, she slipped her bow off her back and readied it in her hand, pulling two arrows from her quiver.

I'm sorry, she whispered to Funakiin.

His response surprised her. *As am I.*

Ashilde let out a breath, nocked her first arrow and, staying on her heels, spun around the edge and released, the arrow flying into the room with a soft, but undeniable whistle.

She'd already let her second arrow fly by the time the first hit its mark, burying itself into Ieka's breast.

The raven let out a surprised caw, raising her wings to fly away, but instead, fell off to the side, onto the ground, her dead form falling through the glowing scrying circles Róta had created. Róta's head whipped around, her eyes alight with real flame as all the scrying circles disappeared instantaneously. Yet even the attention of the god wasn't enough to distract Ashilde from glancing at the victim of her second arrow. Funakiin's head fell forward, the arrow buried into his heart—a perfect shot, only available because the wolf had sat up and opened himself up to her as a target.

Finally, she met Róta's eyes as the Ravenmother stood, her entire form shaking with rage, causing her golden glow to begin to fade.

"How *dare* you—"

Róta's own words were cut off as she raised an ethereal hand to her chest, staring at it as her hand didn't pass through, but instead, landed on something solid. Ashilde watched, fascinated and unable to move, as Róta's physical form slowly overtook her ethereal one, starting with her torso before spreading out to her arms and legs at the same time.

The god's skin still maintained a golden glow around her, despite becoming a solid form. She wore a dark black dress that complemented her features—while accentuating others—with slits up the side that rose all the way to her torso, showing off her thick, muscular legs. As her head finally materialized, revealing long silver hair and glowing eyes to match, Róta threw her head back and laughed, deep from her stomach, before she offered a dark smile Ashilde's way, her lips painted red.

"Oh, Waldemar, I should have expected this from you," she said, shaking her head. With a wave of her hand, a spear appeared beside her, already firmly gripped in her hand. Where Ashilde's spear strapped on her back was black and gold, Róta's was completely white for most of the shaft, only the last third of it the same color of the sharp blade attached to it: a blood red that matched her lips.

She turned and looked at Ashilde, who was still crouched down, another arrow already nocked and aimed for the Ravenmother's heart. "You didn't truly think that this form makes me weak like you? Surely not."

She snapped her fingers.

Ashilde's cramps returned, buckling her to the ground.

She screamed, slamming her bow against the ground as she landed, sprawled against her stomach, lacking the strength to pick herself back up. Her arrow lay broken in front of her and she lifted her eyes, stuck watching as Róta slowly descended with bare feet down the stone steps from her throne, her dress swishing lazily from side to side as she moved.

With a snap of her fingers, the forest within the

room vanished, leaving it empty aside from rock, stone and Rota's throne, the frightened bird calls within the trees silencing instantly; an enclosed battleground. Ashilde tried to push herself up, but another wave hit her even harder. Her stomach felt like it was being ripped out of her while someone stuck a knife into her uterus and swiveled it around, tearing it into shreds while she was still conscious to feel it. She gasped, struggling to breathe against the onslaught of pain.

"I'm not surprised my husband decided to reveal my intentions to you," Róta said, her voice closer now. She spoke with a lazy drawl, obviously enjoying the torment she inflicted on Ashilde, not caring how long she drew it out. "He always liked to steal my fun. I *was* going to tell you. If his soul didn't kill you, first, and I had to do the job myself." She paused, though Ashilde no longer watched to see what she did. She was too busy focusing on not blacking out herself. "I can see it within you, you know. Two halves, made whole again. I'm honestly surprised your soul hasn't combusted at the very nearness of such power."

Ashilde let out another shaky breath, drawing deeper from her reserves. She didn't feel the soul Funakiin carried flow into her, but she had to believe that she carried the entire being of a dead god within her. Obviously, she was strong enough to bear the soul of a god.

But how did she wield it?

Ashilde tried to push herself up, getting up on her knees. She glanced up, threads of her hair slipping free and getting in the way of her eyes, but she didn't brush them away, as Róta turned to look at her, pausing her pacing to make a *tsk* sound.

"Did I say you could get up?"

She snapped her fingers once more.

This time, the pain exploding within caused her vision to blacken and all the white noise in the room to disappear for a few seconds as she landed prone on the ground once more, her spear hitting the back of her head as she landed.

"There, that's better," Róta said, like she was praising a pet. "I'm almost intrigued enough to see how much pain I can inflict within you before your heart gives out. I haven't had this strong of a toy in *ages*."

Ashilde pressed her head against the ground as she tried to dig her fingers into the stone, wanting to grip onto something else, find a way to release her pain. The tips of her fingers came back bloody as she flailed, fighting back against a pain which she'd never been victorious against. As her eyes rolled back, she saw Róta had walked over to stand directly in front of her, her head cocked as she placed a finger against her lips, as if she was in deep contemplation.

"But your body is strong. Stronger than any I've seen in a long time." Róta knelt down, still gripping her spear. "Perhaps I should try to break your spirit, instead. Tell me, Ashilde: how much would you like to hear Davyn cry your name as his own life is robbed from him?"

Ashilde screamed, a surge of strength helping her to lash out at the goddess, her arm swiping toward her throat as if she had claws instead of hands. But a sharp pain in her abdomen made her arm suddenly fall short of her target, instead coming back and curling up around her stomach, her own fingers digging into her flesh, begging her own body to stop.

Róta didn't even flinch.

Instead, she laughed. "Oh, now there's a pleasant sound. So raw, so feral. Barely more than an animal, really."

Ashilde lifted her head to glare, filling the look with something darker than hatred. "I will kill you," she whispered.

Róta chuckled. "An endearing thought. But you made two mistakes short of any such victory." The goddess leaned closer, looking down over Ashilde's shaking form so that she appeared to be upside down. "First, you trusted the advice of a dead man. And second..."

Suddenly, Ashilde was wrenched upward, Róta's iron grip fisted in her hair, pulling hard as she lifted Ashilde off the ground and up until their faces were perfectly in line with one another, the Ravenmother still crouched. She could feel the heat coming off of the god's silver eyes and she didn't look away, no matter how badly her heart wanted to. Sweat dripped off Ashilde's face and neck, creating a small shower of droplets onto the stone ground beneath her.

"You killed Visindi, echoing my dead husband's mistake," Róta said, spitting the words out like poison. "So I won't only kill you..." Róta put her hand on Ashilde's stomach. "I will make you suffer for it."

Heat flooded against her abdomen, but it didn't relieve her pain.

Instead, it intensified still further, causing Ashilde to scream until her own voice gave out. But Róta refused to let her go, keeping her still, holding her top half hovering off the ground while her legs lay beneath her, lost of all strength and worthless to help her get away from her god's torture.

"Do you truly think you could abandon me to become Waldemar's pet, *his* champion? You belong to me, child. To *me*."

Ashilde forced her eyes open once more, swallowing her rage. "I don't belong to him," she hissed, unable to do anything else. "And I definitely don't fucking belong to you."

Róta's eyes blazed, a white fire. She threw Ashilde onto the ground. "Fool," she spat, standing as Ashilde rolled over onto her side, groaning. "I *created* you. I made you what you are. No matter what you try to do, you'll always belong to me."

Not anymore.

Ashilde blinked. That voice wasn't hers and it definitely didn't belong inside her head. Funakiin was dead, his voice much deeper than the airy whisper she'd just heard—or most likely imagined she heard. Once, during a more ignorant time, she'd have thought it was the comforting voice of her gods, there to guide her to Skírrdrauin as she clung between life and death.

What a blissful and ignorant fantasy that was.

Instead, Róta continued to taunt her, Ashilde's cramps escalating once more, to the point where she could no longer scream, no longer move; instead, remained frozen on the ground, unable to breathe, with silent tears slipping down her face, as she struggled to not pass out.

This was the end.

How fitting, to die from the pain that she so often cursed the Ravenmother for while she lived.

Get up.

Ashilde couldn't move. The pain had immobilized her and her vision started to blur, though she could still make out the Ravenmother's form standing above her, looking down at her, ever smiling. Whoever decided to interrupt her dying moments by making ridiculous commands could go to the Pit. She—

Get UP, the voice commanded again, a command so powerful, it shook her entire core. *I give you my blessing—and the power of my child—to resist her power, and do what must be done.*

Kill her.

Ashilde gasped, her eyes widening as she could finally inhale once more.

The cramps were gone.

She pushed herself up onto her elbows, her entire body slick with sweat and still shaking with a weakness she'd never felt so utterly before. But for the first time since Ashilde met her, Róta no longer wore a smile on her face and the fire in her eyes had dimmed, just slightly.

It might not be fear, but Ashilde drew strength from it, pushing herself up to stand, drawing her spear out in one motion.

It was then that she noticed a soft, golden glow around her hands, her arms, her legs.

Similar to the glow the Ravenmother herself had.

Ashilde looked up at the god, spitting blood onto the ground before she wiped her mouth clean with the back of her hand. "I don't belong to you," she whispered once more. "I belong to those I choose: the Slátra and the rest of the clans of Armadin. And you will rule over us no longer."

Lifting her spear, Ashilde charged toward her remaining god, who got over her surprise at her sudden recovery much faster than Ashilde would have liked, using her own spear to easily catch Ashilde's thrust and shove it aside, before twisting and offering a thrust of her own. Róta's speed was matched by Ashilde's grace, by the fluidity of her movements. Never before had Ashilde blocked a thrust so expertly executed. Her spear knocked Róta's weapon back with the same amount of confidence and strength the god had just denied her a second before. The god swung out at her again, quickly, and Ashilde caught it, spears locked against one another.

Ashilde met the Ravenmother's eyes over their weapons, her expression stunned.

Ashilde grinned, showing all her teeth.

Then, they began to dance.

Ashilde swept her spear from underneath the god's, swinging upward as she did so, aiming for her throat, hoping to catch her chin, perhaps snap her neck, if the force was strong enough. Róta knocked aside the attack as she skirted to the right, scoring a hit with the backside of her spear against Ashilde's leg, but she barely buckled. She'd never felt such strength before, within herself. She had never felt such *power*. But she had no desire to command it. Instead, she wanted to harness it, use it to best Róta at an artform that she very well might have invented herself.

Lunging at Róta, she attacked with a flurry of blows, forcing the god to retreat backward, barely keeping up as Ashilde attacked her, again and again, no longer worrying about blocking and protecting her own body, but instead, focusing every effort on finding the one brief moment when Róta slipped and gave her an opening for a killing blow; embracing the years she spent training, capitalizing on every second she'd lost sleep, every moment she practiced, trying to become a warrior strong enough that no one would ever die on her watch.

She might not have had the strength to save the lives of those she loved.

But she had the strength to kill a god.

With the tip of her spear, Ashilde managed to nick a dozen places on Róta's body in quick succession, like sharp, violent kisses: her arm, her leg, cut a gash into her chest, none deadly enough to kill. Still, Ashilde didn't hesitate, didn't surrender. She continued pushing, swinging, dodging and lunging in response to Róta's defenses, always a move behind the god, but Ashilde didn't care. She ignored her arms when they started to weaken, gritted her teeth when her legs tried to buckle against the strain, the chaffing between her thighs rubbed raw as she danced. For no matter how tired her body was becoming, she saw similar strains in her opponent.

And that was the time to strike.

Redoubling her efforts, Ashilde pressed again, spinning away from a jab that felt desperate on Róta's part. As she turned back around to face the Ravenmother, Ashilde did a move she hadn't tried since she was a child first learning the art of spearplay. She let one of her legs collapse beneath her, falling low to the ground, the air of Róta's latest swing *whooshing* over her head. Instead, she lunged out with her front leg, thrusting her spear forward and upward, leaving herself open and completely defenseless. Róta took the bait, quickly jabbing downward.

Both spears connected at the same time.

Ashilde felt her arm slacken as the spear went straight through her elbow, breaking through skin, muscle and bone. She gritted her teeth, Waldemar's strength allowing her to ignore the pain, instead staring at where her own spear had found purchase.

Buried deep into Róta chest, adjacent to her sternum.

Róta looked down, her silver eyes wide. Her mouth was agape, one hand hovering near Ashilde's buried spear as the other released her hold on her own.

"You cannot kill a god," Róta whispered, her breath suddenly becoming shallow.

"Of course not," Ashilde said through gritted teeth. "I've killed two."

Reaching up with her good arm, she grabbed Róta's shoulder, jutting her spear that far deeper, earning a grunt of surprised pain before, rocking back, Ashilde ripped her spear back out, pushing herself away from the god. Ashilde fell to her knees, holding her spear beside her, breathing heavily, as Róta stumbled backward, blood trickling down the widened hole in her chest. She wobbled, took a step forward, before also falling to her knees. Her mouth opened and closed, as if trying to remember how to properly function, but no words came out. Instead, stunned eyes looked upon Ashilde as her mouth opened one last time before her eyes lost their focus, and her god, Róta the Ravenmother, fell onto her side, unmoving, forever staring straight at the corpse of her dead raven.

This time, Ashilde didn't shed a tear.

Finally, she released the tension in her body she'd

maintained during the fight, her shoulders slumping as her entire body went slack. She lifted the spear and held it in both hands, staring down at it with wonder, her own injury forgotten for the moment as adrenaline and inhuman power helped her ignore it. Before she could think of what to do next, dizziness overwhelmed her, alongside the intense desire to puke, and Ashilde collapsed, letting darkness consume her.

***

She awoke to a pile of corpses and a smell to match.

Ashilde blinked, not sure which she noticed first: the putrid stench or the overwhelming soreness that covered every inch of her body. A soreness that she couldn't feel if she were dead. But as her mind caught up with her consciousness, she immediately doubted the reality she woke up to—for how could she have lived through any of *that*?

Pushing herself up onto her good elbow, however, Ashilde took in the scene around her, her reality confirmed. Funakiin lay beside the throne, over to her left. Ieka, to the throne's right.

And Róta, beside her, eyes open, glazed over.

Unblinking.

Ashilde looked down at her bloodied spear, one hand still wrapped around its shaft. She'd done it. She'd come to Skírrdrauin, made it to the gods' realm. She discovered her answers, before realizing her true task, killing not only Waldemar, but Róta as well.

The gods were no more.

She pushed herself up all the way, standing, one arm hanging limp and broken against her side. As she did so, she noticed a familiar, sticky wetness between her thighs, staining her pants. She knew before she even checked what had happened while she was unconscious.

She'd started her *dolorsandri.*

Ashilde couldn't help it. She laughed. She laughed until her insides hurt—which didn't take much—and she had to wipe the tears from her eyes. Because *of course* that would happen, after all of this. That was what started it all. Why shouldn't it end the same way? She'd come here looking for answers, asking why the gods had suddenly tainted her. Instead, she wasn't tainted at all.

No, she thought, glancing down at the still mortal body of Róta laying there and thinking back to how Waldemar had disappeared entirely, leaving Armadin suddenly without their gods.

Her problems were so much bigger than that.

Waldemar's followers were still out there, now without a guiding hand to reign them in—yet, supposedly prepared for a world without gods and what came after, with answers that Ashilde needed. The rest of the clans, however, were still lost. Everyone still believed in the lies the gods had told them, unless some of the Seidsians knew of what had happened here. Or, all of them could still be blind to the lies, ignorant of the day their gods died. Learning the truth would change them in ways she could not see the ramifications of, but she couldn't imagine *not* sharing with them what she knew, either. That task was clear before her. It would no longer be a simple journey home. Instead, she'd become the messenger to what had transpired here.

But what would happen, when they learned the truth? What would they do about *her*, no longer just a warrior, but a god killer?

You're assuming you'll survive the return journey.

Ashilde frowned. She still had her physical form— and she no longer glowed, she noticed with a more intense inspection. But she had no food, no water and her body had taken a beating unlike anything she'd ever experienced before. Not to mention her still bleeding, broken arm, with a massive hole in her elbow, the pain all but numbed. All of those things, issues that couldn't even be worried over, not until she braced the first obstacle: climbing back down Skírrdrauin, swimming through the ocean without the ability to breathe underwater and somehow climbing back *up* Falos—a fall that felt like an eternity.

The weight of that impossibility overwhelmed her, making her stagger back until she fell once again on her knees, the hard stone sending jolts of pain that ricocheted up her spine. After everything she'd been through, after everything she'd done; *this* was the end she was faced with?

To die here alone, the only one to discover the truth? She couldn't even go home?

Suddenly, Ashilde heard it. A soft whispering, in the back of her head, the same light, airy voice that commanded her with such force, right before the battle with Róta had truly begun. The same voice that helped her to access Waldemar's power and overcome Róta's torture.

Cocking her head to the side, Ashilde opened herself up to the voice, focusing on it until it was all she could hear, inside her head.

You did well, child, it whispered. *Events I did not foresee, challenges I never expected and a new hero to thank for it all.*

Who are you? Ashilde thought, her voice a whisper inside her head. *Can you ... can you help get me home?*

You've done so much, the voice said, the tone taking on a melancholy air that instantly felt hollow. *Yet we both know Armadin can't be left without a god.*

Ashilde felt her entire body sink, any joy, relief or worry she'd felt since awakening replaced with a single feeling: dread. *And I take it you, as the supreme god, have an answer for that.*

Laughter echoed in her mind. *Quick, you are. I can*

see why my children saw fit to use you.

Ashilde swallowed.

Not an answer, *the god continued.* Hard to have an answer to a question you never thought to ask. But a consequence? That I am always prepared for.

Ashilde closed her eyes, sagging against the stone floor as her entire body felt heavy and her heart, broken. She wanted nothing more than to return home. To storm the Rhuanics' base, steal Anóra away from them and ask her to live with her. To walk through the gates that kept the Slátra safe and run into Davyn's arms and ask him to marry her.

But, it seemed the gods weren't done with her yet.

With the last thread of will she possessed, Ashilde forced her eyes open, straightening until her entire body was rigid, her mind set, her heart determined. Whether she agreed with it or not, her actions set in motion the events that led up to this moment. *She* killed the gods of her people. She had harnessed Waldemar's power and used it. She had gained notice of gods she didn't even know existed.

Her wants didn't matter. They never had, never did. Perhaps, they never would.

She owed it to those she loved to see this through.

No matter where it led her.

And what consequence would you demand of my actions? Ashilde asked.

No greater price than you've already paid. Perhaps.

She felt the god's smile and it left her body chilled. In the mere moments before her mind went dark and her body limp, she understood the supreme god's intentions even if she didn't know the path to get there.

It was time to reshape the fate of Armadin.

EXTRAS

PRONUNCIATION

Names, major characters:
- Ashilde - [Ah-shield-day]
- Brynhild - [Brin-hild]
- Davyn - [Dav-in]
- Freydis - [Fray-dis]
- Dagfinn - [Dag-fin]
- Anóra - [Ah-nor-ah]
- Róta - [Row-tah]
- Waldemar - [Wall-den-mar]
- Funakiin - [Fun-na-kin]
- Ieka - [E-ka]

Names, minor characters:
- Moria - [More-e-a]
- Unna - [Un-na]
- Ingrit - [In-grit]
- Torunn - [Tour-rune]
- Bodil - [Bow-dil]
- Magnhild - [Mag-hild]
- Hildrid - [Hill-drid]
- Arnvid - [Arn-vid]
- Sod - [Sod]
- Torhild - [Tor-hild]
- Gunnvor - [Gun-vor]

Clans, titles and locations:
- Seidsian - [Said-eh-sin]
- Faethegnar - [Fae-theng-nar]
- Slátra - [Slaw-tra]
- Dreyma - [Drey-ma]
- Solskin - [Soul-skin]
- Rekja - [Wreck-ya]
- Dirheil - [Deer-hail]

- Hvass - [Ha-vast]
- Hreysti - [Hear-sti]
- Skalda - [Skald-da]
- Fundi - [Foon-di]
- Armadin - [Arm-ma-din]
- Segan - [Sea-gan]
- Flatrí - [Flat-tree]
- Hafleden - [Half-fled-den]
- Falos - [Fowl-los]
- Skírrdrauin - [Sker-drawn-nin]

Conlang:
- Dolorsandri - [Dool-lar-sa-ond-dri]
- Sangrild - [Sond-grilled]
- Sangrendi - [Sond-grend-di]
- Rhuanic - [Rune-nah-hic]
- Borinn Day - [Bore-in Day]
- Kallen Day - [Kay-lin Day]
- Wyrdan Day - [Word-dan Day]
- Asttan Day - [Ash-tan Day]

CREDITS

A book cannot come to life without the work of so many people. Here's who helped this make this dream a reality:

Beta Readers: thank you to the following people for reading one of the nth drafts of this book and helping it take shape (some of you, reading multiple drafts). I couldn't have done this without you.
- M.A. Crosbie
- R.K. Brainerd
- A.Z. Pascoe
- Jo Ladzinski (Ladz)
- Robert F. Nugent

Editors: without these editors, this book would have a lot more typos, spelling mistakes and misuse of commas than those that survived. I recommend them wholeheartedly.
- Jeni Chappelle, developmental
- Danai Christopoulou, proofread

Cover Design: a cover can be a book's downfall or its lifeblood. I am so beyond grateful that mine falls in the latter category.
- Zoe Badini, artwork
- Norman Olasiman of Stardust Book Services, typography

Interior Formatting: turning this manuscript from too many Google Doc pages into something actually readable is a skill I don't have. Thankfully, I got wonderful support here.
- Rae Davennor of Stardust Book Services

Patreon: Last, but certainly not least, I must thank each and every one of my Patreon supporters, both paid and free, no matter how long you were a Patreon member for. Without you, I would not have been able to afford getting this book published. Below are those who were comfortable being named:

- M.A. Crosbie
- Brendan Williams-Childs
- Dini K.
- ShadowsProxy

RECOMMENDED AUTHORS TO SUPPORT

Inspired by my friend and fellow self-pubbed author Ashe, I also wanted to take a moment to also highlight some other authors I think absolutely deserve your support. Word of mouth is everything to anyone with a small business. Writers are absolutely included in that.

So, if you're looking for another fantastic book to read, review and share, I'd recommend any of the following:
- R.K. Brainerd, *Jagged Emerald City*
- Timandra Whitecastle, *Queens of the Wyrd*
- Veo Corva, *Books and Bone*
- Ashe Armstrong, *A Demon in the Desert*
- Mike Sliter, *Solace Lost*
- Joyce Chua, *Land of Sand and Song*
- J.D. Evans, *Reign and Ruin*
- Robert F. Nugent, *The Fallen Banner*
- J.A. Andrews, *A Threat of Shadows*
- Steven McKinneon, *Symphony of the Wind*
- Krista D. Bell, *A Magical Inheritance*
- M.L. Wang, *The Sword of Kaigen*

To the following trad authors: thank you for writing books that sustained me and filled my soul when I needed it most.

Megan E. O'Keefe, Tasha Suri, Fonda Lee, Marina Lostsetter, Devin Madson, E.J. Beaton, Lisbeth Campbell, Evan Winter, Nicholas Eames, Melissa Caruso, K.B. Wagers, Andrea Stewart, Kimberly Lemming, Erin M. Evans, C.L. Clark, Becky Chambers, Sarah Gailey.

ACKNOWLEDGEMENTS

I have dreamed of writing these acknowledgments since I was eleven years old. I told myself I wasn't allowed to write them until it was right before my book was to be published; a dream I held throughout my entire life finally realized.

I'm 31 as I write these now, just a month out from 32 at the time of publication. It took over two decades, but we did it. We're here. That 'we' is not just me speaking to my younger self, with her ink stained fingers from overfilled notebooks and over half a dozen shelved novels under her belt. Though so much of this craft and dream is solitary, I did not get here alone. Without the massive support I've been given, I don't think I would have ever gotten here at all.

Two decades is a really, really long time to work at this. I am so spoiled to have so many people to thank. In no particular order, let's dive in.

To those who have been here since the beginning. My parents, who still buy me books every birthday, drove me to the library weekly to max out our library card and (only) once questioned the validity of my desire to get two degrees in English before supporting me wholeheartedly. My dreams could have so easily been crushed by you, but you didn't. Thank you.

To my siblings, Tanna and Trey. To Tanna, thanks for watching Lord of the Rings with me on repeat and letting me do all the "cool" lines when I forced you to recite the films verbatim. That obsession was instrumental to me and my craft. To Trey, who helped me get into video games, a hobby that may continually interrupt my reading and writing streaks, but gave me depths of storytelling I never would have gotten, otherwise. And to Harley, my first dog who was the bestest girl in the world. I love you all.

(To the newest family members who couldn't have been there in the beginning—my nieces, Roxanne, Isabella and Madison—I love exploring my creativity with you all and making up stories so effortlessly together. You're definitely not old enough to read my books, but I hope you all grow up to be readers who might want to, one day.)

I have been blessed with friends beyond measure. First, some "in real life" friends who I couldn't do this without. Amber: you have been my rock in ways no one else in my life has. Life without you in it would be awful. My stories are possible because you help me live and believe in a world that so often hates us. Thank you. I love you. Lyndsey: you never once made fun of me or questioned my love for writing, and used your own artistic talent to bring my earliest characters to life in middle school. I'll never forget that (and I still have the drawings). (PS: we're both still funnier than anyone believed.) Beth: though we didn't meet until I was in college, your steadfastness in our friendship and your utter belief in me has been astounding. Thank you for championing my books and helping me believe in myself.

Olivia: I survived college because of you and I am so, so thankful for our once-a-year chats that make me laugh more than anything else (let's continue to send each other books that aren't the first in the series, yes?).

To everyone in the "Queers Talk Here" friend group—Amber, Wes and Claude—thanks for providing a space where I can be unapologetically myself and always affirming my queerness.

Though it took me two attempts to do grad school, I came close so many times to becoming a second-time dropout. The following people made it so I wasn't. Brendan, Erika, Meleah, Kit, Tiffany, Whit, Logan and Garrett: I believed in my writing because of you. Thank you. To my committee, Kij Johnson, Misty Schieberle and Darren Canady, thank you for fighting for me, advocating for me and believing in me. I cannot wait to publish the book you all helped me write (once I finish it, that is). Also, special shout out to R.M. Lemberg, who's kindness and accommodations showed me how important it is to focus on the individual, not the institution. I'm lucky to have been taught by you.

Also, while we're talking about school, shout out to two English teachers in high school that were so formulative to me, to not mention them would be a travesty. Mrs. Barton, thanks for reading my absolutely awful first YA novel and not telling me it was trash (even though it was, by gods, let's burn it). Mrs. Kelly Peterson-Miranda, you were the best teacher I ever had. Thanks for not only teaching me what juxtaposition, cacophony and synecdoche meant, but also what it means to stand up for yourself.

As if I wasn't lucky enough in-person, the online space has been just as incredible for me. Thank you to my first writing group, the Muses, with M.A. Crosbie and Joyce Chua. Our WhatsApp messages, diving into short stories together and companionship was a boon I will never forget.

To my discord crew, The Restricted Section—Meredith, Reece, Ashe, Nicole, Rebekkah, Tim, Ally, Ana, Greta, Marie and Kate. Y'all are the real deal. Thank you for coming together when we (correctly) feared that Twitter would implode so I could still have other writers to bemoan the bullshits of publishing with.

Most especially, thank you to my current writing group, Meredith and Rebekkah. You both have been some of the greatest friends I've ever had. Your support has meant so much to me and I am so glad we found each other through Twitter over a decade ago. Our writing check-ins, sprints and rants have kept me afloat when otherwise I'm drowning. I love you both so, so much.

This gush-fest would not be complete without shouting out my partner, Edward. We've been together almost a decade and yet you never once questioned me when I told you I was a writer. You've supported my late night writing sessions, my crumpling-into-a-ball-and-crying-in-the-shower post latest agent rejection breakdowns, my self-publishing panic attacks. To you, my dream of being an author was never an if, only a when. I love you.

To our pets, Sasha and Dovahkiin, I love you so much. Sasha, thanks for watching the birds with me and stealing all my mac and cheese. Dovah, my obsession with you is borderline unhealthy but I don't care. You're the best dog in the world. Please live forever. And to Flynn, who passed over the rainbow bridge a few months before this book was published. We miss you, asshole.

Thanks again to everyone in the credits section, from my beta readers, my Patreon supporters, my incredible cover artist, Zoe Badini; my fantastic editors, Jeni Chapelle and Danai Christopoloulou; my amazing formatter, Rae Davennor and my awesome typographer, Norman Olasiman, both of Stardust Book

Services. This book exists thanks to the amazing work you've all done!

The issue with waiting until my dream was realized to write these is that there are most likely many people I've forgotten to mention, despite pouring over these words a dozen times over. That is an error on my part and not reflective at all with how much your help meant to me. I hope to catch you in the next one.

Thank you. I love you.

Finally, to my readers, both old and those I've yet to meet, as this dream is, even being realized, just getting started. Thank you. I am so excited to finally get to share this with you, and all the stories to come. I hope you love them and tell me that you do. If you hate them, go ahead and tell all your friends so they can check it out for themselves (you can leave me out of it, thanks).

Absolutely lastly, thanks (perhaps foolishly) to me. Your stubbornness got us here, even if it was the voices of our stories that wouldn't give us any other option. This is, and always will be, for you.

Author Bio

Nicole Evans (she/hers) is a queer, disabled SFF writer with an MFA in Fiction who's been stuck in the midwest of America since birth, but hopes to escape to a forest someday. Her earliest memories writing stories were from 6th grade, where she wrote an epic tale of her entire class fighting off flying pigs and skeletons with red eyes that carried buckets of bloody-red daggers. (Her creativity still flourishes, but she has ((hopefully)) learned how to incorporate plot.) Since, she has written eight novels, countless short stories and lots of smutty fanfiction. Her ninth novel, Blood Price, made her authorial debut in 2024.

When not writing, she can be found bemoaning the size of her TBR pile, avoiding the main mission in RPGs until every side quest is done, obsessing over trees, watching birds she can't name, getting another tattoo and eating a lot of sharp cheddar cheese.

She lives with her sci-fi streaming partner, Edward, and their two pets: Sasha the cat and Dovahkiin the dog. You can find her online via her LinkTree: https://linktr.ee/thoughtsstained

www.ingramcontent.com/pod-product-compliance
Lightning Source LLC
Chambersburg PA
CBHW060607300726
48975CB00005B/1474